FORWORD

THE STORY YOU ARE ABOUT TO READ is about the relationship between two men, their adopted sons and extended families. If that bothers you, then feel free to change it to two women and their adopted daughters, or a man and woman with their kids, boys or girls, adopted or natural. It covers a wide variety of topics and themes, some of which may be uncomfortable to the reader. Some of those topics include same-sex relationships, adoption by gay adults, gay youth and the risks of suicide by young people, childhood sexual abuse and religion, along with others. All these topics need to be discussed openly in the world to foster a more peaceful and harmonious relationship among all people.

While I don't expect any reader to change their minds based solely on my writings, I am hoping at least a few of you will take pause and possibly reconsider some of your long-held beliefs. By working together to better understand the needs and lives of others, we can make this planet a much better place to call home.

1

I had a quiet, comfortable life living in a large house surrounded by eighteen acres of trees. I'd bought the property and built the house twelve years ago, after the success of my first book. It's my oasis from the rest of the world and I loved the home's location. I'm situated about three miles from a small town that has a couple of restaurants, a gas station and a Dollar General, and twelve miles west of the state capital of Springfield. I just couldn't imagine living anywhere else with neighbors only ten feet away.

The solitude provided by living in the middle of eighteen acres of trees also allowed me the freedom to enjoy a nudist lifestyle. I rarely wore clothes at home and enjoyed the comfort, both indoors and out. I had created several trails through the trees and enjoyed regular walks as a form of exercise and relaxation. About the only time I ever wore clothes of any kind was when I had to leave the property, or on those rare occasions I had guests to the house. After considerable success with four books, I am now essentially retired, living off my investments and residual income from the books. I may write again in the future, but only time can answer that question.

And I was alone. The 4500-square foot house contained four bedrooms for the rare guest and the family I had originally planned to have one day. Those days were rapidly fading away and the family was no closer to becoming a reality than it was when I'd had the house built. I realized shortly after moving in that I had to come to terms with myself before I could even consider marriage and children. And that meant less writing in the future, so I would have more time available for the family I wanted. Despite the success of my first book, I decided I should write a few more before taking a break to work on the family thing.

As I worked on the next three books, I also spent a lot of time analyzing my feelings, needs and desires. A lot of time was spent lounging by the in-ground pool, my brain swirling with thoughts of what I wanted out of life and what I needed to do to achieve my goals. By the time the fourth book had been published, I had finally accepted the fact I was gay and the hopes of having any kind of family were rapidly dwindling. In reality, I always knew the truth, I had just refused to accept it. There were inklings of being different from other boys I knew much earlier in my life, and those inklings became undeniable forces during my early teens, but I had buried them deep inside me in some vague hope they could be squashed like a bug and I could live a so-called 'normal' life.

Now, at thirty-four, the feelings of my true self could no longer be denied, and I was glad that I had never decided to marry. I could not envision the hell life would have been when any possible spouse discovered who I truly was. Everyone involved would be miserable in that situation, especially any kids, and I was glad that I was the only one who was miserable now. I fought depression because I couldn't just delete the thoughts of having a family from my brain. I desperately wanted someone else in my life who could enjoy what I had to offer.

After much thought and introspection, I came to a decision one cold January afternoon while blindly staring at the sun glaring off the snow covering the pool outside the living room. I finally decided to investigate the possibility of adopting a child to help give some meaning to my otherwise sad and lonely existence. I contacted my attorney, Clarence Cantrell, and asked for a meeting to discuss some personal business, telling him to allow a couple of hours for the meeting. Since I was one of Clarence's more prominent clients, we set an appointment for early the next week.

I was so excited to be doing something positive for once, I arrived for the meeting thirty minutes early. Clarence's receptionist, Julie, asked me to have a seat and said he would be with me shortly. I waited impatiently on the edge of my seat for the appointed time and at ten, Clarence escorted his previous client out of his office and motioned for me to follow him inside.

Once the door was closed and we both were seated, he looked at me and said, "Good morning, Max. How's my favorite literary hack doing these days? Still pumping out the cheesy romance stories, I assume. I hope you've been well."

"I'm not doing too badly, you old horse thief, how about yourself?" I retorted, returning his attempt at witty banter.

"Well, when I'm not busy stealing horses, I manage to keep myself busy with divorces, trials, wills and such. You know, the lifeblood of a being a lawyer."

"Glad to hear it."

"You were pretty cryptic on the phone last week. What possible personal business do you have to discuss that requires my services?"

I steeled myself and said, "Clarence, I'm lonely and bored and I need to make some changes in my life."

"Well, why don't you get the hell out of that shack you call a home occasionally and find yourself a nice lady with whom you can share your good fortunes?"

"That might work for most guys, but it won't work for me. I'm glad this conversation is happening as attorney and client, so you can't repeat this to another living soul without my permission. I've only told my parents, sister and brother-in-law so far, but since it will, I'm sure, have some bearing on our discussion, you need to know I'm gay." Despite knowing and working with me for many years, this was certainly news to Clarence and the surprise showed on his face. "I know you weren't expecting to hear that particular tidbit of news today, but it's important to our discussion," I continued.

"Well, I'm glad you feel you could tell me and trust me to keep it confidential. I'm sorry for the 'deer-in-the-headlights' look, but you caught me off-guard, Max. I've known you for years, since before your first book was released, and I never would have suspected you to be gay. That was the absolute last thing I expected to hear when you said you wanted to meet about some 'personal business'."

"It took me a long time to come to terms with that fact, Clarence, and it wasn't easy to say to anyone else since I only settled that battle in my own mind recently. But, that's not the big news. I'm sure the fact that I'm gay will influence the main subject of this meeting."

"Well, now you have certainly piqued my interest, Max. What could you possibly want to discuss that your sexuality will have any bearing."

I took a deep breath and blurted out, "I want to adopt a kid."

"What!?" Clarence asked as he stuck a finger in his ear as if to clear some blockage that was messing with his hearing.

I inhaled and slowly repeated, "I want to adopt a child. I have always wanted a family and since I won't scam any woman into a farce of a marriage to accomplish that goal, I want to adopt. Now, can you see how my being gay will have some bearing on how best to make that dream a reality?"

"Most certainly, Max. It's rare that a single male is allowed to adopt, and even rarer for a single gay male. In fact, it's practically unheard of in this state, anyway. I'm sure you realize that's the case or you wouldn't be here. But, I'll be glad to help in any way I possibly can. I guess the first question I have to ask you is what age child you were thinking about?"

"That's the first question?? I figured you'd be asking if I wanted to adopt a boy or girl. Isn't that what everyone else will be asking?"

"You're probably right about that, but I think the age is more important."

"Well, I hadn't really thought that much about it, but now that you've asked, give me a moment." I looked out the window and pondered the question for a few minutes, then brought my focus back to Clarence and said, "Okay, after some quick thought, I think maybe a child in the six to ten-year-old range."

"Why that age, Max? Most folks who adopt prefer to adopt babies."

"Well, to be quite honest, while I have always wanted to have a family, I was never that thrilled about the whole diaper-changing, middle-of-the-night feeding, toddler aspect of having a kid. And if I can skip over that period of life, it would be perfect."

"Okay, that's one important question down. Now to the second important question. Would you prefer to adopt a boy, girl, or does it matter?"

"Now this one, I have thought about. A lot. And despite how it sounds, I think I would prefer to adopt a boy. I may not be the manliest man, but I'm definitely not a girly-man either. I could offer a lot to either a boy or a girl and will accept either as my child, but I think I would deal better with a boy. I just don't think I would handle all the girl stuff of puberty and beyond very well."

"That's a good, honest answer, Max, and it will definitely be important as we proceed. My next question is how soon you would like this to happen? This is January, and adoptions under normal circumstances can take a year or more. And we really aren't dealing with what you would call *normal* circumstances, now, are we?"

"No, we're not, and that's why I wanted you involved from the very beginning. I had hoped that we could accomplish this by June, so the kid and I would have the summer to get settled in and get a routine established before we have to deal with starting school and all that."

"So, June next year, right?" Clarence asked.

"Oh, no, June this year," I replied. "Now that I've made this decision, I don't want to put it off any longer than I have to. I'm not getting any younger, you know."

"Well, that's certainly pushing the time frame, but let me make some inquiries and see what I can do. Now, I'll need to provide some detailed personal information about you to whomever I talk to, things like income, debt, health, and so on. Do I have your permission to do so?"

"Since you're my attorney, you have access to all that info and you are free to share anything and everything necessary to help move the process along."

"Including your sexuality?" Clarence asked.

"Everything," I replied. "I don't want to hide anything. I fear if we hide that and it comes out later, then folks will get the wrong idea and I'll be unjustly persecuted for being a sick pervert. I don't want that happening. The only request I have is that you hold that particular detail until after things look promising."

"Max, if we don't disclose your sexuality up front, then it will most assuredly look like you are trying to do something devious. How about we disclose all the important information, including your sexuality, first and withhold just your name until we can meet with someone?"

I thought about that idea for a moment and replied, "That should work, Clarence. Me being gay will eventually come out and be news for a while, but I'll deal with it as needed. Since I'm still working on that acceptance process myself, I don't want to have to deal with the media hype and bullshit while I'm trying to adopt. I should have a firm handle on the situation by the time it becomes public and I'll be in a better frame of mind

5

to cope with it."

"That sounds like a fair plan to me, Max. I don't think there's anything else I need from you at this time. Why don't you go home and start thinking about what you need to do to prepare your home for life as a parent. I obviously can't promise quick results, but I'll do my best."

"I know you can't make any promises, but get started, Clarence. Now that I've made this realization and decision, I'm anxious to get started with the rest of my life. It'll be nice to finally have something to look forward to."

I left Clarence's office with a new attitude and a bit of a bounce in my step. I felt the meeting went well and was looking forward to finally making some changes in my life for the better. On my way home, I stopped by a furniture store to get some ideas for new furnishings for a kid's bedroom. I didn't buy anything because I didn't want to get my hopes up only to have them dashed later. I also stopped by the local toy store to just wander around and get some ideas on things I may need there.

Upon returning home, I parked my Shelby Mustang in the garage and suddenly realized that as much as I loved the car, it wasn't going to be very practical when I had a kid to haul around. I first headed to my bedroom and undressed to get comfortable, then went to my study and fired up the computer to do some car shopping. Since I am a diehard Ford guy, I headed to their website and started perusing the selection of available vehicles.

After spending some time looking, I decided on a Flex Limited with all the available options. I figured if I was successful in adopting, he or she is going to have friends and I would, at times, need to transport more than one kid on multiple occasions and they might as well be comfortable.

My decision made, I called the Ford dealer where I bought the Shelby and asked if I could order a car over the phone. The salesman balked at the idea, but when the sales manager, Herb, got on the phone and discovered who was asking, he gave his absolute approval. I told him what I was looking for, thanked him for his help and told him I would be in the next week to make payment arrangements.

While I was buying a new car, Clarence got on the phone and started making inquiries of adoption and family service agencies in the area. On his fourth call, he finally had some luck. The agency did, indeed, have some children available for adoption to the right couple, a girl and several boys. Clarence provided some basic information to the agency's director and asked if they thought I would be an acceptable parent.

The director, Anna, stated they usually only dealt with couples, but she would be willing to discuss a single parent situation in more detail. When asked if they would have any problem with the parent being a gay man, the director suddenly lost all interest. Clarence persisted, though, and was finally able to persuade the director to agree to an interview with us the next Monday. Once he'd sweet-talked our way into the meeting, he called me to pass on the good news.

"Max, it's Clarence and I have some news for you."

"Already? I just left your office a few hours ago," I responded. "I can't believe you have been successful this quickly."

"It wasn't easy, Max. She wasn't too impressed with the idea of a single gay man adopting, but after talking to her for some time, I finally got her to agree to at least give us an interview. Are you doing anything next Monday at one that would prevent you from attending?"

"Hmmm, I don't know, give me a moment to check my calendar. Well, I was thinking about weeding the garden, but since it's January, and the weeds are covered with six inches of snow, I guess I can put that off until later. Hell no!! You tell me where and I'll be there."

"Well, here's my thought. Why don't you come to my office and we'll go to the interview in my car? It's about a half-hour drive, so you should be here no later than twelve fifteen. That should insure we're at their office a bit early."

"No problem, Clarence. I'll be there. Thanks for the quick action and results."

※ ※ ※

The rest of the week and weekend seemed to drag, but when Monday arrived, I was champing at the bit and stressed beyond belief. I arrived at Clarence's office at noon and we headed to the interview shortly afterward. We arrived at the agency's office with ten minutes to spare and headed into the lobby. After waiting for a few minutes, the director came out to greet us.

"Good afternoon, gentlemen. My name is Anna Stewart and I am the director of the agency."

Clarence extended his hand, introduced himself and said, "It's a pleasure to meet you, Anna." He then turned to me and added, "I'd like to introduce my client, Maxwill Sanders. Max, this is the wonderful woman I had to sweet-talk on your behalf last week."

I shook hands with Anna and said, "It's nice to meet you, Anna. I'm looking forward to working with you."

"I'm pleased to meet both of you, as well," Anna replied. "Won't you please follow me, and we can talk in my office."

Once in her office, Anna took a seat in a comfortable chair away from her desk and offered the couch to us. Anna quickly and silently studied both of us to get a feel of our personalities.

Clarence started the meeting with, "Thanks for seeing us today, Anna. As we discussed on the phone last week, my client, Max, is interested in adopting a child in the six to ten-year old range. In our conversation, I relayed most of the information you would need in making your decision except for Max's identity. As I'm sure you can understand, he preferred to keep his name out of the decision-making process until he was able to talk to someone face-to-face."

"That's not how we normally do things here, Clarence, but upon meeting your client, I certainly understand the need for discretion. May I say to you, Mr. Sanders, that it is certainly a pleasure to finally meet you. I didn't realize you lived in the area. I have read all four of your books and I am looking forward to number five."

I looked at the floor for a moment, then back to Anna and replied, "First, please call me Max, everyone else does. Second, I'm afraid you are going to have a long wait for a fifth book, Anna. I have stopped writing for the time being. My writing was a kind of therapy for myself while I dealt with the issue of who I am. It took me a long time to accept the reality that I'm gay. You are only the second person outside of my family who knows that, and I would appreciate it greatly if you would keep it to yourself.

"That realization has not dampened my desire for a family, though, and I feel adoption is the only realistic way I can achieve that goal. I have a lot to offer to any child and have stopped writing so I can devote my time in that direction. I may write again later, but for now, that emotional outlet has been shut down."

"I'll certainly do that, Max. As with most all adoptions, virtually everything is kept sealed and confidential, but in light of your notoriety, I don't know how long we would be able to maintain that confidentiality."

"Understood, Anna. I expect the news that I'm gay will come out in due time, I just want to be the one to do so, on my own terms, not someone else's."

"Well, the news will not come from this office. I guarantee that to you right now."

"Thank you."

"Now, on to our interview. Clarence tells me you are hoping to adopt a boy in the six to ten-year-old range. Please tell me why a boy and why that age range."

"Like I told Clarence when I first talked to him, I picked the age based on the realities of raising a child from a younger age. Let's face it, I'm a single guy and in all honesty, while I really want to have a family to share in my life, I don't think I'd do well dealing with the very early years all by myself.

"I would like to avoid having to hire someone to help me, not that I couldn't afford it, but I just like doing things myself. I also know that older children tend to be more difficult to place in homes and I truly think that's a shame. It's almost like they are being punished just by growing up, which they obviously can't help.

"As to why a boy, again, in all honesty, I don't think I could adequately and properly care for a girl from puberty on through the teen years. Since I'm gay, all the things you have deal with while girls are growing up would make me very uncomfortable and I would be a very bad source of information or inspiration to a girl. There is no doubt in my mind that she would end up hating me, and I just couldn't accept that."

"Well, I appreciate your candor, Max. Now, let me be just as candid back. I understand your misgivings about raising a girl and would rule that option out for you because I think you are 100% correct as to how things would turn out, given your feelings as you stated them.

"That said, I also have serious concerns about allowing a gay man to adopt a boy. I know it's not politically correct to say this, but I'm going to anyway, as politely as I can. I would always worry that a gay man would take advantage of his position of authority over a boy and force him to do things that would land the man in prison for a very long time and the boy back in the system."

"I would *never* do anything to a child that would be considered improper. I understand your thoughts and I don't hold them against you. I knew that would be a concern and you're doing your job in looking out for the best interests of the child. That is my intention, also. I have a lot that I can share with any child and I would love to do so. I am hopeful that we can work together to give a child a happy, stable and loving home."

"You've certainly given me something to think about, Max, and I'll have some discussions with our case workers this week. I'll keep your name out of those discussions as long as possible. If I think we have a child that would fit well in the situation, I'll let Clarence know on Friday and we can have you come back to meet the child next week. I will warn you now, if we proceed and you are successful in adopting, we will be keeping a very close watch on you for some time. At the very first hint of anything improper, you will lose the child and be in jail. Do you understand?"

"I most certainly do, and we'll be waiting for your call. Thanks for your time today and I hope to be seeing you again soon." We shook hands with Anna, left the office and headed for Clarence's car. Once we were on the way back to his office, I asked him, "Well, how do you think that went?"

"Better than what I expected after talking to her last week," Clarence replied. "At least she didn't shoot you down right out of the gate, which I was sure would happen. We'll just have to wait for Friday to see if she was serious about helping."

I headed for my lonely home and, after getting comfortable, I started making list after list of things to do before any kid could move into this home. Bedroom furniture was first on the list. While the other three bedrooms were already fully furnished, they weren't exactly what you would call kid-friendly. That would have to change. And not just the furniture, but probably some paint and other decorating, also. Clothes were the next major item on a list, but those would have to wait until I knew what sizes would be needed. I would also have to acquire some things for entertainment purposes, but again, I would need to know what the child wanted before I went too far.

As the week passed, the lists and plans were worked on and organized as best as could be expected. When Friday finally arrived, I was wound tight in anticipation. I thought about calling Clarence several times throughout the day but didn't want to appear overly anxious. Finally, at four, when I just couldn't wait any longer, I headed to the study to call him. Just as I opened the study door, the phone started ringing. I eagerly sprinted to the desk and answered on the third ring.

"Hello," I panted while trying to catch my breath.

"Max, it's Clarence. I have some news for you. Are you sitting down?"

"Yes!" I exclaimed. "Just spit it out."

"I just got off the phone with Anna and she believes she has some good candidates for consideration. She would like us to come to the agency Monday afternoon, so you can meet them and see how things go. Are you available then?"

"Hell, yes! Should we meet at your office again and go together?"

"That would probably be the easiest. Why don't you get here about one? That will give us plenty of time to be there for our meeting at two."

"That's perfect, Clarence. I'll be there with bells on."

"I'll be waiting for you, but you just might want to leave the bells at home," Clarence laughed.

"Okay, no damn bells. Thanks for making this happen."

"No problems. That's why I get paid the big bucks. Just remember, Max, this is just a meet and greet type of thing. That does not mean anything is going to happen. Try to have a good weekend and I'll see you Monday afternoon."

I knew this was going to be the longest weekend of my life.

As the Monday dawn crawled into existence, I started getting ready for the most important meeting of my life. I left home at noon for the trip to Clarence's office and after a quick lunch, arrived promptly at one.

After being led into Clarence's private office, he asked, "Are you ready for this meeting, Max?"

"Readier than I've been for anything else in my life."

"Then let's not waste time sitting around here. Get your things and let's go."

We rode to the meeting at the agency's office in silence, both of us lost in our own thoughts. I was anxious to meet my possible son and Clarence worried about my reaction if things fell through. We arrived at the agency with plenty of extra time and headed inside for our meeting. After a short wait, Anna came out of her office to greet us and then lead us back to her office.

Anna started our meeting with, "Welcome back you two. I want you to know that there have been some very lively discussions around here this past week about your request. While a few expressed concerns about allowing a gay man to adopt a boy, I think we are all finally of a mind that there is no reason why this can't be successful. We just have to be cautious and aware that every decision made from here on will face severe scrutiny by the public at large."

"I completely understand," I responded, "and I'll do whatever's needed to calm any concerns that anyone may have. I've waited way too long to reverse course now."

"I'm glad to hear that, Max. During our discussions this week, we were also creating a list of potential adoptees for you to meet today. We've narrowed the list down to four boys. They are Alexander and Joseph Allison, Thomas Stults and Michael Reynolds. Alexander and Joseph are eight-year-old twins in third grade, Thomas is seven, in second grade, and Michael is six and in first grade.

"All four boys attend the same school as all their foster parents live on the far west side of town. All of them are doing well and maintaining decent grades despite their circumstances. I also want to give you a bit of background on these boys before you meet them. All of them, unfortunately, come from situations that no longer require the severing of parental rights, so you won't have to worry about that.

"Alexander and Joseph came to us after their parents were killed in car accident about four years ago and they have lived in the same foster home the entire time. They have adjusted as well as can be expected after losing their parents. They miss their mom and dad terribly, but due to their age, we have been unable to find an acceptable adoptive family to take both of them. I know you were expecting to adopt only one child, but I'll tell you right now that we have no intentions of allowing these two to be split up. They rely on each other way too much to let that happen. They have just been in the system too long and truly deserve a forever home and family.

"Thomas' mother has been incarcerated for some time now and his father is unknown. It is highly unlikely that his mother will be released from prison until well after Thomas has reached the age of majority and that's why her rights have been severed. There is a slim possibility his biological father may show up at some point in the future, but without knowing who he is, it's nearly impossible to be certain of anything. He may not even know he has a son, which would probably be the best at this point in Thomas' life.

"Michael has had a rough six years in his short life. He was severely abused by his parents and removed from their home only seven weeks ago. Due to the severity of the abuse, his parents' rights have already been severed and there is no chance he will be going back to live with them. He will need some very special care in the near term, and possibly in the long term, also. When he came under our care, he was malnourished and quite behind in his education. He is very withdrawn now, but we are hoping that the proper environment will help pull him out the protective shell he has created around himself. Only time will tell how that turns out.

"I think that's all I have for now. I'll let the boys provide any more information you may want. How does that sound, Max?"

"That sounds just fine. I'm glad I got that information from you as I hadn't considered the reasons you would have these kids under your care. I'll make sure to tread lightly when we talk to them. It sounds like they all have some challenges in their futures, but I'm more than willing to help them in any way possible."

"Very well, are you ready to meet them?"

"Very ready, Anna."

"Do you want to meet them one at a time or all together?"

A crazy thought had been forming in my mind during our conversation, so I replied, "Why don't we meet all four at the same time. While I'm anxious to meet them, I'd also like to see how they interact with each other."

Anna reached for the phone on the end table, dialed her secretary's extension and asked, "Marcy, would you please bring the boys in? Thank you."

2

After just a few moments, the office door opened and in walked four boys. They filed into the room with a minimum of pushing and prodding, and sat together on the couch while Clarence and I moved to separate chairs at each end of the couch.

Anna began the conversation with, "Boys, this is Mr. Maxwill Sanders and he is hoping to adopt a child. We thought you four might be interested in meeting him and we can see what develops."

With a sheepish look on my face, I gave the boys a little wave. All four faces lit up with anticipation and hope at the news that they were being considered for adoption.

Anna continued, "Now before you all get wild ideas and dreams going on in your heads, there are a few things you need to know. Mr. Sanders is not married so he will be a single parent. While he is not the type of person we regularly consider as being an adoptive parent since he is single, we feel that whichever one of you he decides to adopt will be taken care of very well.

"He lives alone in a large house that sits in the middle a large copse of trees. He built the house some years ago in the hopes of marrying and having children. But, since those plans have not worked out for him, he is now trying to adopt. Out of all the children in our system, you four, we felt, were the most likely candidates to become Mr. Sanders' son.

"The gentleman with Mr. Sanders is his attorney, Mr. Cantrell, and he is here to help Mr. Sanders work through the process. Now, I'll turn the rest of this meeting over to Mr. Sanders. If you need anything, I'll be at my desk right over there, dealing with some paperwork, okay?"

Anna received affirmative nods from all six of us and moved off to her desk.

I looked at the four boys and started our chat with "Hi guys, it's great to meet you. As Anna said, my name is Maxwill Sanders, but you can call me Max. Though I'm a single guy, I have always wanted a family. I'm thirty-four and life has kept me very busy to this point. I feel like now is a good time to get started on that dream.

"Anna thinks one of you four might like to become my son. I'd like to talk to you a bit, find out a little bit about each of you, and see how you would feel about having me as your dad. Anna and I have told you a bit about me, why don't you each tell me a little bit about yourselves?"

The four boys looked at each other with a look in their eyes that said, 'I'm not going first, you do it.' All four looked back at me, mute, and I decided I was going to have to give a little prod to get things going here. I looked to the twins and asked, "Why don't you tell me a little bit about yourself, Alexander?"

He stammered, "I don't know what to say. I've given up on being adopted. Since Joey and I are twins, we've been here a long time 'cause nobody wants to take two kids and I won't go anywhere without him. He won't go anywhere without me, either."

"Well, I'll be honest with you. I had planned on adopting only one child at this time, but if things work out and it seems like we'd be a good fit, I wouldn't have a problem taking both of you into my home."

Alexander and Joseph looked at each other with relief in their eyes as they took in the news that this just might work out for them. Joseph looked back at me and asked, "Really? You'd be willing to adopt both of us? Wow, that'd be great."

"I sure would," I replied. "Now, can either or both of you tell me a little bit more about yourselves?"

Alexander started, "Well, our parents died when we were four. They were in a bad car wreck and they were killed while we were at home with a babysitter. We've been hoping to be adopted by someone ever since."

Joseph added, "Me and Alex do everything together and always have. That's why we won't leave the other one behind. We couldn't stand being separated."

"Well, you don't have to worry about that, boys. Like I said, I would be willing to adopt both of you."

"Would we get our own bedrooms?" Alexander asked. "We've never had separate rooms and the people we've lived with thinks that since we're twins, we should always be in the same room together."

"Well, I have three unused bedrooms in my home, so yeah, I don't see why you each couldn't have your own if you wanted."

"Cool," said Joseph.

"What about you, Michael? Would you like to come live with me and have me as your dad?"

"I guess," he said meekly. "I never really thought about it much. I just figured I'd live where I am 'til I got out of school."

I looked at Thomas next and he started talking before I could open my mouth.

"Why ain't you married? Are you one of them fags? I ain't gonna to live with no damn fag! Is that other guy queer, too?" he demanded.

I was stunned at the questions from the youngster and I looked over at Anna to see how she reacted. Anna gave me a slight nod that I took to mean it was a valid question and one that deserves an answer.

I looked Thomas straight in the eyes and replied, "While I didn't expect that question today and the way you worded it was quite rude, I'll give you an honest answer. First, the words fag and queer are not ones I like, and I don't want to hear them again. Second, to answer your question, yes, I'm gay." I caught a quick, knowing look pass between Joseph and Alexander, but they remained silent.

"I prefer the company of another man. Since I just recently settled that question myself, I have been alone as I dealt with my feelings all these years. It would not have been fair to marry some nice lady while I was still figuring things out for myself. Now that I realize the truth about myself, I can move on with the rest of my life.

"As to Clarence, I'm pretty sure he isn't gay since he's been married 25 years and has three kids. Heck, he didn't even know I was until I told him just last week. Clarence is my attorney and he is here to help me through this process. Does that answer your question?"

"Yeah, I guess. I still don't think I want to live with you," Thomas replied.

"Let me tell you all something. You would all be perfectly safe. If you become my son or sons, I will protect you with every fiber of my being and do my best to make sure no one hurts you ever again. Does that sound okay to you?"

I received nods from all four boys, though Thomas still seemed a bit reluctant to accept what I said at face value.

Joseph asked the next question, "Are you talking only to boys or you gonna to talk to girls, too?"

Again, I glanced at Anna and received a nod to continue. "Well, over the years, I've thought a lot about the type of family I would like to have, and I really don't have a preference as to whether I adopt a boy or a girl. But to tell you truth, I just don't think I would do very well dealing with some of the issues girls have as they grow up. I think I would be much more comfortable and helpful dealing with boys as they grow up. I'm much more familiar with their issues."

All four looked at each other again and seemed to accept this. The questions returned to the type of questions you'd expect from six to eight-year-old kids and we chatted about a bit of everything for the next hour. At the end of our time, Anna excused the boys and asked them to wait with her receptionist for a bit while we talked a bit more. Each boy came to shake my hand and thank me for talking to them. Thomas was last and he added in a small whisper, "Sorry for being rude. I think I might like to live with you after all. If I didn't make you mad and you'll let me."

"Thanks, Thomas, I appreciate and accept your apology. As far as I'm concerned, it never happened." Thomas wrapped his arms around my neck and gave me a quick hug. I hugged him back to show there were no hard feelings and then patted him on the back letting him know he needed to catch up to the others.

After the boys left the office and Anna rejoined Clarence and myself, she asked, "Well, Max, what did you think of the boys?"

"I think they're all great. Thomas seems to be a bit rough around the edges, and his first question really surprised me, but I still think he's a great kid."

"I must say his question shocked me quite a bit, also. But then again, Thomas has always been quite outspoken and not afraid to share his thoughts. You handled your response very well, though, and I appreciated your honesty and candor. I think that really helped put an end to that line of questions in a very tactful way."

"Well, I didn't know what else to say so I figured the truth was the best way to go. I know they're just kids, but kids today seem to know so much more than we give them credit for."

"Too true," replied Anna. "Now that you've met the boys, what are your thoughts?" asked Anna.

"My first thoughts are that I could see myself adopting any of them. It's really kind of hard to form a real opinion based on such a short conversation with the four of them together. But I really liked the way they treated each other. They all seemed pretty comfortable together," I said.

"That's true, but this was meant to be just a quick meeting to see how things went. If you have particular interest in any of the boys, we will schedule a couple more meetings and perhaps an outing or two, just so you can get better acquainted with all four individually. Plus, we must do inspections of your home to make sure we approve of the living conditions and other things before we could proceed any further."

"That sounds great, Anna, but I have another idea for you to consider."

"And what would that be?"

"As you know from the information sent over by Clarence, I have a large house just waiting for someone to help me finally make it a real home. What would you think of all four boys coming out and spending a weekend with me? That would give us a better chance to get to know each other. They could see where they'd be living, do some swimming, walk through the woods on some of the trails I've created and get a few days away to have some fun.

"One of your staff would be welcome to come along. With three empty bedrooms, Alexander and Joseph could use one, Thomas and Michael could use one and your staff member could use the third one. That would give me a good chance to see how the boys react to life in the woods and give you someone onsite to see how things go. That would kill two birds with one stone."

"Well, now, I hadn't thought about that, but it could possibly work. Let me talk to my staff about it. I'll get back to you in a few days and let you know what we decide."

"Don't hesitate to contact me if you need. You have my phone numbers and if you can't get in touch with me, you're welcome to contact Clarence. I can't imagine not being available for anything, but just in case. Feel free to work with him as you do your investigation, background checks and whatever else you need to do."

"I'll do that, Max. It was a pleasure to meet with you two again today and I'll be in touch as soon as possible."

"Come on, Clarence, let's get out of here so Anna can get to work."

We left Anna's office and as we passed the boys sitting in the lobby, they each came up to us to say goodbye. I told them all that I hoped to see them again soon, and Clarence and I headed out for the ride back to his office. It was a very quiet trip as my brain swirled with thoughts of suddenly becoming a father after living alone the last twelve years. I was anxious and scared all at the same time. Clarence tried to start a conversation with me several times, but I was too lost in my own mind to engage with him.

When we arrived back at his office, Clarence invited me in to chat for a bit. I accepted his offer, and we headed inside. Once we were both seated, Clarence asked, "So, what thoughts are percolating through that gray matter you laughingly call a brain, Max?"

"Everything, man. Am I sure about this? Am I doing the right thing? Can I really provide a good home to any of those kids? Am I in too deep? What the hell am I doing?!?"

Clarence came back with, "Yes, yes, yes, damn right and losing your mind. I think I got 'em all."

I shook my head to clear the fog from my mind and asked, "Huh? What sort of gibberish is that?"

Clarence smiled and said, "I was just answering your questions. Yes, you're sure about this or we wouldn't be here, having this discussion. Yes, you are doing the right thing. Yes, you can give a good home to any of those boys and will be happy doing so. Damn right you are in too deep, but you can swim back to the surface anytime. As to what the hell you're doing, that is losing your mind, but in a very good way, Max."

"God, I hope so. This is happening so fast, I keep having to pinch myself to make sure it's not a dream. After our first meeting, did you really think we'd be making this kind of progress already?"

"Absolutely not. I was certain nobody would even talk to us once I informed them of your sexuality. Like I told you during our first meeting, it's extremely rare that a single male, especially a gay one, would even be considered for adoption."

"But you made the calls anyway. Why?"

"I'm your attorney, Max, and it's my job to do as you request, no matter the result. Still, I tried several other agencies before finding Anna and her group. The others were semi-willing to consider a single parent but once I told them the person was a gay man, they quickly lost all interest. One even said, and I quote, 'You've gotta be fucking kidding me. Take a hike, pervert. I hope you rot in hell.' Even Anna wasn't thrilled at the prospect, but, having met you, I think she's coming around. I must say I'm nicely surprised."

"I'm just surprised as hell. I didn't think this would be easy, but Anna sure does seem willing to help."

"Yes, she does. I think the need for adoptive parents is great and that's why she's considering it for you. We'll just have to wait and see how things go the next few weeks and months before we declare victory."

"That's not a problem, Clarence. I've waited this long, I can wait some more. It won't be easy, but I'll survive it. Well, I better get going and let you take care of some other clients, though you probably won't need them with all the money you're charging me right now. Thanks for all your help, and if anything comes up, let me know."

"I'll keep you updated with any new developments, Max. Now, go home, keep working on your lists and getting ready to be a father."

We shook hands and I headed outside for my car. Once ensconced in the leather seats of the Shelby, I rested my head on the steering wheel for a few minutes before trying to drive. I had to collect my thoughts before I headed out so I wouldn't be a hazard to the other folks with whom I'd be sharing the road. Once I pulled myself back together, I drove out of the parking lot and, instead of heading directly home, I turned in the direction of the Ford dealer so I could talk to Herb and check the status of my new Flex.

Twenty minutes later, I arrived at the dealership and asked the receptionist to see Herb, the sales manager. She checked and told me he was in a meeting with a customer and it would be about fifteen to twenty minutes before he'd be available. With nothing else to do, I wandered the sales floor while I waited.

After seeing the other cars Ford was currently offering, I decided that I had made a good decision on selecting the Flex. It looked like it would have plenty of room and be comfortable for everyone. It wasn't nearly as big as the Expedition, but I really didn't want anything that big. Driving that monstrosity would feel like driving a semi after tooling around in the Shelby the past several years.

Herb finally freed up about thirty minutes later and called me into his office. After taking seats, Herb asked, "How ya doing, Max? That Shelby still treating you well?"

"It's great, Herb. Best damn car I've ever had. I wanted to stop by and see what's up with the Flex I ordered last week."

"Well, the order's been placed with the factory, let me check the production schedule and see what we're looking at for delivery. Give me just a moment." Herb punched some keys on his computer and pulled up the schedule. After a moment and a few more keystrokes, "At this time, the computer's showing the start of production is scheduled for three weeks from yesterday. It usually takes a few days to build and quality check the vehicle, then about two to three weeks for delivery to the dealership."

"That sounds like it should be just perfect, Herb. I can't wait to get it."

"Can I ask a question, Max?"

"Sure, what do you want to know?"

"Well, it just seems a bit odd for you to be buying a Flex when you have the Shelby. You're not planning on trading it in, are you?"

"Oh no, I love that car too much to consider doing that. I'm just going to need a bigger vehicle shortly and want to be prepared when the time comes."

"Okay, now my curiosity meter's pinging off the dial. Why would a single guy like you be needing a bigger vehicle?"

"Well, I hate to say anything for fear I'll jinx it, but I'm hoping to adopt. And I figured that with a kid and friends and their stuff, the Shelby would be quickly packed to the gills. I want to be ready with a bigger car when the time comes."

"Congratulations, that's great, Max. And the Flex is the perfect vehicle for a family. Plenty of room for you, a couple kids and whatever else you will need to haul."

"I just figured it would make more sense than trying to stuff it all in the 'Stang. Now, how do you want to handle payment? I've brought my checkbook, so I can give you a deposit on the car."

"Don't worry about that. I know you're good for it. With tax, title, license and other fees, you're looking at about fifty-two to fifty-three grand. If you can bring a cashier's check for the final total once the car comes in, I'll even knock a few grand off the price for ya."

"That sounds fine, Herb. Let me know the total when the time comes, and I'll do just that. But, instead of reducing the price of the vehicle, would you consider donating to a worthy organization in the same amount?"

"That's a great idea, Max. It's not like you need the money yourself, is it?" he chuckled.

I laughed along with him. "No, I don't, but I do know a place that would make good use of a donation."

"Once we have everything settled on the car, we'll make the donation in your name."

"Oh no, you can't use my name. I want the donation to go to the agency I'm working with on the adoption process and I don't want them thinking I'm trying to buy their decision in any way. You'll need to send the money in either your name or the dealership's name. My name can't be involved in any way, shape or form with it."

"Gotcha, Max. No problem. We'll use the dealership then, that way I can reduce my tax bill next year."

"Thanks, Herb, I knew you'd understand. Well, I'll get out of your hair and let you get back to selling some cars."

"Happy to help. I'll be in touch as we get closer to delivery of the car."

"Sounds good. Have a great afternoon."

I drove home while my brain was swirling with thoughts of what I had to do to prepare for four boys to spend a weekend at my house. Of course, I assumed Anna would be agreeable with the idea and wanted to be prepared for whatever happened. After parking the Shelby in the garage, I undressed and headed to my study to start creating new lists of what needed to be accomplished and making the phone calls to make it all happen.

The first item on my list and, therefore my first call, was to the company that installed and maintained my pool. If the boys wanted to go swimming when they were here, I would have to have a cover for the pool that would allow us to be comfortable despite the freezing winter temps and six plus inches of snow on the ground.

Mike Wilson answered the phone when I called. "M&M Pools. How can I help you?"

"Mike, Max Sanders here. How are you this fine, frigid day?"

"Bored as hell, Max. Nobody wants a pool installed in January and we have nothing to do. Can't even sell a spa to anybody right now and there sure isn't any pool maintenance to deal with this time of year. You gonna fix that for me?"

"As a matter of fact, Mike, I'm sure hoping to. I've been thinking about this for a while and I'd like to see what it would take to have an enclosure installed so I can enjoy the pool all year. Think you can help me with that?"

"You bet. It's about time you followed through on my suggestion from a few years ago. I wish more people would do that. We might be able to stay busy during the winter if more folks could swim all year. What type of enclosure are looking for?"

"I want something that can be heated for winter use, obviously, but then be taken down or opened up to enjoy the fresh air during the summer. Is there anything like that available?"

"There are a couple of different options that would serve your purpose. How about I come out tomorrow morning? I can take some measurements and show you some brochures of what's available, then we can discuss it in more detail."

"That would be perfect. What time do you want to come out?"

"Well, I'm not sure, my schedule's pretty full," he chuckled. "But seriously, how does nine sound to you? That will give me a chance to come to the office, see what's not happening here and then I'll head out. It takes about thirty minutes to get to your house from here."

"That's perfect, Mike. I'll have some fresh coffee on when you get here. I'll see you then."

Scratch item one off the list. My next call was to a cleaning service. While I'm not a slob by any stretch of the imagination, I felt it would be a good idea to have someone come do a thorough cleaning before my hoped-for guests arrived. I hopped on the internet to look for cleaning services in the area. After finding one with excellent reviews, I got on the phone and dialed the number.

"Thank you for calling Merry Maids, this is Joyce, how may I brighten your day?"

"Hi, Joyce, my name is Max Sanders and I need some cleaning done at my home."

"Good afternoon, Mr. Sanders, we'd be glad to help out. What type of cleaning do you need?"

"Well, I have a rather large house in the center of a small woods. I try to keep things up, but it's been quite a while since I've given the place a thorough cleaning. Under normal circumstances, I'd take care of it myself, but I'm expecting some houseguests in a few weeks and won't have the time I need to take care of everything that needs done."

"What services are looking for, sir?"

"Pretty much everything, I guess. Vacuuming, mopping, cleaning windows, dusting, and I need the linens in three bedrooms either cleaned and the beds remade, or changed with the current linens cleaned later. Do you think you can help me out?"

"I'm sure we can, sir. You say it's a big house. Approximately how big and is it a one or two-story home?"

"I have a total of 4,500 square feet of living space and it's all on one level. Oh, and as weird as it sounds, I'd also like my outside pool area cleaned up with all the snow removed and furniture cleaned off."

"We can certainly take care of all that without any problems. I think a crew of four people should be able to accomplish everything in a day. If we clean the bed linens with the intentions to use the same ones, would we be allowed to use your laundry machines, or would we have to take them elsewhere?"

"If your people think they can get them all washed, dried and the beds remade the same day using my machines, I'm happy to let them do so. All three beds are king size, so the comforters are pretty large and would probably have to be washed one at a time unless they are taken to an outside service with larger machines. I'll let your people decide on how best to handle the situation once they get here and have a chance to see what they're in for."

"That sounds fine, Mr. Sanders. When would you like us to come out?"

"Well, I have a meeting tomorrow that could take quite a bit of time so why don't we shoot for the next day? We'll be going in and out the whole time he's here and I don't want to be in your crew's way."

"That will work out just fine. I'll have a crew of four of our most experienced people there at nine in the morning, ready to work. We'll bring all our own equipment and supplies except for a washer and dryer. Will you be staying at the home while the cleaning is happening?"

"Probably, yes. I have some other things to take care of that day, but I'll stay out of the way. When your crew gets here, I'll have them take care of my study first, then I can get out of their way while they work on the rest of the place."

"That sounds fine. Everything is all set on this end. You have a great day and we'll see you the day after tomorrow."

"Thanks, Joyce, you have a good day, also." Item two checked off, ready for number three.

I next started a shopping list of the food and supplies I would need to get to cover the needs of six people for a weekend. Figuring out meals to feed six people that would suit everybody turned out to be more time consuming than I anticipated. I assumed the boys and Anna's aide would be here from Friday night to Sunday afternoon.

I finally decided we would stop at Steak 'n Shake on the way out of town for supper Friday evening. That would allow us to spend all our time at home getting to know each other a little better. Then Saturday morning, I would do scrambled eggs, bacon, sausage and toast for breakfast, grill hot dogs and hamburgers for lunch along with a variety of chips, then, for supper, we would have pizza from Capone's just a few miles away. They don't deliver, but it would take only ten minutes to pick it up and bring it back home to eat. That left just Sunday to figure out. I settled on waffles for breakfast and spaghetti with my homemade sauce, along with garlic toast in the middle of the afternoon for lunch.

I would also have to lay in a supply of drinks of various types. I basically drink only coffee, Pepsi or water at home, but I thought I should also have tea available along with a variety of soft drinks. I also planned to get an assortment of juices for the boys to have with their snacks. Snacks! Damn,

I almost forgot munchies of some kind. I well remember when I was the age the boys are now how much I liked getting a snack of some kind in the afternoon and again in the evening before going to bed. I was sure these boys wouldn't be any different. I guess I better add some cookies, crackers and maybe some apples or oranges to my shopping list, too. Since I didn't know what drinks or snacks any of the boys would like, I planned to get a wide variety of both just to cover my bases. I also added a note to my other to-do list to clean out the refrigerator in the garage to make room for the drinks. That way they would all be cold and reduce the need for ice through the weekend.

Check number three off the list of things to do.

My next list concerned entertainment. While I have a very nice entertainment system in my home theater, I really didn't have any movies in my collection that I thought would be appropriate for the boys to watch. They were all either too violent, riddled with inappropriate language, or the subject was what I thought would be above their age level. I absolutely love *2001: A Space Odyssey*, but I wasn't prepared to explain it to six, seven and eight-year-olds. I decided a stop at Walmart or Best Buy would be required to pick up a few movies that would be more appropriate for the intended audience. I thought about getting some board games, also, but decided I would be better off to wait until later when I knew more about what they might like.

Item four done, ready to move on.

After a couple of hours working on and refining my lists, I saved them all to the computer so I could print them out later when it would be time to do the actual shopping. After closing my eyes for a moment of relaxation, I realized that time had gotten away from me and it was now dark outside and much later than I thought it should be. It suddenly hit me that not only did I skip lunch today, but I'd also missed supper. That explained the empty feeling I had in my gut. I wandered into the kitchen and browsed for a few minutes before I decided just to fix myself a burger and fries. Not great food, but it would fill me up and get my stomach to stop aching. I cleaned up the kitchen after eating and then headed to the home theater to watch a movie before going to bed.

I popped *National Lampoon's Vacation* in the player and kicked back in my lounger to enjoy a few laughs. I've seen the movie so many times, I wasn't really paying much attention to it and my mind kept drifting back to the four boys I had met just a few hours ago. Alexander and Joseph are as identical as any twins I had ever seen. They both have light blonde hair and blue eyes, were about four feet tall and weighed about eighty pounds. Both were your classic cute lads and I could see them breaking some serious hearts later in life.

Thomas has dark hair and brown eyes, was just a bit shorter than the twins and weighed maybe seventy pounds. He seemed to have a very up personality, but I could see where his being so outspoken and not afraid to say what he's thinking could be a possible issue if he couldn't learn to control it.

Michael has red hair, hazel eyes and his face is covered in freckles. He was about three and a half feet tall and looked to be pretty skinny. I assumed his small stature was due to the abuse and neglect he suffered at the hands of his parents. He was also very timid, but I think that was a trait that could be worked on as he grows up.

Based on our short meeting today, I really couldn't decide which one, or two in the case of the twins, I most wanted to adopt. The thought that popped in my head during our meeting that I kept to myself was why don't I just adopt all four? I knew it was premature to think that way since adopting any of them was not yet guaranteed, but there it was anyway. I would have to seriously consider the option as things progressed.

In my mind, if I was allowed to take in one of them, then why wouldn't they permit all four to become my sons? I tried to reason with myself that I really wasn't prepared for one, let alone four, but I kept coming back to my biggest concern: if I wasn't allowed to adopt all four, then what would happen to the others? Would they end up living in foster homes until they turned eighteen? I wasn't prepared to let that happen, but I knew the chances of adopting all were slim to non-existent. I would have to wait until after their weekend visit and then discuss the possibility with Anna and see what she thought.

I finally realized that the movie had ended, and the television turned itself off. I was so deep in thought about the boys that I totally missed when it happened. If I'm this scatter-brained now, I can't imagine what I will be like when there are kids in the house all the time. It was getting late and since I had a meeting in the morning with Mike, the pool guy, I headed for my bedroom, crawled under the covers and hoped for a peaceful night's sleep.

3

I slept rather fitfully that night. I kept having dreams about the four boys living here and driving me crazy with demands. I would awake with a start, sweating profusely and shaking with fear about what I was contemplating. I'd toss and turn for about fifteen minutes each time, and then drop back off to sleep, only to awaken again about an hour later. By the time the sun was coming up, I'd managed about five and half hours sleep out of the nine I'd been in bed and I was still tired. This day had long day written all over it.

I fixed myself a quick breakfast, then cleaned up my mess to get ready for Mike to show up. I took a shower to help me wake up a bit more, got dressed and headed to the kitchen to start the pot of coffee I had promised to have ready when he arrived. The last of the coffee was dripping into the carafe when I heard the ding announcing someone had turned into the driveway. Since I was expecting only Mike this morning, I headed to the front door to meet him, a fresh cup of coffee in hand. I opened the door just as he was about to ring the chimes. He wasn't expecting me so quickly and he jumped back a bit in surprise.

"Jesus, Max, you scared the hell out of me. You really should give your guests at least a *chance* to ring the bell or knock before you open the door."

"Sorry, Mike, didn't mean to spook ya, but I heard the driveway sensor ding when you turned off the road."

"Oh, that's right. I keep forgetting you have that. That's probably a good thing to have living out here in the boonies like you do."

"I wouldn't be here without it. While I love the property, I'm just a bit paranoid about folks popping in without warning. The sensor keeps that from happening. Come on in and warm up a minute before we go out to measure things."

"Now, there's a plan, Max. Get outta my way, man."

I closed the door and while handing Mike the coffee, I said, "Here's that fresh coffee I promised. It just finished brewing. Why don't we sit at the kitchen counter and you can show me what types of shelters you can get while you drink a bit. Then we can go out and get some measurements."

"Good idea," Mike replied. On the way to the kitchen bar, Mike asked, "So tell me, Max, why, after all these years, have you decided to enclose the pool? If you remember, I suggested that same idea about five years ago."

"Oh, I remember, all right. That's why I called you and not someone else. The main push behind it happening now is I am hoping to adopt soon and I thought it would be nice for us to have the pool available all year."

"Adopt?? I've never thought of you as having a family. I assumed you would go through life as a dedicated bachelor."

"I kinda thought that's where I was headed, also, but I've discovered I'm getting pretty bored living out here all alone and decided to change that."

"But why adoption? Why don't you get married and have kids the way everyone else does?"

"To be honest with you, Mike, I'm gay and the *normal* way of doing things wouldn't work out too well for me. Or for any potential wife, either."

"Whoa, sorry for being so nosy."

"It doesn't bother you, does it? Me being gay, that is?"

"Not a whit, Max. Some of our best clients are gay. You should see some of the pools we've done. They'd blow your mind. Waterfalls, slides, fancy tile work in the pool and on the deck. It seems the sky's the limit with you folks."

"Just what do you mean by that!?" I exclaimed.

"Ah, shit, that didn't come out right. Sorry, Max, I didn't mean anything other than the gay folks we've done work for always seem to have plenty of money and have no hesitation in spending it. And I'm happy to let them do just that. I apologize if I've offended you."

"Oh, hell, don't worry about it, Mike. I've just recently accepted who I am, and I guess I'm a little more defensive about it than I should be. Sorry for jumping down your back. I know you didn't mean anything by it."

We each took a stool at the bar counter and Mike pulled some brochures out of his case. He handed them to me and I started looking at them while Mike described the different shelter styles.

"The system you are looking at now is an aluminum framework with triple-glazed glass. We place anchors in the concrete deck around the pool and then the frames are bolted to the anchors. Despite how that sounds, the anchors are designed so that when the shelter is taken down, no part of the anchor sticks up above the surface of the concrete. And there are stainless steel caps to place over the anchors to make them flush with the concrete. That makes it safe for anybody walking around, no bolts or studs sticking up to trip over."

"This looks pretty good, Mike. What kind of pricing are we looking at?"

"Of course, it all depends on size, but around 25-30 thousand, installed."

"That's about what I expected. What's this next one?"

"This is similar except it's a redwood framework instead of aluminum. The anchors are similar in design so that when the shelter is taken down, none of the anchor sticks up to cause problems. Again, the glass is triple-glazed and installing, taking down and storage is pretty easy for a group of four or five guys. Personally, this one's my favorite because I'm partial to the wood framing.

"Each section of the walls and roof is four foot by eight foot and there are custom-made triangle pieces on each end to tie the walls into the roof. That makes it easy to order whatever is needed for each installation. You just decide how much area needs to be covered and go from there. The only pieces that take a bit of time to manufacture are the custom triangle pieces to close the ends. But they only take about three or four days to fabricate, so the delay in shipping isn't too bad."

"What kind of pricing are we looking at for this setup? Is it similar to the aluminum-framed shelter?"

"It costs a little more than the other, but for the wood framing, it's worth every penny. Again, it's my favorite of what we have available."

"And what's this third one like?"

"This last one is a what we call a roll-away shelter. We install tracks in the concrete deck and then the sections simply roll in or out depending on what kind of exposure you want on any given day. The advantage to this system is you can roll it over the pool one day to enclose it and then the next, you simply roll it back out of the way. You can also just partially cover the pool if you want.

"The disadvantage to this system is that once it's put up and the rollers are bolted to the shelter sections, you really don't want to take it down because aligning the whole thing is a nightmare. What that means is, even when you are not using the shelter, there's a stack of sections at the far end of the pool. Once you have so many sections nested, the visibility through the end and sides becomes pretty lousy."

"I don't think I'd like that. It sounds like I'd be killing the view out the glass wall of the living room with that thing."

"Yep, you'd be doing just that. That's why I prefer one of the other two systems. With them in place, the view wouldn't be too bad, and when you take them down for the summer, your view is exactly what you have right now."

"What about heating them? Would it be difficult to add supplemental heat if I wanted it?"

"Not really, Max. With the triple-glazing, the shelters are basically solar heated. If you want to add some heaters to the shelters, we can have electric, gas or both run to the far corners and either type of heater can be installed. That would be handy to have on those winter days that are cloudy or cold enough outside that the solar gain can't counteract the cold."

"Well, I'm leaning toward the wood frame system, depending on cost, of course. I really like the looks of it compared to the aluminum. It would blend in a lot better with the cedar siding on the house."

"I tend to agree with you, Max, and I'm not saying that just because I'll make more money off you. If this were my house, that's the shelter I'd pick. Now, you ready to go outside so we can see how big we need to make this?"

"No time like the present, my friend. Let me grab my coat and boots and I'll meet you out there." I headed to my bedroom to get bundled up and met Mike outside by the pool.

"How much area were you looking to get under cover, Max? Just the pool itself or do you also want to cover part of the deck?"

"I also want to cover a pretty good area of the deck up towards the house. That will give us a decent area to sit in and watch whoever might be swimming, or just take a short break without having to go inside the house."

"That sounds like a good idea. I think we should start measuring from the house out to the end of the pool then. We can leave a four to six-foot gap between the house roof and the shelter, just so you can get outside and go around the pool without having to go through it. Make sense to you?"

"Sounds perfect, Mike. Let's get measuring and back inside."

We took some quick measures as best we could with the snow on the deck, but we got what we needed and headed back inside. After taking off our coats and boots, we headed back to the bar counter.

"Well, Mike, what are we looking at?"

"The pool measures twenty-four by fifty feet and the concrete deck is about forty by one hundred feet. I'd recommend we plan for the shelter to cover thirty-six by seventy-two feet. That gives you an extra twelve feet on the width, which allows for six feet on each side of the pool and twenty-two feet extra for the length. If we stick with six feet of coverage at the far end of the pool, you'd have sixteen feet on the end up here by the house and that allows plenty of space for your chairs and table inside. That also leaves you just about five and a half feet between the shelter and the roof of the house. It's almost like the guy who put the pool in originally knew what he was doin'," Mike snickered.

I laughed along with him, "Yeah, I guess he did. I was kinda worried about him when I called the first time, though. I wasn't too sure if he even knew what a pool was."

Mike punched me in the shoulder for that crack and joked, "That smart comment just jacked the price up an extra ten percent, bubba."

"Okay, okay, I take it back. You and your guys did a great job and always have, and I thank you for it. Now, let's get serious. How big of a dent is this gonna put in my bank account?"

"That all depends on when you want it installed. If you want it now, it's going to cost more because the company that makes the panels runs only half their normal crew in the winter and our guys are running about half-time, also. Most are working split days from our normal summer schedule."

"Let me tell you what I'm thinking, Mike, and you tell me if you can make it happen. I've met with an agency in Springfield this week and met four kids needing homes. I suggested that they all come out for a weekend with one of her staff so we could all get to know each other better. I thought it would also give the agency a chance to inspect the home and make sure they approve of the conditions. After suggesting the visit, I thought it would be great if we could go swimming while they're here. With all that said, I'd like to have the shelter in place by next weekend or the weekend after that. Is that possible?"

"Next weekend's not gonna happen, Max. I know the panel factory isn't what you'd call busy right now, but we have to allow for the time it takes to build any special panels and then another week to get them delivered. So, the earliest we could have everything here and installed would be the weekend after next and that's the best-case scenario. I wouldn't plan on having your guests anytime in the next three weeks. If you want to swim, that is."

"Well, that kinda sucks, but I'll live with it. Do you have the information you need to get the anchors installed before the panels are delivered?"

"Oh, yeah, that's not a problem. This company always ships the anchors when they receive the order along with the installation instructions and locations. That way, we can have everything ready on-site before the shelter panels are delivered and we usually install them as they come off the truck."

"Well, that should help. I'm having a cleaning service come out tomorrow and one of the things I'm having them take care of is cleaning off the pool deck area. That should help you guys out when you have the anchors. Providing, of course, we don't get any more snow between now and then. And if we do, I'll call them out again. Do you have any heaters to make working out there a little better for you?"

"You bet we do. If we try to install the anchors with the concrete as cold as it right now, we're more likely to crack it in places we don't want. I know we poured a good slab when we did the pool originally, but I'd rather be safe than sorry. The heaters will also cut the wind chill effect out here in the middle of nowhere."

"That sounds fine. Now, get your butt back to your office and get that shelter ordered."

"One more thing, Max, and I hate to ask, but this time of year, cash flow is tight. Do you have a problem with making a deposit payment of forty or fifty percent?"

"No problem. You've always been good to me. Once you have a total, let me know and I'll have my bank wire you seventy five percent. I'll pay the balance once the installation is completed. Would that be okay with you?"

"Perfect, Max. I knew there was a reason I liked working with you. You just reminded me what it is."

"Happy to help you out, Mike. Well, you better get moving and get your work schedule lined out. This should make your guys happy, too."

"A little late for Christmas, but still a very welcome present. Thanks for calling me on this. I'll make sure you're taken care of."

"I know you will. Thanks to you, too. Call me if you run into any problems or delays. Have a good day and be careful out there."

I waited to hear the ding of the driveway sensor to make sure he didn't get stuck leaving, then once I was sure he wasn't coming back, I got undressed and headed to my study to look over my lists to see if any changes were needed. After a few minutes of review, I couldn't see anything to update so I headed to the home theater to kick back and relax for a bit. If things worked out the way I was hoping, I probably wouldn't have much relaxation in the future, so I should probably enjoy it while I could.

I awoke the next morning, well-rested and ready to attack another day. The cleaning crew would be here shortly, and I wanted to be ready for them. I ran through the shower, got dressed, and fixed myself a quick breakfast. After cleaning up my breakfast mess, I heard the ding of the driveway sensor announcing, I hoped, Joyce's cleaning crew. I met them at the door, let them in and directed them to where they could stash their coats and boots. I then led the crew on a short tour of the house while giving them directions on what needed to be done. I saved the pool deck area for last. As it turned out, I should have done the pool deck first as one of the crew, Ron, was there specifically to take care of that project and he wanted to hit it early.

The crew went back out to their van to retrieve their equipment and supplies and got straight to work. Three of them attacked the study while Ron passed through the house with a what looked like a leaf blower. I followed him outside and pointed out a power supply he could use. He started blowing the snow at the living room doors and worked his way out to the end of the pool deck. It took him about half an hour to clear the area and it looked like a blizzard while the blower was running. When he was done, I asked him about the device and he told me it was basically your regular leaf blower with a larger motor and fan in it to help displace heavier materials. It was the first time he had tried to use it on snow, but he was glad he did because it performed flawlessly.

With that chore completed, we headed back into the house to warmth and comfort. The work in my study had been completed and I could hear the washer running so I assumed they were working on the bed linens from the other three bedrooms already. Ron found the team's leader, Dawn, and she gave him his next task. It turned out his job was to take the three comforters to an outside service to be cleaned. Dawn told me that with washing and drying the sheets from the other three bedrooms and the towels in the bathrooms, she thought they could finish quicker if the comforters were taken out. I let her know that was fine with me.

While Ron was gone, the rest of the crew dusted, vacuumed, mopped and worked like dirt demons to finish up the rest of the house. Ron returned with the comforters about two hours later, just as the rest of the crew was finishing up. The beds had already been re-made and the comforters were back in place in very short order.

Once they were done with the job, Dawn came to my study to let me know they were ready to move on to their next client. I headed out to the kitchen with my checkbook so I could pay them. After a quick review of their work, I was nicely surprised at the job they had done in a very short period time and I let them know how happy I was with the results. I wrote out a check to cover the charges quoted to me by Joyce. I then gave each crew member a $100 cash tip to thank them for their excellent work. All four were stunned at the tip, but happily accepted the unexpected gift.

I quietly slipped Ron an extra fifty bucks for taking care of the pool deck and let him know how appreciative I was for the extra work he'd done. I also told him he was welcome to come back and use the pool any time he wanted. Ron was a nice-looking guy about twenty-five to thirty years old and I silently hoped he would take me up on my offer.

Dawn, Ron and the others loaded up their equipment and supplies and headed down the drive to their next job. Just after the drive sensor dinged to announce their departure, the phone rang. I grabbed it in the kitchen after noticing from the caller ID it was M&M Pools calling. "Good afternoon, Mike. I assume you're calling with good news," I answered.

"Well, I think it's good, but I'll let you be the judge. I just got off the phone with the shelter people and they were ecstatic at getting an order like yours this time of year."

"Great, glad I could help them out."

"I told them the size of shelter we need, and it looks like they have enough of the regular wall panels already built and ready to ship out. They only have to assemble a few roof sections and the triangular wall sections for each end of the shelter."

"That sounds great. Did they give you any idea when they'd be ready to ship everything?"

"Like I told you yesterday, the anchors will be shipped tomorrow so we can get them installed before the panels arrive. They expect to have the special sections built in about a week and should be shipping everything else next Friday or the following Monday."

"Perfect. Now, I have some good news for you. The pool deck is cleaned off as promised. You wouldn't believe how they did it. Actually, it was just one of the crew who took care of it. He had this thing like a leaf blower on steroids and once he started, it was cleared off in about half an hour. Now you guys won't have to deal with that when you come out to install the anchors."

"Thanks for that, Max. We could have done it, but having it done before we get there will save us some time. Just hope it doesn't snow more between now and then. We'll bring the heaters out when we receive the anchors to help ward off the chill while we install them. Considering the size of the shelter, it will take at least a day to get all the anchors in place and ready. It won't be much fun this time of year, but I won't complain about the income. Speaking of which, the total for the shelter and everything comes up to $47,500. I know that's more than what you probably expected when you started this project, but it is what it is. That's not a problem, is it?"

"No problem at all. I'll call my bank this afternoon and have $36,000 wired to your business account. Sound okay to you?"

"That'll work just fine. Thanks."

"When do you think your guys will be here to install the anchors?"

"As long as UPS doesn't have any issues, we should have them Monday or Tuesday next week. I'll schedule the guys to come out Thursday, if that works for you."

"Thursday should be just fine. That will give me time to deal with some other things I need to take care of."

"It's a date, then. We'll see you next Thursday about nine in the morning."

"I'll be here and have everything ready for you, including a fresh pot of coffee. Have a great weekend, and we'll talk to you soon."

After ending the call with Mike, a thought popped in my head and I made another quick call to help Mike and his guys. I called a local party rental company and arranged to have a tent erected over the pool deck. I figured heaters without some way of cutting off the wind wouldn't be much help in keeping the guys semi-comfortable. I know it's their job to deal with the elements, but if I could help, I would.

I also had to make sure they had a tent that could be set up on concrete without damaging it and, fortunately, they had just what I was looking for. I scheduled them to install the tent Tuesday afternoon and they should expect me to have it for about two to three weeks. While they didn't much enjoy the thought of erecting a tent in early February, they were happy to have the income from the rental.

I next checked in with Herb about the status of my new Flex. He let me know it was still on schedule and I should expect delivery a little over a month from now. I knew nothing should really change in a couple days, but I was just trying to avoid any surprises. I had more than enough happening in my life that surprises would not be welcome. I finally got undressed again and called Clarence to see if he had heard anything from Anna. Unfortunately, he was in a meeting with another client and had to call me back. I waited for about an hour before the phone rang.

I anxiously answered, "Clarence, have you heard from Anna yet?"

"Hi, Max, I'm just fine. Glad you asked. How about yourself? You hangin' in there?"

"Sorry, Clarence. I'm getting a little nervous and freaked out. I'm just fine and glad you are, too. Now, answer my question, have you heard from Anna, yet?"

"As a matter of fact, I talked to her just about ten minutes ago. Anna and her staff have had several discussions about your proposal and it sounds like they approve of the idea. One of Anna's staff is single and has agreed to give up one of her weekends to come out and supervise a visit with all four boys. They agree that the visit would not only give each boy a chance to see where they would be living, but also give Anna a person on-site to evaluate your home and the living conditions for an adoptee, or two in the case of the twins."

"That sounds great. Did she give any hint as to when they would like the visit to happen?"

"The date seems to be up to you and the staff member. Her name is Carol Ward and it will be up to you to call her and arrange the date and time. It sounded to me like it could happen any time as long they have enough notice for Carol and the boys to prepare for the weekend."

"Perfect. Why don't you give me her number and I'll get in touch with her to make arrangements?" Clarence gave me the number and we said our goodbyes. I called Carol's number next.

"This is Carol Ward, how can I help you?" she answered.

"Good afternoon, Carol, this is Maxwill Sanders and I just got off the phone with my attorney, Clarence, and he said I should talk to you to make arrangements for a weekend visit."

"Good afternoon to you, also. You sure didn't waste any time calling, did you? Are you just a bit anxious, Mr. Sanders?"

"Well, I guess maybe a little bit. First, please call me Max. Everyone else does and I think as we work through this process together, you'll get tired of calling me Mr. Sanders. Clarence tells me that you and Anna have agreed to a weekend visit with the boys and that you would be coming along to make sure everything goes smoothly."

"Yes, sir. And you can call me Carol. I'm not too big on the formalities, myself. And, yes, I agreed to be the supervisor for your case and will be coming out to spend the weekend with you and the boys."

"Thanks. Is there anything special I need to do for or during the weekend?"

"Not really. From my discussions with Anna, I understand your home has four bedrooms. You, of course, have your own, the twins will use one, Thomas and Michael will use one and I'll be in the third bedroom. Is that correct?"

"Exactly. All the bedrooms currently have king-size beds and I figured, for the weekend anyway, the boys wouldn't mind sharing a bed for a couple of nights. You don't see a problem with that, do you, Carol?"

"No, I don't think it will be an issue. I mean, Joseph and Alexander already do everything together, so sharing a bed shouldn't be a problem with them, and I don't think Thomas and Michael would mind sharing the same bed, either."

"Excellent. I've already created a list of meals for the weekend, but I can make changes if you think it's necessary." I quickly went through my meal plans with her and then added, "I assumed you'd be leaving sometime Sunday afternoon, so I haven't planned anything for supper."

"It certainly sounds like you've given this a lot of thought, Max. Your meals sound fine and I don't see the need to change anything. You've selected a decent variety of food that should appeal to anyone. The boys and I will be just fine with your choices. As far as when we would leave, I had planned on Sunday afternoon, probably around four. That gives me time to get the boys back to their foster homes and me to get home for a relaxing evening. I think I'll need it after what sounds like is going to be a busy weekend. Now, the only other question I have for you is when would like to have this visit happen?"

"Well, it won't be this weekend or the next as I'm having some work done that will be a surprise for the boys."

"I hope you're not doing anything crazy, Max."

"That depends on what you consider crazy, Carol."

"Hiring a circus, going racing, swimming, you know, that kind of crazy. I don't think anyone would enjoy those things in February."

"You're safe with the first two guesses, but you struck out on the third."

"What?? You're planning to go swimming? In this weather?" I had to laugh at her reaction.

"To be honest, Carol, I have an in-ground pool at my home and I am having a shelter installed to allow us to do just that."

"You're not doing that just because of our visit, are you? That's going way too far, Max."

"No, it's not just because of your visit. I've wanted a shelter over the pool for a long time so I could use it in the winter, I just never got around to it. This seemed to be the perfect excuse for me get off my butt and make it happen. However, the shelter won't be installed and ready for use for a couple of weeks. I want to make sure the boys can go swimming while they're here, if they want to."

"Well, from what Anna has told me, if any of our clients can afford to do such a thing, it's you. Oh, I'm so sorry, Max, that sounded crass. I hope I didn't offend you."

I laughed and replied, "No Carol, I'm not offended. It's hard to be offended by the truth."

"Thank you. I'll try to abstain from any further such comments."

"No problem. So how does the third weekend from this one sound to you?"

"That sounds just fine, Max. It gives us plenty of time to arrange things with the boys and their foster families, and also allows me to prepare myself for a weekend with four active boys. I'll talk with Anna in the morning, let her know what the plan is, and we'll be all set."

"I'll look forward to it, Carol. Don't let the boys know about the pool, please. I want it to be a surprise when they get here. If you can get me their sizes, I'll get them some new swim trunks. I'm guessing they don't already have any."

"No, I'm sure they don't. I'll double-check on the sizes you'll need to get and let you know so you can have them when we get there."

"One more thing. How do we want to handle transportation? Right now, my only vehicle is a Shelby Mustang which would only hold two or three of the boys along with their bags. I have a new Ford Flex ordered, but it's not even built yet. If you want, I can meet you at your office in the afternoon, then we can head out to pick up the boys together. I could take two in my car if you can take two in yours. Does that sound okay?"

"That'd be fine, Max. Well, it sounds like we have everything set. I'll let you go and I'll start getting things arranged on my end."

"Thanks, Carol. I'll look forward to your visit and if anything comes up, I'll be sure to let you know. Have a great evening."

We ended our conversation and I sat back to think a bit. I wanted to make sure I had everything ready for Carol and the boys when the time came for their visit.

4

The rest of the week passed quietly, just me alone with my thoughts. I was still trying to convince myself I was doing the right thing. Not just for me, but for the boys also. I really wanted a family of some kind so my life would mean something, but was it right to bring boys into my home with me being gay? How would they deal with it and how would other kids deal with it? I finally decided we would just have to work through any situations that popped up as time went by. Hopefully, the boys would learn that it's important for a person to be themselves, whoever they may be.

The next Tuesday morning, I called Wesley at the party rental company. "Party Creations, this is Wesley, how can I brighten your day?"

"Wes, this is Max Sanders and I was calling to make sure the tent I requested is still going to be set up today."

"Max, good to hear from you. The crew is just about loaded up and ready to head your direction."

"Great. I have another favor to ask if it's not too late."

"Shoot. If we can do it, we sure will."

"I wanted to see if you had any heaters available to rent with the tent. My pool guys are going to be coming out sometime in the next couple of days to install anchors in my pool deck for a new shelter. I'd hate to see them freeze to death while they're doing it."

"Good thinking. We have electric and propane heaters available. Which do you think you'd prefer?"

"Well, I'm not sure. Which do you think would work best considering the size of the tent?"

"If it were me, I'd use the propane heaters. They'll put out more heat. Granted, with the outside temps, it won't be like Florida inside, but they'll still be better than the electric heaters."

"That sounds, fine, Wes. Can you have your crew bring them along and just add them to the rental contract. Oh, and will you provide propane tanks to go with the heaters?"

"You bet. We have fifty-pound tanks ready to go. We'll refill them when they're returned and add the fuel charges to your final total."

"That sounds like a plan. I'll let you get off the phone so you can let your guys know to bring the heaters. I'll be here when your crew arrives. Just have them pull up to the garage doors and they can move materials through there to the pool deck."

"No problems, Max, we're happy to help. It's pretty quiet with tent rentals this time of year and this will help stave off some boredom for a day."

We hung up and I headed out to the garage to make sure the crew would be able to move their materials through it without problems. I decided to move the Shelby to the other side of the garage so I wouldn't be worrying about it getting hit by stray items. Once that task was completed and a few other items moved out of the way, I headed back inside to wait for the crew to arrive. Just as I sat down with a fresh cup of coffee, I heard the driveway sensor ding and I carried my cup out to garage to meet the crew. I directed them on where to park and then met the leader of the crew.

"Good morning. My name's Max. I'm glad you could get here today," I said as I greeted them. "Did you have any problems finding the place?"

"Morning, Max. I'm Al, this is Frank, and the straggler there is Ken. Your directions were perfect. I hope you're ready for a tent."

"Sure am, Al. I had the pool deck cleared last week and fortunately we haven't had any more snow to clean off, so you should be good to go. Let me show you where the tent goes." I led Al and his crew through the garage and out the back door to the pool area. "This is it. Think you'll have any problems."

"We shouldn't. The area's nice and clean, just like you said. You won't mind if we set up the heaters first just to take the chill off, do you?"

"Nope, go right ahead. I don't need anyone freezing today. If you want, I also have a fresh pot of coffee in the house for any takers."

"Thanks, Mr. Sanders. I don't think we need any right now but will probably want some when we're done." Al turned to Frank and Ken and said, "Okay, guys, start hauling stuff and get it back here, the heaters first."

"Well, I'll head back inside and leave you guys to it. Just come on in if you need coffee, a bathroom, or just to warm up for a few. Oh, and no falling in the pool. I don't want any popsicles hanging around after the tent's up."

All three gave a quick laugh and then Al said, "Before we get started, I assume you want the clear end panel facing the house."

"Yes, please. That way I can watch anybody working inside the tent in case they fall in the pool or need some help."

"Will do, sir. Thanks."

I headed back inside, picked up the book I'd been reading and took a seat where I could keep an eye on the progress of the tent. Al and the guys wasted no time getting things going. I'd never seen a tent like this set up and it was interesting to watch. I ended up paying more attention to that than I did reading.

The poles to support the corners of the tent were placed in large rubber blocks to protect the concrete, and then weights were placed outside the poles to keep them standing up straight. Next to go up were the tent's roof supports, and they just slid over the tops of the poles to a stop about eight inches down from top of the pole.

Once the basic framework was in place, they were ready to pull the top over the roof supports. They laid the roof section on the ground on one side of the frame and then tossed ropes over the roof supports so they could pull it into position from the other side. They walked to the other side of the pool, grabbed the ropes and began pulling. The roof section must have been heavier than it looked as I could tell they were straining to get it in place. Once the roof was properly positioned, they attached it to the tops of the posts, then started attaching the sides to the frame. From start to finish, the project took just over two hours. While Frank and Ken loaded up their tools and equipment, Al came inside to let me know they were done.

"Okay, Mr. Sanders, we're all set. The tent's in place and so are the heaters. We shut the heaters off as we didn't want to waste the gas if you weren't going to be outside."

"It looks great, Al. My pool guys will be nicely surprised to see they'll have a tent to work in. Do you guys need a coffee to warm up?"

"I'd sure appreciate a nice warm cup and I don't doubt Frank and Ken will, too. They're loading up our tools, but I'll have them come in when they're done."

"Why don't you go tell them and I'll get it ready for you."

"Be right back."

I set the guys up at the bar counter and had everything ready when they came back in. "Here you go fellas, cream and sugar are here, also, if you need either or both."

All three took a stool, sat down and fixed their cups as desired. While they drank, and warmed up, I said to Al, "Wes asked for a payment of fifty percent of the rental once you were done. Let me know how much you need and I'll get you a check." Al gave me the amount and I headed to my study to get the check they needed. After handing the check to Al, Ken said, "That's a damn nice Shelby in the garage. How do you like it?"

"I love it, Ken. It's a blast to drive. Not much fun in the winter, of course, but as long as you're careful, you can get where you need to go."

"Yeah, I'm sure it's a handful in the snow and I bet you can forget goin' anywhere with that thing when there's ice on the roads."

"Oh, yeah, when there's ice, I'm stuck at home for a few days. Of course, there are worse places to get stuck," I added with a chuckle.

"It might be okay for you, out here on your own, but when I'm stuck at home, I have a wife and five kids to deal with. All in all, I'd rather be at work," Ken laughed.

Al interrupted, "Well, Mr. Sanders, I think we'll get out of your way. Wes has us scheduled to remove the tent in two or three weeks, is that right?"

"That should work out. The pool shelter I'm having installed is due to be delivered in the next week or so and they think they'll have it completed by the next Friday."

"Well, if that doesn't work out, we'll come back whenever you're ready for us. If you need anything else, don't hesitate to call."

"Will do, Al. Thanks to you, Ken and Frank for your work today. Hope you all enjoy the rest of the day."

I followed them out to the garage and after they left, moved the Shelby back to its regular spot. I closed the door and headed back inside to finish my own cup of coffee and read my book a bit longer. After a quick lunch, I gave Mike, the pool guy, a call. "Afternoon, Mike. How ya doing?"

"Dandy, Max. How 'bout yourself?"

"I'm not complaining. I just called to see if the shelter anchors had arrived and if your guys were still coming out Thursday to install them."

"As a matter of fact, they just showed up. I'll have the guys out there about nine Thursday morning to start work. Is that all right with you?"

"That'd be just fine. I have a little surprise for them when they get here."

"I hope it's a good one, 'cause they're not looking forward to working in the cold."

"Oh, I think they'll like it. I had a tent set up over the pool deck with propane heaters. I was told it won't be quite as warm as Florida, but it should make the job a bit more comfortable for them. I'm hoping maybe forty-five to fifty degrees inside with heaters running full blast."

"Well, that was a mighty nice thing for you to do. We were going to bring out some small portable enclosures, kinda like the ones the phone company uses, just to block the wind, but they aren't heated. A full tent will probably blow their minds."

"Look, I know how miserable it is to work in these weather conditions and I don't want to have worry about anybody getting frostbite just so I can get a pool enclosure installed. I have the tent for however long we need it, so it'll still be up when the shelter's panels are delivered, also. That should make that a lot easier to deal with."

"It sure will. I may actually come out with the guys tomorrow to see what it looks like and get them started on installing the anchors."

"That'd be just fine. I'll have the coffee on and warm for ya. You and I can sit inside and 'supervise' the work."

"Ha! I like the sound of that idea. The guys won't like it much, but I sign their paychecks, so what're they gonna do? We'll see you Thursday morning, then, Max. Have a good afternoon."

"Thanks, Mike, see you then."

I spent the rest of the afternoon, relaxing and reading. I felt I had done everything I could so far. All my lists were ready and waiting to be acted on once I knew for sure what was going to happen and when. I just had to try and not get stressed out about it.

I got up early Thursday morning, showered and dressed, then headed out to the pool to crank up the heaters so they could start doing their job. While the heaters were cutting the chill over the pool, I headed back inside and fixed myself a quick breakfast. I had just finished cleaning up my mess and started a fresh pot of coffee when the drive sensor dinged promptly at nine announcing the arrival of Mike and his guys. Hopefully the heaters had done their trick and the guys wouldn't suffer too much. The concrete would still be cold as hell, but I didn't have any way to warm that up, also.

I answered the doorbell and let Mike and his crew in. "Morning, Mike, guys. Hope you're ready for some bone-chilling work." They grumbled unhappily at the thought while Mike chuckled quietly to himself. I led them through the house to the glass wall facing the pool and said, "There ya go, fellas. Tented, heated and ready to roll." Their eyes grew wide with surprise and Mike busted out in full laughter this time. "What's so damn funny, Mike. You knew I'd done this."

"I sure did, but I somehow forgot to pass the word on to them," he replied while pointing over his shoulder to his crew. "I've been giving them grief all day yesterday and this morning on the way out about how cold, windy and miserable it was. They were starting to get really pissed at me. It took everything I had to maintain a straight face the whole time. By the way, this is Ted and John."

"That was cruel, Mike. Funny as hell, but still cruel. C'mon on guys, follow me and I'll show where you can get power, then you can bring the anchors and your tools out." I stepped through the door to the pool deck and showed them where the power outlets were located, then led them through the back door of the garage so they could retrieve their equipment from the truck.

Mike and I headed back inside to have some coffee and conversation while Ted and John got to work. We settled into some comfy chairs where we could 'supervise' and watch as they started measuring and marking anchor locations. I was glad I'd requested the clear end panel on the tent so we could watch their progress. They were soon ready to start cutting holes in the concrete to install the anchors.

Mike cracked the door and hollered out, "Double-check all those locations before you start drilling. I don't want to have any mistakes or holes that need to be filled. I'm pretty sure Max doesn't either." Mike sat back down with a contented look on his face as he watched the crew do exactly as instructed.

"What's with the smile, Mike?", I asked.

"I just love to give them hell. I know they're all good guys and know what they're doing, or they wouldn't be working for me. But, sometimes, I still like to remind them who's the boss."

"Boy, I'm glad I don't work for ya, I'd have snapped a long time ago. One of the perks of working alone is not having to deal with asshole bosses like you," I laughed as I punched him in the shoulder.

"Oh damn, Max, that's cold. I think I'm seeing an additional 'jerk' charge being added to your final bill for this shelter," he retorted.

"Sorry, man, couldn't resist. I'll take it back if you'll forget about the 'jerk' surcharge."

"Done. Now, speaking of work, when's your next book due out?"

"It's going to be a while, Mike. I put my writing on hold while I came to terms with being gay. Once I did that, I decided I still wanted the family I'd dreamed about for so long, but for obvious reasons, going the *normal* route isn't going to work for me. It wasn't easy, but I've managed to talk to a child service agency in town. While they aren't really excited about the thought of a gay man adopting, they're at least thinking about it."

"Why would you even dream of giving up the life you've got just to complicate it? You needing some new challenges in your life?"

"I don't look at it as new challenges, though I'm sure there will be some. I have a good life, Mike, and I want to be able share that life with someone. Also, I'm not going to live forever, and I sure don't want the government getting my estate when I die, so I'm hoping to have someone in my life who I can pass it on to."

At that moment, Ted popped the door open and asked, "Hey, Max, can I use a bathroom, or should I just whiz into the pool?"

"Aw, c'mon, Ted. You know there's no peeing in the pool. Bathroom's right down the hall toward the garage, last door on the right."

"Thanks, man. John will probably need it when I'm done."

"No problem. You guys need any coffee or anything else to drink?"

"I don't right now, but I can't say for John. He might when he comes in."

"I've got a fresh pot on the warmer whenever you want some."

"Thanks, maybe in a bit."

After Ted headed back outside, John came in to take his turn, then said on his way back out, "Max, we can't thank you enough for the tent and heaters. It's making the job much easier to deal with. I really wasn't looking forward to working in those little enclosures we have."

"Glad I thought of it, John. I almost called too late to get it set up in time for you, but the party place was happy to take care of it. I'm guessing they don't do much tent rental in February."

"No, I bet they don't. Oh, Ted said you had some drinks available. Do you mind if I grab one?"

"Not at all. Coffee's in the pot on the counter and soft drinks and tea are in the fridge. Help yourself."

John grabbed a Pepsi and headed back outside after thanking me for the drink. After he closed the door, Mike and I resumed our conversation.

"So, tell me, Max, how many kids are you planning to take in?"

"Well, I was originally planning on adopting only one, but after meeting with Anna, the director of the agency I'm talking to, she introduced me to four boys in need of good homes. I haven't said anything to her just yet, but if things go as I hope they do when they come out for a visit, I'm going to see if I can adopt all four."

"FOUR!?!? And all four of 'em boys, have you lost your freakin' mind?"

"You're not the first to ask that question, Mike. I'm still asking myself the same thing a couple times a day. But, the more I think about it, the more it feels like the right thing to do."

"You're a braver man than I and I wish you luck. May I ask why you're doing this without appearing to be a nosy Nellie?"

"Ha, sure you can. I've have a great life, Mike. I'm a successful writer who's had four best-sellers, I've invested my earnings well and obviously live a very comfortable life. I've finally figured out that life with wealth and comfort is meaningless without someone to share it with. Since marriage and kids aren't going to be possible, I thought I'd check into the kids' part by itself and see how that would work. So far, so good, but I'll have to wait and see if it really happens."

"Well, I truly do wish you luck 'cause you're going to need it."

"I know I am and I'll willingly accept any extra luck you have and are willing to share."

At that moment, Ted and John came back inside announcing they were done with the anchors and ready for Mike to take a look. We all headed out to inspect their work and Mike verified the placement of the anchors and agreed that everything looked good. Ted commented, "We both really want to thank you for the tent and heaters. It made the job go so much easier."

"Yeah, we would have frozen to death out here without that," John added with a bit of a shiver.

Mike looked at his guys and said, "Why don't you two get the tools loaded up while I talk to Max a minute, then we'll be on our way."

"Sure thing, boss," Ted replied.

Mike and I headed inside while Ted and John started loading their tools through the garage and into the truck. Mike turned to me and said, "Well, Max, it looks like we're ready to install the wall panels and heaters when they get delivered. I checked with the manufacturer before leaving the office and they tell me they are still on schedule to be shipped the middle of next week."

"That's good news, Mike. Any idea when you and your guys will be out to set it all up?" I asked.

"We're expecting the delivery truck to arrive sometime Thursday afternoon. The driver's going to check into the Hampton Inn and get some rest after a long drive from New Mexico. We're planning to come out Friday morning, leading the delivery driver, to unload and start setting it up. The driver also works for the company. He'll supervise the installation and be on hand to make sure everything goes the way it should."

"That sounds just great. I'll start the heaters when I get up and have the coffee going when you get here. How many of you will be here?"

"Well, the panels aren't that heavy and usually two guys can handle them, but since we're going to haul them through the garage, I figured we'll bring four crew guys, myself and the delivery driver for a total of six of us. That going to be a problem?"

"Not at all, I just want to be prepared so everything's ready to roll when you get here. I'll open the rear garage door to make it easier to get the panels through without having to fight the regular size door."

"Now, I have one other thing I want to talk to you about, Max. While we appreciate the tent and heaters, you really didn't have to do that. We had planned on bringing our portable enclosures and I had calculated your price based on that plan. I now think since you went to the extra lengths and expense to rent the tent, I owe you a discount or rebate on the total price I quoted after placing the panel order."

"Nope, not gonna happen, Mike. I was happy to help. I know how cold it can be out here in February with the wind and everything, and I didn't want to have to worry about anybody freezing on my account. I could have easily waited until it warmed up to have the shelter done, but I wanted to have it available for the boys when they come out for a visit in a couple weeks."

"Well, I still feel like I'm overcharging you and want to discount the price anyway."

"If you feel that strongly about it, I have an idea for you to consider."

"What's that?" he asked.

"Instead of refunding the money to me, how do you feel about making a donation to a group that could certainly use some financial assistance?"

"Hey, that's a good idea, how'd you come up with that so quickly?" Mike asked.

"Herb at the Ford dealership is doing the same thing on the new Flex I've ordered. He's willing to give me a rebate if I pay cash for the car when it comes in instead of financing the thing. I told him I'd be happy to pay cash, but he could donate the rebate to someone else."

"I like it, Max. Who's the donation going to?"

"Whoever you want, but Herb is sending the rebate to the adoption agency I'm working with. With the state budget being what it is lately, they are always fighting to find the funds they need to ensure they place kids in good homes. It takes a lot of money to do the inspections and investigations required by the state, but the state apparently doesn't think they should have to pay for them, so it's up to the agency to raise some of the funds they require as the need arises."

"Sounds like a great cause to me, Max. I'll personally deliver the check to the agency and tell them you sent me."

"Go right ahead with the personal delivery if you like but leave my name out of it. I don't want them knowing I'm involved in any way with the donation because I don't want them to think I'm trying to 'buy' my way through the process. I want to be treated just like anyone else, no special favors or consideration."

"Gotcha'. Mum's the word. Well, it looks like Ted and John have everything loaded up. I guess we'll get out of your hair until the panels are delivered next Friday morning. Thanks again for the tent and heaters."

"I'm always happy to help, Mike. Tell the guys thanks, too, and we'll see you next Friday. If anything changes, just let me know."

"Will do, Max. Have a good weekend." With that, Mike headed out to the truck and they headed down the drive. Since I wasn't expecting any other visitors today, I got undressed and enjoyed the remainder of the day relaxing.

✳ ✳ ✳

The next week passed slowly but steadily until Thursday afternoon when Mike called. "Afternoon, Max. Hope I didn't wake you from your much-needed beauty sleep."

"Nope, I'm awake and dealing with some financial shenanigans trying to increase my wealth. You know, your typical retired, rich guy fun and games. What's up?"

"The delivery driver just called to let us know he's checked into the Hampton Inn. He was going to head out to get some supper then head back to get some much-needed shuteye. We plan on meeting at the shop in the morning about eight and then heading your way shortly after that. We should be at your place about nine or so. You still want to do this?"

"You bet. I'll have the heaters running and the coffee going when you get here."

"Sounds great, Max. I have an electrician scheduled to show up about two in the afternoon to run the wire for the shelter heaters. I figure we'll have most of the shelter bolted down by then and he can get started on his part of the project."

"Perfect. It sounds like you have everything planned. I'll just sit back and 'supervise' again. I'll see you guys in the morning."

"We'll be there, Max. Have a great evening."

I kicked back the rest of the evening, watching a movie and letting the mind unwind for a bit. Bed came early that night so I could be up early in the morning to get things ready for Mike and his guys. Morning reared its ugly head much quicker than I thought it should, but I still got up and headed out to start the heaters. Too bad my brain wasn't in gear before I went out there because it was colder than hell with no clothes on. I cranked up the heaters anyway, then headed back inside to pull on something warm before Mike showed up. I found some sweats and headed to the kitchen to get some food. I was just about done with breakfast when the sensor dinged to announce the arrival of my shelter.

I opened the front and rear garage doors and waited for the guys to show up. Mike pulled past the driveway, then got out and directed the truck driver into position to unload the panels. Once he was in position, Mike's guys began hauling tools through the garage and Mike introduced me to the truck driver, "Morning, Max. I'd like you to meet Phil. He works for the pool shelter company as their delivery driver and installation supervisor."

We shook hands and I said, "Nice to meet you, Phil. I can't believe you drove all the way from New Mexico. That's one heck of a long trip."

"It sure was, that's why I went to bed right after supper last night. I'm feeling more alive now."

"I imagine you spend a lot time away from home delivering and setting up shelters. Bet your wife hates your job."

"She doesn't really hate it, but she doesn't really love it either. It pays well since I get paid 24 hours a day while I'm on the road. That lets us save enough money through the summer that we can survive the winter with minimal income. There's usually not a lot of shelters being delivered in winter. I think the last winter delivery I had was 3 years ago."

"Well, I'm sorry if I ruined any plans you had with my order."

"Aw, don't worry about it. It's all part of the job. Not gonna be much fun today with the temperature where it's at, though."

"Follow me, Phil, and I'll show you where the pool is." I led Phil and Mike through the garage and when we stepped out the back side, Phil couldn't believe his eyes.

"A tent?! Are you freaking kidding me? Did you set this up, Mike?" he sputtered.

"Wasn't me, Phil. You have to thank Max for that."

"Well, thank you, Max. I've never had a winter install happen in a tent before. Guess there's always a first time for everything. Maybe this won't be as bad as I thought." Phil came over and wrapped me up in a giant bear hug. He suddenly backed off and said, "Sorry 'bout that, man, I don't usually go 'round huggin' guys, but for some reason, I couldn't help myself. That tent is about the nicest thing a customer's ever done for me."

"No worries, but I didn't do it just for you", I laughed. "I was thinking about Mike's guys as well."

"Of course, you were."

"I'm glad you like it, though. I'll get out of your guys' way and let you get on with it. Coffee and bathrooms are inside, which is where I'll be. You need anything, just ask." I headed on in and let them get to work. Mike got them started, then came inside, also. He helped himself to a cup of coffee and sat in a chair next to me where he could watch the work as it progressed. "Is the electrician still scheduled to show up this afternoon?" I asked.

"Yep, I talked to him yesterday afternoon and he said he had all the materials he needed. He should show up shortly after lunch."

"I hadn't thought about lunch yet, Mike. What do you guys want, or did you bring something with you?"

"I was going to send one of the guys over to the Subway at the truck stop to pick up some sandwiches for everyone and have them brought back here. If you don't mind, that is."

"Good idea. If you find out what everyone wants, I'll call the order in and pick it up for you."

"I'll let them work a while before I bring up food. If I do it now, that's all they're gonna think about until they sit down to eat," he joked.

"I know what you mean. Now that you've brought it up, it's all I can think about. And I just finished breakfast."

We sat in our chairs and watched while the guys made short work of getting the wall panels in place and bolted down. As they were placing the last wall panel at the far end, Mike went out to get their food orders. He came back in and handed me the list of sandwiches to order. I had all the drinks here, so I didn't have to worry about that. I called the order in and told them I'd be there in fifteen minutes to pick it up.

Ten minutes later, I got up to grab my coat and Mike asked, "Mind if I go with? I'd like a ride in that car. I've seen it several times, but never gotten a ride."

"Why not? Grab your coat and let's go."

He stuck his head out the door to let the guys know we'd be back shortly with lunch, then met me in the garage. He climbed in the passenger seat and pulled on his seatbelt. After we got out of the still slick drive and on clean, dry roadway, I punched it a bit. "Wow, this thing really kicks you in the ass, doesn't it?" he asked.

"That, it does. And quite nicely, I might add. It stops on a dime, too. It's a blast to drive. I'm gonna miss driving it if I'm successful with the adoption."

"You're not selling it, are you?"

"Hell no, but if I accomplish my goal and adopt all four boys, this car, as nice as it is, ain't gonna be big enough to carry all five of us anywhere."

"Ooh, didn't think about that. That's why you ordered the Flex you told me about, isn't it?"

"Exactly. Actually, it was one of the first things I did after my first meeting with Anna. Of course, that was only a couple weeks ago, and it takes about a month and half to two months from order to delivery. Especially with one optioned out the way I wanted it."

"I assume you got the all-wheel drive version, what with the drive you have to deal with."

"You bet. I love this car, but when it snows more than a couple inches or ices, I'm stuck at home until I can get someone out to plow and salt the drive, and that ain't cheap. I should have had a four-wheel or all-wheel drive long ago, but I figured since it was just me stuck out here, it wasn't that big a deal. With a couple kids or more, I can't be stuck anymore."

"No, you're right about that. You never know when you might need to deal with an emergency."

"My thought, exactly. Well, here we are, let's go get lunch." We headed into the Subway and up to the counter. I told the girl what I was there for and she let me know they were still making the last sandwich. Mike pulled out his wallet and I told him, "Put that away, Mike, your money's no good here."

"Now, that's not right, Max. You shouldn't be buying our lunch, too. The tent's more than enough."

"Not to worry, it's my treat today." I paid for the order, we got back in the Shelby and headed back home. I honked the horn as I pulled into the garage to let the guys know we were back and we headed inside. We met them coming in the glass door from the pool deck and I directed them to the bathrooms so they could clean up before eating. We all met back in the kitchen where Mike and I had all the food laid out and ready for them. They took seats on the barstools, then dug into their meal while I got everyone's requested drinks and we settled in.

After swallowing my first bite, I asked, "Well, Phil, how's everything going out there?"

"Perfect, Max. These guys did a great job installing the anchors and everything's lining up just like it should. You should be proud of your crew, Mike."

"Oh, I am. They don't hear it enough, I'm sure, but I think they know how I much I appreciate the work they do."

"I'd like to hear some of that appreciation in my paycheck, Mike. Think you could arrange that?" Al asked with a chuckle.

Mike laughed and responded with, "We'll see what we can do, Al. Any other complaints?"

A resounding chorus of 'Nope' rang through the house and we all enjoyed a good laugh.

"Now that that's settled, what's left to do?" I asked.

"Next, we start on the roof. I'll roll out the lift so we can get the panels up there safely. I just have to make sure I don't drive the thing into the pool."

"Good plan, Phil."

"Yeah, I thought so. Once the roof is in place, then we get to go over all the bolts again to make sure they're properly tightened and the thing won't collapse. Once we do that, we'll be done."

When the feeding frenzy ended, Phil, Al and the others headed back out to start work on the roof panels. They were moving right along when the drive sensor dinged.

"That should be the electrician, Max," Mike said. "I'll meet him out in the drive and show him where everything is."

Once the electrician had started his work, Mike came back in and re-settled in what had become his chair. Four hours later, the roof was completed, and the electrician had the heaters up and running. Mike and I headed out to inspect the job and we were both happy with the way everything worked out. The temperature inside the shelter was already on the rise and I could tell the heaters were going to do a fine job when the skies were cloudy. I thanked all the guys for their hard work under such difficult conditions.

Phil said, "Thanks again for the tent, Max. Without that, we'd have been here tomorrow finishing up. Now, I can get started on the long drive home today, so I'm going to hit the road. Mike, thanks for the order, pleasure to work with you again. Hopefully, the next one will be a spring or summer install. Max, thanks for everything. I hope the shelter works as well as you expect."

"I'm sure it will, Phil. I'll walk you out." I followed him out through the garage and before he could get in his truck, I handed him $500 cash.

"Max, thanks, but that's not necessary," he objected. "I'm well paid and I'm just doing my job."

"Take it, Phil, you've earned it. Take your wife on a nice weekend trip somewhere once you get back home. You've done a great job today and I appreciate it."

The next thing I knew, he had pulled me into another great bear hug. When he backed off, he said, "Damn, I don't know what's come over me. I got to quit doing that."

"Hell, don't worry about it. Nothing wrong with a hug now and then. Thanks again for all your work, have a safe trip home and don't forget, you owe your wife a trip."

"I won't, Max. Enjoy your new shelter." Phil climbed in his truck and headed down the drive for his long trip back home to New Mexico.

I met Mike and his crew inside to finish up my business with him. "Okay, Mike, time to settle up. Let me call the bank real quick." I placed the call and arranged to have the final payment wired to Mike's account in the morning. "Okay, all set. The balance due should be in your account by noon tomorrow."

"Thanks, Max. Been a pleasure doing business with you, as always."

I handed each of Mike's crew a crisp, new $100 bill as thank you for a job well done and asked them to wait for Mike at their truck. After the last one was out the door, I turned to Mike and asked him, "Were you serious about the discount?"

"Of course, I am."

"Well, you know how to handle it. Thanks, again, for the great work, Mike. You and your guys go above and beyond for your customers."

"We aim to please, Max. I want to thank you for the work. Winters always suck, and this just made it a little less sucky. Enjoy your new shelter."

"Oh, I will. If you have any other customers looking for a shelter, you're welcome to bring them out so they can see one in person before ordering it."

"That'd be great. We'll get out of here, now. Enjoy your evening. If you need anything else, you know where to find us. And good luck with the adoption. I'll be expecting an invite to the celebration once it happens."

"You'll definitely be on the list, Mike."

"See you later," he called over his shoulder as he headed down the hallway to the garage.

Mike climbed in the truck with his guys and followed in Phil's tire tracks as they headed back to town. I closed the garage doors and headed inside to make another call. I got a hold of Wes at Party Creations to let him know I was done with the tent and they could come take it down any time. He told me his tent people didn't work weekends and it would be Monday before they came back out. I let him know that was fine and I would see his people Monday afternoon.

I headed to my bedroom and got undressed. I'd been out and about so much lately and with all the people coming to the house the past few weeks, I was getting really tired of wearing clothes as much as I had been. I headed to the kitchen to fix something for supper, then to the theater to watch another movie.

As I watched the movie, a depressing thought slowly creeped into my conscious mind. I realized I was probably going to have to start wearing clothes around the house after years of not doing so. While it wouldn't bother me for the boys to see me nude, I was certain Anna and her agency would have a problem with it. To them, it was bad enough I was gay. I bet if they knew I liked to lounge around the house, swim and take walks in the woods sans clothing, I wouldn't stand a chance of being successful in adopting any child, especially the boys. I was going to have to be extra careful when they were here for their weekend visit, keep my brain engaged and not stroll around nude. I guess if that was one sacrifice I would have to make, I'd do it. Only time will answer that question.

The Party Creations crew arrived on Monday as scheduled to remove the tent. They took extra care taking things down to ensure they didn't damage the new pool shelter. The new heaters in the shelter were running, I had removed the pool cover and turned on the pool heater over the weekend so the pool was ready to use when Carol and the boys got here. The crew liked what I had done and couldn't believe the change from what it looked like before they put up the tent.

I thanked them for their service, tipped each person another $100 and gave them a check for the balance of the rental charges, including enough extra to cover the cost of any propane used. After they had everything loaded up and were on their way down the drive, I closed the garage and headed back inside.

The Wednesday afternoon before the boys' visit, I called Carol at the agency to see if everything was still on schedule for the boys coming out the upcoming weekend. She confirmed that she and the boys were all set, and we made plans to meet at her office at three-thirty Friday afternoon, then head out to pick up the boys. The rest of Wednesday and Thursday seemed to crawl by. I made a shopping trip into town Thursday afternoon to pick up everything on my food list for the weekend. I was about to head for the checkout when the five-watt bulb in my head suddenly clicked on.

I had barely remembered I needed to find swimsuits for the boys and had forgotten to get their sizes from Carol. I called her real quick and after I had the info I needed, I headed to the boy's department to find new suits for all four. I don't know what I was thinking, but have you ever tried to buy a swimsuit at Walmart in February? Let me tell you, it can't be done, at least, not at one in Illinois. What I ended up getting were some basic loose-fitting exercise type shorts with drawstrings that they could wear and could then be tossed in a dryer after a thorough wringing.

Substitute swim-shorts in hand, I finally headed to the checkout. $538.27 poorer, I headed out to the Shelby to load everything in and hit the road for home. I filled the trunk completely and had to lay down the back seats to make room for everything. It was a good thing I had a larger car on the way as I could tell the Shelby would not work for long. If I succeeded in adopting all four boys, I could be spending that much money and probably more every week just in food. I didn't even want to think about what clothing four growing boys would go through. Not yet, anyway.

After I got home, I unloaded the car and got everything put away. I was glad I had cleaned out the garage refrigerator earlier this week as I needed it in addition to the space in the Sub-Zero fridge in the kitchen for everything. I laid the boys swim-shorts in the bedrooms I thought they would be using.

I then got undressed and spent what was likely to be one of my last nude evenings watching movies and browsing the latest magazines I subscribed to before heading to bed about midnight. I spent a restless night trying to sleep. I just couldn't stop thinking about the changes I was about to make in my life and, with luck, the lives of four boys. I finally fell asleep around four in the morning and woke up to the sun streaming through my window at nine. That's why I had my bedroom on the east side of the house, I liked to wake up to the sun filling my room with the light of the new day.

I took a shower, headed to the kitchen to fix some breakfast and suddenly realized my stomach was not going to cooperate. I ran back to the bathroom and promptly lost what little I had managed to swallow. I really needed to get my nerves under control or I would not survive the upcoming weekend.

I cleaned up the kitchen and after spending most of the day in nervous expectation, I ran through my lists for the weekend one more time and, satisfied I had everything covered, got dressed and headed to Springfield to meet Carol. I arrived at the agency's office thirty minutes early and while waiting for Carol to finish some work before she could leave for the weekend, I talked to Anna for a bit.

"Good afternoon, Max. Are you ready for your weekend with the boys?"

"I think I have everything covered, Anna. I've got the food we'll need and shorts for the boys to use while swimming since the pool shelter is completed. I tried to get actual swimsuits for them but discovered that's an impossible thing to find in Springfield in February."

Anna laughed heartily and said, "I could have told you that. But other than that little glitch, it sounds like you have everything well under control."

"I sure hope so. I really want this weekend to go well."

"I'm sure you'll be just fine, Max. And Carol will be there to provide some help and guidance. Of course, her main job during the weekend will be to see how you deal with boys and any situations that come up. She'll also be looking at the house and property to make sure they'll be safe and well cared for."

"I think she'll find everything in good shape."

"I'm sure she will. She'll also be closely watching how you interact with the boys and being especially observant of anything she feels might be inappropriate. You probably won't like that much, but I warned you up front we would be going to extra lengths with your case to ensure the boys would be protected."

"You're right, Anna, I don't like it much, but I do understand. Just because I'm gay, it doesn't mean that I will molest the boys at the first opportunity. I know you must think that way with your job, but from my side, it's rather ridiculous that everyone believes the worst of people like me. I'm gay, not a pedophile."

"I'm sorry, Max, but we always have to think in terms of the worst-case scenario, regardless of who we're working with. We don't like it much it either, but history has proven to be the best indicator of the future. Especially with the children we work with. Our paramount concern is their well-being."

"I know it is, Anna, but that doesn't mean I have to like the methods or assumptions we must live under."

"To some brighter news, Max, all our investigations and background checks have been completed and I must say you are, by far, one of the best candidates I have ever seen for either fostering or adopting a child. I don't think I've ever seen an individual as squeaky clean as you are."

I chuckled at that comment because I knew there was nothing to find. "That's good to hear. That was the one thing I did feel confident about because I knew there was nothing to find. I know you couldn't take my word for it, but still, it feels good to know that a person can live a good life and not get in trouble."

A light knock on the door was followed by Carol popping her head in saying, "I finally have everything wrapped up, Max. I'm ready to go when you are."

"Be right there, Carol." I shook hands with Anna, "Thanks for your time today, Anna. I'm sure you'll receive a complete and detailed report from Carol Monday morning. Have a great weekend."

"You too, Max. Don't let the boys drive you crazy."

I met Carol in the lobby and we headed out to our cars. "Shall I follow you, Carol, since I don't know where we're going to pick up the boys?"

"That shouldn't be a problem, Max. I've arranged with their foster parents to meet us at the Steak 'n Shake on Veteran's Parkway at five, that way we don't have to drive to three different houses to pick them all up."

"That just makes too much sense. I should have thought of that. I know the way there, so if we get separated, I'll see you there."

We hopped in our cars and headed out to meet the boys. Carol and I were the first to arrive and were a bit early, so we headed inside and arranged for a large table to accommodate the two of us, the four boys and any others who came along. Thomas was the next to arrive with his foster mom. I saw him point us out and she led the way over to our table. Thomas walked up to me, stuck his hand out and said, "Hi Mr. Sanders. Did you know I was spending the weekend at your house?"

"As a matter of fact, I did, young man. Are you looking forward to it?" I replied as we shook hands.

"Yeah. It'll be neat to be somewhere else a couple days," he chimed as he climbed up in the chair next to me. He leaned in and whispered in my ear, "You aren't still mad at me, are you?"

"Never was and never could be, Thomas. We're fine," I whispered back. I looked up at the young woman with Thomas and introduced myself, "Good afternoon, I'm Max Sanders. You must be Thomas' foster mom."

"Nice to meet you, Mr. Sanders. I'm Nancy Hamilton and yes, I'm Thomas' foster mom. My husband, George, couldn't make it. He had a late-afternoon meeting and it's running long."

"That's too bad. Would you like to join us for dinner?"

"Thanks for the invite, but I left the other kids at home and have to get back there to fix them supper. Hopefully, George's meeting will end soon, and he can be home in time to have a meal with his family for once."

"Well, it was nice to meet you. I'll take good care of Thomas the next couple of days and he should be back with you late Sunday afternoon, right Carol?"

"That's right. I plan to leave Max's about four Sunday afternoon to bring all the boys back to their foster homes and then get to my own home and relax before heading back to work Monday."

"Oh, I just assumed you were Mrs. Sanders. You two aren't married?" Nancy asked.

"Um, no," Carol replied. "I work for the agency Max is working with on the adoption. Thomas is one of four boys spending the weekend with Max to see how things go. If all goes well, one of them will end up becoming Max's son."

"It's a shame your wife couldn't make it to dinner with you, Mr. Sanders. It seems to me that adopting a child is more important than anything else and she should have made the effort to be here."

"I'm sure she would have done just that if there was a Mrs. Sanders," I replied.

"Oops, open mouth, insert foot time, Nancy," she muttered to herself. "I'm so sorry, I just assumed."

"No worries, Nancy. I'm sure to run into that much more in the future."

Nancy turned to Thomas and reminded him, "You be a good boy. I'll expect to hear from Carol that you behaved yourself this weekend."

Thomas blushed and responded with, "I know, I'll be good. Thanks for bringing me out. See you sometime Sunday." Nancy turned and left the restaurant just as Michael arrived with his foster dad. I waved them over to our table and Michael hid behind the man as they headed our direction.

"Good afternoon, Carol, what are you doing here?" the man said.

"I'm going to be spending the weekend with Michael and the other boys at Mr. Sanders' home."

He turned to me, stuck out his hand and said, "That must make you Mr. Sanders. I'm Paul Kirkland, this shy lad's foster dad. Michael, quit hiding behind me and say hi to Mr. Sanders."

Michael edged his head out from behind Paul's leg, squeaked out a quick, "Hi," and then pulled his head right back behind Paul.

"Hi, Michael. I'm glad you're here." I turned my attention to Paul and asked, "Would you like to join us for supper, Paul?"

"Sure, thanks for asking. The wife's having a 'girl's night out' with some friends of hers, so the house is empty. I might as well stay so I don't have to cook anything for myself when I get home." Paul and Michael took chairs on the other side of the table.

We waited just a few more minutes before Joseph and Alexander showed up with both foster parents. The boys spotted me and immediately ran to our table, leaving the adults to follow in their wake. As they trailed the twins, I had a feeling I knew these two people from somewhere, but I just couldn't put my finger on how or where. I finally put the feeling down to having met them at a book signing event I held in town a few years ago.

"Hello, Joseph, Alexander. It's good to see you again. Would you introduce me to your foster parents, please?"

"Sure," started Joseph, "This is Mr. and Mrs. Mueller."

"Or, Frank and Iris, depending on if you're old enough to use first names," finished Alexander. That weird sensation that I should know these people returned to haunt me, but I was no closer to solving the riddle, so I put it out of my mind.

"It's a pleasure to meet you both. Will you be joining us for the meal, also?"

They gave each other a quick glance and Frank said, "Sure. Not exactly what we had planned for tonight, but what the heck. Gotta stay flexible."

"Then, pull up a chair and make yourselves comfortable. Let me introduce the others. This young lady is Carol, she works at the agency with Anna and will be spending the weekend at my house also to make sure everything goes okay. This young man is Thomas," I continued, patting him on the head, "then, over there is Paul and the shy one trying to crawl under the table and hide is Michael."

Frank replied, "It's a pleasure to meet you all. Carol, I don't believe we've met, which is odd considering how many kids we've fostered and how much we've dealt with Anna over the years."

"Oh, I've only been in Springfield for a few months. I used to live in Chicago but moved down here a while back to be closer to my parents. I guess I got volunteered for this weekend duty since I'm the youngest in the office. Honestly, I think they think I'm naïve or something and don't know what to expect. I've never told them I grew up the youngest of six, four boys and two girls. I have a pretty good feel for what this weekend will be like."

We all enjoyed a quick laugh. "Well, I'm hoping it won't be too wild. But if they get too crazy, I have plenty of duct tape and rope." You could've heard a pin drop at the table after that comment. "Whoa, just kidding, folks. Take a breath and relax."

"Sorry, Max, I should have warned you. We don't make jokes like that, not with what we deal with."

"I apologize, everyone. I should have known better." Desperately looking for a change in topic, I said, "Oh, look, here comes our waiter. Does everyone know what they want?"

The waiter patiently took our orders and when he asked if it was all on one check, I nodded and signaled that it should come to me. He nodded his understanding and turned to get the order in the kitchen, then returned shortly with our drinks.

After the drinks were served, Frank asked, "The twins tell us you're looking to adopt, and this weekend is chance to get to know the boys a bit before you do. Do you mind if I ask why you're adopting?"

"Not at all, Frank. I'm thirty-four years old and, while I've always wanted to have a family, it doesn't look like I'll ever achieve that dream the regular way. Adoption seemed like the next logical alternative."

"Well, just what do you do to support yourself and do you intend to continue doing it to support yourself and a kid?"

Iris interjected, "Frank, don't be rude."

"No, it's a fair question, Iris, and deserves an answer. I'm an author, Frank, and have four books that have sold quite well. I've invested wisely with good advice from my broker and now, I essentially live off those investments."

"Wait," Iris interrupted, "you're that Max Sanders?"

"I suppose I am."

"I knew you lived in a Springfield, but I always thought it was in Massachusetts or Pennsylvania, not Illinois. I've read a couple of your books and they were excellent. The book club I belong to is planning to read the third one starting next month. I can't believe I'm having dinner with you. Wait 'til I tell the others, they won't believe me."

"Thanks for that rousing endorsement, Iris, but trust me, it's not that big of a deal."

"Yes, it is. Don't belittle yourself that way, Max."

"So, where is Mrs. Sanders this evening?" Frank asked.

Before I could respond, Joseph or Alexander, I'm not sure which, stated, "There isn't any Mrs. Sanders 'cause he's not married, Mr. Mueller, he's gay."

The other twin helpfully added, "Yeah, I thought we told you that." I could feel the heat rising as I blushed as red as a lobster just out of the steamer.

"And you two don't have a problem with that?" Paul asked incredulously.

"Why should we? We are, too," the twins chimed together.

I looked at Carol to see her reaction to that statement and saw nothing but surprise. Frank replied, "Now, how could you possibly believe you two are like that? You're only eight, and that's too young to know something like that."

The twins looked at me and one asked, "When did you know, Mr. Sanders?"

I was really red now and about ready to join Michael in his search for seclusion under the table but decided to hold my ground. "I was probably about seven or eight when I first realized I liked boys instead of girls. I didn't know what, exactly, those feelings meant, but I knew who I liked. The feelings didn't leave as I grew up and I suppressed them for a long time. Part of the time I spent writing was dealing with those feelings and finally realizing who I was in my heart. Now that I know and accept who I am, I'm ready to move on with the rest of my life. And I'm hoping to share that life with some lucky kid or kids."

"See, we can, too, know who we are," one of the twins shot back at Frank.

Frank retorted with, "Well, that ain't right, a pervert adopting kids."

"I'm sorry you feel that way, Frank, but being gay does not mean I'm a pervert."

"C'mon Iris, boys, we're out of here."

Iris stood to leave, but the twins remained in their seats. "Sorry, Mr. Mueller, but we're staying here and going with Mr. Sanders to stay with him this weekend."

"Well, if you two think you're like that also, then Ms. Ward can find somewhere else to dump you on Sunday as you won't be welcomed back in our house. I won't stand for it."

"That's fine, Mr. Mueller," I heard as Carol joined the conversation with a certain amount of frost I'd not heard from her before. "If you can't deal with your charges as needed, then we'll make different arrangements. I will, nonetheless, be stopping by Sunday afternoon to retrieve the boys' other belongings. And when I talk to Anna Monday morning, I will be recommending that you be removed from our list of acceptable foster families."

"That's fine with me, Ms. Ward. If you approve of this nonsense, I don't think we'd like to continue as a foster family with your group." With that, Frank and Iris stormed out of the restaurant.

"So much for 'staying flexible'," I said.

"Bet Iris' little club won't be reading your book, either," Paul chuckled. After they were gone, the table got very quiet until Paul finally broke the silence with, "Don't worry 'bout them, Max. Closed-minded folks like them don't have the brass to realize the world's changing and they either change with it or they'll get left behind."

"Thanks, Paul. If you don't mind me asking, why are you so open-minded?"

"Because my dad's gay. He'd suffered through thirty-three years of a loveless marriage to my mom before he finally decided to tell her the truth. He got my mom pregnant with me when they were eighteen and nineteen, and at that time, if you got a girl pregnant, you got married. End of story.

No big surprise I'm an only child. When he finally came out of hiding, it was a relief to us all. All the weirdness of the past years suddenly made some sense to mom and me. They actually have a better relationship now than they did when they were married."

"Better late than never, I guess," I replied. "Since we're on the subject, what are your feelings, Carol?"

"To be honest with you, I have a sister who lives near San Francisco and she and her wife have adopted two beautiful girls over the years. I'm the one who pushed Anna to give you a chance because I know that things can be fine with gay parents, married or not."

"I guess I should say thanks, Carol, for believing in me."

Our waiter appeared at that moment with a helper to deliver our food. He started to set each plate in front of the proper person and suddenly realized we'd lost two people. "Did I bring too much food, or did we lose a few while my back was turned?"

"Sorry, they decided they didn't want to eat with us. They both had a sudden illness take them and they left."

"What should I do with their food?" he asked.

"Why don't you check around the restaurant and see if anybody who hasn't ordered yet would like it? If anyone does, they can have it and you can leave it on my check. They'll get a free meal and the food won't go to waste."

"Will do, sir. Thanks. If y'all need anything else, don't hesitate to ask. Enjoy your meals." With that, he moved on to see if anyone wanted a free meal.

"So, now that the excitement's over, what do you guys want to do this weekend?" I asked. Three out of the four started reeling off suggestions at the same time and I couldn't catch any of them. "Whoa, boys, one at a time. Why don't we start with Michael and work our way up in age?"

Michael quietly muttered, "Don't know. Whatever you guys do, I guess," looking at the other three.

Thomas came up with, "Watch some TV or movies, play some games. Whatever."

"What about you two?" I asked the twins.

"Get to know you better and see if we really want to live with you," Alex answered.

"Especially now that we can't go back to the Muellers," Joey added.

"I know what I want to do," I said, "That's come up with some way to figure out which one of you is which without getting it wrong all the time. Maybe I could paint an 'A' on Alexander's forehead and a 'J' on Joseph's."

Everybody laughed at that and we got down to eating our meal. About the time we were finishing up, an older couple stopped by the table. I looked up and asked, "Yes, can I help you?"

"We just wanted to stop by and thank you for the meal. We sure didn't expect to get by that cheaply tonight."

"No problem, I'm glad you enjoyed it." They then turned and headed out the door.

"Well, boys, I think it's about time we get out of here, too. Let me take care of the bill and we'll be on our way." Paul followed me to the cashier. "Paul, it was a pleasure to meet you. I hope to see you again sometime."

"I'm sure you will. Thanks for the meal, also. I wasn't looking forward to eating alone tonight. Hey, let me give you my number real quick, just in case you have any questions about Michael. You obviously know how withdrawn he is and I might be able help you out this weekend if you have any problems."

"Thanks, Paul, that'd be great. Hopefully, I won't need it, but better safe than sorry." He gave me his home and cell numbers and then headed out the door. I settled the bill with the cashier, then headed back to the table to leave the tip for our waiter and gather my guests. Once the tip was taken care of, I turned to the rest of the group and said, "Grab your things boys, and let's go." Once outside, I let them know, "Okay, guys, my car is too small for all four of you, so two will ride with me and the other two will ride with Ms. Ward."

The twins immediately responded with, "We're with you, Mr. Sanders."

"I guess that's settled, then. Carol, do you think it's okay for you to follow me or should I give you directions?"

"I know where we're going, Max. I looked up your address on the internet and have a pretty good idea how to get there."

"Okie-dokie, then. If you do get lost, you have my cell number, don't you?"

"Sure do. We'll see you there."

As the twins and I crossed the lot to my car, they suddenly realized we were headed directly for the Shelby. They both started jumping around and running in circles with excitement.

"This is your car?" Joey asked.

"Sure is. You like it?"

"Yeah, it's hot," Alex replied.

"I hope you both fit in the back seat. It's pretty darn small."

"We'll be just fine, Mr. Sanders, don't you worry."

We climbed in the car and after ensuring the twins were safely buckled in, left the parking lot for the twenty-minute drive to home.

5

As I made the turn into my drive, one of the boys asked, "Where the heck are we going? This looks like a great spot to dump bodies."

"Home," I responded with a chuckle. "And you're right, these woods are filled with the bodies of all the people who've pissed me off over the years. You be careful this weekend or you'll end up joining them," I joked.

"Yeah, right. You sure look like a killer to me. Big, bad, gay man with a big, bad knife I bet. What do you call yourself? 'The Gay Blade'?" Both boys were laughing hard now.

"Wow! You got right it on the first try. I'll have to change it now, for sure. Something more manly, perhaps."

"Don't you dare. 'The Gay Blade' is perfect."

I made the turn to the house and what I heard from the back seat shocked me.

"Holy shit! This place is yours?? What'd you do, rob a bank?"

"First, watch your mouth, second, yes, this is my home, and third, I didn't rob any banks. Not that you know of, anyway." I pulled into the garage and opened the second door so Carol could park inside, also. We'd no sooner gotten out of the car when Carol, Michael and Thomas arrived. I signaled for her to pull inside and she did as we made room for her. They got out of the car, the boys grabbed their bags and I picked up Carol's bag as the garage doors were closing. We headed into the house and I directed the boys to the first of the three spare bedrooms.

"Okay, boys, this is the first bedroom for you to use. All three have king-size beds at the moment, so I hope you don't mind sharing a bed."

Joseph or Alexander said, "No big deal with us. We always sleep in the same bed, even though the Muellers didn't like it much."

"Okay, why don't you two take this room, Thomas and Michael can have the next one, and Ms. Ward can take the third. Sound okay, everyone?"

"Sure, Mr. Sanders. Where's your bedroom?" Thomas answered.

"Mine is on the other side of the house. Why don't you put your things in your rooms and then meet us in the living room right down the hall?"

"Okay," they responded.

Carol and I headed on down the hall and, after dropping her bag in her room for the weekend, headed on into the living room. "I gotta tell you, Max, this is one very nice house. I wish I lived here."

I laughed as I responded, "All my visitors think the same thing, Carol. To me, it's just a house. I'm hoping with a boy or two in it, it will finally become a home."

"I'm going to do everything I can to help make your dream become reality, Max."

"Thanks, Carol. I think I'm going to need it."

Shortly, the boys came in to join us. Alexander, I think, asked, "Hey, Mr. Sanders, there were some grey shorts on the bed in our room. What are those for?"

"Yeah, there were a couple in our room, too. What's the deal?" Thomas added.

"We'll get to those in a few minutes, boys," I replied. "Have seat for just a moment." I pointed to the couch and had them sit so we could chat. "Okay, I have a few ground rules for this weekend. The first one is that you are expected to have fun and enjoy yourselves. Think you can all do that?" I received nods from all four. "Good. Second, if you want something or want to do something, ask. If you don't ask, I won't know what you want. Sound all right?" Again, four nodding heads. "Third, please call me Max. For this weekend, at least. I don't want to hear Mr. Sanders all weekend. Mr. Sanders is my dad and I'm Max. Got it?"

"Yes, Max," I heard from all four.

"Now that we all know what to call me this weekend, what about you guys? Do you want me to use your full names as we have so far, or do you prefer something else?"

"Joey for me, and my brother likes Alex," he answered.

"Yeah, Joseph and Alexander are way too long," Alex added.

"Okay, we have Joey and Alex, what about you two?" I asked looking to Thomas and Michael.

Thomas answered, "I like T.J. My middle name's James and all my friends call me T.J."

"Well, since I want to be your friend, too, T.J. it is." I turned to Michael, "And you, Michael?"

"Mike, I guess" he whispered.

"It's your choice young man. If you want Mike, then Mike it shall be. If you want to be called Chuck, we'll call you Chuck, or Tim or Sam or anything you want."

Mike gazed at me with a puzzled look in his eyes. "Why'd you want to use any of those other names? They aren't mine. My name is Mike."

"Okay, Mike, you got it. Now that we have that out of the way, let me show you the rest of the house. This is obviously the living room and you've seen those three bedrooms. Across the hall from your rooms is a small bathroom, a storage room, and the laundry room. Over here is the kitchen and eating area. I usually eat at the counter, but since there aren't enough stools for all of us, I figure we'll be using the table over there for most of our meals this weekend. Follow me and you'll see the rest."

After going down the hallway from the kitchen, I continued, "This is my bedroom and bathroom and the room across the hall is my study. Each of the other three bedrooms have their own bathrooms, also, in case you didn't notice." Moving on and passing through the kitchen and dining room, I added, "And down this hall," I paused as I grabbed the knob and pushed the door open, "is the home theater."

"Whoa, this is cool, Max. You mean we can watch TV and movies in here?" Joey asked.

"Movies, TV, music, Xbox games, you name it. I have satellite for the TV, a large collection of movies and a fair assortment of games, not that I play them that much, and a wide variety of music. Each of the bedrooms is connected to the satellite, but the music and games are limited to here for now. If you guys want to listen to music more, I'll make some modifications to the systems to allow it to be played in any room. There's also a pool table in the back of the room over here, but I'll have to limit your play to when I'm here to help. At least for a while."

From T.J. I heard, "This is one cool house, Max. I'm glad you asked us to come out for the weekend."

"I'm glad you like it so far."

"So far? Does that mean there's more?" asked Alex.

"Yes, there's something else, but I'm not sure you're ready for it just yet."

"Why not?" came from Joey.

"C'mon, Max" added Alex, "Quit holding out on us. What else you got?"

"Okay, follow me." I led them to the glass doors at the back of the living room and had them line up facing the outside. All four pressed their noses against the recently cleaned glass, straining to get a better look at what lay in the darkness beyond. I glanced at Carol and grinned as she smiled back. I walked to the end of the glass and flipped the switch to turn on the outside lights.

"Oh, man, you've got a pool out there!!" T.J. screamed.

"I know. You want a closer look?"

"You bet, let's go."

We grabbed our jackets and headed out to the pool where I unlocked and opened the door so we could enter. "One rule with the pool. Nobody, and I mean nobody, swims alone. I will always be out here while you are in the pool. The doors to the shelter will be locked and I have the only key. If I'm not here or busy, no swimming. Understood?"

A chorus of four "Yesses" told me they got it.

"I love to swim. Can we go swimming now, Max? Ple-e-e-ase!!?" begged Mike. That was the loudest he had spoken so far, and I was starting to feel a bit better about him and his reaction to being here.

"Now you know why the shorts are on your beds. You guys go get changed and I'll do the same. Carol, are you going to join us in the pool?"

"Darn," she giggled, "I forgot my suit. Guess I'll just have to sit on the sidelines and watch," she smiled.

"Okay, boys, we'll meet back in the living room. And grab towels from the bathrooms when you come back. GO!" They scurried off to get changed while Carol and I slowly walked back to the house. "You sure you don't want to join us, Carol?"

"I might hang my legs into the pool, but I won't get in. I'm terrified of the water and it just wouldn't be a good scene."

I chuckled and said, "No problems. If you want something to drink or a snack or something, help yourself. I stocked up on a bit of everything for the weekend."

"Thanks, Max. I'll be waiting here for you guys."

I headed to my bedroom to change, thanking my lucky stars I'd held on to my old swimsuit from college. If I'd been thinking at Walmart, I would have gotten myself new shorts like I got for the boys, but I was lucky to remember them, let alone something for myself. It wasn't until I pulled open the dresser drawer that it hit me my college suit was a Speedo. Oh, well, it wasn't too embarrassing in college, I guess I could deal with it again. This would be my first-time swimming with anything on in a long time and I hoped it wouldn't be too uncomfortable.

I headed out to the living room with a towel wrapped around my waist, found Alex and Joey sitting patiently on the couch and Carol was sitting on the loveseat drinking a diet Pepsi. I asked about T.J. and Mike and all I got was shoulder shrugs from the twins. I called to the other two and out came T.J. in his shorts and Mike was hiding behind him. I said, "Come on, guys, the pool's waiting and I'm not getting any younger."

T.J. said, "We are, but Mike's got a problem with his shorts. The strings are all boogered up and we can't get it undone."

I sat in a chair and said, "Come here, buddy. I'll help you out." I expected him to still be wearing the pants he had on when we got here, but he popped out from behind T.J. stark naked, one hand holding his new shorts and the other covering his crotch. Joey and Alex busted out laughing and when Carol turned to see what was so funny, she sprayed her Diet Pepsi all over the coffee table with her laughter. "Sorry, little guy, no suit, no swimming," I chuckled.

He came up to me, maintaining his cover, handed me his shorts and said, "Then you better fix these, 'cause I'm swimming, shorts or no shorts."

"Okay, munchkin. Sit down and let me see what I can do." I expected him to sit on the floor or on the couch with the other boys, but instead, he climbed up in my chair and sat next to me. After a few minutes of fighting the jumble of strings, I finally got the knot undone. I handed the shorts back to Mike and told him he could get dressed now.

He stood up right in front of me, grabbed the shorts with both hands and pulled them on. Once they were in position, he asked me to tie the string for him. I hesitated for a moment, but realized I was stuck with Carol intently watching the whole thing. I pulled him closer, tied the string and gently tucked it inside his shorts, making sure not to touch any more skin than I absolutely had to. "Everybody got their towels and ready to go, now?"

Affirmative nods all around and we headed out to the pool, Carol and I in the rear. The boys jumped into the shallow end while Carol and I took a seat at the table. "You guys stay in the shallow end tonight. Joey and Alex, help T.J. and Mike, please, until I climb in, okay?"

"You got it, Max," they replied together.

"You handled that well, Max. Better than I did, anyway. I lost it when I turned around and saw him standing there with nothing on but a hand covering his crotch. I should have warned you that a lot of kids his age, boys especially, aren't particularly body-shy. They think nothing of taking their clothes off anytime, anywhere. You should probably get used to it, for a couple more years at least. Once they hit nine or ten, they start to realize that it's no longer appropriate to wander around naked all the time."

"A little warning would have been nice, Carol, but it was pretty funny."

"So, tell me, Max, why the towel wrap? Embarrassed to be seen in a swimsuit?"

"Well, not really, it's just that I didn't think fast enough to get some new shorts for myself when I got them for the boys and I'm wearing my old suit from college."

"Are you wearing a Speedo?" she chuckled.

"Yes, it's all I have. I probably shouldn't tell you, but I normally don't wear anything when I swim. It's a very private pool, after all. Though, I'm sure that's going to have to change if I'm successful with the adoption, isn't it?"

"Why would you have to change that?"

"I just assumed you and your agency wouldn't think it's quite kosher with me swimming nude with the boys."

"Max, you worry too much. Sure, Anna would probably have a cow and nix the whole thing if she knew, but she's going to be relying on my reports to her in making her decision. Nothing says I have to tell her *everything* I know."

"So, you seem pretty relaxed about the whole situation. Why is that?"

"Well, I already told you about my sister and her wife. I've been out there several times and seen their lives. They live out in Marin county on property much like yours and are very relaxed about the whole nudity thing. Their girls are now twelve and fourteen and they don't have a problem with it, either. I've even joined them when I've visited. It's the most liberating experience I've ever had. I think they're pretty much like you, out here in the woods. If I had to guess, I'd say you don't wear clothes about ninety-five percent of the time, am I right?"

"Guilty as charged. I've lived out here almost twelve years now and nobody knows how I live. Except for you, now. Oh, and my sister and brother-in-law."

"Your secret's safe with me Max. I don't have a problem with nudity as long as it's not forced on someone against their will. And as I've just told you, kids are natural nudists, you actually have to force them to wear clothes most of the time. There's nothing wrong with people of any age being nude together as long as there's no sexual behavior between adults and children. That's where I draw the line. You pull that shit and you're going to jail."

"Nice to know where I stand. I'll abstain for the weekend, though, if it's all the same to you."

"Whatever floats your boat, Max. If you want to be nude now, it wouldn't bother me at all. I've seen it all before at some of my sister's parties. I'm sure it wouldn't bother the boys, either."

"Thanks, Carol, but I think it would better for all, for now anyway, to remain at least minimally covered. This is just a 'get to know each other better' weekend, not a visit to a nudist resort. Although, on second thought, if the boys thought it was cool, I probably wouldn't say no to going to one. I've always wanted to see what it was like."

Carol laughed and the boys spun around to see what was so funny. I turned back to Carol and said, "Well, I guess I better join them and get wet. You sure you don't want to?"

"I'm sure, Max. Go have fun with your boys."

'Your boys'. I liked the sound of that. I stood, removed my towel wrap and was greeted by a chorus of whistles from Carol and the boys. I jumped in the pool and was immediately attacked by four wild monkeys. We spent the next hour swimming, diving and just generally having some fun. After about an hour in the pool I was starting to get tired and decided it was time to get out.

I climbed out and told the boys they had five more minutes before their pool time was up for the night. I grabbed my towel and started to dry off before rejoining Carol at the table. She surprised me when I sat down and quietly asked, "Why are all the hot guys gay?"

"You talkin' about me?" I sputtered in surprise.

"You see any other gay guys here?" she asked.

"Well, if my ears were working correctly at supper, Joey and Alex say they're gay, although I think they are really too young to know for sure one way or the other."

"Oh, they know. They told me a couple months back when they came to the office to meet me. You said that you knew about yourself at that age, you just suppressed it. Why do you think I recommended them as two of the boys you should meet? Did you think that was a fluke?"

"Wait, you purposely set me up with them. And you sure looked surprised at supper when they told the Muellers why they were staying."

"You bet I did. The surprised look was just that they said it out loud like they did. I can't think of a better person for gay boys to grow up with than a wonderful, kind and loving gay man. Who else is better qualified to provide the guidance and help they'll need as they grow older? Certainly not the Muellers."

"You're right about that. Those two would probably think conversion therapy would be appropriate."

"I'm sure they would. I'm glad you came through when you did because I knew I had to get those two boys out of that house. I just didn't know where they could go until you showed up."

"Glad I could help," I replied sarcastically. "What about T.J. and Mike. Have they told you they're gay, too?"

"Not in so many words, no, but T.J. was caught at school in the bathroom with another boy. There was a huge stink raised over it and we had to move him to another home and school to calm everyone down. I had a serious and private talk with him to let him know that his behavior is not appropriate for a bathroom at school, or anywhere else for that matter, except in the privacy of his own home. He understands that now, so I'm pretty sure he's gay as well."

"And Mike?" I asked.

"Mike probably has no clue yet what gay even means. He could go either way. However, most of the abuse dumped on him by his parents was due to his wanting to play with dolls and the fact he liked to play dress up with his mom's dresses and shoes. They couldn't accept that and tried to beat it out of him. You know as well as I do that that just won't work."

"I was never beaten, but, no, that won't work. So, you've set me up with three and possibly four gay boys. You're a piece of work, Carol Ward."

"I'm sorry if you think I've used you, Max, even though I kinda have, but I'm thinking only of the well-being of those four boys. If anybody can take care of them properly and help guide them on their life's journey, whatever it may be, it's you."

"Well, it looks like I have my work cut out for me, don't I? What do you think Anna will do or say?"

"It's hard telling, but I'm going to recommend you be allowed to adopt all four as soon as possible. It's the best outcome I can think of for all of you."

"Thanks, Carol. I appreciate your help in making this happen, though it was pretty devious. I'd been thinking about trying to adopt all four since our first meeting in Anna's office, but hadn't said anything yet. I didn't want to spook her." I turned to the pool and yelled, "Come on boys, it's time to get out and ready for bed."

"Five more minutes, Max," Mike begged.

"No. Now, please."

"Okay," they moaned in defeat. They climbed out of the pool and I handed them towels so they could dry off a bit before we headed back to the house.

After reaching the living room, I said, "Joey, Alex, take a shower in your bathroom and T.J., Mike, same goes for you. I'll take mine and then be down in a few minutes to check on you. Carol, make yourself at home." The four boys headed to their rooms and I headed to mine. After my shower, I came back out to the living room to check in with Carol. "Heard anything from the others yet?"

"No screaming, if that's what you're asking about."

"Not really, but I'll check in on them anyway." I stopped in T.J. and Mike's room first and found they were both still under the water. When I asked if they had everything they needed or if they needed help, T.J. asked for help washing Mike's hair. I slid the shower door open just enough to reach Mike and keep the water from spraying everywhere in the bathroom. I lathered up his hair and while doing so, took a moment to smile at T.J. As I scanned him from head to toe, I noticed that he wasn't circumcised and decided I needed to educate myself on proper care and hygiene to avoid issues later. After finishing with Mike's hair, I told them to finish up, dry off and meet me back in the kitchen after they had their pajamas on.

I headed in to check on Alex and Joey next. "Boys, you okay in there? You need anything?" I asked after cracking the door open.

"No, we're good, Max," they answered.

"Well, hurry up. I've got a snack for you guys before bed. Get dried off and into your pajamas, then come back out to the kitchen."

"Be there in a few, Max."

I headed back to the kitchen where I found Carol, T.J. and Mike waiting. I asked the boys what they wanted for a snack and both asked if I had any cookies. "I have Oreos and Nutter Butters, your choice." Mike opted for Oreos and T.J. went for the Nutter Butters. I set both up with four cookies each and a glass of milk. After I put the milk away, I turned around and found Alex and Joey turning the corner into the kitchen, naked as the day they were born. "Okay, what gives guys, I asked you to put on your pajamas and then come out for a snack, not the other way around."

Carol turned around and about fell off her stool in shock at the sight before her. I guess she should start listening to her own warnings.

"These are our pajamas, Max. We sleep naked and have for years. Is that a problem?" said Alex.

"Yeah, the Muellers just hated it," Joey added with a giggle.

"I don't care if you sleep naked, but when you're out in this part of the house, you should have something on, even if it's just underwear. Especially when there are other people around."

"Oh, don't be so uptight, Max," said Carol, "Leave them be. If they're comfortable in their own skin, let 'em do so."

"You're really testing me, aren't you, Carol?"

Carol hopped off the stool she was using and said, "Maybe a little. C'mon on boys, hop up here and get your snacks."

Mike and T.J. finally took a break from their cookies and discovered the other two climbing up on their stools.

T.J. asked, "Hey, if they don't have to wear pajamas, why do we? I wanna be naked, too."

"Well, T.J., I just assumed they wore pajamas to bed. Apparently, they don't. If you want to join them, don't let me stop you."

T.J. hopped off his barstool, stripped right there, dropping his pjs on the floor in the kitchen, then climbed back up on the stool to finish his snack. Mike, however, stayed in place and seemed content to remain dressed. I asked the two latecomers what cookies they wanted and they both went for the Oreos. I set them up with their cookies and milk and poured a glass of milk for myself. We chatted idly while they finished their snack and when all were done, I suggested they head to bed and I would follow along shortly to make sure they were comfortable. All four headed to their bedrooms, T.J. grabbing his pajamas off the floor, and after they were out of earshot, Carol started laughing.

"I warned you, didn't I?" she manage to say between her snorts.

"You sure did. And you're still testing me, aren't you?"

"Sure am. And you passed with flying colors. Those boys couldn't be any safer in a monastery."

"I'm glad you have faith in me, Carol. One good thing happened tonight."

"Oh, what's that, Max?"

"I finally found a way to tell the twins apart."

"What? How?"

"Alex has one of those liver-colored birthmarks on his right behind. Of course, I can only use that clue at home, but I'll take any advantage I can get." Carol snorted in laughter at my comment.

"Well, I'm going to turn in, also. It's been a long day and tomorrow's going to be even longer. See you in the morning, Max."

"'Night, Carol. I'll check on the boys to make sure they're settled in and head to bed also."

I followed Carol down the hall until she turned for her room and I headed to the next room to check on T.J. and Mike. I crept into the room to find both boys already snoring lightly. I pulled the covers up to their chins, gave them both a kiss on the forehead and then moved on to check on Alex and Joey. The two were in bed with the covers pulled up to their chins but they weren't asleep just yet. I leaned in and kissed both their foreheads and said goodnight.

"Did you guys have a fun night with T.J. and Mike?" I asked quietly.

"Yeah, Max, we had a blast," Joey answered.

"We ain't never had so much fun," Alex added.

"I'm glad to hear it. Get a good night's sleep and we'll have some more fun tomorrow."

As I flipped off the light, they chimed, "G'night, Max. We hope we never have to leave." Little did I know at that moment how prophetic their simple words would be.

6

Saturday morning rolled around and I was awake early. I pulled on some shorts and a shirt and headed out to the kitchen to get some coffee brewing and start working on some breakfast. The smells of fresh coffee, bacon and sausage were finally influencing my house guests and I began hearing noises from the other end of the house. Carol was the first to emerge from her bedroom and she came into the kitchen and sat at a stool at the counter.

"Anything I can do to help, Max?"

"I don't think so, Carol. Everything's about ready. I'm just about to head down and wake the boys." I took off down the hall and stopped at T.J. and Mike's bedroom first. After knocking, I pushed the door open to find both boys sitting on the edge of the bed, T.J. still nude and Mike in his pajamas. "Are you two ready for some breakfast?"

"Just about," T.J. answered. "Mike's been to the bathroom and I'm just heading there." He stood up and ambled slowly to the bathroom.

"Sounds good. Make sure you both wash your hands, come out to kitchen and have a seat at the table. And T.J., please put on of pair of shorts. I was serious last night about wearing clothes in the rest of the house when other people are here."

"Sure thing, Max."

I turned and headed to the twins' bedroom to repeat the process and heard light snoring through the door. I opened the door, looked in, and found the boys all tangled up with each other and the covers on the floor. How they could sleep tied in a knot like they were was beyond my ability to comprehend. I walked to the bed to wake them, then gently shook Alex's shoulder, told him it was time to wake up and come have some breakfast. As he untangled himself from his brother, Joey started to open his eyes, also. I told them to hit the bathroom, wash hands and come on out. I also reminded them to pull on a pair of shorts before they came out to the kitchen. They mumbled they would and I headed back to finish up and get food on the table.

When I returned to the kitchen, T.J. and Mike had joined Carol on a stool at the counter and were talking. Mike was still in his pajamas and T.J. was shirtless, but at least he had on a pair of shorts. I pulled plates out of the cabinet, handed them to T.J. and asked him to set the plates on the table. I then handed Mike silverware and napkins for everyone and had him add those to the table. Both boys seemed happy to help and the table was soon ready for our breakfast. Joey and Alex slowly stumbled around the corner into the kitchen. Amazingly, they both had listened to me and had on shorts.

I asked them to get some glasses out of the cabinet for the four of them, while pointing to the cabinet, then fill them with milk and set them on the table. Everything was finally ready and we sat down to eat. Talk was light as the boys plowed through the eggs, bacon, sausage and toast. I had to help Mike put some honey on his toast as he was having a hard time squeezing the silly bear. Once we were all done eating, I asked the boys to take their dishes to the sink and then had them come back to the table. When they had done as I asked, they returned to the table and took their seats.

"Okay, boys, what would you like to do today?"

T.J. was first to answer and he, of course, wanted to go swimming. Mike wanted to play on the Xbox and the twins said they wanted to see more of my property.

"Okay, how does this sound to you? Why don't we take a walk through the snow and the woods for a while? When we get back to the house, we can take a swim to warm up, then have lunch. After lunch, we can relax in the theater and watch a movie and have some popcorn. We can figure out the rest of the day after that."

"Yeah, let's go!"

"Whoa, buckos. None of you are quite dressed for a walk in the snow. Why don't you head to your rooms, get on some warmer clothes, including two pair of socks? When you're changed, come back to the living room and we'll head out." The four scampered to their rooms to get ready and I turned to Carol and asked, "How about it, Carol, you going to join us?"

"I'll pass, if you don't mind, Max. I've never been much for the cold. If my parents didn't live here, I'd probably be in Florida, Arizona or somewhere else warm. Besides, I need to call Anna, tell her about the Muellers and see if she has any thoughts on where the twins will go next."

"No problem, Carol. I'm the same way with the cold. I don't usually wander the woods this time of year, but I thought it would occupy the boys for a while. Besides, your call is important. I'll be interested to hear what Anna says. When you're done with your call, if you'd like, feel free to grab a book from my study. There's plenty there to choose from."

"I'd like that, Max. I'll curl up by the fireplace and read a bit. You guys go have some fun out there and I'll see you in a little while."

I headed to my room to get bundled up for a snowy trek through the woods and then met the boys by the front door. We headed out and I led them to the nearest trail I had cut through the trees, one that usually took about a half-hour to hike in good weather. As we walked, the boys were constantly chattering about the things they were seeing.

After a bit, I suggested they might want to quiet down as we were coming to a point on the trail where I frequently found deer. The boys got all quiet and started tiptoeing through the trees. As we turned a corner in the trail, we were not disappointed. Six deer were straight ahead of us, grazing through the underbrush. The boys were awestruck, but T.J. started to creep closer and I quickly grabbed his shoulder to hold him back.

"Hold on, there, T.J.," I whispered. "They might look tame, but they're as wild as they can be. They'll tolerate us being here as long as we don't get any closer."

"Aw, man, I wanted to pet one."

"Sorry, but these guys and gals aren't pets that you can touch or hold. If you tried, they'd either run off or knock you silly with their hooves."

"That's too bad," Joey said, "I bet they'd make great pets."

"Yeah, we could put up a fence in the yard and corral them," added Alex.

"What's this *we* stuff? You don't actually live here, you know. Not yet, anyway."

"Yeah, we know," Alex mumbled. "Soon enough though, I bet."

"I'm hoping for that also. Well, you guys getting cold yet? Ready to head back to the house and go for a swim?"

"Yeah," they all screamed, scaring the deer who bolted deeper into the trees away from the source of all the noise.

We turned around and headed back to the house. When we got back to the house, we headed in through the garage so we could remove our snow-covered clothes there instead of tracking it throughout the house. We all stripped down to our underwear, headed into the house, then dropped our snow packed clothes in the laundry for me to deal with later. I grabbed a towel from Joey and Alex's bathroom so I could get through the house and past Carol without embarrassing myself or her.

While the boys got changed in their rooms, I headed to my bedroom to get changed for a swim, hearing a whistle behind me as I passed through the living room. We met up in the living room to head out to the pool. Carol joined us and caught up with the group as I unlocked and opened the door to the pool. The boys tossed their towels on the table and jumped in the pool while I sat with Carol to ask about her call to Anna.

"So, did you get in touch with Anna and, if so, what did she have to say?" I asked.

"I did. She was less than thrilled about the Muellers skipping out on us, but when I told her why they did, she didn't seem too unhappy about it. I think she's finally moving into the current century with her thinking."

"And ...?" I prodded.

"I gave her my thoughts and, surprisingly, she agreed with me."

"Quit holding back," I uttered, "What's going to happen with Joey and Alex? I can't stand not knowing where they're going tomorrow afternoon."

"Well, Max, I have one more call to make to finalize the new plans, but I have to wait until I know the person's available before I call."

"When will that be?" I pushed.

"About an hour or so. I'll make the call as soon as I can."

"It sounds like you've done all you can for now. I guess I'll join the boys in the pool for a bit."

"You go right ahead, I'll be right here reading and watching you guys play."

I jumped in the pool, much to the delight of four rambunctious boys. We spent the next hour swimming and playing. I spent some time with Joey teaching him to float and once he seemed to have it figured out, I moved on to help Alex. Alex caught on to floating very quickly and it was T.J.'s turn. The whole time I was working with those three, Mike was just swimming back and forth across the width of the pool. He'd take a short break every 5 or so laps and then start up again.

Once T.J. had floating mastered, I waded over to Mike and said, "You swim pretty well for a munchkin, Mike. How'd you get so good?"

"It's the one thing I liked to do that my mom and dad liked, too. We lived in a trailer park that had its own pool and I'd go there every day I could. Last summer, the park arranged to have YMCA lifeguards come in to give lessons to all the kids in the park. It was great. When the classes were done, I got a ribbon for being the best swimmer in the park."

"I can see you learned a lot. You might be able to help the others learn to swim better."

"I can't do that, they're all older than me."

"Just because they're older, Mike, doesn't mean they can't learn from you. I bet you'd do just fine helping them."

"I don't know, Max. You think they'll listen to a pipsqueak like me?"

"If I tell them they have to, they won't have a choice, will they?"

"No, I guess not," Mike giggled. "Thanks, Max."

Turning so the others could hear me, I asked, "You guys getting hungry, yet? I'm starving."

"Yeah, let's eat," they screamed. Man, they were loud inside that shelter.

"Okay, let's get dried off, showered, dressed and fix some grub." We climbed out of the pool, grabbed our towels, and did a quick wipe-down before darting for the house. Once inside, we headed for our bedrooms to get cleaned up. After I was dressed, I headed to the kitchen to start the grill built in the stovetop so I could cook hamburgers and hot dogs for lunch. After getting the meat on the grill, I swung by T.J. and Mike's room to see if they were okay and finding they were, headed to check on the twins. They were just drying off, so I headed back to the kitchen to continue cooking.

When the boys returned to the kitchen, I again had them set the table like they had done for breakfast. I had to reach the plates for T.J., but the others were able to get the items they needed by themselves. I offered Pepsi as drinks with lunch and that option was well-received. Alex had gotten the glasses and Joey poured the drinks, then they each took two glasses and carried them to the table. The table was set and ready in very short order, we just needed the food. I asked Carol to get the chips out, then had Joey and Alex get the ketchup, mustard, dill pickles and relish out and on the table. By the time those were ready, the meat was ready to serve.

I set the platter of burgers and dogs on the table, then grabbed the buns. Between Carol and me, we pretty quickly had the boys' plates all set, and it was our turn to fix our own plates. Lunch was a fairly quiet affair and the meat platter was soon empty, signaling cleanup time had arrived. I had the boys take their dishes to the sink while Carol and I started cleaning up the remaining items. Alex and Joey took charge with the dishes, first rinsing their own, then T.J.'s and Mike's and stacking them all in the sink. They went back to the table to get the last of the plates and proceeded to rinse and stack them with the others. The kitchen was cleaned up in a heartbeat with all the help the boys supplied to the effort.

"Great job, guys. Thanks for your help. I could get use to this."

"We're just trying to do our part, Max," Alex remarked.

"Yeah, we're doing everything we can to have you pick us as the ones to adopt," added Joey.

"Hang on there, hotrods, this is not a competition or a test. Come here, all of you, take a seat on the couch. We need to have a chat." I could tell that T.J. and Mike were unhappy with what the other two had said. Just as I sat down to start the conversation, the phone rang. I was going to ask Carol to grab it and take a message, but she had disappeared for a bathroom break, I assumed. "Hang on guys, I have to answer that. Don't go anywhere. We're still going to have a chat."

I grabbed the phone in the kitchen on the fourth ring, "Max Sanders."

A deep voice asked, "Is this Maxwill Sanders, the famous author?"

Great, I thought, a lunatic fan. "Nope, sorry, you have the wrong number." I looked over at the couch and saw I had four pairs of eyes watching me intently as the boys kneeled on the couch, peering at me over the back and through the window in the kitchen wall. I turned around so they couldn't see my face as the call continued.

"Are you certain? I was sure this was the right number," the deep voice continued. "Aren't you the Maxwill Sanders who's hosting four young guests for the weekend?"

"Well, yes, I am, but how could you know that?"

The voice abruptly changed to one I immediately recognized, "Max, it's Carol. I'm calling from the bedroom," she chuckled.

"Might I ask why you are doing this?" I quizzed her while trying to sound disinterested so as not to attract any more attention from the boys.

"Sure," Carol continued. "As I understand it, those four young guests are all looking for a new and forever home. Is that correct?"

"You know it is."

"Well, I thought you'd like to know that after our conversation this morning, Anna has given her approval for you to adopt all four. Do you think you can handle that?"

"Are you serious?"

"As a heart attack, Max."

"When?"

"Well, the final paperwork needs to be completed and you will all have to go court in about six months for the official hearing in front of a juvenile judge, but with my recommendation, that's just a formality. And, if you want, the boys can go ahead and move in now."

I was working really hard to maintain my composure and sound natural. "Sounds good. Can I ask why we're having this conversation over the phone and not in person?"

"I thought you'd like to tell the boys by yourself."

"Thanks, I'll do that right now."

I hung up the phone and took a moment to catch my breath, and my wits, before turning around and walking back to the couch to finally have my chat with four very nervous and anxious boys, a very different conversation than the one I had originally planned. I sat on the table facing them, took a deep breath and began the talk that would forever change our lives.

"Well, boys, it's a good thing I answered that call because it was very important."

"It was about us, wasn't it?" asked Joey.

"You're not going to adopt us after all, are you, Max?" added Alex.

T.J. dropped his head and I could see tears forming in Mike's eye.

"You're right, Alex, I'm not going to adopt one of you."

"Why not!? I thought you liked us," T.J. whined.

"Oh, I do. More than I should after such a short time together. But that's why I'm not adopting *just* one of you."

"Huh? Watchu spoutin', Max?" Joey asked.

"Nope, I decided picking just one of you wasn't going to work because I could never decide on which one. So, I'm doing the only logical thing and I'm going to adopt all four of you."

"No shit!? Yee-ha!!" yelled Joey as he jumped off the couch and started dancing like a demon. He abruptly stopped and said, "Oops, sorry Max, that slipped."

"It's okay this time, young man."

"When do we get move in?" asked Alex.

"Last night," I said.

"Really, we get to stay here and not go back to our other homes?" Joey asked.

"Yep. You guys good with that?"

"You bet!!" T.J., Joey and Alex cheered.

The three had started a little happy dance when I finally noticed Mike was still curled into ball on the couch and appeared to be crying. I sat down next to him and pulled him up in my lap. When I finally saw his face, I could see he was most definitely crying.

"Hey, Mike, what's up? Didn't you hear, you get to stay here with T.J., Alex and Joey and be my sons."

"Yeah, but I like Mr. and Mrs. Kirkland. I'll miss them," he whimpered.

"I'm sure you will, buddy. Don't worry, you'll still get to see them. I'll make sure of that."

"You will?" he sniveled.

"Of course, I will. Would you like to call and tell them the news?"

"Really? I can do that?"

"Of course, you can. Come on. You other three, quiet down for a minute, Mike needs to make a phone call."

"Who's he callin'?" T.J. asked.

"Mr. and Mrs. Kirkland. He wants to tell them the good news about being adopted. And when he's done, I think T.J. should call the Hamiltons and let them know, too, okay?"

"Sure thing, that's a great idea," T.J. answered. "They were hoping things would work out this time."

"Wait, you've been through this before and nobody followed through?"

"Yep, this is my fourth home visit."

"I'm sorry you've had to deal with that, T.J., but no more. You have a home now! And three new brothers, to boot."

"I get to kick 'em!? Cool, come here you two, Max says I get to kick you."

"No, I didn't, T.J., you misunderstood."

"Rats. I was lookin' forward to it. Maybe later," he laughed.

"Come on you two, let's go make those calls." I turned to Carol who had finally rejoined us and asked, "Carol, would you do me a favor and make sure these other two don't tear down the house while we call the Kirklands and Hamiltons. These two want to tell them the good news."

"Sure, you go on," she answered with a smile.

"Thanks. I think we'll use the phone in the study. It should be quieter in there."

"Ha! I have no doubt."

Mike, T.J. and I headed for my study. I took my seat at the desk and asked, "Who wants to go first?" Mike raised his hand. I pulled him over and set him in my lap, then put the phone on speaker and dialed the number Paul had given me last night.

"Hello?" Paul answered.

"Good afternoon, Paul, this Max Sanders. How are you today?"

"Good, Max, how are you and the boys doing? We're worried about Michael."

"We're all doing just great, Paul. Thanks for asking. Is your wife close? Michael has something he'd like to tell both of you."

"Sure, hang on a second." Paul covered the phone and I heard him call, "Joy, come here, Michael's on the phone and wants to tell us something." He came back to our call, "She's coming."

"No problem, Paul, do you have a speaker on the phone so she can listen, too?"

"Sure, let me switch it on." Paul made the switch just as his wife came in the room. "Okay, Joy's here and we're on speaker."

"Michael, it's Joy, how you doin'?"

"I'm great, Mrs. Kirkland. Hi, Mr. Kirkland."

"Hi, Michael. What's this news that couldn't wait?"

"Well, Max, um, Mr. Sanders just got a phone call and after the call, he told us he gets to adopt all four of us."

"Wow! That's great news," Paul said. "Congratulations Max and Michael."

"Oh, Michael, that's just wonderful. We're going to miss having you, though," added Joy.

"I'll miss both of you, too, but I'm getting a new dad and three new brothers. I never had brothers before. It's gonna be great!"

"Paul, Joy, Max again. Michael wanted to be the one to tell you the news. I got off the phone no more than five minutes ago, and he couldn't wait to call."

"When will he be moving in with you, Max?" Paul asked.

"Well, that's what's gonna be a bit weird. According to Carol, he moved in last night."

"Oh my, that's awful quick. Are they sure about this?" Joy asked.

"Yeah, they are, guys. After the incident with Frank and Iris at Steak 'n Shake last night, Carol made some calls this morning and made arrangements for Joey and Alex to just stay here instead of trying to find another foster family for a couple of weeks or months. Since they were bending rules for those two, they decided to bend them for the other two, also."

"What incident, Paul? You didn't tell me about anything that happened," Joy commented.

"I'll tell you later, Joy. Listen, Max, what do you want us to do with Michael's other things that are still here?"

"Well, we could come in later this afternoon or evening to pick them up, if that's okay with you? The only problem is, my car's a Mustang and doesn't have a lot of room, so we'd probably have to make a couple of trips to get everything."

"No problem, Max, but it sounds like you have plenty other things to deal with today. How 'bout we pack his things up and bring them out to you? That would give us a chance to say goodbye to Michael."

"Yeah, you're right, I have more than enough to take care of now. It'd be a great help to us if you don't mind making the trip."

"Not a problem, we'll be happy to help any way we can. I can bring Joy up to speed on last night as we get his things put together. Shouldn't take us too long and we could be there in a couple hours."

"That would work out fine, Paul. Say, I was planning to order pizza for supper tonight, would you two like to join us?"

"Sure, Max, we'd like that. Should we bring anything with us?"

"Just your appetites, I'll have everything else covered. Let me give you directions to the house."

"Just give me the address, Max. We have satnav in the car and I'm sure it can find you."

"Okay, here it is." I gave them the address and my phone number just in case their navigation unit wasn't updated and needed to call. "Thanks, again, folks, we'll see you in a while."

I punched the button to disconnect the call and asked Mike go out to the living room with his new brothers while we called T.J.'s foster parents. Mike scooted off my lap and ran out of the study. T.J. then hopped up, filled my lap again and I dialed the number for the Hamiltons.

"Hamilton house, who do you want to talk to?" a young voice answered.

"Hi, is your mom or dad there? This is Max Sanders."

"Yeah, hang on." I heard a clunk as the phone was laid down and a kid yelling, "Mom! Phone's for you. Some Sandy dude."

T.J. laughed, "That's Olivia, no manners at all."

Nancy picked up the phone, "Hello? Max?"

"Hi, Nancy, yes, this is Max Sanders. We met last night at Steak 'n Shake when you brought T.J. out."

"Is everything alright? I wasn't expecting to hear from anybody until tomorrow afternoon."

"Things couldn't be better, Nancy."

"Oh, thank goodness."

"T.J.'s here, too, and he has something he'd like to tell you himself. Is your husband home so he can hear this, too?"

"No, George is at work, again. Hi Thomas, what's going on."

"I got some great news, Mrs. Hamilton. Mr. Sanders can adopt me! And the others, too!! I'm finally getting a real home," T.J. squealed with joy.

"Oh, that's great, Thomas. I'm so happy for you and the others. This is a wonderful thing you're doing, Max. Life-altering, but wonderful."

"It will surely change life around here, no doubt about that. For the better, I'm hoping."

"Oh, for sure, Max. There's nothing better in this world than being a parent."

"Now, what arrangements can we make to pick up T.J.'s other belongings? Mike's foster-parents are going to bring his stuff out in a while and they're going to join us for a pizza dinner. Would you and your family like to join us? We have plenty of room for everyone."

"I'll have to call George and ask him, but I think that'll be fine. To be honest, T.J. didn't have a lot when he came to live with us, so it won't take long to pack it up."

"You'd be doing me a huge favor, Nancy. I appreciate it."

"Oh, happy to help. I'm just so happy for Thomas. I'll call George right now and let him know our evening plans have changed. Give me your address, Max, and we'll see you in a little bit."

I gave Nancy the address and we hung up. I lifted T.J. off my lap and we headed back to the living room, me walking and T.J. dancing the cutest little happy dance I have ever seen.

7

When I returned to living room, I got the boys settled down and had them sit on the couch.

"Okay, guys, it looks like this is your new home and as of last night, you all now live here." They all cheered loudly, and Carol gave a small round of applause. I was quickly surrounded by all four boys as they attempted to hug the stuffing out me. "Thanks, fellas, I love you, too. You owe a great big thank you hug to Carol, also. I don't think this would have happened if it hadn't been for her help. Especially, not this soon." They turned as one and smothered Carol in big group hug, all saying thanks.

"Okay, have a seat, again. There's a few more things to tell you." Once all four had returned to the couch, I continued, "Mike and T.J.'s foster parents are going to be bringing the rest of their stuff out later this afternoon and they are going to stay for pizza as a bit of a celebration."

Joey got a worried look on his face and asked, "The Muellers ain't comin', are they? I don't ever wanna see them again."

"Absolutely not. I have no intention of them ever having contact with you and Alex again."

"But what about our stuff?" asked Alex. "We only brought what we needed for the weekend and left a whole bunch at their house."

"Don't worry, I'll take care of that. I'll go there this afternoon and retrieve your belongings myself."

"Whoo, that's good, we left a bunch of stuff that we don't want to lose," said a relieved Alex.

"Yeah, the only picture we have of our parents is there," added Joey.

"Like I said, don't worry about it. It will all be brought back here in a little bit. I just need to draft a little bit of help." I turned to Carol and asked, "Would you be willing to stay with the boys this afternoon while I deal with this?"

"Sure thing, Max. I'll arrange some help for you, too."

"How are you going to do that?"

"No worries. I just to need to make a couple of quick phone calls. Be right back." She turned and headed to her bedroom, leaving me with the wild bunch.

"Okay, guys, since we're having pizza tonight, I need to find out what you like so I can order them when I get back. And remember, one at a time so I can hear. Let's start with Mike."

"I don't want nothin' but cheese."

"Sausage and pepperoni for me, please," from T.J.

"Whatever meats they got, no green junk or fungus for us," added Alex.

"Okay, we can handle all that. I'll make sure to cover all the bases when I order. Do you guys like breadsticks, too?"

"Oh, yeah, those are great" Joey answered.

"Okay, that's settled. When I get back from the Muellers, we'll get things put away and I'll order supper. I'll head out just as soon as Carol is done with her phone calls."

As if the words were magic, Carol appeared at my shoulder. "Okay, Max, everything's all set. Here's the Muellers address. You'll be met there by Brian Marks, a man who works in our office, and a county deputy, Tom Wright, who owes me a favor. They've both been told about last night, so they know what to look out for."

"Thanks, Carol. I can understand the guy from your office, but why the deputy?"

"I just want to ensure there aren't any problems. After last night's incident, I think it's a good idea. I think the Muellers could be a problem if you went without backup."

"Well, I hope I won't need it, but thanks."

"I've also told Brian the things that I know belong to the twins he needs to help look for. I don't want anything left in that home."

"Okay, I'll be on my way, then." I turned to the boys and said, "You four be good for Carol. I don't want to hear of any problems while I'm gone."

A chorus of "Okay, we'll be good, get outta here" came from the boys.

"Thanks for helping, Carol. I owe you more than I could ever repay. I'll be back as soon as I can."

"Take your time, Max, and don't let the Muellers get in your way."

I grabbed my coat, hopped in the Mustang and headed out to retrieve the twins' belongings. I hoped the Muellers wouldn't cause any problems, but I was also concerned that I didn't have enough room in the car for whatever the boys had left there. I knew they were just being fostered at the Muellers, but they'd lived with them since their parents had died over four years ago, so I had no clue how much might be there. The drive to their house was only about fifteen minutes as they lived on the far west side of Springfield. As I turned onto their street, I saw a man I assumed to be Brian getting out of a truck and a county deputy was getting out of his car.

I pulled into the driveway and was met by both men as I got out of my car. When I turned around to introduce myself, I was met by what could be best described as a cloth-covered boulder. The man was well over six and a half feet tall and weighed in the neighborhood of 300-325 pounds, and all of it appeared to be nothing but muscle. I had to seriously strain my neck as I looked up to make eye contact.

"Are you Mr. Sanders?" the mountain grumbled.

"M-mayb-be," I stammered, "it all depends on who you are."

"My name's Brian. I work at the agency with Carol. She called and thought you could use my assistance this afternoon."

"Well, thank god for that, 'cause if you weren't Brian, I was outta here. Carol said you'd be here, but she didn't warn me you were so damn big. It's good to meet you, Brian, and I thank you for your help today. Sorry to bring you out on a Saturday."

"Not a problem, Mr. Sanders. It's all part of the job. Carol told me what happened last night and I'm here to make sure nothing like that happens again today." He pointed his thumb over his massive shoulder and added, "This here's Deputy Tom Wright and he's here to help me, not that I really need it, but he makes it official."

I shook hands with both men, "Thanks for joining us, Deputy Wright. I'm hoping there won't be any issues, but it's better to be safe than sorry."

"Nice to meet you, too, sir, just sorry it has to be under what could be troubling circumstances. Like Brian said, I'm here to reinforce whatever he says. He has the paperwork showing you as the rightful and legal guardian of two boys, Joseph and Alexander Allison. If the residents dispute that, I'm here to enforce the rules laid out in his paperwork and keep the peace, if needed. Hopefully it won't be, but you never how these situations will turn out."

"Well, thanks, again. Shall we make our presence known, gents?"

"Yes, let's," Brian said in a voice that grated like rocks in a blender.

I led the way to the front door and rang the bell with Brian and Tom flanking me. Iris opened the door and exclaimed, "Just what the hell are you doing here? We got nothin' to say to you." She turned and yelled, "Frank, get in here, it's that pervert from last night!"

"Hi, Iris," I responded politely. "It's nice to see you, too," I added sarcastically.

Frank arrived at the door and took charge. "Get outta here you sicko. We got no business with you and I don't want people the likes of you on my property."

"I'm sorry to hear that Frank, but I'm here to pick up the rest of Joey and Alex's belongings."

"Well, that's just too bad. You wasted your trip because you're not stepping foot in this house."

"Um, before you say anything else, Frank, let me introduce these two gentlemen. First, the giant on my left is Brian. He works with Carol and has the paperwork appointing me as the new legal guardian of Joey and Alex Allison. The kind gentleman on my right is Deputy Wright of the Sangamon County Sheriff's department. He's here to ensure you comply with the orders as stated in Brian's paperwork. Now, do you have anything else you'd like to say?"

"Fine, whatever, they can come in, but you get the hell off my property."

"That is *not* the way it's going to be, Frank. Either I'm allowed to come in and retrieve my sons' belongings or Deputy Wright, here, is going to put handcuffs on you and your sweet little wife, then park your ignorant asses in the back seat of his car until we're done. My, what will the neighbors think when they see you sitting in his car for the next hour or so?" I turned to the deputy and winked. The evilest grin I've ever seen split the lower half of his face and he nodded as he pulled a set of cuffs from his belt. I turned back to face Frank and added, "Your move Frank, what's it gonna be? Cooperation or confinement?"

"Fine. Be an insufferable ass. Get in here, get those little fags' shit and get the hell out."

"Whoops, Frank, I think you just stepped over the line from jerk to outright asshole. Deputy Wright, would you kindly do me a favor and get this individual out of my sight?"

"With pleasure, Mr. Sanders. Mr. Mueller, please step outside."

"I don't think so. If you're helping him, you must be one of them, too."

"Sir, either step outside, or I'll have to come in and remove you."

"You can't do that! This is *my* home," Frank bellowed.

"Excuse me, Mr. Sanders." I stepped aside and Deputy Wright took my spot. "*Now*, sir, or I *will* come in and remove you by force," he growled.

Frank seemed to lose all his bluster after that. His head drooped to his chest and he stepped outside. "Fine, do what you have to do," he mumbled.

"You, sir, are going to sit in my car and not cause any trouble. Can you do that without the cuffs, or do I have to cuff you? I can tell you that it will be much more comfortable without them. And once you go in, you're not coming back out until these two gentlemen have completed their task. Understood?"

"I don't like this at all, but I understand. No cuffs, though."

"That's fine, sir. As long you're good, no cuffs. Any hint of trouble, I'll not only slap the cuffs on ya, I'll hogtie you, too, and toss you back in on your gut. Got it?"

"Got it."

"Good, let's go." Tom led Frank to his car at the curb, placed him in the back seat and slammed the door in his face. He then came back and rejoined Brian and me on the porch. "Okay, he's dealt with. He ain't happy, but then, neither am I. I hate dealing with homophobic assholes like him."

"Thanks, deputy, shall we try the door again?"

"You bet, let's get this done."

I rang the bell, again. Iris cracked it open and peeked through. "Hi, again, Iris. We're still here and we *are* going to get my sons' belongings. Are you going to let us in so we can do that or will you be joining your husband in Deputy Wright's car?"

"Oh, fine, get in here and get it done," she snarled.

"Thank you for cooperating, Iris." The three of us stepped inside and while Tom took a position by the door to keep an eye on Frank and his car, I asked, "Will you show me where their room is, please?"

"This way," she hissed. We followed her lead down the hallway to a closed door. "In there," she said as she pointed to the door.

I tried to open the door, but discovered it was locked. I turned to iris, "Unlock the door, Iris."

"I don't have the key."

"Well, who has the key?"

"How the hell should I know? Those little faggots musta lost it."

"Fine, Iris. We'll just have to try something else. Deputy Wright!" I called down the hall, "We have a slight issue. Could you please help us here, for just a moment?"

Tom came down the hall with a frown on his face. "What seems to be the problem, Mr. Sanders?"

"The door to the boys' room is locked and Iris says the key is lost. Do you have an easy way to remedy that situation?"

"You bet your sweet ass I do. If you'll step back, I'll fix this in a jiffy." We backed down the hall a few feet and Tom positioned himself with his back up against the wall opposite the door. "I absolutely love this part of the job." He took a deep breath, raised his right foot and firmly planted it directly on the knob. Iris screamed as the door flew open into the room.

"There ya go, Mr. Sanders, problem solved."

"I like your style, Deputy. I think we could be great friends."

"No doubt about it, sir. I'll be at the front door keepin' an eye on the car. You need anything else, just holler."

"Why'd you go and do that, you ignorant ape? You tore up that door for no reason!" Iris wailed like a bitch in heat.

"Ma'am, the door was locked. I thought I heard a cry for help and, without the key, that was the quickest way to get in and provide any assistance that may have been needed. As it turns out, my hearing deceived me, and the room was empty. Can you imagine how embarrassed I am about this?" The smile that crossed his face was absolutely wicked. "Please accept my apologies for the damage. If you file a claim with the department, I'm sure you'll be reimbursed for the damages. Now, let's you and I go back to the living room and stay out of the way. Please, ma'am, lead the way."

A fuming Iris stomped back to the living room with Tom following two steps behind her. "Now, plant your skinny little behind on the couch right there and don't move. You move, you join your hubby in the car, got it?"

"Yes, SIR," she spat, then quietly added, "asshole."

"That's it, lady, I'm done with you, too." Tom grabbed her arm and dragged her out to his car. When they arrived at the car, he cuffed her, opened the back door, sat her down with her husband and slammed the door in her stunned face. He then returned to the house and came down the hall. "Okay, they're both on ice. You can go about your business without any further interruption."

"Thanks, Deputy. You've been extremely helpful."

"You two got this? I need to keep an eye on the jerks in my car."

"Sure, go ahead." Tom headed back to the front door while Brian and I got busy. "Brian, why don't you work on the dresser while I take care of the closet?"

"You got it, Max." He opened the top drawer and closed it immediately, then the next drawer, which he also closed and continued on through the remaining drawers. "Uh, Max, we got a problem, man. The dresser's empty."

I had just opened the closet and realized it was also empty. "So's the closet, Brian. What the hell's going on here?" I stood back and after a quick look around the entire room, realized it was basically a shell with just two beds, a dresser, four walls, a floor and a ceiling. I headed out to the living room to tell Tom what was going on.

"Uh, Deputy, we've got an even bigger problem, now."

"What now, Mr. Sanders?" he asked with exasperation flooding his words.

"The room's been emptied. No clothes, no toys, nothin'. Even the picture of their parents that was supposed to be on the wall is gone."

"That's it, I'm done being a nice guy." He got on his radio and requested his supervisor be dispatched to his current location. The three of us chatted on the front porch as we waited for his supervisor to arrive and the more we talked, the more I was liking Tom. We could see Frank and Iris in the car and they were stewing. Their faces were red and glistening with moisture despite the cool temperatures. The supervisor finally arrived after a 30-minute wait. A rather large African-American man in uniform met the three of us on the porch.

"Afternoon Deputy, what's up?" he inquired.

"First, let me introduce Brian Marks and Max Sanders. Brian, Max, this is my supervisor and sergeant, Sheriff Dylan Brock." We shook hands and Tom continued, "Here's the scoop, boss. Mr. Sanders is in the process of adopting two boys that, until last night, lived here with Mr. and Mrs. Mueller, who, at this moment, are chilling out in the back seat of my unit." Dylan turned and saw the two of them through the fogged windows.

"Mr. Marks works for the family service agency helping Mr. Sanders with the adoption process and has the paperwork designating Mr. Sanders as the boys' legal guardian. The boys in question are currently at Mr. Sanders' residence under the supervision of Ms. Carol Ward, who works at the agency with Mr. Marks. Mr. Marks and Mr. Sanders arrived here this afternoon to retrieve the belongings of the two boys and we've had some issues, sir."

"Hang on a minute, Wright. How did the boys come to be at Mr. Sanders' house already?"

"I think I'll let Mr. Sanders explain that part, sir, as I wasn't there."

"Fine. Mr. Sanders, please fill me in."

"Okay, here goes. I had planned with the adoption agency for the boys to spend the weekend at my home, along with Ms. Ward in her official capacity. We were to meet the boys, along with their foster parents at Steak 'n Shake last night, to have supper before going home."

"Wait, why meet there instead of picking the boys up here?"

"There are two other boys I'm adopting at the same time are from two other foster homes. Ms. Ward thought it would be easier to meet there instead of going to three different homes to pick up the four boys."

"You're adopting four boys? You got balls, mister. Go on."

"Okay, when Frank, Iris, Joey and Alex arrived, I invited them to join us for dinner and they accepted. We had just placed our order and were chatting when Frank asked where my wife was. Before I could answer, one of the boys told Frank and Iris that I wasn't married because I'm gay. Frank flipped out and told Iris and the boys that they were leaving. The boys refused to leave and said they were going with me because they're gay, also."

"Wait a sec, Mr. Sanders. You're gay?"

"Yes sir."

"And the boys you're adopting are gay also?"

"That's what they said. I honestly don't know. They're only eight, so they may not be."

"From my experience with people, at that age, they probably know. Sorry for interrupting you, go on."

"Well, after that was said, Frank told Ms. Ward that Joey and Alex would not be welcomed back into their home tomorrow and she would have to find somewhere else for them to live. After his little speech, Frank and Iris left. This morning, Carol talked to her boss, Anna, and convinced her that I should be allowed to adopt all four of the boys. And since they were already at my house, they should be allowed to stay instead of being moved to another foster home for a few weeks or months.

"So, that left me with four boys who only had the things they needed for a weekend. I've arranged with the other two families to bring the other boys' things out later this afternoon. Since I didn't feel I'd get the same cooperation from these two, I decided to come in myself to get their stuff."

"All right, that explains your presence, what's the explanation for Mr. Marks and Deputy Wright being here."

"That would be Ms. Ward's doing. Before I came here this afternoon, she arranged for these two to be here to prevent possible problems. She was there for the incident at Steak 'n Shake last night. I guess she had a feeling this wasn't going to go well and provided 'backup' for me, as she called it. I think it best to let Deputy Wright tell the rest of the story."

"You're doing just fine, but I'll let him pick it up from there." He turned to Tom and said, "Go."

"Yes, sir. Mr. Marks and I arrived shortly before Mr. Sanders and we waited in our vehicles for him. When he arrived, we introduced ourselves and then rang the doorbell. Mrs. Mueller opened the door and told Mr. Sanders to leave, he had no business here. She turned back in and yelled to

Mr. Mueller 'Frank, get in here, it's that pervert from last night.' Mr. Mueller then came to door and again told Mr. Sanders to 'get off my property.' Mr. Sanders politely explained that was not going to happen and that he was only here to pick up the boys' belongings. Mr. Sanders then introduced Mr. Marks and myself and explained our presence.

"Mr. Mueller said he would allow the two of us in the house, but, again told Mr. Sanders to get off his property. I informed Mr. Mueller if he did not allow Mr. Sanders in to retrieve the boys' property, I was going to place him in my car until we were done. He still refused Mr. Sanders' entry into the home. After two more warnings and refusals, I placed Mr. Mueller in my unit, without handcuffs."

"That explains his cooling it out here. Care to explain why the wife's out here with him?"

"I'm gettin' there, boss. After placing Mr. Mueller in my unit, I explained how things were going to be to Mrs. Mueller and she started to be slightly cooperative. She led Mr. Marks and Mr. Sanders to the boys' room while I stood at the front door to keep an eye on my unit and Mr. Mueller. Very shortly, Mr. Sanders called for my assistance. When I arrived at the door to the room, he told me it was locked, and Mrs. Mueller had said the key was lost. So, I kicked the door in."

"You kicked the door in!?" Dylan interrupted. "You mind explaining what led you to that brilliant course of action?"

"Yes, sir. I thought I heard someone yell for help from inside the room and thinking we might have an emergency situation, that seemed to be the most expedient way to gain access."

"You expect me to believe that, Deputy?" Dylan asked as a slight grin broke his otherwise stoic face.

"That's exactly what will be in my report, sir."

"Fine, continue. I still haven't heard how Mrs. Mueller ended up in your unit."

"Yes, sir. Unfortunately, after we gained access to the room in question, I discovered nobody was inside. My ears must have been playing tricks on me. I led Mrs. Mueller back to the living room, told her she needed to sit on the couch and remain there until Mr. Marks and Mr. Sanders had the boys' property packed and were on their way. She responded with, and I quote,

'Yes, sir, asshole.'

"It was at that point I decided to place her in my unit with Mr. Mueller. I came back inside in case Mr. Marks or Mr. Sanders required additional assistance. Mr. Sanders called me back to the bedroom again and explained that none of the boys' possessions were located within said room. I decided at that moment to call in the 'Big Dog' and made the radio call requesting you be dispatched to this location. And that's how we got here. Sir."

Dylan turned to Brian and asked, "You have anything to add, Mr. Marks?"

"No, sir, I think they've covered everything pretty well."

"Very well, let me have a discussion with the Muellers and see what they have to say." Dylan headed to Tom's car and opened the back door. A very heated and animated discussion took place that we couldn't quite hear, but I could see Dylan's face getting redder and could tell he was not happy with the Muellers.

After five minutes of listening to the Muellers yell at him, he'd apparently heard enough as he slammed the car door in their faces, turned and came back to the three of us on the porch.

"Those two are a real piece of work, let me tell you. Mr. Sanders, Mr. Marks, you will find what you came for in the garage. These two have spent a lot time since returning home last night, attempting to remove all traces of, and I quote, 'those little bastard pervert faggots' from their home. All the boys' things have been thrown into garbage bags and put in the garage.

"They had planned to take it out to the country tonight and burn it all. Have themselves a nice little bonfire. Said they even used rubber gloves to bag it all so they wouldn't get any 'viruses or other sick shit' by touching their things. Go through the house, open the garage door and load it up. Deputy, I'd like to have a word with you."

Brian and I headed back into the house and followed his instructions while he had his discussion with Tom.

"Deputy, I think you've done excellent work here today. With the possible exception of kicking in the bedroom door," he chuckled. "That particular move may have been just a notch or two high on the scale of acceptable actions, but I understand why you did it."

" 'Scuse me boss? You're okay with it?" he stuttered.

"Look, Tom, I've known since you joined the department you were gay." Oh, shit, here it comes, Tom thought. "I haven't said anything about it to anybody because, quite frankly, it's none of their damn business and you do an excellent job. I wish I had more guys with your level of competence out here. And if I'd been in your position here this afternoon, these two would be lucky to have just a door to fix."

"Are you kidding me, sir?"

"Not at all, Tom. You've shown remarkable restraint today. Dealing with folks like the Muellers isn't easy for any of us, but I can only imagine what it was like for you having to endure that level of homophobic abuse. Now, is there anything we can charge them with? Did they assault anyone that you witnessed? Anything besides being disgusting individuals which, unfortunately, isn't against any law I'm aware of?"

"Uh, no sir. About the only thing I can think of we might be able to charge and make stick would be obstructing a police officer while attempting to enforce a court order."

"Oh, I like that, Tom. Write it up and I'll see that it's done. I'll deliver the papers to them myself after I see the judge Monday morning."

"Yes, sir. And thank you, sir."

"For what, allowing you to do the job you were hired for?"

"No, sir, I'd fully expect that. About not saying anything about who I am. I'm sure the others in the department wouldn't like it much."

"Oh, don't be too sure about that, Tom. You're not the only gay man in the department."

"I'm not? Who else?"

"Oh, no you don't, mister. Just like I keep your confidences, I don't talk about other's either."

"Understood, sir. Thanks again. Um, what about the door thing. I told them if they filed a complaint with the department, they could probably get reimbursed for the repair charges."

"Oh, they can file any damn complaint they want to. Doesn't mean I have to do anything with it. I have a very special file under my desk just for stupid crap like that. If they think they are getting any money from the department after the way they've acted, they're smoking some really good shit."

"Thanks again, sir. I'll go help Mr. Sanders and Mr. Marks."

"No problems, Deputy. When you have everything loaded up, you can let those two out and leave them here to stew in their own filth. After that, take the rest of the day off in recognition of your good work this afternoon. And remember, don't take no shit off nobody."

"Thank you, sir. For everything. Have a great afternoon."

While Dylan and Tom had their discussion, Brian and I had managed to get everything loaded into our vehicles and were ready to leave. "Deputy, we're ready to get out of here. I'd like to get this stuff home and to the boys so we can start putting it away. What's going to happen with them?" I asked pointing to his car.

"Sounds good, Mr. Sanders. Those two are going be charged with obstructing an officer enforcing a court order. Don't worry, they'll get what's due them," he grinned. "As soon as you two are on your way, I'm supposed to leave them here. Will you need any help unloading when you get home? I suddenly have the afternoon off and nothing else to do."

"I think we can handle it, but you're welcome to come out anyway. We're going to have a little pizza party to celebrate today's good news. Since you helped here, I'd be happy if you joined us."

"That sounds like fun. Go on, you two, get outta here so I can kick those two to the curb. I'll be right behind you."

"Great. See you soon." I turned to Brian and said, "Let's get the hell out of here, Brian. I don't want to hear from them when they get out of the car."

"You lead, I follow, Max."

I hopped in the Shelby and headed down the street with Brian right behind me. In the rear-view mirror, I watched Tom get the Muellers out of his car and he was quickly settled in on Brian's bumper for the parade to my house. We pulled in my drive 20 minutes later. While I parked in the garage, Tom and Brian took spots on the concrete outside, stopping just short of the garage door. I was immediately surrounded by four jumping and whooping boys, Carol smiling in the background and two very confused looking gentlemen standing behind me.

8

"You guys miss me or something?" I asked.

"Yeah, you was gone forever, Max," cried Mike. "I didn't think you was ever coming back."

I knelt in front of Mike, wrapped my arms around him and whispered in his ear, "I won't ever leave you guys."

"You better not," he said.

"Well, it looks like we have plenty of help here, let's start taking things in and get it stashed in Joey and Alex's room." The boys worked on the smaller bags while Tom, Brian, Carol and I carried the bigger bags.

"Wow, what a mess, Max," Joey said.

"Yeah, what's the deal?" asked Alex.

"Let's just say we had a few small problems and leave it at that. Why don't you start emptying bags and sorting things while we go in the other room and chat? T.J., Mike, would you like to help them?"

"Sure, Max, c'mon T.J. Let's dig in."

All four boys started dumping bags to sort while the four adults headed to the living room.

"I need a drink, people, can I get one for anybody else?" I asked.

"Hard or soft, Max?" Tom asked.

"I'd like a hard one right now, but I better stick with soft."

"I'll take a soda, whatever you have."

"You got any tea, Max?" asked Brian.

"Sure thing, what about you, Carol?"

"I'm fine, Max. So, tell me what happened."

After retrieving the requested drinks, I sat and relayed the story to Carol with Tom and Brian filling in missed details.

"Oh, my God, what a scene. I'm glad I wasn't there, or I would've slapped that bitch silly. I'm glad Anna agreed to remove them from our list of foster homes. I wouldn't want to put any kid through that nightmare again."

"Tell her the good news, Tom."

"Oh, yeah, they're going be charged with a felony for obstructing. That should get them blocked from ever being able to foster kids again, for anybody, right?"

"It sure will. They'll never pass the background investigation with that hanging over their heads. Good work, guys." Carol turned to me and asked, "So, how'd you and Brian get along?"

"Yeah, I wanted to thank you for having him there. You should have warned me how big he was before I left, though. I about needed a clean pair of shorts when I turned around and saw this mountain standing there. He was great help, though."

"Ha, I wish I could have seen the look on your face."

"It was priceless, Carol," Brian laughed. "He really did look like he was about lose it. He thought I was there to maybe help the Muellers and not him. Once I told him who I was, the color slowly returned to his face."

At that moment, I heard a scream of anger from the other end of the house and I bolted down the hall to see what had happened. When I got to the twins' room, all four were staring at a small pile of paper shreds laying on the floor and tears were streaming down Joey and Alex's faces. I entered the room, grabbed the boys in a hug and asked, "What's wrong boys. Whatever it is, we'll fix it."

"Those nasty fuckers tore up our mom and dad's picture!" Joey screamed. "It was the last thing we had of them. I can't fucking believe they fucking did that." He buried his face in my shoulder and sobbed. I stroked his and Alex's back for a few minutes while they continued to cry. Mike and T.J. came around behind them and joined in the hug.

It took several minutes, but once they started to calm down, I leaned back, looked into their eyes and said, "I don't know how I'm going to do it, but I'll get this fixed. I promise." I gently picked up the pieces of the picture, asked them to continue their sorting and headed back to the living room.

"What was that all about?" asked Carol.

I held out my hand, showing them the scraps of paper.

"Was that the picture of their parents?" she asked.

" 'Was' is right, Carol. I can't believe they did this."

Tom piped up, "Well, now there's another charge I can throw at those scumbags, destruction of private property. Not a big one by any stretch, but it'll cost them. Probably the only way to hurt folks like that since they obviously don't have hearts."

"Can they be forced to pay to have it repaired?" Brian asked.

"Possibly. If they're charged and either found or plead guilty, they'll be fined at a minimum. Sometimes, the judges will add damages to the fine. All depends on the judge and his mood."

"I might be able to help with that," Carol said. "I know a friendly judge or two, especially when it comes to dealing with kids and their issues."

"Good, I want to see them pay through the nose for this," I replied. "I'll put this in an envelope for now and be right back." As I entered my study to get an envelope, I heard the ding of the driveway sensor announcing someone pulling in the driveway. I asked Carol to meet whoever it was at the door and I'd be right back. Carol was just opening the door when I came back into the living room. "Paul," I called out as I crossed over to the door, "it's good to see you again. And you must be Joy, pleasure to meet you. Any problems finding the place."

"Nope, satnav had you pinpointed. I love tech when it works right."

"You both know Carol, right."

"Of course, afternoon, Carol. We have a load of stuff for one lucky young man, should we bring it in now?"

"Let me get some helpers and we'll make quick work of it." I stepped to the hallway and shouted, "Boys, grab your coats and shoes, Paul and Joy are here with Mike's things. Let's help them unload and get it all in Mike and T.J.'s room."

"On the way, Max," Alex yelled back.

"Let's go guys," I heard Joey say.

With everybody hauling boxes, it took only five minutes to get all of Mike's things moved into his room. The sorting of Mike's stuff would begin once they were done with Joey and Alex's sorting. As the boys returned to the twins' room to continue their task, the adults gravitated to the living room.

"Paul, Joy, let me take your coats and I'll hang them up." Once all the coats were hung up, I headed to join the others while asking, "Can I get you two something to drink?" I fielded the drink requests from Paul and Joy and headed to the kitchen. I returned shortly, handed them out and took a seat in my chair. "The Hamiltons should be getting here shortly with T.J.'s stuff. Once his stuff is in his and Mike's room, I'll order the pizza. Anything you do or don't want when I order?" The general consensus was anything but anchovies. Once that was settled, I made introductions.

"Paul, Joy, you already know Carol, the man in uniform is Tom Wright from the Sheriff's department and the large man next to him is Brian. Brian works with Carol and they met me at the twins' former foster parents to pick up their belongings."

"Were you expecting trouble, Max," Paul asked.

"I wouldn't be surprised after Paul told me about what happened at supper last night. It's a shame the boys had to be there for that."

"No, I really didn't think I'd have a problem today, but Carol did, and, thankfully, she called in Tom and Brian for reinforcements. As it turns out, it's a good thing she did. We had some fun this afternoon, didn't we, boys?"

"Oh, yeah, I live for days like this," said Brian sarcastically.

"Just doing my job, Max," added Tom. "I see shi—, um, junk like that every day."

"I'm sorry you both got dragged into that today, but I'm glad you were there. So, tell me Paul, Joy, how's Mike doing? I know he's only lived with you a couple months, but I'd like to know whatever you can share."

"Well," Joy began, "he was very withdrawn and scared when he was first brought to us. We knew about the abuse by his parents, so we just tried to show we cared."

"He hasn't talked about it much," Paul continued, "but the last couple of weeks, he seems to be doing a little better. Physically, it looks like all the bruises have finally faded, but mentally, I think he's still pretty fragile and probably will be for a while to come. One of the reasons the agency placed him with us is I'm a licensed child psychologist and they thought if he wanted to talk about it, I'd be in a better position to help. Unfortunately, we didn't get that far."

"He seems to have attached himself to you a bit judging by the way he hid behind you last night. Would you be available and willing to talk with him if he wants to?"

"I'd be happy to, Max. Let's give him a little bit to adjust to his new home and surroundings and see how he feels about it later. If he wants to talk, I'm more than willing to listen."

"Speaking of new homes," Joy interrupted, "your house is beautiful. How big is it?"

"About 4500 square feet and set in the middle of eighteen acres of nothing but trees."

"I'd love to see the rest of it, can we get a tour?" Joy asked.

"Sure, tours are a quarter per person," I laughed, "but how about if we wait for the Kirklands so I only have to do it once?"

"Deal, Max."

"Is that a pool or a greenhouse out there?" Tom asked while pointing through the glass wall.

"Pool, Tom. Just had the shelter installed last week. I'd been wanting to have one for several years so I could use it in the winter and with the boys coming out, it seemed like the time was right to finally follow through."

"Must be rough to live like this. I wouldn't know, though, not on a cop's salary. How'd you swing it?"

"I'm an author, Tom. I had four successful books. The royalties from the first one paid for it all."

"Damn, I knew you looked familiar. Now it clicks where I've seen you, your picture on the dust covers of your books. Your first name is Maxwill, isn't it?"

"Guilty as charged."

"I've read a couple of your books, but never realized you lived in the area."

"Been here almost twelve years, but I like to keep a low profile." Ding!

"What the heck is that?" Brian asked.

"Driveway sensor," I explained. "Let's me know when someone's turned into the drive. Probably the Kirklands"

"That's a good thing to have out here in the middle of nowhere, Max. Good security," Tom commented.

I headed to the door, but, on my way, I called down the hallway, "Boys, coats and shoes, again. The Kirklands are here with T.J.'s things." I opened the door to greet George and Nancy just as the boys came charging in. "Hi Nancy, nice to see you again, and you must be George. Nice to meet you, also. The boys are ready, so why don't we get unloaded real quick?"

"Sure thing, Max, come on boys, let's go," George called as he waved his hand. We followed George to their car and in just a few trips had all of T.J.'s stuff moved into his and Mike's room.

Once we were done unloading, I asked the boys, "Do you have all of Joey and Alex's stuff sorted out?"

"Yes, sir, we're about to start putting it all away," T.J. answered.

"Well, why don't you take a break and come meet these folks. I'm sure they'd like to know who they've been helping today."

"Okay," Joey said and they all followed me to the living room. When we arrived, I lined them up, standing in front of me.

"Okay folks, I know some of you already know each other, but I'd still like to go around and introduce everyone." I started with the boys, tapping each one on the head as I said their names. "I'll start here with Joey, I think, then Alex, maybe, who knows for sure, T.J. and, finally, Mike." The boys giggled at my confusion on the twins. "Boys, you all know Carol, who has helped make this possible, then we have Paul and Joy Kirkland who were Mike's foster parents, Nancy and George Hamilton, T.J.'s foster parents, the big guy over here," I said pointing out the human mountain by the fireplace, "is Brian Marks and next to him is Tom Wright."

"Who are they?" Alex asked, "And why is a cop here?"

"Brian and Tom met me to help get your stuff from the Muellers."

"Really, did they get arrested?" Joey asked.

"No, not yet, anyway," Tom answered.

"Well, they should be after what they did," from Alex.

"What'd they do?" Paul asked.

"They were a royal pain in the ass," Brian commented.

"And they obstructed me in doing my job," added Tom. "Add destruction of property to that and they're going to have some nice fines to pay."

"What property got damaged?" Joy asked.

"They shredded a picture of Joey and Alex's parents. It was the last thing they had of them."

115

"Oh, that's just horrible," cried Nancy.

"I'm going to try and get it repaired, but I don't know if I can. We'll see. Well, let me get supper ordered and then we can go on the house tour I promised Joy. Why don't you boys go start sorting T.J. and Mike's things while we wait." I called Capone's, placed the order, then asked, "I know you don't normally deliver, but would it be worth an extra 100 bucks to you to get this order brought out? I have a house full of people and don't want to be a rude host and leave."

"Let me check, hang on," the young lady replied. She came back in a minute, "Yeah, the boss says he'd allow it this time, especially for the extra you're willing to pay. Where do you live?"

"Is Joe working tonight? He's been here before to work on my mowers and knows the way."

"You bet. We'll have him on the way as soon as everything's out of the ovens."

"Great, I appreciate the service. Thanks."

"Thank you, Mr. Sanders. Have a good evening."

I turned to my guests and said, "Okay, the food's ordered, who's ready for the tour?" Everyone but Carol raised their hand. "Follow me." Joy was the first to join me and held her hand out. "What's this, Joy," I asked.

"It's my quarter, for the tour," she laughed.

"Put that away. You know I was kidding."

"I know, but it's still funny. I couldn't resist."

"Yes, it was, and I needed a laugh. Thanks." We headed down the hall to my study where I opened the double doors to the room and stood aside as my guests entered, "This is my study. This is where I've spent the better part of the last twelve years while writing my last three books." The room is paneled in light oak and the walls are covered with floor to ceiling shelves crammed full of books.

"You could start a library out here, Max," commented George.

"I like it, Max. I would love to spend time in here reading," added Tom.

"I'll get you a library card with full privileges then, Tom," I laughed. "Books are due back two weeks from checkout with a dime a day late fee." They all laughed at that. "Let's move on. This next room," I said as I opened the door, "is my bedroom and bathroom. I separated mine from the others so guests wouldn't have to hear me snore all night long." Next, we headed back through the kitchen and dining area to the home theater and gaming room. "This, obviously, is the home theater and gaming room. I really haven't used it much over the years, but I think it's going to be seeing a lot more use with four boys in the house."

"Are those leather chairs, Max?" Paul asked.

"Yep, recliners with cup holders, massagers and heat. Great place to spend a cold winter's night, let me tell you."

"Where's the screen?" asked Brian.

"Let me show you." I walked to the recliner I normally used, grabbed the remote and pressed a button. The ten foot wide screen lowered from a slot hidden in the ceiling by the end wall of the room while the projector dropped from its hidden cubbyhole.

"Freakin' cool, man. I could get used to this," Tom enthused.

"Well, I need to upgrade the projector to handle the new 16k resolution, but since I don't use it a lot, I haven't been in a hurry to do so." I punched the button and the screen and projector returned to their hidden positions. "Let's move on." I headed to the glass wall in the living room, turned on the outside lights and opened the door, waving a hand to direct my guests outside. I unlocked the pool shelter and led everyone in.

"Wow, Max, this is wonderful," said Nancy. "Nice and warm. Have you been swimming since they completed it?"

"Last night and again this morning with the boys. They love it, too. Probably a wise investment since they're going to be living here, now."

"I really could get used to living here, Max" Tom said. "If you're interested, I'm available for adoption, too," he laughed. "My parents surrendered their parental rights years ago." We all laughed along.

"Let's head back inside and I'll show you the other end of the house." We headed back inside after I had re-locked the pool shelter and turned down the hallway towards the other bedrooms and garage. We entered the bedroom Carol used last night, "I have three bedrooms on this side of the house. They're all about the same size and each has its own bathroom. I didn't want guests to have to share." We passed by the two other bedrooms, saying hi to the boys while they continued sorting stuff and headed on to the garage. "On this side of the hall is a half-bath and separate utility room. I also have a fairly good-sized room here that I currently use for storage."

The door at the end of the hall opened into the garage. "And this, of course, is the garage. Nothing much to see in here."

"Are you kidding me, Max?" asked George. "Your average Joe doesn't get to walk in his garage and see a Shelby like that every day."

"It's just a car, George. And now, it's too small. When it was just me, it was great, but with four boys, I need something considerably bigger than this."

"I'll trade you my ten-year-old minivan for it, even up," he joked, which elicited another laugh from everyone.

"Yeah, I just bet you would. Actually, I have the problem already solved, but it won't be here for another month. I'll have to check with the Ford dealer to see if they have something I can rent until my new Flex comes in."

"Well, the offer's still open, if you change your mind."

"George, stop that. You're embarrassing me," Nancy scolded as she slapped the back of his head. "I'm sorry, Max, I don't know what's come over him."

"No worries, Nancy. If our places were swapped, I'd be making the same offer," I laughed. Ding!

Tom yelled, "Incoming!" which garnered another laugh from everyone.

"Good timing for the food to show up, right at the end of the nickel tour."

"Wait just a darn minute, Max, I paid a quarter. Where's my change, dang it?" Joy asked with a giggle.

We headed back into the house and as we passed the boys' rooms, I hollered, "Boys, wash faces and hands and come eat." That was followed by a resounding cheer from all four. When we got back to the living room, Carol was already waiting at the door. I met her there and pulled out my wallet to pay for our pizzas and breadsticks. After Joe rang the bell and we let him in, he handed the food to Carol while I settled the bill with him, including a generous tip to him for making the delivery.

"Thanks, Mr. Sanders, appreciate it. Enjoy your supper."

"We will, Joe. Thanks again for making a delivery. I'll try to not make habit out of it."

"You keep tipping like this, I'll deliver every night," he laughed. "See you later." He then hopped back in his car and headed back to work.

When the boys came in to the kitchen, I had them set the table for everyone after getting the plates out of the cabinet for T.J. Joey and Alex asked everyone what they wanted to drink, fixed them and set them on the table. We were soon ready to sit and chow down.

"That's quite the little work crew you've got there, Max. I wish our kids were that helpful," Nancy commented.

"I started that this morning with breakfast, I asked the boys to help set the table and they were happy to do so. They did the same at lunch, also."

"I still wish our kids would help like that."

"Well, Nancy, when I was growing up, our parents instilled in me and my sister that we had to work together to live together. I intend to pass that on to these guys."

"Can I send our kids out for a week or two this summer and see if you can work a miracle with them?" laughed George.

"I can't promise a miracle, George, but I'd be happy to do what I can." The rest of the meal passed quietly and when the boys had emptied their plates, they took their dishes to the sink, rinsed and stacked them. Then, they came back to take the adults' dishes and do the same thing.

Nancy commented, "Oh, yeah, our kids are definitely coming out sometime this summer."

We all laughed, including the boys.

T.J. asked, "Can they really come out. Even though I'm not going to be living with you any longer, I'd still like to be friends with them. We always had fun together."

"I'm sure we can work something out, T.J.," I said. "I don't want you to lose your friends just because you live here now. After all, we have the pool, the trails and lots of other things to do out here. They might enjoy the occasional visit. Why don't you guys keep sorting Mike and T.J.'s things and we'll get stuff put away in a little bit."

"Okay, Max. See y'all later." Alex said as they turned and headed down the hall.

"Max, you are one lucky son-of-a-gun," Paul said. "And those are four lucky boys, too." He turned to Joy and said, "Dear, I think it's time we head for home and let Max help his sons get organized."

"Paul, what you just said, 'his sons', I really like the sound of that. I hope I get used to it."

"Oh, you will, don't worry. C'mon Joy."

Nancy was next with, "I think George and I will be on our way also, Max. You have a lot of organizing to do and we'll just be in the way. Thanks for supper and good luck. You're going to need it."

"Thanks to all of you for helping out today. I really appreciate it and if we can ever do anything for you, just let me know. Paul, I'll be in touch after a while about counseling for Mike." I shook hands all around and reminded my new friends to not be strangers. As I turned around to head back to the others, I found Carol and Brian standing behind me with their coats and Carol's bag. "You two are leaving, also?" I asked.

"Yeah, Max, you have plenty to deal with at the moment and we don't need to be in your way, either," Carol said.

"But aren't you staying tonight, Carol?"

"That was the original plan, but the way things happened today, I really don't need to since we've approved the adoption and this paperwork transfers legal custody and guardianship of all four boys to you. I think you have everything under control."

"Yeah, right, that remains to be seen. Carol, I don't think I'll ever be able to adequately thank you for your help."

"No need, Max, it's my job and we have a good result. Don't worry, you'll be just fine. I'll stay in touch with some follow-up visits, but I'll give you a couple days' notice before showing up."

"I'll look forward to it." I turned to Brian and said, "Brian it was a pleasure to meet you and I want to thank you for helping me at the Muellers today. Sorry for picking on you about your size, but that's Carol's fault for not warning me." Carol and Brian both chuckled.

"Yeah, she does that to a lot with folks, loves to see their reaction when I show up."

"Well, thanks again. You two enjoy your day off tomorrow. We'll see you later." Carol and Brian turned and headed to their cars to leave.

I closed the front door and turned around to find Tom still sitting on the couch with what appeared to be a rather pensive look on his face. I walked over and sat next to him, which seemed to rouse his from his thoughts.

"Looks like it's just you, me and the boys, Tom."

"Yeah, it does."

"What's up, Tom, you seem a bit lost?"

"I'm not sure, Max, can we talk?"

9

"Privately?" he quietly added.

"Sure thing, after what you did for me earlier, I owe you. Let me make sure the boys are okay and we'll go to the study, okay?"

I went to T.J. and Mike's room where the boys were still sorting stuff. "Are you four still doing okay? You got enough to keep yourselves busy a while longer?"

"Yeah, we're great, Max," Joey answered. "We're having a blast."

"We got a lot to dig through, too," added Alex.

"Good, Tom wants to talk to me about something, so he and I are going to the study. If you need anything, come knock on the door."

"Will do, Max," answered T.J.

I headed back to the living room and called out, "Let's go, Tom," as I continued on. Tom followed me to the study and after we entered, I closed the door. "Okay, what's on your mind. You seemed to be in pretty deep thought out there."

"Can I ask you a personal question, Max?"

"Well, you can sure ask, but that doesn't mean I'll answer it."

"Fair enough," Tom replied. "I was wondering, how did, I mean, when, uh ... Oh, hell, I don't think I wanna do this now."

"Spit it out, Tom. Whatever it is, it can't be that bad."

"Okay, just know I'm not real comfortable with this. What I want to know is, I guess, is how long it took you to get so comfortable with being who you are."

"What, the fame and fortune thing?"

"No, the being gay thing."

"Oh, that."

"Yeah, that."

"It wasn't easy, let me tell you. I've told you how I've lived out here twelve years, alone, writing my last three books. What I didn't tell you about is the amount of time I spent those twelve years figuring out who I really am and what I wanted to get out of life. It wasn't until just recently that I came to understand myself to the point that I was finally willing to accept I'm homosexual."

"Twelve years? That long? Damn, how'd you do it?"

"Very slowly, obviously."

"Well, when did you first think you might be?"

"I was about seven or eight when I first realized I was different from most of the other boys I knew. When they started talking about girls and things, I was still thinking about my best friend's body and how I'd like to know that body much better than I did. I suppressed all those feelings for an awful long time and finally realized it was killing me. I mean, here I am, a successful author, nice house, money, whatever I could want except for what my heart desired. I guess I've finally decided to let my heart have a say in how I live the rest of my life."

"Yeah, that sounds about right."

"What do you mean, Tom?"

"That's about when it happened with me, too. I guess I was ten or eleven, so a little later than you, but not by much."

"Wait, are you telling me you're gay, too."

"I guess I am. I've hidden that side of myself, I thought pretty well. Until this afternoon."

"How so, Tom, what happened today that changed your mindset?"

"First, it was dealing with those sanctimonious, uptight assholes, the Muellers. I mean, I knew you were gay because Carol told me when she called about being there today to help, but seeing the shit they put you through, for no reason except for you being who you are, it really pissed me off. And you stood up to them. You were way more polite than they deserved. And then, with what my sergeant said, I guess that kind of finished it off for me."

"Dylan? What'd he say?"

"He told me he knew I was gay from the moment he hired me. I guess I haven't been as successful at hiding it as I thought I was. Being a cop is tough, but being a gay cop is even tougher, puttin up with the bullshit from the other guys on the force if they knew. I just didn't want to deal with it, so I buried it. If they knew about it, they'd make my life a living hell."

"Well, you're secret's safe with me. It's not like I'm going to run around town telling everybody I see that Deputy Tom Wright of the Sangamon County Sheriff's department is a flaming fag."

"God, I hope not. I'd have to bury your body among all those trees out there." I had to laugh at that. "No, seriously Max, how should I handle this?"

"Just be who you are. If somebody asks, tell the truth. I haven't told many people about myself, but the ones I have don't seems to care. Except, of course, the Muellers, and I don't give a shit what they think. In the grand scheme of my life, they mean nothing."

"Just be myself. Yeah, right" he chuffed.

"I know it's a whole lot easier saying it than doing it. But let me tell you, once you start living your life that way, there's no turning back the clock."

"I know, I guess that's why I keep hiding behind the uniform. It's easier to deny it."

"I wish I could have accepted it long ago, then I could have started on a family much earlier. Better late than never, I guess."

"Thanks, Max. I'm feeling better about things now."

"Is there anything else you wanted to talk about?"

"Yeah, but not yet."

"Oh, hell, you've already dropped one huge bomb, get it over with and move on."

"I guess I have, haven't I? Okay, here goes. You remember those not so subtle comments I made during the tour about getting used to living here, you adopting me, and so on?"

"Yeah, that was pretty funny," I chuckled.

"I hope the others thought so, too, but, deep down, I was kinda bein' serious."

"Wait a minute, what are you really saying."

"I guess I'm saying I'm attracted to you. And I think I'd like to get know you better, much better."

"Whoa, hold it right there ..." I started, but Tom interrupted.

"I knew it, damn it, I went too fucking far. Son-of-a-bitch. Okay, Max, I'll be going now."

"Sit your ass back down, you're not dropping a bomb like that and running away from it. Let me finish what I was going to say." He returned to his chair and I continued, "I know we just met this afternoon, under lousy circumstances, but when I said that I thought we could be great friends, I meant it, 100%."

"What, you really meant that?"

"I sure did. Obviously, I didn't know you were gay when I said it, but that doesn't change how I feel. I think we truly could be great friends, but we need to take it a day at a time and see how things go. I've got a lot of changes happening in my life right now and I need to really think hard about it before I add anything, or anyone, else to the mix right now."

"So, you're saying not now, but someday, maybe, right?"

"Exactly. I need to think about what's best for the boys first, before I try to add to that. At least for a while. I really would like to know you better, but you have to give me some time. Plus, you need to know what you'd be getting yourself into."

"What do you mean, Max?"

"You remember that comment from Frank this afternoon about getting any trace of 'those little bastard pervert faggots' out of their home."

"Yeah, what about it?"

"Well, that comes from something the twins said last night at Steak 'n Shake. The boys told the Muellers they were staying with me because they're gay, too. In fact, they said it loud enough, they pretty much told everybody there."

"You're shittin' me!"

"Not a bit. And there's more you need to know."

"Now, I know you're shittin' me. What more could there possibly be?"

"Not at all. T.J., so I've been told, was caught in the bathroom at his school with another boy and he was moved to a new foster home and school as a result." Tom's eyes grew wide with surprise. "Wait, there's more. Mike was removed from his parents because he was being severely abused. You wanna guess why?"

"Not really, but you're gonna tell me anyway, aren't you?"

"He liked to play dress-up with his mom's things and his parents didn't like it, so they tried to beat it out of him. How do you think that would have turned out for Mike?"

"He'd probably end up dead with his parents rotting in jail for the rest of their lives."

"Exactly. Those four boys were placed with me because I'm gay and they all four have shown they are most likely gay, too, either through what they've said or done. Carol has been looking for a good home or homes for all four of them for quite a while and when I showed up at the agency's doorstep, it was like her prayers had been answered. She couldn't believe her luck when she found out who I was."

"Unbelievable. So, you've gone from a confused single guy to being a gay father of possibly four gay boys in the space of what, five, six months?"

"Precisely. Can you now see why I need to take things a little slower and see how life shakes out? I'm dead serious about getting to know you better, but I just need to take it slowly. And you need to know what you're getting yourself into. Are you willing to give me some time to sort things out?"

"Yeah, I guess. I'm not going anywhere."

"Thanks, I appreciate your understanding." I stood up, walked to his chair and held my arms out. Tom slowly stood up and we wrapped our arms around each other in a warm embrace. At that moment, there was light tapping on the door and it popped open. I turned to see four pairs of eyes looking at the two of us and heard lots of giggling.

"See," Alex said, "I told you guys the cop was gay."

"And I told you he had the hots for Max," Joey added.

Tom and I guiltily broke our embrace. "Boys, come here. How long have you been listening at the door?"

"Um, the whole time," Alex mumbled.

"We're sorry, Max," added T.J. "We know we shouldn't have, but we couldn't help it. Please don't send us back," he cried.

"I'm not sending you anywhere. But you all need to understand what privacy is and you have to respect peoples' need for it. When a door is closed, you knock on it and wait for a response before you just come on in."

"Yes, sir," they all mumbled.

"Well, since it seems you've heard everything we said to each other, what do you have to say about it?"

"I think it's great, Max, you guys look good together," Joey said.

"Yeah, you deserve to have someone to love, like Joey and I do," added Alex.

"T.J., Mike?"

T.J. answered, "I like Tom. He seems like a nice guy, for a cop, anyway."

"Nice to know I have your approval, T.J.," Tom chuckled. "And Mike?"

"I don't know. I guess if you two like each other, that's all that matters."

"Well, boys, it's not *all* that matters, but yeah, it's a big step in the right direction," I replied. "It also matters how you guys feel about the two of us getting to know each other better. You four have just moved in and I don't want to do anything you're not okay with. I have to think about what's best for you and not just myself."

"I think I can say for all us, Max, that we'd be good with it," Joey answered. "Tom proved he's a good guy when he stood up to those assholes we lived with."

"Yeah," added Alex, "we always wanted to do it, but knew if we did, they'd probably kick us out. Then, we'd probably end up getting separated, and we weren't gonna let that happen."

"Does anybody besides me need a snack or drink?" I asked. "I'm thirsty and we can continue this discussion in the kitchen."

"Yeah," chorused four boys.

"I could sure use a drink. A hard one if you've got any," Tom added.

"The hardest thing I have is some Corona, but no limes."

"I'll take it," he said as we all headed to the kitchen.

I got the boys set with their milk and cookies and grabbed a Corona for Tom and me. The boys sat at the counter on the stools while Tom and I stood on the other side of the counter.

"Okay, guys, here's what we'll do. Tom and I will spend some time getting to know each other better while the five of us do the same. I'm sure Tom will be spending some of his spare time around here, are you cool with that?"

"Yeah, that's fine, Max."

"Okay with you, Tom?"

"You bet."

"Good. Now, if a door is closed, you will knock and wait for an answer before opening the door. If a door is open, we'll assume we're welcome to come in without knocking. Does that sound reasonable?"

"Yep, what's next?"

"If you ever want to talk about anything, and I mean anything, you come to me and ask. No subject is off-limits. If you want to talk alone, we'll talk alone, if you want a group chat, we'll do that. Anything else you want to know about right now?"

The boys looked at each other and broke into wide grins. Alex finally said, "We all want to know one more thing, but they're too chicken to ask, so they told me I have to."

I had a feeling of what was coming, but it was too late to stop since I'd already said no subject was off-limits. "And what's that, Alex? It is Alex and not Joey, right? I'm not sure since you're both dressed." Tom raised his eyebrows and gave me an odd look at that comment.

"Of course, it is. Last night, you said that when we were out in this part of the house, we should be wearing something, even if it was just underwear, especially when other people are here. Is Tom 'other people' or is he one of us now?"

Tom had picked the wrong moment to take a drink as he spewed Corona all over the counter when he heard the question. I just rolled my eyes, shrugged and answered, "I guess we should ask Tom and see what he says." I turned to him and asked, "So, Tom, are you 'other people' or are you 'one of us'?"

"I guess that all depends on what you're talking about, Max. You want to give me a few details before I answer?"

"Even the boys don't know this yet, but, for the last twelve years I've lived here, I've rarely worn clothes." Five sets of eyes opened wide at that statement. "I know, but I lived here alone, in the middle of nowhere for a reason. You can only see the house from the air. It's a great way to live. I thought I would have to change that with boys moving in, but after last night, I'm not so sure."

"Why, what happened last night?" Tom asked.

"Oh, it was a sight, for sure. I thought Carol was gonna die."

"Quit stalling and tell me."

"Okay, we'd gone for a swim. After we were done, I told the boys to get showered, dress in their pajamas and come back to the kitchen for a snack before they went to bed. T.J. and Mike were first out, and they showed up in regular jammies. They'd just started eatin' their cookies when here come Alex and Joey, struttin' into the kitchen in their birthday suits, not a care in the world." Tom sputtered wildly as he processed that image and the boys all snickered. "I told them it was pajamas first, snack second, not the other way around. That's when Carol turned around and about fell off her stool. They told me, rather bluntly, that they *were* wearing their pajamas, that they'd slept nude for years. But that's not all of it."

"It gets better? How?"

"Well, T.J. said that if they could be naked, why couldn't he? When I told him and Mike they were free to join the twins if they wanted, T.J. got off his stool, peeled off his pajamas, then sat back down to finish his snack. The three of them just sat there, munchin' their cookies like nothing weird was going on. So, that's the story and now they want to know, I guess, if they have to wear clothes around you or not. That *is* what you're asking, right?"

"Exactly, Max," Joey answered and looked at Tom for an answer to the question.

"Well," Tom started, "I've been known to lounge around my apartment in the buff. And I don't have any aversion to being seen nude or seeing others nude. I can't tell you how many locker rooms I've been in and nobody seems to care. If they want to go naked around here, it won't bother me a bit."

At that, all four boys hopped off their stools, stripped their clothes off and hopped back up to their stools. Then Alex looked at me and said, "Your turn, guys."

"Um, I don't think that's a good idea, Alex."

"Why not, if we're naked, you should be, too. You said you used to be like this all the time before we moved in," T.J. argued.

"That's true, but there weren't any kids around, either. I don't think the adoption agency would look too favorably on adults being nude around young kids."

"I won't tell 'em," Joey said, "will you?" he asked, looking to the other boys.

"I ain't tellin' no one," came from Alex.

"My lips are sealed," added T.J.

"Watchu' talkin' 'bout?" asked Mike.

I looked to Tom, said, "When in Rome," and started to remove my shirt.

10

Tom looked at me and said, "Oh, what the hell?" as he started to remove his belt. I carefully watched Tom as he disrobed and was liking what I was seeing. Apparently, so did the boys as they whistled and hooted as we undressed in the kitchen. It took him longer because of his uniform, but we had soon joined the boys in comfort. When we were both finally naked, we stayed behind the counter, though I'm not sure why.

"Okay, we're all nude. I hope you're happy. Now what, guys?" I asked.

"Let's go swimming!" Mike squealed with joy.

"Why not?" I asked. I grabbed the keys from my pants pocket and we headed out to the pool. As soon I unlocked the shelter door, the boys were off like a bolt of lightning and jumped in the pool. They were just getting their heads back above water when Tom and I reached the pool.

That was when Alex asked, "Max, how come Tom is all hairy and you're not."

Before I could respond to his question, Joey asked, "How come my, uh, thingy got hard comin' out here?"

Tom and I climbed in the pool and I called the boys over for another chat. "Let's talk about a few things real quick. Every guy's penis will get hard for any number of reasons. Even when you're used to being nude like I am, it still happens."

"Yeah, we know that, but why does it happen?" Joey asked. "It happened to both Alex and me just now."

"Okay, so you know what I'm talkin' about. What about you two?" I asked, looking at T.J. and Mike.

"Yep, me too," T.J. said with a grin.

"Uh-huh," mumbled Mike.

"Okay, when your penis gets hard, it's called an erection. As I said, it happens to all guys and it's nothing to be ashamed of because it's simple biology, you just don't attract attention to it, understand?"

"Yeah," they all replied.

"Okay, now, where's all your hair? Especially around your, well, you know?" asked Alex.

"Well, that's an entirely different subject. I don't have much hair on my body because I shave it or trim it very short."

"Why," asked T.J.

"It's just a personal preference. I prefer very short or no hair over longer hair. I like the look of it and I like the way it feels, too."

"I like the way it looks on you, too, Max," smiled Tom.

"Do you shave it 'cause you're gay. Will we have to shave ours when we finally start growing some," asked Joey.

"No, it not a 'gay' thing. Lots of guys, gay and straight, shave their bodies. Any other questions before we actually start to swim?"

"I got one," whispered Mike. "How come Tom's pee-pee is so much bigger than yours?"

My first thought was, six years old and already worried about size, but I answered, "It's just genetics, Mike. As you go through life, you'll see all kinds of body shapes and sizes, and that includes penises. Some guys are bigger than others, that's just a fact of life and there's nothing you can do to change it. As you get older and start taking P.E. in school, you'll see just about every shape and size of penis imaginable, from small to huge. As long as it works properly, size doesn't matter."

"I got a question for ya, Max," said T.J.

"Shoot, young man."

"Well, I ain't never seen another naked guy in my life and I wanna know why my, well, you know," he stammered as he pointed down into the water, "looks different from all of yours."

"Ah, yes, your foreskin. T.J., Alex, would you both stand on the steps for a minute?" When both boys were on the step and turned around to face us, I called the other two over. "You guys see this piece of skin on the end of T.J.'s penis?" I asked as I pointed to T.J.'s penis.

"Yeah, why is it like that?" asked Mike. "I saw it was like that when we took our showers but didn't want to say nothin'."

"Well, that is called the foreskin. Most guys, like the rest of us, had it removed shortly after we're born, usually before we leave the hospital to go home. That's called circumcision. Some others, like T.J. here, are left intact."

"You mean we all looked like that when we were born?" Joey asked in surprise.

"We sure did."

"Why do they cut it off?" Alex queried.

"It's just some goofy old custom that started so long ago, nobody really knows where it came from or why people started doing it. There are lots of people who don't believe in it today and it's not happening quite as much as it used to. Most people who continue to circumcise their boys do so for religious reasons."

"What does it look like under that skin," Mike asked.

"Just like us. If T.J. doesn't mind me touching him, I can show you. Is that okay with you?"

"Sure, go ahead," he giggled.

I reached over and grasped the end of T.J.'s penis between my thumb and forefinger.

"That tickles," he giggled again.

"I know it does, and you might get an erection, but you said it was okay." I slowly slid T.J.'s foreskin back to expose his glans, and I was right about him getting an erection again. "There, that should be what you other three are used to seeing, right?"

"Look, I'm the same as you guys, now," T.J. laughed.

"Actually, T.J., you're the one with the normal penis. It's the rest of us who are different."

"Yeah, Max, that's cool," Joey said. "T.J., can I touch it?"

"Sure, go ahead," T.J. answered.

I grabbed Joey's hand before he made contact and said, "I don't think that's such a good idea, young man. Why don't we do what we came out here to do and actually swim?"

"Yeah!!" the boys screamed. Alex and T.J. jumped back in the water and the boys started horsing around.

Tom and I slowly moved to the deeper end of the pool to relax and watch the boys play.

"Max, those four are going to be a handful. I hope you're ready for it."

"I hope I am, too, Tom. When I started this process, I was hoping to adopt just one kid, I never dreamed it would turn into four."

"Just how did you end up with four?"

"When I first met Anna at the agency and explained what I hoped to do, she was very skeptical. They rarely worked with single guys and never with a single gay guy. I wasn't at all hopeful. After she talked to her people, including Carol, she finally decided that maybe I'd be okay. She arranged for me to meet the boys at her office. Little did I know at that moment, but Carol had stacked the deck in my favor. She had these four in the system, all needing good homes. Anna told me at that first meeting she would not consider separating the twins, and once I'd accepted the idea I could adopt two of them, taking all four didn't seem too far-fetched. They all seemed to be good boys, except …"

"Except what, Max?"

"I just remembered something I wanted to ask T.J." I turned to the other end of the pool and called, "T.J., come here a minute!" He slowly made his way to Tom and me while holding on to the edge of the pool.

"Yeah, Max, what do you want?" he asked when he joined us.

"I wanted to ask you a question about the first time we met in Anna's office."

"Oh, crap. I knew this was comin'."

"Oh, c'mon, don't be like that. I'm just curious. You seemed pretty sure that day that you didn't want to live with me. I know about what happened at your school and the fact you had to move to a new home and school because of it, but you still didn't want to live with, wait, what'd you call me? Oh yeah, 'a fag'. What made you change your mind?"

"You want the truth?" he asked.

"Always, T.J."

"Well, I'd been feeling different from the other boys I know for a while. That kid in the bathroom at school was just playing around, trying to figure it out. When I first met you, I tried to push you away, so I wouldn't be gay. I still didn't think I wanted to be like that, but after meeting with you, Joey and Alex, I started to think maybe it's okay. I've talked to the twins at school a lot the past couple weeks since we met. They're pretty cool dudes and really not any different from the other boys, except for the whole likin' boys thing. They got me thinkin' maybe I wasn't so weird after all."

"Okay, my curiosity is satisfied. I want you to know something, though. You can't *not* be gay just because you don't want to be, you either are or you aren't. Take that from someone who fought it for years. You just have to be who you are. If you're gay, fine, if not, that's fine, too."

"Thanks, Max. I love you," he said as he gave me hug.

"Love you, too, T.J. Now, go play with your brothers." He pulled himself along the edge of the pool until he could touch bottom, then rejoined the others in their ongoing tomfoolery.

Tom asked, "Max, how did you get so damn smart?"

"Lots of alone time writing and thinking. That's why it took twelve years to write three books. So, now you know how I ended up adopting all four boys. Anything else you want to know?"

"Lots, Max, but this may not be the right time."

"Why not? Ask away. I'm in an answering mood. I don't get that way often and you better take advantage of the opportunity."

"Okay, you ever been with another guy?"

"Wow, right for the juicy stuff, huh? Okay, you asked for it. Not since I was twelve or thirteen and that was just a quick jerk-off with a friend. After that, I started to suppress the feelings because I didn't want to be gay and I thought I could be *normal* like all my other friends. It's so easy to lie to yourself at that age and I just continued the lying and suppressing until very recently. Your turn, Tom, same question."

"Once, and only once, before I joined the force. As an adult, anyway. From eleven to about fourteen, I was constantly in circle jerks and mutual blowjobs with *really* good friends. Then, they switched to girls and I lost all my horny buds. From then to about twenty-one, I got by with my fantasies. Then, one night, I met this one guy in a bar, one thing sorta led to another and we ended up in the same bed. Worst night of my life. He just wanted to get off and didn't give a shit about me. When he was done, he just fucking left. Never saw him again and I joined the force shortly after. Since then, I didn't want even a hint I was gay out there."

"Not easy out there for us, is it?"

"Not a bit. But I think life is starting to get better." He moved closer and put his arm around my shoulder. I'd never been held like this by another man, especially a naked one, but I had to admit to myself that the closeness felt good and right. "Okay, Max, ready for the next question?"

"Sure."

"Do you think you're ready to be with a man any time in the near future?"

I turned to look into his eyes and replied, "It would have to be the right guy. I'm not going to just hop into bed with any old Tom, Dick or Harry, or even with Tom's hairy dick," I laughed. Tom jerked his arm from my shoulder, put both hands on the top of my head and pushed my head under the water. When I came back up, sputtering for air, I asked, "What the hell was that for?"

"Ha, very funny, asshole. How about Tom's hairless dick?"

"I'd consider it if you could find me one," I laughed again.

"We'll just have to see about that."

"That's definitely something I'd like to see. What about, you, Tom? Do you think you're ready to sleep with a guy?"

"Yeah, I am. Now that I know the boss is okay with my sexuality, I think I'm ready to find some nice, good-looking, and really smart guy, fall in love and have kids with him. To hell with rest of the world, if they don't like it, tough shit."

"Let me know when you find that guy, I'd like to meet him," I cracked.

"Dammit, Max, I'm trying to be serious here and all you can do is make jokes."

"I'm sorry, Tom. That's how I've dealt with my life the last twelve years, an endless stream of shitty jokes. It's a really bad habit and I'll make a serious effort to stop."

"Thank you. So, where do you see us going forward?"

"First, I have to be really careful until the adoptions are finalized. Now that the boys are here, I can't put that at risk."

"Well, how long will that take?"

"According to Carol, about five or six months."

"Well, damn, now that I've found you, I don't think I can wait that long."

"Hey, I didn't say we couldn't see each other and get closer during that time, just that I need to be careful. I still want to be with you and I want the boys to be comfortable here and get to know you better, also."

"Uh, Max, look down there," he said, pointing to the other end of the pool, "I don't think they could possibly get any more comfortable. They obviously had no problems stripping down right in front of us, no hint of modesty by any of them. And now, they're playin' naked in the pool with two naked guys watching them. If that ain't comfortable, I don't what is."

I laughed and said, "I guess you're right. It looks like they all just needed a place to live where they can be themselves. And I'm glad I can provide that place. As Carol put it last night, 'if they're comfortable in their own skin, leave 'em be.' They certainly seem to be content."

"No doubt about it, Max. You think we'll ever be like that?"

"I sure hope so, Tom, I can only hope."

11

"I think it's time to get out of here and get these munchkins in bed. It's been a long day and I don't know about them, but I'm beat." I turned to the other end of the pool and yelled, "Boys, time to call it a night. Run inside, hit the showers and get ready for bed." They took off like shots from cannons, covering the gap from the shelter to the house very quickly. "Good thing I used wood floors when I had the house built since we forgot to bring towels out with us."

"Point me to a mop, Max, and I'll follow along behind to clean up water trails," Tom chuckled.

"Then who's going to clean up your water trail?" I kidded back at him. "I'll grab us some towels and meet you in the twin's room."

"Works for me."

I directed Tom to the mop and headed to my bathroom to grab a couple towels for the two of us, then turned back towards the twins' room. I met Tom just as he was coming back out, "Here's your towel," I said as I started drying myself.

As he put the towel to good use, he said, "Maybe I'm not ready for this."

"You better get ready, bubba, 'cause your part of the family now."

"That sounds good. Seriously, Max, I never dreamed that I would ever be part of a family again. I'm glad I found yours today."

"Me too, Tom, me too. Shall we get our clothes off the kitchen counter and get their snacks ready?"

"Might as well. Should we get dressed?"

"You really think they're going to come back out here with a stitch of clothes on?"

"Probably not. From what I've seen so far, I'd be amazed if they did."

"See, you're catching on already." Leaving the mop in the utility room, we headed to the kitchen, grabbed our clothes and took them into my bedroom. After we dropped them on the bed, we headed back to the kitchen for a snack with the boys. Tom and I got back just as T.J. and Mike came in from their room and hopped up on their stools. "Cookies again, boys, same as last night?" Both nodded and I got out the cookies while Tom poured the milk. By the time the twins reappeared, the first two were done. Joey and Alex wasted no time in inhaling their snack. Tom and I cleaned up and I turned back to the boys. "So, tell me boys, do you really think you want to live like this?"

"Like what, Max?" Joey asked.

"In this house, in the middle of nowhere, with me, and at the right time, Tom?"

"Sure, we do. Why wouldn't we?" responded Joey.

"Yeah, I don't ever want to live anywhere else for the rest of my life," added Alex.

"Me either," said T.J. "We got a great house, a pool, trails to explore, a giant yard and we don't have to wear no stinkin' clothes."

"What about you, Mike, you've been awfully quiet."

"I think, so, Max. It's different, but I like it here, too."

"Are you as okay with the no clothes thing as the others are?" I asked. "I don't want you to feel like you're being forced to do something you don't want to."

"That's really different, and it felt kinda weird at first, but I can get used to it. If it was just me with no clothes on, I wouldn't like it, but since all of us are, I think it's cool."

"Okay, now that that's settled, why don't we watch a movie before bed?"

"Yeah! Can we have popcorn, too?"

"Why not? Let me get some popped while you guys go grab some clean towels."

"What're they for, Max?" asked Mike.

"To sit on. Nudists always carry towels with them to sit on, usually draped around their necks like a scarf. I'll expect everyone to have a towel in their chairs before they sit. There are clean ones in the dryer. Why don't you go grab six so we all have one, then head into the theater? Tom and I will bring the drinks and popcorn. Go!" They took off in a flash and flew back by us on the way to the theater with towels for everyone.

"We better get the popcorn and drinks and get in there." I tossed a bag of popcorn in each microwave while Tom pulled drinks from the refrigerator, sodas for the boys and Coronas for us. I was glad I had the two microwaves though I rarely used both at the same time, but it was a real time saver now. When the corn was popped, I poured each bag into separate bowls so each boy had their own. I didn't want any food fights in the theater because it's a bear to clean with the way it's furnished.

Tom and I headed to the theater with the refreshments and found the boys seated and ready for a movie. Towels were placed in two chairs behind the boys for Tom and me. I selected the first Star Wars movie for tonight because let's face it, who doesn't love a good science fiction flick? I started the movie and took my seat next to Tom. After I was seated, Tom reached over and took my hand in his. God, it felt good.

"I'm not pushing you, am I, Max?"

"Not at all, Tom. I was just thinking how nice this was. I could really get used to this."

"Good, I could, too."

We settled back to enjoy the movie and the boys seemed be enjoying it, too. I hadn't realized when I picked this movie that the boys were young enough they probably hadn't seen it before. It was well after eleven when the movie ended, and I realized I had two sleeping boys and two more who were about to join them. "Joey, Alex," I whispered, "you two head for bed."

"What about them?" Alex asked pointing to T.J. and Mike.

"We'll get them to bed, don't worry, and we'll check on you two after we do."

"Okay," said Joey, "Come on, Alex."

They stumbled out of the theater on the way to bed and I looked at Tom and asked, "Which one you want?"

"Doesn't make a lot of difference really, neither one weighs much. Why don't you get Mike and I'll grab T.J.?"

"Works for me, let's go." We carried them to their room, carefully pulled the covers back, laid the boys down and then covered them back up. I then leaned in, kissed each on the forehead and said, "Love you, guys, sleep well." To my pleasant surprise, Tom followed suit. I was starting to really like this guy. We headed to the twins' room to find both laid out on their backs, covers at the foot of the bed and lightly snoring. We each grabbed a corner of the cover and pulled it up to their chins. When I bent to kiss Alex on the forehead, I saw Tom do the same to Joey. We swapped sides and repeated for each boy, then headed back to the living room.

"Max, I want to thank you for a wonderful day. It had a pretty shitty beginning, but the ending has been one of the highlights of my life." Tom headed down the hall to my bedroom and I followed along.

"You're leaving already."

"Yeah. I don't really want to, but I've got an early shift tomorrow and all my clean uniforms are at home. I'd have to leave here by five to get home, change and then get to work on time. I don't want to bother you guys that early in the morning. Besides, I'm not sure I'm quite ready to spend the night. I hope you understand."

"I do," I replied with a touch of sadness. "A lot has happened to both of us the last couple days and we both need a little time to assimilate. But let me leave with you something to think about." I grabbed his shoulder, turned him around, wrapped my arms around him in a loving hug and gave him a kiss. He was shocked at first, but soon began to return the kiss. My tongue soon invaded his mouth and he willingly returned the gesture. We separated a minute later, both breathing heavily.

"Okay," Tom breathed heavily, "I really need to get out of here, now. You certainly know how to give a guy something to think about."

"I do my best," I smiled. I sadly watch him get dressed and when he was ready to go, I followed him to the door. "Good night, Tom. We'll miss you in the morning."

"I'll gonna miss seeing you all, too. Good luck keeping those four in line, Max, you're gonna need it."

"Wait, when can you come back?"

"My shift ends at three tomorrow and I'm off Monday. I'm gonna pack some extra clothes when I go to work in the morning and I'll be out about three-thirty. We'll see what happens after that."

"You be careful out there tomorrow, you hear me? Now that I've found you, I don't want to lose you."

"I'll be careful, Dad," he replied sarcastically. "See you guys tomorrow. Sleep well."

"Oh, I'll sleep, just not sure how well." I watched Tom as he pulled away, then locked the doors and turned off lights on my way to bed. After a quick stop in the bathroom, I crawled in my bed hoping I wouldn't be sleeping alone for much longer.

12

It was a long night filled with many weird and wild dreams. If even one of those dreams comes true, I was gonna be a very happy man. When I finally woke up, I rolled over to look at the sun streaming through the window, only to find my view blocked by four boys.

"Uh, morning guys, what's up?"

They all giggled and Joey said, "Judging by the tent in your blanket, I think it's you."

"Good dreams this morning, Max?" asked Alex.

"Wouldn't you like to know?" I chuckled. "So, why are you all here, blocking my morning rays?"

"C'mon, Max, it's almost ten and we're hungry," T.J. said.

"Yeah, get up and feed us. Please and thank you," whined Mike.

"It's nice to know at least one of my sons knows the magic words. Okay, you four head on out to the kitchen and I'll be there in a minute." The boys took off while I climbed out of bed and took care of my morning bathroom needs. Hands and face washed, I headed to the kitchen to fix something for breakfast. "Good morning, boys. Is cereal okay for breakfast? I don't feel much like cooking this morning."

"Sure, Max, what ya got?" asked Joey.

"Let's see." I opened the cabinet and gave them their options. "I have Frosted Flakes, Honey Nut Cheerios, Corn Flakes and Rice Krispies. What's your choice?" Joey and Alex picked Frosted Flakes, T.J. went for the Cheerios and Mike settled on Rice Krispies. "Y'all want some toast with your cereal?" A chorus of 'yeahs' filled the kitchen so I pulled out the toaster, bread, honey, cinnamon sugar and apple and grape jellies. I buttered the toast and set it next to each boy so they could select their preferred topping. All except for Mike, and I had to help him with the honey, again. I was going to have to find something easier for him to use.

Once we were all done chowing down, we cleaned up the kitchen together and I gave the boys a quick lesson on stacking the dishes into the dishwasher.

"So, what are we doing today?" I asked.

"We talked about it before you woke up and we just want to relax and take it easy today. If that's okay with you?" Alex said.

"You guys sure?"

"Yep," said Mike, "Yesterday was busy and we're all kinda wiped out."

"Sounds good me, guys. How about another movie, we could watch the next Star Wars?"

"Cool, let's go," said T.J.

As I was getting the movie set up, the boys settled in their chairs and Mike asked, "Is Tom coming back today?"

"He's planning to. He had to be at work real early this morning, so he went home last night after you were all in bed."

"Good, I like Tom," T.J. commented.

"I do, too, and I'm hoping we see a lot more of him."

"Uh, Max," Joey said, "I don't think we can see much more of him than what we saw last night," he laughed, and the others joined in.

"Ha-ha, very funny. We could say the same about the four of you." That really got them laughing. "Okay, you guys settle down and enjoy the movie. If you need a drink or something, you know where all that stuff is. I need to go make some phone calls and I'll be back.

"Sure thing, Max," Joey replied.

I headed to my study and made my first call to Carol.

"Hello?"

"Good morning, Carol, how are you this bright and beautiful day?"

"Ah, morning, Max. I'm great, how are you doing? I have to assume you survived the first night alone with the boys."

"I did, though I'm not quite sure how."

"No, seriously, is everything okay?"

"We're just fine. We all got a good night's sleep after a very long and busy day yesterday. We watched the first Star Wars last night, T.J. and Mike fell asleep before it was over, and Joey and Alex were barely awake. They're watching the second Star Wars now so I could make some calls. You're the first one."

"I'm honored. What can I do for you?"

"I was hoping you had time today to talk. I need to ask some questions that kinda slipped my mind before you left last night, and I don't think I want to deal with them over the phone. I know you were looking forward to a day off, but if you don't mind coming out, I'd really appreciate it."

"I think I can do that. I have some running to do this afternoon but could come out before I start those errands. Would sometime around one be okay?"

"Oh, that would be perfect. You could join us for a spaghetti lunch. Does that sound alright?"

"Sounds wonderful. I love spaghetti. Can I bring anything?"

"Nope, I have everything else covered. Thanks, Carol, we'll see you around one."

"See you then."

My second call was to my parents. We hadn't talked much lately because they were less than thrilled when I told them I was gay back in November of last year. I figured I should probably clue them in on my adopting the boys. I didn't want to show up one day, out of the blue, with four boys tagging along and them not having some warning.

"Sanders residence," Mom answered.

"Good morning, Mom, how are you today?"

"Just fine, Max, how are you?" she answered frostily.

"I'm great. Is Dad there, too? I have to tell you something and I'd like you both to hear it at the same time, directly from me."

"I suppose, hang on while I get him on the other phone." I heard her in the background, "Jim, pick up the phone, it's Max and he has more *news* for us ... I don't know what it is, just pick up the damn phone."

I heard the phone click as he picked up in the other room. "Hi, Dad, how ya doing?"

"Fine, Max, what's this big news you have to tell?"

"Well, I know we haven't really talked much for a while, but I first want you both to know I love you."

"We love you, too, Max, it's just a little difficult right now," dad said.

"I know it is and I understand. I hope what I'm about to tell you won't make things worse."

"Well, go ahead and spit it out."

"Okay, I hope you're both sitting down."

"Yeah, we are, get on with it."

"Well, I thought you should know that I'm in the process of adopting four boys."

"Are you fucking kidding me, Max? Please, please, please tell me this is some sick joke. A man like you shouldn't be adopting any kids, especially boys."

"Dad, we've been over this before. Being gay does not make me a child molester. They're not the same damn thing."

"How old are the boys, Max?" Mom asked.

"The twins, Joey and Alex, are eight, T.J. is seven and Mike is six."

"Oh, my, I figured they'd be older."

"Nope. And the other thing you need to know is that all four of them are probably gay, too."

"Bullshit!" Dad yelled. "They can't know what the hell they are at that age."

"Dad, I told you both when I came out to you that I was seven or eight when I knew, I just hid it. If I knew at that age, they can, too. You both realize that we can't change who we're attracted to, don't you?"

"So you say, I never believed that shit. It's a choice you make, like what color car to buy or what book to read."

"Okay, Dad, let me ask you this. Exactly when did you *choose* to be straight?"

"I didn't choose, I always was."

"Exactly. It's the same with being gay, you don't choose, you just are. Who in their right mind would fucking *choose* to be gay when we are forced to put up with the bullshit that gets dumped on us. I'll tell you who, NO ONE!"

"Don't you yell at me, young man," Mom cried.

"Look, I know you guys don't like or accept the fact I'm gay yet, but it's not something I can or would change. You'll either learn to accept it or you won't. The other thing you need to think about, now, is these four boys will be your grandsons and I'm not going to have them around you until you change your attitude."

"Is that a threat, son?"

"No, Dad, it's a promise. These boys have come from some tough situations and I won't allow them to be abused by you two."

"Abused? What the hell are you talking about, I would never hit them."

"Dad, words can be just as abusive, if not more so, as hitting. I will not subject them to anti-gay slurs and shit like that. You can't take back the words once they pass your lips."

"Fine, son, if that's the way you want it." Mom replied.

"It's not how I *want* it, Mom, but it's the way it's going to be. I just wanted to let you know you're going to be grandparents and as soon as you think you can be decent, I'll have you out and you can meet your new family members. Goodbye, I'll talk to you later." I fairly slammed the receiver down as I hung up. I had really hoped they'd have softened a bit, but I guess that was too much to ask for. Oh, well, it's their loss, not mine. The next person I called was my sister, Lee.

"Yo, sis, what's up?" I asked when she answered.

"Not much, bro, what's up with you."

"Same shit, different day. Just got off the phone with the 'rents."

"Ooh, bet that was fun. NOT!"

"You hit the nail right on the head, as usual. They were even more pissed when I gave them something new to think about. If that's possible."

"What, did you tell them you'd found a really nice man and the two of you were getting married in Vegas next week?"

"Ha, I wish. That probably would have been better received than what I told them, though. No, I let them know they're becoming grandparents. And, by extension, I guess, you're gonna be an auntie."

"WHAT!?"

"I told them I'm in the process of adopting four boys. I could practically hear the old man shittin' his pants through the phone," I laughed.

"Max, that's wonderful. I'm so happy for you. You'd said you were going to think about it when you came out to me six months ago. I guess you're done thinking, huh. When can I meet them?" she giggled with glee.

"Well, Carol from the adoption agency is coming out about one to have lunch, and so I can ask her some questions. That'll probably take up a couple hours, so if you wanted to come out about three, that'd be cool. I'd really like you to meet them."

"I wouldn't miss it. I'll see you then."

"Thanks, Lee, love ya."

My next call was to my car dealer, Herb.

"Hello?" he answered.

"Herb? Max Sanders, here. I hate to bug you at home on a Sunday, but I have a problem."

"No problem, Max, what's up?"

"You remember me telling you I ordered the Flex because I was hoping to adopt?"

"Like it was yesterday. Oh, please don't tell me it fell through, that'd really suck."

"Oh, no, it's still happening, in spades."

"What's that mean?"

"Well, it happened yesterday afternoon and it turns out I'm not getting one kid, I got four."

"Yesterday? Four? What the heck?"

"Yeah, Herb, I now have four boys, ages six to eight, living with me. The actual adoption won't be final for several months, but the agency worker arranged to have the boys stay here after their weekend visit instead of going back to their foster homes."

"Well, congratulations, Max. That's great news. You're gonna be a great father."

"We can always hope, can't we?" I chuckled. "So, now, we come to my problem. I now have myself and four boys that need transportation and I really don't think the Shelby's designed to accommodate more than two for any length of time, is it?"

"No, it sure isn't."

"Do you have a vehicle on the lot I can rent until my Flex comes in?"

"You bet I do. We have a Flex in the rental fleet and it was returned earlier this week. I can let you use it until yours is delivered. I'll even give you a discounted rate since you've ordered the new one from me."

"That's great, Herb. And you know what to do with the discount. Bill me the full price and forward the discount somewhere else. Now, I just need to figure out how I can get it."

"No big deal, Max. I'll bring it out tomorrow morning and have one of my guys follow along to bring me back to the showroom. Will that work okay for you?"

"Service above and beyond, as always. Thanks. Just give me a call when you're ready to come out and I'll see you then. Thanks again."

That was all the calls I could think of at the moment and decided to check on the boys to see how they were doing. The movie was close to ending, so I told the boys I was going to head to the kitchen to start making lunch since the sauce was going to need some time to simmer.

"When the movie's done, punch the big red button on the remote to shut everything down and then come out to the kitchen, okay?"

"Okay, Max, we'll be there in a little bit," Alex replied.

I headed to the kitchen to start browning the ground beef and sausage for the sauce. While it was cooking, I started up a large pan of water for the noodles and the rest of the sauce in a smaller pan. As I kept an eye on the meat, the boys came in and joined me at the counter to watch while I cooked.

"What're we havin'?" asked Mike.

"Spaghetti with garlic bread. Sound good to you guys?"

"Yeah, I love s'getti," Mike said.

"Okay, why don't you all go wash your hands real quick and when you come back, bring a pair of shorts with you."

"Why do we need shorts, Max?" asked T.J.

"Carol's going to join us and I'd prefer for you to be dressed when she's here, please. You won't have to put them on until we hear the drive sensor, but you should have them close by. I'll grab a pair for myself in a minute." The four took off and were back shortly with their shorts. I grabbed a pair for myself along with a shirt and laid them on the end of the counter.

After I returned, I had the boys set the table and get drinks for themselves, each taking care of the same tasks as before. As I watched T.J. struggle to get the plates, I decided I was going to have to move the plates and bowls to a lower cabinet to make them easier for the boys to reach.

I had just dropped the spaghetti into the water when the sensor dinged. "Shorts, kids." We all pulled on our shorts and I added my shirt as I headed to the door to meet Carol. I opened the door as she was coming up the walk, took her coat and hung it up in the closet. "Good afternoon, Carol, how are you?" I said as the boys ran up to us.

"I'm great, Max. I hope you're good, too." The boys wrapped her up in a five-way hug and she added, "And judging by the reception, I have to assume these guys are all good."

"Yeah, we're great, Ms. Ward," Alex said.

"Thanks for finding Max for us," Joey added.

"It's great, we all love it here," from T.J.

"How about you, Mike?" she asked. "Is Max being good to you?"

"The bestest, ma'am."

"You're timing is perfect, Carol, I just dropped the spaghetti in to boil. We'll be ready to eat in about eight minutes. Joey, would you get Carol a drink, please?"

"Sure thing, what do you want?"

"Tea would be fine. Thanks, Joey."

The spaghetti was soon ready, so I drained it, carried it to the table and put some on everybody's plate. I then went around the table adding sauce to each plate. With the garlic bread in a basket and the parmesan cheese added to the table, we were ready to eat. "Grab a chair y'all and dig in."

The room was quickly filled with the sounds of slurping spaghetti and crunching garlic bread as we ate. There wasn't much discussion during the meal, for which I was grateful. I wanted to talk to Carol alone after we ate. When we were done stuffing our faces and the boys had cleaned the table, I had them go to their rooms and start putting away all the stuff they'd sorted yesterday so Carol and I could talk. We headed to my study after I reminded the boys about knocking before coming in.

After getting comfortable in the study, Carol asked, "So, Max, how did it really go last night after I left? They didn't burn down the house, so I have to assume you had a good night."

"We had a great time. We went swimming again, then a snack during a movie and bed. It was a long, emotional day for everybody and we were all wiped out."

"So, what did you want to talk about that you didn't want to deal with on a phone call?"

"First, I wanted to ask about school. Should I let the boys finish off the year at their current school or what do you think I should do? I'd hate to move them to a new school in the middle of the year but getting them to school in Springfield could present some problems."

"Oops, I forgot to tell you, didn't I? All four lived far enough west of Springfield that they already attend school out here. You'll just need to contact the principal and make arrangements to have the bus stop here to pick them up."

"Well, that makes life quite a bit easier than I thought it was going to be. I'll call first thing in the morning to let them know they won't be there tomorrow and to start picking them up Tuesday morning. Herb is bringing me a rental tomorrow so I can get all four down to the end of drive to meet the bus."

"Okay, that's one problem solved, what's next on your list of concerns?"

"The Muellers. Can they, in any way, cause problems with the adoptions?"

"I don't see how. They can try, for sure, but I'm going to angle for a specific judge to deal with their cases and I don't think he'll have any problems with having you as their father. He doesn't much care what anyone else thinks and really does look out for the best interests of the child."

"Good, so my parents shouldn't be able to cause any problems either."

"I didn't know they lived in the area, you'd never mentioned them before."

"No, I didn't. They weren't too happy with me when I came out to them. We haven't talked much since then until I called them this morning to let them know I was adopting four boys."

"Bet that went over like a lead balloon."

"Even worse. They still think that since I'm gay, I'm some sort of sick, bastard, pervert child molester. I also reminded them that being gay isn't something a person can change just like you can't change being straight. You either are or aren't."

"That's very true, Max."

"I also told them that even though they will be grandparents to the boys, they won't be allowed around them until they change their attitude. I'm *not* going to give them the opportunity to abuse the boys."

"As much as that must hurt, I think it's the best thing. For you and the boys."

"Yeah, it sucks, all right, but those four have been through enough already. I'm not going to put them through even more just to try and have a relationship with my parents. They'll either figure it out or they won't."

"We'll make sure the judge knows that if we think it will make a difference."

"Now, my sister, on the other hand, was ecstatic with the news. She couldn't wait to come out and meet her new nephews. She's supposed to be here about three."

"Ahh, now it makes sense."

"What?"

"Well, the boys are wearing shorts, as are you. I just assumed that after everyone left last night, this became a nudist household. I know the boys weren't at all concerned about being nude around me. They made that very evident Friday night."

"They sure did, and they asked about it last night, too, when it was finally down to just the five of us and Tom."

"Tom stayed longer after I left?" she asked with surprise.

"He did, and the boys asked if the rule I laid out Friday night about clothes and when 'other people' were here included Tom? When Tom asked what they were talking about, I told him about what happened the night before at snack time, with you sitting right there, and the rule I laid down. His eyes bugged out in surprise."

"Oh, I wish I could've seen that. I bet it was priceless."

"It was, let me tell you. It was then that Alex asked if Tom was 'other people' or is he 'one of us'? Tom had picked a bad time to take a drink and sprayed his Corona all over the counter," I laughed as the sight flitted through my mind. "Tom wanted to know more before he would answer, and when I added that you were okay with it, Tom finally said he'd been known to lounge around nude and didn't have a problem with it if the boys didn't. I bet you know what happened next. I'll even give you three guesses and the first two don't count."

"I would imagine all four hopped off their stools, took their clothes off and hopped back up without a care in the world."

"Bingo, we have a winner. But that wasn't the end of it. Not by a long shot. After all four were seated again, Alex looks me square in the eyes and said 'okay guys, your turn'." Carol laughed at that.

"I told them I didn't think it was such a good idea. I didn't think your agency would look too favorably on me being nude, too, even if they were. They said they weren't ever going to tell anyone. I finally looked at Tom, said 'when in Rome' and started to pull off my shirt. Tom hesitated, but finally gave in and we both got undressed, right there in the kitchen."

"Oh, my, I bet that was a sight to behold."

"It kinda was, Carol. Tom's a very good-looking guy, in more ways than one." I smiled at the pleasant thought. "We spent the rest of the night nude, went for a swim, had snacks and watched a movie together. None of us cared we weren't dressed. The only kinda weird thing was when T.J. asked why he was different from the rest of us."

"What the heck was that about, Max?"

"Think, Carol, what's something you could only see on a naked guy? Something that would make him different from a lot of other guys."

"I don't have a clue, Max."

"Well, he's not, you know, um, circumcised." I don't know why, but I was embarrassed to say it out loud.

"Oh, my, I'd never have thought of that."

"It wasn't a big deal, but I had T.J. and Alex stand on the steps in the pool so I could explain and they could all clearly see the difference. There was some worry among the other three that T.J. was somehow deformed. Mike said he had noticed it when the two took their shower, but he didn't want to say anything about it. I asked T.J. if I could touch him to show the others that, under the foreskin, he was just like us. He said go ahead, so I did and, of course, he developed an erection. I hope I didn't step over a line."

"No, Max, I think that kind of touch was fine. First, you asked for his permission and he gave it. That's very important. Second, you were answering a question they all had and they deserved an answer. I think you handled it the best way possible. Third, they are all going to have questions about their own and other's bodies, especially as they get older. I think it's best they be given true and accurate answers. I just hope you're ready for them."

"Well, Alex asked one I wasn't ready for, but I answered it anyway."

"And what was that?"

"He wanted to know why Tom was hairy all over and I wasn't."

Carol chuckled and asked, "Did he really mean 'all over'? I noticed your body, of course, Friday night when you came out in those tiny Speedos. I wondered about the rest of it."

"Well, you can quit wondering. Yes, I shave or trim *everywhere*. You don't have a problem with that, do you?"

"Absolutely not, Max. Whatever floats your boat."

"I'm glad to hear it. Later, during the movie, T.J. and Mike had fallen asleep. We got Alex and Joey on their way to bed, then Tom and I carried the two sleeping beauties to theirs. Tom helped me tuck the boys in bed and followed my lead in giving them each a kiss on the forehead to say good night."

"Sounds like everyone had a nice evening, including Tom. Makes me glad I called him to help you with the Muellers yesterday."

"Wait, you set that up, too? Did you know he was gay?"

"I did," she answered with a slight blush of embarrassment. "I found out by accident the first night we met. I thought you two would make a cute couple and Lord knows you're going to need all the help you can get." We shared a laugh at her observation.

"No doubt about it, Carol, and I can't think of anyone I'd rather have helping me. Tom's a really nice guy, in so many ways. The boys all like him and he seems to like them just as much. Those four just worm their way right into your heart."

"I knew they would. That's why I'm glad you came into the agency when you did. I knew you'd give them a good home. So, when is Tom coming back?"

"He said he's off shift at three and should be here about three-thirty if all goes well. Oh, shit!" I exclaimed while slapping myself in the forehead.

"What?"

"My sister's coming out about three to meet the boys and I bet she'll still be here when Tom comes back."

"Is that a problem, Max?"

"It shouldn't be, she was great when I told her I was gay, didn't bat an eye. Just hugged me and said it was about time I faced reality. I just don't think I'm ready for her to meet him just yet. Hell, I've only known him for a day."

"And yet, you've only known the boys for two days, but you don't have a problem with her meeting them."

"Stupid, huh. I guess I'd better get over it."

"Yep, I think so. Well, if that's all you had for me, I'll be on my way so you can be ready for your sister."

"Thanks for coming out, Carol. I'm glad I have your support and I appreciate all your help in making this happen."

"Happy to help, Max. If you need anything else, don't hesitate to call. And thanks for lunch. It was delicious."

We headed to the front door and I called for the boys to come say goodbye to Carol. As I retrieved her coat from the closet, the boys came charging down the hall, sans shorts. They wrapped a laughing Carol in a hug to say their goodbyes. "Boys, what did I tell you just last night about that?"

"We didn't think Carol was 'other people', Max," volunteered Alex.

"Yeah, it was okay Friday night, why not now?" asked Joey.

"It's fine, boys," Carol answered. "I grew up with four brothers so, trust me, I know what naked boys look like." She turned to me and added, "Lighten up, Max. Really, I'm okay with it. After all, boys *will* be boys."

"Ain't that the truth. Thanks again for coming out, Carol. I hope you enjoy the rest of your afternoon."

A chorus of 'byes' rang out behind me as I opened the door. No sooner had the drive sensor dinged to announce Carol's departure than it dinged again. I thought maybe Carol had forgotten something, but I soon saw my sister's car pull in the drive.

"Boys, go put on your shorts, a shirt and come back here. There's someone new you need to meet."

13

I waited at the door until Lee got closer and then opened it before she could ring the bell. "I hate that damn sensor, Max. I can't sneak up on you with that thing."

"Precisely why I have it, sis, and you know that." I took her coat and was hanging it up when the boys rounded the corner and, fortunately, they were dressed as I'd requested.

"Who's she, Max?"

"Boys, this my sister, Lee. Lee, these four wild monkeys are going to be my sons. From left to right, we have Alex, Mike, T.J. and Joey. Boys, say hi to your new aunt."

"Hi, Aunt Lee," they all said.

"Oh, aren't you guys just the cutest? Come give me a hug," she said as she knelt down to their level. All four gathered around her and enveloped her in another five-way hug. "Let's go sit on the couch and you can tell me all about yourselves."

"Lee, you want anything to drink," I asked as she headed to the couch with the boys in tow.

"I wouldn't say no to a cold Pepsi," she replied as she took a seat in the center of the couch with two boys on each side. "Okay, guys, let's start with your ages."

"Joey and I are both eight, Mike's six and T.J.'s seven."

"And how long have you been here?"

"We got here Friday night, after we met Max at Steak 'n Shake for supper," Joey said.

"Yeah, that was a fun meal, wasn't it guys?" Alex asked with a chuckle.

"Really, what happened that made it fun?"

"Our foster parents pitched a fit when they found out Max was gay like us and stormed out."

"Well, that sounds familiar, I wonder if they know Mom and Dad?" she asked me as I handed her the Pepsi.

"With my luck, they do."

"So, Max, how does it feel to finally be a dad?"

"So far, so good, but it hasn't even been two days yet and they're already giving me a run for my money."

"I bet, so tell me, guys, how did you end up here in my brother's home?"

"Our parents were killed in a car wreck when we were four," Joey said.

"Yeah, and we've lived with those scumbags, the Muellers, since then. Max rescued us from living in hell," Alex added.

"Alex, that's not a nice thing to say about anybody," I reprimanded.

"It's true, isn't it?"

"Be that as it may, it's still not nice."

"What about you, T.J., how'd you end up here?" Lee asked.

"My mom's in prison and not bound to get out any time soon. She don't know who my dad is, and I've lived with a couple different foster families since she went away. Max is the first one who had me for a home visit who said he'd still 'dopt me."

"Mike, you want to tell me how you got here?"

"Not really," Mike mumbled.

"I'll fill you in later, sis."

"So, what do you boys like to do?"

"Watch TV and movies, swim, play games, skateboard, lots of things."

"Hey, you guys missed one," I said.

"What'd we miss, Max?"

"You forgot all about driving me bonkers," I laughed.

"That's just the nature of kids, bro, any age, any number, they're going to drive you crazy. We sure did our fair share of driving Mom and Dad crazy, don't ya think?"

"Some of us still are," I replied proudly. "Hey, have you boys finished putting all your stuff away?"

"We got most of it done, Max, except for the little bit that needs hung in a closet," Alex answered. "We can't reach the bar."

"You've still made good progress. We'll take care of those things a little later."

Ding!

"You expecting someone else, Max?" Lee asked.

"Yeah, looks like he's a little early though."

"He? Anyone I should know about?"

"Well, not really, but you will soon enough."

Tom came in the front door without ringing the bell, carrying an overnight bag. He started to say hi, saw Lee and stopped abruptly. Instead, he said, "Whoops, sorry folks, I must be in the wrong house. Sorry for the intrusion." He turned and reached for the doorknob to leave.

"Tom, you bonehead, get your ass in here. I want you to meet my sister, Lee."

"Oh, maybe I am in the right place." The boys took off and wrapped Tom in giant hug. "Hi guys, good to see you again. Uh, can I walk now?" They finally released him and he was able to make his way over to Lee and me, followed by the boys.

"Tom, I'd like you to meet my sister, Lee. Lee, this is my new friend, Tom."

Tom stuck his hand out for a shake as he and Lee greeted each other. "New *friend*, huh, Max? So new that I haven't even heard about him yet."

"Calm down, sis. We just met yesterday afternoon and I've been a little busy. Please forgive me for being so remiss in not keeping you updated on my social status."

She laughed and said, "Don't have a cow, Max, I'm just giving you grief. Tom, is it? Tell me how you two met."

"Do I have to?"

"Well, Max obviously isn't going to, so yeah, it looks like it's up to you."

"Okay, Max went to Joey and Alex's foster parents yesterday to pick up the things they'd left there. Max's case worker, Carol, thought there might be some problems, so she called me, I'm a sheriff's deputy, and another guy, Brian, who works with her, to help your brother. Good thing we were there, or you'd have probably ended up bailing Max out of the pokey. Since my sergeant gave me the rest of the afternoon off for my exemplary service, Max invited me to join the mini-celebration he had last night with the other boys' foster parents and Carol and Brian."

"Wait, you had a party last night and didn't invite me. You're a piece of work, dear brother."

"I'm sorry, Lee, things happened kinda fast Friday and yesterday." I relayed the details of how the boys ended up staying here instead of going back to their foster parents this afternoon.

"Wow, you've certainly had some weekend, Max. But next time you have a party, my name better be on the list of invitees."

"It will be, Lee, for sure. Thanks for understanding."

"Now, back to you, Tom. You met Max and the boys for the first time yesterday and you already feel comfortable enough to come back with an overnight bag? Explain, please."

"I plead the fifth, ma'am," he laughed.

"I'll handle this, Tom. Lee, you know how I've lived here the last twelve years and why I have the driveway sensor."

"Yeah, free as a bird. Wait, you didn't. Did you?"

"Yeah, we did. These four are naturals, apparently," I said, waving my hand in the direction of the boys who were all grinning madly. "They have no shame or inhibitions, not that they should. You can ask Carol about that. They'd be bare-assed right now if I'd let them. I've told them they have to wear at least underwear in this part of the house when other people are here. After everybody else left last night and it was just the six of us, they asked if Tom was other people or one of us. When I explained to Tom what they were asking, and he finally decided he didn't care what they wore, they got off the bar stools, undressed right there in the kitchen, and climbed back up."

"Oh, man, I don't believe this."

"Believe it, Sis. I'm not done yet, though. After they were sitting down again, Alex looked me straight in the eyes and said, 'okay guys, your turn'. I told them I didn't think that was such a great idea, but they all said they weren't telling anyone, so Tom and I joined them."

"Jesus, Max, are you freakin' nuts? A gay man running around naked with four supposedly gay, naked young boys and another naked man who I assume is also gay. That agency's gonna kill you if they find out about this."

"No, they're not, Lee. Carol was here just before you and I asked her about it to make sure it's not going to be an issue. She's fine with it." I explained in further detail about Carol's sister and her wife and kids' life so she'd know who I was working with.

"Well, you sure got lucky with her, didn't you?"

"In more ways than one, Lee."

"Don't you think I've forgotten about you, Tom," she said as she turned to face him again.

"Oh lord, I hoped you were done with me," he laughed as he mockingly cowered behind me.

"Not by a long shot, bubba. Is my assumption about you being gay correct?"

"Yeah. Max and the boys are the first to know. Well, besides my sergeant, I guess. I still don't know how he knew. Oh, and my parents, of course."

"Well, Tom, I obviously don't have a problem with it, but you need to know I'm very protective of my little brother, here, and I won't accept anyone playing with his emotions. It's taken him way too long to get comfortable with who he is to get screwed over by a lunatic."

"Not to worry, Lee. I've been hiding in the closet way too long myself. I'm ready to start living my life the way it was meant to be. After meeting your sweet and smart brother yesterday, everything just seemed to click. I know it seems sudden to others, but I feel like I've known Max my whole life."

"Good, just so long as we understand each other."

"We do, Lee. I promise I won't hurt anybody. I've waited way too long to find someone like your brother to love. I'm not going to blow it."

"WHAT!!" I exclaimed.

"Okay, bad choice of words," he snorted, "I won't screw it up. Oops, did it again. Damn, I think I'll shut up now." Everyone was laughing hysterically by the time he finally quit talking.

"Good idea," I agreed.

Lee turned back to the boys and asked, "So, do you think you guys will like living here with Max? And, Tom, it looks like."

"You bet, Aunt Lee," answered Joey.

"We love it here," added Alex.

"Yeah, we're not leaving, ever," Mike threw in.

"I think we'll be just fine, Aunt Lee. We know Max loves us and we're pretty sure he's falling in love with Tom, too. We all like Tom and I think it's great they've found each other," said T.J. as he added his two-cents to the conversation.

"Well, Max, you've got your work cut out for you, but I'm so happy for you. I don't envy you, but I'm happy. I'm happy for all of you. Yes, even you, Tom," she grinned.

"Well, miracles do happen. Praise be!" Tom exclaimed.

"Now, what are you going to do about Mom and Dad?" Lee asked looking at me.

"Boys, now might be a good time to go watch TV in the twins' room."

"But we want to talk with Aunt Lee."

"In a bit, please. Go." They grudgingly left the room as I called out, "Thank you," to their retreating backs.

"What about your parents, Max?" Tom asked. "You didn't say anything about your family last night, so I wasn't aware they were still around."

"What's going on, bro, you tryin' to act like you don't have a family. I mean, Mom and Dad, I can kinda understand them, but me, your favorite sister, you can't tell your new family about me? Now, I'm hurt," she joked as she play-acted a pitiful pout.

"C'mon, Sis, I've had bigger fish to fry this weekend. Besides, you're my only sister so you have to be my favorite, don't you? This has all happened so fast, I'm just now catching up myself." I turned to Tom and added, "Let's just say our loving (cough, cough) parents and the Muellers could be bosom buddies and leave well enough alone. I want to move forward with life, not dwell in the past."

"Max, I'm so sorry, I had no clue."

"I know, Tom, and it's my fault for not saying anything. They were furious when I came out to them. They said there's no way in hell their only son was a queer. I told them 'I guess you don't have a son, then', and walked out."

"Ouch."

"Yeah, it wasn't a pretty scene," Lee said.

"Well, we haven't really talked much since then, but I called them this morning to let them know I was adopting the boys and they were going to be grandparents."

"Didn't go well, I take it."

"Not at all. I thought maybe their frozen hearts had thawed a bit, but no such luck with that. I told them, flat out, that they would not be allowed to have anything to do with the boys until they changed their attitude and slammed the phone down. God, I was pissed."

"I'm sorry, Max. My parents were the same way, at first, but they've slowly come around and we're pretty good now. Maybe yours will, too."

"How long did it take them, Tom?" Lee asked.

"I first told them when I was twenty-three, so four and a half years ago. It took a couple of years for life to get back to normal between us."

"Shit, you're only twenty-seven? You weren't kidding when you said you wanted me to adopt you, were you? You're still a damn kid."

"Thanks, Max, I try," he laughed. "I've always said you have to get older, but you don't have to grow up. By the way, how old are you?"

"Thirty-four," I answered.

Lee started laughing hysterically and we both looked at her in surprise. "Now, wait just a dang minute, you two. You're telling me you spent an evening together, naked no less, and you had no clue how old each other was? That's a hoot!"

"I guess it didn't seem that important, sis."

"It wasn't to me, either, Max. I just felt a connection with you that I've never felt with any other person, male or female. From the very first moment we met in the Mueller's driveway."

"I felt it too, Tom. We're obviously on the same wavelength."

"That's good to know."

"Well, I'm glad you two found each other. And that you found the boys, Max. They are so sweet and special. Your life is going to change in so many ways, you have no idea. Is there anything I can do to help you out?"

"Can't think of anything at this moment, Lee, unless you can bring Mom and Dad into the 21st century. Think you could swing that?"

"Yeah, right, you don't want much."

"I had to try, didn't I? The only thing I'd like to ask is if you'd be available for babysitting services if I need some? If you don't mind hanging out with four boys in their birthday suits."

"You bet. I'd love to spend time with my nephews. I like the sound of that, 'my nephews'," she smiled. "And they can wear whatever they want or don't want, I'll deal with it. I dealt with you growing up, didn't I? I think I'll remain dressed, though, I don't want to scare them to death," she joked. "Hopefully, someday, they'll be able to know their grandparents. I'll do what I can with them, you know that. And while Tom, here, thinks I'm a miracle worker, there *are* limits to my powers." We all enjoyed a good laugh with that comment.

"Thanks, Lee, you're the best sister a man could have."

"And don't you ever forget it. Well, guys, I'm gonna get out of your way and let you enjoy your evening. I can't wait to get home and tell the hubby your good news, Max. I tried to get him to come with me, but the Bulls were playing this afternoon and he wouldn't leave the damn house. Tom, it was a pleasure to meet you, I think you'll be good for Max. Let me say goodbye to the boys and I'm outta here. Then, you can all get comfy."

"Boys, you can come back out now, Aunt Lee is leaving," I called down the hall.

They came running down the hall and surprisingly still had on their shorts and shirts.

"I thought she was gonna stay longer," Joey complained.

"Don't worry, guys, she'll be back. She's even agreed to babysit when we need her."

"Cool, we'd like that," Alex said.

"And she's approved you guys being nude when she's here."

"Even better," said T.J., "we hate having to wear clothes."

"We'll be just fine, won't we, boys?" Lee asked.

"Yeah, Aunt Lee," Mike said, "And we promise we'll be good."

"I know you will. Now, give me hug so I can get home and fix supper for me and my husband." The normal five-way hug ensued as I got Lee's coat for her. She kissed my cheek, then surprised Tom with a kiss on his cheek, too. "Y'all be good. Maybe next time, Carl can join me. He'll love you guys. You, too, Tom," she added as she patted Tom's cheek.

Tom blushed as Lee walked out the door. As I closed the door, he leaned in and gave me hug that squeezed the air out of lungs. "What was that for?" I asked after getting my breath back.

"Do I need a reason to hug you? Besides just being the good man you are?"

"No, I guess not. You have my permission to give me a hug whenever you want to." I turned to tell the boys to get ready for supper only to see four bare behinds turning the corner down the hall to their rooms. Tom and I chuckled and I said, "I think we're behind the times, Tom. Why don't we take your bag to my room and we'll join them?"

"Best thing I've heard all day, Max. Lead the way."

I led the way down the hall, removing my shirt in the process and I was unbuttoning my shorts as we reached to doorway to the bedroom. As I turned into the room, I could see that Tom had his shirt in his hand and was kicking his pants towards the bed.

"You in a hurry, big guy?"

"I'll tell you what, Max, after spending last night out here, I was itching to beat hell all day. Every time I turned around, my clothes were binding me up. I hated every minute of it and couldn't wait to get here this afternoon so I could get comfortable with you guys."

"I'm glad you're here, too. I missed having you around today. Although the morning wasn't too much fun, the afternoon made up for it. What do you think of Lee?"

"She's funny. And cute, too. If I wasn't gay, I consider making a run at her," he laughed, and I joined him. "Seriously, though, I like her a lot. I like her attitude on life, too, live and let live. That's the way it should be for everybody."

"I agree. Shall we go see if the boys are hungry?"

"Yes, let's. I know I am, I didn't get a lunch today and I'm starving."

"Busy day?"

"Not too bad, there was just never a good time to take a break."

We got back to the kitchen to find the boys sitting at the bar counter with hunger written all over their faces. "Ready for supper, I take it?" Nods all around. "This is going to sound weird, but how do y'all feel about waffles for supper? I had planned on having them for breakfast but didn't want to cook."

"Yeah!!" echoed through the house.

"Okay, while I get the syrup made and the waffle batter mixed, will you guys set the table, please, and Tom, can you retrieve the waffle iron?"

The boys got busy and Tom said, "I would if I could, Max, but I ain't got a clue where you keep stuff."

"Bottom, right cabinet over there."

"Thanks." After a moment's digging, "Got it. Anywhere particular you want it set up?"

"Wherever you can find an empty outlet."

"Got it. So, you make your own syrup?"

"Yep. One of the few useful things I got from my dad. Two cups of sugar, one brown and one regular, a cup of water and a teaspoon of maple flavor. Let it simmer a bit and you've got a pretty decent syrup. We have so many people here now, I'll double it so we have some left over."

Joey came over and said "Table's set, Max. Take a look and see if we missed anything."

I inspected their work and commented, "The only thing I think you missed is the butter."

Alex called out, "I got it."

We were soon ready to eat and sat down to a breakfast for supper. The boys and Tom loved it. Apparently, none of them had ever had waffles for supper before. I guess there's a first time for everything, and if I had my way, it wouldn't be the last. When we were done eating, the boys cleaned up the table and had all the dishes rinsed and stacked in the sink while I cleaned the syrup pan and Tom put the waffle iron away.

"Boy, that was easy. I could get used to having all this extra help. You guys did a great job. How about we get your hang-up things put away real quick? I'll help Joey and Alex, and Tom can help T.J. and Mike. Then we can relax for a bit before we go for a swim. Sound like a plan?"

"Works for us, Max." Alex said.

"Yeah, I wanna swim," yelled Mike.

"Okay, let's go. You don't mind helping these two, do ya?" I asked while looking to Tom.

"No problem, man. Gotta start doing my part around here," he replied.

Tom, Mike and T.J. turned into their room while Joey, Alex and I continued on to theirs. I gave the room a quick inspection and said, "You've done a good job, boys. The room looks great. Where's the stuff that needs to go in the closet?"

"We laid it in there already, we just couldn't reach the hangers."

"I'll hand you the hangers, you put the clothes on them and I'll hang 'em back up. We'll have this done in a jiffy." Alex and Joey worked right along with me and we soon had everything put away. "Where'd you guys put everything else?" They took me around the room, opening and closing drawers and cabinets until I'd seen everything. "You did a great job. Tomorrow morning, we'll sit down and go through your clothes and figure out what new things you need. We'll make a list for all four of you and then we can go get some of it in the afternoon."

"That sounds great, Max. All our stuff was starting to get small and the Muellers didn't like to take us shopping. They said it was too much hassle."

"Well, you don't have worry about them any longer, do you?"

"No, thank god," they agreed as they wrapped me in a hug.

"Let's go check on the others," I said, breaking up the hug and heading for the door. We turned into Mike and T.J.'s room and found Tom and Mike sitting on the bed, hugging each other and crying their eyes out. T.J. was kneeling on the bed behind them, holding their shoulders. I went to them, knelt in front of Mike, took his hands in mine and asked, "Hey, what's wrong, little guy?"

Tom answered, "We were talking while putting their things in the closet and Mike told me why he's here. I just don't understand how parents can do that to their own kids."

I sat next to Mike and wrapped an arm around his shoulder, "Mike, I'm sorry you had to go through that, but you're safe now. You're here, with me, your new brothers and your Uncle Tom. We all love you and won't ever let anyone hurt you again." I brushed the hair off his forehead and he looked up at me with tear-filled eyes. "I promise, okay."

"Yeah, I know, but I still hate my mom and dad for what they did."

"I know you do, but you don't have to worry about them anymore. Okay?"

"Okay, thanks, I love you guys, too," he sniffled.

I looked back to Tom and said to him, "C'mon, Tom, you, of all people, should know how low some people can be."

"Yeah, I know, I see it almost every day, but it still pisses me off. I just don't get it, what the hell is wrong with people?"

"I don't know, but if I did, I'd sure try to figure out some way to make it stop. The important thing is, Mike is here now, and his parents can't hurt him ever again."

"Good thing, otherwise, their bodies wouldn't be found, ever."

"So, how did these two do with their organizing?" I asked in a weak effort to lighten the sullen mood that had fallen over us.

Tom wiped his eyes dry on his arm and answered, "Pretty good, Max. They split the dresser, each taking one side, all their toys and other stuff are in the cabinets over there and their other things are all hanging up in the closet now. They were great help in getting that done."

"Great. Mike, T.J., tomorrow we'll go through your clothes and see what needs to be replaced. Then tomorrow afternoon, we'll all go shopping to get all of you what you need. I sure hope Herb shows up early with the rental car. Can't go shopping for and with four boys in the Shelby."

"What about me, Max, you just gonna leave me here?"

"Oh, I forgot you have tomorrow off, don't you?"

"Thank the lucky stars, yes."

"Then you are most definitely coming with us to help run herd. Can you bring your cuffs with you?" I laughed.

"Hey, that ain't funny, Max!" Joey fairly screamed.

"I know, Joey, I'm sorry. I'll make a serious effort to stop saying things like that. Well, let's head to the living room for a minute. I have one more thing I'd like to talk about before we jump in the pool." As we headed out the living room, I could hear the boys whispering, 'any idea what this about', 'not a clue', 'guess we'll know soon'. Once the boys were all sitting on the couch and Tom and I had taken a seat on the table in front of them, I started, "Okay, boys, I know on Friday night, I asked for you to call me Max. And for the weekend, that seemed okay, but since it now seems you're all going to be here for a long time, I'm re-thinking that."

"You don't want us to call you Max no more?" asked Alex.

"I don't know, what do you guys think?"

"You are adopting us, aren't you?" Joey asked. "That means you're going to be our dad for real, right?"

"That's exactly what it means, Joey."

"Well, can we start calling you Dad, then?" asked T.J.

"I'm going to leave that up to you. I'd consider it an honor. What do you think, Mike?"

"I'm gonna do it, I don't ever want to be reminded of my real dad."

"What about you three?"

"Yeah!" they cheered.

"But what about Tom. What should we call him?" T.J. asked.

"Well, Tom?" I asked as I turned to face him. "What say you?"

"Well, I think Dad might be rushing things a little bit, even though I hope that's where we all end up. What do you guys think about Uncle Tom? At least until we're sure where things go."

"That's cool. Uncle Tom. Yeah, I can get used to that." Alex said.

"Okay, now that that's all settled, what say we jump in the pool?"

"Lead the way, *Dad*, you've got the key." Joey said.

I patted my hips where pockets would normally be had I been dressed. "Whoops, it seems I left them in my other pair of pants," I joked. "Be right back. You guys grab towels from the laundry room for us and I'll meet you back here." While I grabbed the keys from my bedroom, the boys got towels for all six of us. "Okay, let's go."

"Uh, Max, I think we'll wait right here where it's warm while you get the door unlocked," Tom commented. "Once you have the door unlocked, we'll be right behind you."

"Fine, just be that way, you wimps. A little cold never hurt anyone." I headed on out and once the shelter door was open, the others made a mad dash from the house to minimize their time in the cold. I closed the door behind me once we were all inside. After dropping their towels on the table, the boys ran straight for the warmth of the pool and jumped in while Tom and I headed for slightly deeper water. We slipped in the water and leaned against the wall, just watching the boys have fun.

After about 20 minutes, Mike swam over to us, "C'mon you two, get over here and let's play."

"Okay, munchkin, we're right behind you." Mike swam away while Tom and I followed. Once the three of us had rejoined the others, Tom and I were instantly smothered by four laughing boys. We spent a half-hour tossing and dunking the boys and just generally having a great time. My shoulder began to develop a severe ache from tossing boys, so I begged off any more.

Joey, Alex and T.J. wanted me to see how they were doing with floating on their backs while I provided some minor assistance. While I was helping those three, Mike was showing Tom how he could swim the width of the pool by doing laps for a while.

When he finally stopped to take a break, Tom waded over to Mike's resting spot on the step and said, "You swim very well, Mike. Did you teach yourself?" Mike answered by telling Tom about the lessons at the trailer park. "Well, young man, you learned your lessons well. You should be proud of yourself."

Mike leapt out of the water and wrapped his arms around Tom in a giant hug. "Thanks, Uncle Tom, I wish my real mom and dad could have been as nice as you."

"I wish they could have been, too, but not everyone is nice. But, you're here, now, with three brothers, a dad and an uncle who all love you very much and we'll all make sure nobody can hurt you ever again."

"I know, I wish I'd always lived here," Mike cried.

"Don't cry, buddy, now you can have everything you could have ever wanted."

"I know, that's why I'm crying, 'cause I'm so happy."

"Well, that's a good thing, isn't it?"

"The bestest, Uncle Tom. I love you."

"I love you too little guy. Don't you ever forget that."

I had waded over to see what was going on and heard the tail end of the conversation. I was starting to tear up myself and had to turn away and duck my head underwater to have a reason for a wet face. "C'mon, guys, let hit the showers and have a snack. Then we can watch another movie before we go to bed." Mike let go of Tom's neck and joined the other three in the crush to grab a towel and dry off before making the dash to the house. Tom and I lingered a moment as they took off.

"You're a good man, Tom. I'm so glad you're the one Carol called yesterday. Remind me to thank her for that someday."

"You'll have to get in line, bubba."

We entered the kitchen and I told Tom, "Why don't you go hop in the shower while I get their snack ready?"

"Aren't you going to wash off the chlorine? I don't want to watch a movie sitting next to a guy who stinks like a laundry room," he laughed.

"I will, but I'll let you go first."

"What's with this 'first' crap, Max? Isn't your shower big enough for two people at the same time?"

"Sure it is, I just thought you'd like to go first."

"Oh, no you don't, c'mon, get your skinny butt in here." Tom led the way to my bathroom, although the way things seemed to be going, I was going to have start calling it 'our' bathroom. I stopped just long enough to lock the door and once the water was running and warm, we climbed in together. I'd never, in my life, taken a shower with another person, except for after P.E. in school, and I sure didn't remember those showers being as nice as this one. We spent way more time getting cleaned up than we should have, but it was an experience we'd both been waiting to have for a long time.

"Uh, I think somebody needs another bathing," I chuckled when Tom had finished cleaning the pool off me.

"Not on your life, Max, another right now would kill me."

"Well, we can't have that, but what a way to die."

"No shit. I know we've only known each other a little over twenty-four hours, Max, and I hope I'm not pushing you into things you're not ready for, but I think I love you."

"Trust me, Tom, the feelings are 100% mutual. And you're not pushing me into anything. If I didn't want this, you wouldn't be here right now. Again, remind me to thank Carol for calling you to help yesterday."

"Why don't we thank her together?"

"You're right, of course. I see a steak dinner in the near future for her. Now, we better get the hell out of here and take care of that snack we promised the boys." When we returned to the kitchen, we were greeted by the smirking faces of four cute, young lads. We both blushed from head to toe from the embarrassment of getting caught.

"And just where have you two been?" asked Alex.

"We took a shower just like you did. It takes us longer since we're bigger than you are."

"Yeah, right, likely story, Dad," laughed Joey.

"Taking a shower together is lot of fun, isn't it?" T.J. asked.

"We plead the fifth, boys," Tom answered.

"S'okay," from Mike. "I really like taking a shower with T.J."

"I can only imagine. Now, about that snack, you want popcorn again to munch during the movie?"

"Sure, Alex and I will get drinks," Joey offered.

"I got the bowls," said T.J.

"Mike, why don't you make sure we still have towels on our seats?"

"Be right back." And off he scooted to the theater, only to come back and let us know our towels were still there.

"Perfect, you guys take the drinks and get settled. Tom and I will bring the popcorn when it's done." When they were gone, I turned to Tom and said, "Boy, were we just busted or what?"

"Guilty as hell, and not a damn bit sorry about it, either."

"Funny, neither am I. Guess there's no real reason to hide it. Those four know the score."

"No doubt about it, Max."

"Well, let's get the popcorn and get the show started." We headed to the theater and while Tom handed out the popcorn bowls to the munchkins, I retrieved the next Star Wars movie and got it started. The boys were really liking the movies and Tom and I were enjoying spending time together.

When the movie ended tonight, all four boys had fallen asleep in their recliners. We moved Alex and Joey first, and once they were tucked in bed, we repeated the process with T.J. and Mike. Once all four were snoozing away, Tom and I cleaned up the dishes and retreated to what was now our bedroom. After we entered the room, I closed the door, then we pulled down the covers. Tom laid down and rested his head on the pillows.

I sat down facing him and crossed my legs. He gave me a puzzled look and I said, "Sit up, Tom, we need to talk."

14

"Oh, shit. Here it comes."

"Oh, don't be like that, please. This is a good talk." I waited until he'd sat up and was facing me before continuing. "I don't know how it's possible, but you need to know that I truly love you. It's like you told Lee earlier, I feel like I've known you all my life. When we met yesterday afternoon, something just clicked. I have never, ever, felt like this about anybody else. I want you to know that."

"Max, I'm in love with you, too. I know it sounds trite, but it's real. Sure, I've thought about other guys over the years, but none have made my heart go flip-flop like you."

"Well, you're a few years ahead of me in the acceptance department. I really just figured my life out a couple months ago."

"What!?"

"I know, that's why this is all so unbelievable. To me, anyway. Don't get me wrong, I've known I was gay from about T.J.'s age, but I've suppressed it, hard. I've always wanted a family and felt the only way to accomplish that was to be a straight guy, get married and have kids. There's that part of it.

"The other reason why I buried it so deep for so long is I knew how my parents would react. I knew from a very early age, even before I first wanted to *play* with any of my friends, that they felt people like us should not be accepted as human beings. I'm not sure how I knew it, I just did."

"Well, I told you it wasn't a party with my parents, either. They were totally disgusted when I came out, as I knew they would be. And it's taken them a long time to accept me for who I am. We've come a long way in the past five years."

"I know, and I'm still in the early stage of that parental denial. Do I hope that denial will slowly turn into a grudging acceptance? More than anything, but I can't let them continue to dictate how I live my life. I have to be who I am."

"I'm cool with that. Since I've been through it myself already, if there's anything I can do to help with them, just let me know."

"I don't think there's anything you could really do, but I'll be sure to let you know if I think that changes. I think Lee's my best bet. You saw how accepting she was. She's never had a problem with me being gay. If anyone can talk sense to Mom and Dad, it'll be her. Just bear with me about them."

"Max, your parents are the last thing on my mind. You're first and the boys take positions two through five, okay. Beyond that, I'm not too worried about anybody else right now."

"That's good to hear, Tom, and I appreciate it. Now, I have something really serious to ask you."

"Oh shit, here it comes," Tom chuckled.

"You won't be chuckling when you hear the question. How important is being a cop to you?"

"Well, up until about two yesterday afternoon, it was pretty damn important, 'cause if I wasn't paying attention to things from the first moment I started patrol, I wasn't gonna come back home alive. Not that I much cared if I ever went back to that empty apartment at the end of the day.

"That's all changed now. I worked today but couldn't concentrate on anything. My partner asked me what was up, and I just told him I was dealing with some family issues. I didn't want to outright lie to the guy and that was the closest I could come to explaining where my head was without telling him everything."

"I can only assume you were talking about this family. At least, I hope you were."

"Damn right I was. Now that I have someone I want to see at the end of every day, I damn sure want to make sure I can."

"I really hate to ask this, but would you have a problem resigning from the department?"

"Not really, Max. It's just a job. Granted, it's one I love, but I've found something and several someones I love even more. I was going to talk to you about it tomorrow, but since you brought it up already, I decided on the way out here tonight to turn in my papers to Dylan on Tuesday."

"Oh, Tom, that's such a load off my mind. Now that I've found you, I don't want to lose you."

"Not a chance, man."

"Any idea what you want to do next?"

"Not really. I've thought about doing private investigations before. It doesn't pay that well, but the hours are real flexible. And it's a hell of a lot safer, as a rule, since you can pick and choose the cases you want to deal with."

"I have an idea I want you to think about and it kinda follows the lines of your own agency. And, I'd be willing to help get it started."

"I'm interested, what are you thinking about?"

"Carol's agency is in almost constant need of people being investigated, some background checks and some home checks for abuse and living conditions. Does that sound like something you'd be interested in doing?"

"Hell, yeah. Some of that could still be hazardous, but not near as bad as what I deal with now. And with my background, it could open up some avenues of investigation that they can't currently access. I think Dylan would help with it, also. He's always hated dealing with that aspect of our job and I think I could talk him into funneling some cases my way."

"Would you mind me talking to Carol to see if they'd be interested in using you?"

"Not at all."

"Good. Now, I have one more thing we need to talk about."

"Oh, shit, here it comes," Tom laughed.

"Not yet, but soon, I'm sure. That shower we took together was the most erotic experience I've ever had. I can honestly say I've never had such a whole-body orgasm as I did with you."

"I'm happy to hear it, Max. I'm even happier it was me you had it with."

"That said, Tom, I don't know if I'll ever be able to give you the maximum pleasure you deserve."

"What the hell you talkin' about?"

"Well, I think, even you have to admit that when you get aroused, you definitely put me and many other guys to shame. I'm not sure that monster will ever find its way into my most private of areas." Tom almost rolled off the bed with paroxysms of laughter.

When he got himself under control, he responded, "Max, I don't care about that. Besides, haven't you heard, size doesn't matter."

"Yes, I've heard that, but sometimes it does, and this is one of those times. There is such a thing as too much of a good thing."

"There's so much more to a successful relationship than just the sex."

"I know that, but I wanted you know where I am mentally with this whole thing."

"Don't worry about it. If it happens someday, great, if not, I'm sure we'll think of something else. Besides, with a little patience and work, I think, together, we can make it happen. But only if you want to, I'll never force you to do anything you don't want."

"Thanks, I knew you wouldn't. I would like for it to happen, eventually, but you'll have to be patient with me."

"We have all the time in the world, Max."

"I really hate to ask, especially after what I just said about being patient, but do you think you'd be able to handle me? There, I mean?"

"Oh, yeah, no sweat."

"Gee, thanks. You really know how to boost a guy's self-esteem."

"Okay, I could have said that better, I guess. I wasn't trying to demean or to make you feel inadequate in any way. I think you're perfect. In every possible way."

"Well, that helps. If only a little."

"Will you please stop saying 'little'?" he grinned. "What I'm trying to tell you, is that while I haven't been with anybody before, it doesn't mean I've haven't had the desire or need. In light of that need, and I do mean *need*, I've acquired, how shall I say this, some *aids*, I guess you could call them, over the last several years. And during that time, I've made good use of them."

"Oh, really? That's interesting. Do you think your 'aids' could help me, too? And would you be willing to show me how to use them properly."

"You bet, and I'll cherish every moment."

"Well, I think we've officially skipped over that 'getting to know you better' awkwardness of the next few months, don't you?"

"Assimilation completed," he droned, in what I had to assume was a Borg imitation.

"Good, that's what I wanted to hear. Are you ready to get some sleep, now? We have a lot to do tomorrow."

"Sleep? Are you freakin' kiddin' me? After that 'talk', all I wanna do is make you happy. And from the looks of things, you're half-way there already," he added while pointing to my lap. After seeing he had the same problem, we laid down, rolled to face each other and wrapped each other in a loving embrace. After spending quite some time pleasuring each other in new and inventive ways, we lay back on the bed, spent but happy.

"Oh, my god, Max, are you sure I'm the first guy you've ever been with? That was mind-blowing. Among other things," he chuckled.

"Uh, yeah, Tom, I'm pretty sure. I think I would remember doing that before," I laughed. "But, I had a great teacher," I smiled as I looked into his eyes.

"Well, you're a quick study, I'll give you that. And to think that I've missing out on that all these years. I wanna kick myself for wasting all that time."

"We're in the same boat there, Tom. I can't wait to see what the future holds for us. Now, I don't want to be rude, but could we possibly get some sleep, please? It's been a long damn day, I'm tired and tomorrow's going to a busy one, also."

"I can barely move after that, Max, so sleep should be a piece of cake."

I grabbed the covers and pulled them over us, then laid down behind Tom, wrapping my arms around him. He sighed contentedly and was soon snoring lightly. I was not far behind in falling into the deepest, most relaxed sleep I'd had in a long time.

I woke up Monday morning with a warm body curled up behind me and a lot snickering happening in front of me. I opened my eyes and found a gaggle of nude boys staring at me, eyes wide open. "Good morning, guys, we have to stop meeting like this. Did my closed-door rule go in one ear and out the other?"

"Sorry, Dad," Alex said, "but we did knock, and when you didn't answer, we got worried and thought we should check to make sure you're okay,"

"And you sure look like you're okay to us. Tom does, too. Did you two *sleep* well?" Joey asked.

"We slept just fine, thank you very much. How about you four, did you sleep well?"

"You bet!" Mike yelled.

Tom jumped, opened his eyes, saw the boys and said, "Oh, crap."

"It's okay, Uncle Tom, we know you two love each other. You should be sleeping together," T.J. added.

"Nice to know we have your approval, guys, now get out of here so we can get out of bed and we'll meet you in the kitchen for breakfast in a few minutes." The four scampered out of the room and I rolled over to face Tom. "Good morning bright eyes, ready for a fun-filled day of list-making and shopping? We've got a lot to do and not much time to do it."

"No, I'm not ready, but then I never will be. I absolutely hate shopping, of any kind."

"Well, you better get used to it, bucko, shopping is a family deal."

"Yeah, yeah. Can I pee before we leave?"

"I'll even feed you first," I laughed.

"You really know the way to my heart, Max." He tossed off the covers and headed to the bathroom to relieve his bladder. I decided to follow him and when he stepped in front of the toilet, I slid in behind him, invading his personal space. "You better back off or I'm never going to be able to pee and we'll be stuck at home all day. Not that I have a problem with that."

I laughed and backed away. "Well, hurry the hell up 'cause I gotta go, too." When we were both done in the bathroom, including washing faces and hands, we headed to the kitchen to rustle up some breakfast. The boys had cereal and toast while Tom and I had English muffins. Since we had a busy day ahead of us, part of it outside the house, I suggested we all get dressed and be ready to head out in a bit. The boys grumbled about it, but eventually headed to their bedrooms to get some clothes on while Tom and I followed suit.

When the boys returned to the kitchen, I had them sit at the counter with pencil and paper to start making lists of the clothes they thought they needed. I had Alex help Mike to make sure I could read his list. While they got busy on their task, the phone rang and I answered it in the kitchen.

"Good morning?"

"Morning to you, too, Max. How are you this bright and beautiful day?"

"Herb, I'm great. It's good to hear from you this early. Does this mean you're about to bring the rental out for me?"

"Yep, be headin' that way in about ten minutes. Just wanted to make sure you were awake and functional before I did."

"There're four boys here who apparently don't believe in sleeping in, so being awake isn't the issue. Functional? Not quite yet, but another cup of caffeine should help that along."

"Well, either way, I'll be there in about thirty minutes and my guy will be along about ten minutes later. He's got a stop to make on the way out."

"No problems, Herb, we'll be here. See you soon." I hung up the phone and checked on the boys' progress on their lists when I suddenly remembered another call I needed to make. I looked up the school's number and placed the call.

"New Berlin schools, how may I direct your call?"

"I need to speak to the elementary principal, please."

"One moment, sir."

I was on hold less than a minute before an exasperated female voice came on the line.

"This is Ms. Carling, sorry to keep you waiting, but it's been one of those mornings."

"No problems, ma'am, I'm having one also."

"How may I help you, sir?" she spat out.

"My name is Max Sanders and over the weekend I became the legal guardian for four of your students, Joey and Alex Allison, T.J. Stults and Mike Bell. I was calling to let you know they wouldn't be in school today and make arrangements for a new bus stop to pick them up starting tomorrow morning."

"Ah-ha, I was wondering where those four rapscallions were today. Mystery solved. Thank you for calling to let me know they're okay. Their driver was rather confused and more than a bit concerned when none of them showed up to get on the bus this morning."

"I know I should have called over the weekend, but I didn't have a clue who I needed to talk to, so I decided to wait until this morning."

"That's all right. Now you said your name is Max Sanders, right? And you're the boys' new guardian? What happened to their foster parents?"

"Well, I was hoping to adopt a child and this weekend, these four came to my home for a visit to see my house and see how things went. They apparently went very well and my case worker, Carol Ward, arranged for all four to stay here until the adoptions are finalized instead of going back to their foster parents."

"Ah, yes, the undeniable and relentless Ms. Ward. She is a force to be reckoned with, isn't she?"

I laughed and answered, "She sure is. Fortunately, she's working for me and not against me. I wouldn't want to be on the other side."

"No, sir, you surely don't. So, you're expecting to adopt all four of these young men? When do you expect that process to be completed?"

"According to Carol, five or six months."

"Yes, that sounds about right. Why don't you give me your address and I'll make sure to get it to the drivers' supervisor so we can start picking the boys up at their new home tomorrow morning."

I provided the address and directions since there were no signs of a home at the end of the drive. "My drive is long and in this cold weather, I'll be bringing the boys to meet the bus in my car so they don't turn into popsicles waiting."

"That's probably a good idea, Mr. Sanders. While we strive to be punctual, schedules do occasionally slip."

"Is there anything else you need this morning?"

"I don't think so, but I would like to meet with you. I like to know the parents of all our students. Would you have time tomorrow morning to stop by?"

"Sure thing. I'd like to meet you, also, and their teachers, if possible. Would sometime around noon be okay?"

"That would be fine, Mr. Sanders. The students will be at lunch and their teachers should be available at that time also."

"Great, I'll see you then."

"We'll look forward to it. Again, thanks for calling and letting me know where the boys are. I really was worried about them. Have a good day."

"Thank you, you, too." I ended the call and turned to the boys. "Okay, you're all set. Back to school tomorrow morning. We can't have you playing hooky the rest of the year."

"Bummer, Dad," said T.J.

"Yeah, that sucks."

"Joey, mouth. You really need to learn some self-control young man."

"Sorry, Dad," he pouted.

"It's okay, but we'll work on that. Now, how are your lists doing?"

"I think we're ready, Dad," Alex said. "We both need new socks and underwear. Our pants and shirts are okay for now, but we'll probably need more by summer."

"Okay, what about you, T.J.?"

"I need some new socks, too, and maybe a few shirts. Most of my shirts are starting to get pretty small and tight."

"Good thinking. What's on your list, Mike?"

"Everything," he whined. "I didn't have much to begin with and the Kirklands never had a chance to get me anything new."

"Well, don't you worry about it, munchkin, we'll get you taken care of this afternoon, okay?"

"Thanks, Ma ..., uh, Dad."

"What about you, Tom, anything you need to pick up today?"

"Let me see, Max, I've got my list right here." He theatrically whipped a blank sheet of paper in front of his face, cleared his throat and started reciting, "Socks, shoes, underwear, pants, shirts, shorts, a couple of cool hats, a PS4, new laptop, a Harley and, wait, what's that say, I can't quite read my own writing. Oh, yeah, my own Shelby. Yeah, I think that covers everything." The boys were laughing hysterically by the time he finished.

"Well, that's quite the list you have, there, but methinks you have forgotten one very important thing."

He glanced back over the blank paper, "No, I'm pretty sure it's all there."

"What about the bank we'd have to rob to pay for it all?"

"Well, heck. Just where is my mind, today? Joey, give me your pencil and I'll add that stop."

"Are you done, clown?"

"Yeah, but seriously, Max, I think we should pick up some food, too. We've pretty much wiped you out this weekend."

"Good point, Tom." Ding!

"That's probably Herb with the rental. Why don't you guys work on a food list while I deal with Herb?"

"Sounds like a plan, Max. We'll be right here."

I watched out the window by the front door as he parked the rental on the drive and walked up to the door. I opened it as he stepped up on the porch and invited him in to wait for his guy to pick him up.

"Morning, Herb, how are you this morning?"

"Doing great, Max, how 'bout yourself?"

"As well as can be expected after the weekend I've had. You want a cup of coffee while you wait?"

"That sounds great. Where's the new family?"

"In the kitchen making a shopping list for food. C'mon in and I'll introduce them." I led Herb to the kitchen and when he was set up with a warm cup of coffee, I turned to make the introductions. "Starting on that end, Herb, we have Alex, Mike, Joey and T.J. And this is Tom. Guys, this is Herb, my car dealer."

"Hi fellas, nice to meet you," he directed to the boys, "You sure you want to live with this guy?"

"You bet," they answered in unison.

"Uh, Max," Herb whispered in my ear, "I think the other dude's a little outside adoption age," then laughed.

"That may be, Herb, but he was a great help to me Saturday and I think he's earned his place. You'll be seeing him around quite a bit more."

Herb turned to Tom and held out his hand. "Nice to meet you, Tom. Hope you know what you're gettin' yourself into here."

"Nice to meet you, too, Herb. After the weekend, I've got a pretty good idea. That's all right, though, I like a challenge. After five years in the Sheriff's department, this should be a piece o' cake. Sure couldn't be any harder." He then turned to me and asked, "Hey, Max, is this the guy I need to talk to about that new Shelby?" and laughed heartily.

"Max, he's a keeper. Great taste in cars," Herb replied as he laughed along.

Ding!

"What the heck was that?" Herb asked.

"Driveway sensor," I answered.

"So, you knew I was here before I pulled up to the garage, didn't you?"

"Sure did. Did you think it was just ESP that had me meet you at the door?"

"You never know, Max. Should be my guy, though."

"Thanks for bringing the rental out, Herb. You sure saved me some headaches and a bunch of time today."

"Happy to do it. I wouldn't do this for every customer, but you're one of my better ones. I left the keyfob in it and I'll keep you updated on the one you've ordered." He turned to the boys and said, "Boys, you be good to Max. I hope you enjoy your new home." He turned to Tom, extended his hand again and added, "Tom, I wish you luck with this zoo. And when you're ready to order that Shelby, you come see me."

They shook hands and Tom said, "Don't you worry, Herb. Hope to be seeing you soon," and grinned.

I led Herb to the door, thanked him again and let him out to head back to the dealership. I then returned to the kitchen and asked, "Everybody ready to roll? We've got a lot to do today and the sooner we get started, the sooner we can get back home."

Everybody grabbed their coats and shoes and we met in the driveway. The rental Flex was gleaming in the sun reflected off the snow. The boys climbed in and Tom and I made sure each was buckled in place and that they knew how to operate the belts. We got in and after I started the car, I inserted a movie in the DVD player to help keep the boys entertained. All four were busy checking out all the features, oohing and aahing as each new gadget caught their eyes. I rolled my eyes at Tom as I backed away from the garage and he chuckled in understanding. I was just about to pull out when I realized this car hadn't been programmed for my garage door opener, so I ran back into the house to grab the extra control. I'd have to make sure I retrieved it when I returned the car.

I decided on the way to town that the easiest place to get everything we needed was Walmart. I figured that one-stop shopping was going to be the quickest way to accomplish everything. We'd just gotten in the store when I felt a tug at my sleeve. I looked down to my right to find Mike holding onto my jacket with one hand and he was holding his crotch with the other. I suddenly realized nobody had gone to the bathroom before we left home.

"Uh, fellas, Mike and I need to use the restroom. Anybody else need to go?" Joey and Alex raised their hands. "Okay, Tom, why don't you grab a cart and head to the boys' department with T.J. and we'll find you in a few minutes?"

"Sure thing, Max." Four of us headed to the restroom while the other two headed in the opposite direction. When we joined back up with Tom and T.J., the bottom of the cart was already covered. We spent the next hour loading the cart with new clothes for all four boys. Fortunately, we didn't have to try on much except for a couple pairs of pants for Mike.

Selecting underwear was another story in itself. With the selection available, you would have thought they wouldn't have any problems finding what they wanted. Mike's was the easiest to satisfy as he wanted briefs with characters from his favorite movie, 'Cars'. T.J. settled for basic boxer briefs, but the twins weren't finding what they wanted.

"Come on you two, make a decision already, we don't have all day."

"We've looked at it all and don't see what we want," Joey said.

"Well, what do you want? I'll ask where they are."

Alex came to me, pulled me down to his level and whispered in my ear, "We want some that look like your Speedos. But you can't ask anybody, that'd be embarrassing."

I snickered a moment and quietly drafted Tom to help me search. We dug through the entire rack and finally realized they apparently don't sell bikini briefs for boys at Walmart. While Tom distracted the boys, I asked a clerk, even though I'd been asked not to. The clerk grinned but told me they didn't have anything like that in their size. I thanked her and told the twins to pick something else for now and we'd look somewhere else later. They grumped about it but ended up picking out the smallest briefs available that would fit their waist.

Once finished with the clothes, the cart was overflowing. I decided we should pay for this load, get it stashed in the car, and then come back and deal with the food shopping separately. Tom volunteered to load the car while the rest of us started on the food list. We were about half done with the food shopping when Tom finally found us and we finished rather quickly. With everything loaded up, we headed to Long John Silver's to get some lunch.

While we were eating, Tom asked, "Hey, we're pretty close to my apartment. Would you mind swinging by so I can grab a few things?"

"No problem. I'm sure they won't mind, will you, guys?"

"No, let's go!" T.J. said as he started to get up from the table.

"Um, can we finish eating, T.J.?"

"I guess," he grumped as he sat back down.

"Thank you."

When the food was gone and the table cleaned off, we piled back in the car and headed to Tom's apartment. When we got there, I offered to help, but Tom replied, "I got it, Max. It won't take long to get what I want to grab right now." True to his word, he returned in five minutes with a small box. He placed the box on the floor at his feet and said, "Let's boogie."

"Is that it? Doesn't seem like you got much."

"Just the important things for now. I'll grab more tomorrow after I talk to Sarge."

"Okay. Anybody need anything else before we head for home?" Silence reigned. "Okay, we're outta here."

The ride home was quiet and we pulled in the garage twenty minutes later. Tom carried his small box directly to our bedroom. As we unloaded the rest of the car, the boys took their new things directly to their rooms while Tom and I carried bag after bag of food into the kitchen. I asked the boys to carefully remove all the tags and labels from their new clothes so I could wash them before they wore them. Tom and I got all the food stored and were just about to sit down when four nude boys wandered in.

"Can we go swimming before supper?" Joey asked.

"Sure, just give us a minute to get ready."

Tom and I headed to our bedroom, peeled off our clothes, grabbed a couple of towels and headed back to meet the boys, shelter key in my hand. Once in the pool, Tom and I were attacked by four feisty monkeys trying to dunk us. We spent about a half hour playing around, tossing and flipping boys back and forth. Tom and I eventually needed a break and moved to the deep end and let the boys continue their fun. After another half hour, I decided it was time to get out. I still had to wash the boys' new clothes and supper was coming up soon.

"Boys, hop out and hit the showers. We need to get your new clothes washed and put away." Tom and I waited until they were back in the house to get out of the pool.

We headed inside and while Tom headed to the bathroom to take his shower, I turned towards the laundry room to start a load of the boys' new clothes. As the boys came out of their showers, I told them to start going through their older clothes and pull out anything we replaced this afternoon. By the time I was done dealing with them, Tom was out of the shower and telling me it was my turn. I ran through a quick rinse, thankful at my foresight at having tankless, instant water heaters installed in each bathroom when the house was built. They were certainly getting a workout today and I didn't see that changing in the future.

Supper tonight was what I laughingly called broke food, Kraft macaroni and cheese. While I'm far from being broke, it's an easy meal to fix and clean up. An added bonus was that the boys all said they love it. After the supper mess was cleaned up, the boys wanted to watch the next Star Wars movie, so we headed to the theater to relax for a couple hours. It was 8:30 when the movie ended, and I told the boys it was time to head for bed. When they complained, I explained they had to go back to school in the morning and needed a good night's sleep before they did.

They grudgingly gave in and Tom and I followed them to their rooms to make sure they were all tucked in and had received their goodnight kisses on the foreheads. Once the four feisty monkeys were in bed, Tom and I headed back to the theater to watch another movie. By the time is was over, we were both yawning and headed to our bedroom.

"Are you still planning to talk with Dylan tomorrow about resigning?" I asked Tom.

"Sure am, but it'll be afternoon. My shift starts before he gets in, but we'll talk at the end of the day."

"Are you absolutely sure you're ready to do it? I don't want you regretting the decision later, and it is kinda sudden."

"100% sure. Never been so sure of anything else, ever. Well, except how I feel about you."

"I'm glad to hear that, Tom. I know it's a lot to ask, but I can't stand the thought of you going out every day, placing yourself in danger and maybe not coming back at the end of the day."

"That's the only thing I've ever hated about the job. The uncertainty of knowing whether I'd come back home in one piece at the end of the day. I know it can be an ugly job, but there's more good than bad and somebody needs to do it. I've done my part and now it's time for someone else to take over."

"You think Dylan's going to give you a hard time?"

"I don't think so. We've always gotten along really well. I'm pretty sure he'll understand."

"I hope so. I'd hate to have to call him and give him a piece of my mind."

Tom laughed. "Well, I hope it won't come to that. I don't think Dylan's ready for that."

We snuggled up under the covers with Tom holding me. "Goodnight. I love you, Tom Wright," I whispered.

"Love you more, my angel."

15

Tuesday began way earlier than I was used to. My alarm went off at six so I could get the boys up, dressed, fed and ready to catch their bus. I never realized how grumpy kids could be at that time of day. While I dealt with the four grumplestiltskins, Tom dressed in his uniform and headed out the door, pausing to give each of us a hug and kiss.

"Bye guys, I'll see you tonight. Have a good day at school and learn something new."

"We will, Uncle Tom. Be careful today, we want you coming back home tonight," Alex said.

"I will." With that, he was gone.

"Come on boys, get a move on. Your bus will be here soon and I need to have you at the end of the drive when it shows up."

"We're moving as fast we can, Dad," Alex said.

"Yeah, man, give us a break," added Joey.

"I just don't want you to be late. I'll try to relax, promise."

When they had finished their breakfast, I made sure they all had their coats, hats, gloves and backpacks and got them loaded in the car. We got to the end of the drive with a few minutes to spare. While we waited for the bus to arrive, I reminded the boys that the dress code, or lack thereof, at home was not to be shared with their friends. They all said they understood.

The boys chatted amongst themselves while we waited and when I saw the bus coming our direction, I had them make sure they had everything before getting out. I had to laugh as the bus slowly rolled right past the driveway. Unless you know what to look for, it's pretty easy to miss it hidden among all the trees. I had the boys out of the car and standing in line as the driver backed up about a hundred feet.

When the door popped open, the driver said, "Sorry 'bout that. I was watching for your drive since turning on the road and still missed it."

"No worries, it's easy to miss. By the way, my name is Max Sanders and

I'm the boys' new father."

"Good to meet ya, Mr. Sanders, I'm Cal, the regular driver on this route."

"Please, call me Max. Will you be getting here about the same time every day?"

"Should be, within a few minutes either way."

"Okay, I just wanted to make sure. While it's cold like this, I'll be bringing them down and be waiting in the car with them, just want to make sure when I should be here. About what time will they be dropped off after school?"

"I usually hit this road about three forty-five. There's a few more stops further up the road."

"Sounds good, Cal. I'll be here, waiting for them. The house is about half mile walk from here, which is a little too far to walk in these temps."

"No problem, we'll see you this afternoon." The door closed, and I waved at my boys as the bus pulled away. I hopped back in the car, turned around in the road and drove back to the house. I pulled the car in the garage so it could stay warm until I left for the school later and my meeting with the principal and the boys' teachers. I undressed, laid my clothes on the bed to wear again later and headed into the study to make a few calls. The first was to Carol at the agency.

"This is Carol, how can I help you," she answered.

"Good morning, Carol."

"Well, good morning to you, too, Max. How are things going?"

"Couldn't be better. We spent yesterday getting new clothes for the boys and they're all back to school today."

"Clothes? You think they'll actually get worn?" she laughed. "Seriously, it's progress. Sounds like you're starting to get a handle on being a father."

"Slowly, but surely. Say, I have something I'd like to discuss with you this afternoon. If I came to the office, would you have some spare time for me?"

"Let me check my calendar, Max, one second." She returned a few moments later, "I have some free time about two. Will that work for you?"

"That'd be perfect. I'm going to the school to meet the principal and the boys' teachers at noon, so I'll head your way when I'm done there. Thanks,

Carol."

"No problem, Max, I'll see you then."

My next call was to a local contractor I'd had do some work for me a couple years ago.

"This is John."

"John, Max Sanders, how ya been?"

"Good, Max, long time. How 'bout yourself?"

"Doing well, thanks for asking."

"So, what's up?"

"Well, I'm in the process of adopting four boys and ..."

"Four? Boys? I never took you as a glutton for punishment, Max."

"I know, but what can I say? People change."

"Well, I shoulda' said congratulations. Sorry to interrupt, go ahead."

"Well, you know how far back from the road the house is located, and the boys will need to wait out at the road for the bus."

"That won't be much fun for them, will it? Not in this weather, anyway."

"That's exactly why I'm calling you, John. I'd like to get a small shelter built at the end of drive so they can get out of the wind, snow and rain while they wait. Sound like something you'd be interested in helping with?"

"Gee, I don't know, we're pretty busy right now," he chuckled.

"If you're that busy, do I need to call someone else?"

"Hell, no, Max. This is a piece 'o cake. How big do you want it?"

"I'm thinking maybe 8' X 8'. That'd be plenty big enough to last them through high school."

"Do you want it insulated and heated?"

"That'd be a good idea, but I don't think I'd want to pay to run electrical from the house all the way out to the road."

"What if we put a solar panel on the roof with a battery backup to run the heater. That should be cheaper than running the wire and be almost maintenance-free for you."

"I like that idea. The heater wouldn't have to be that large if the shelter's got enough insulation and sealed tight enough to keep the heat inside."

"That's what I'm thinking."

"I'll also want a real, lockable door and a window in it. The window doesn't need to open, just be there so they can keep an eye out for the bus without having to go outside."

"Good idea. How soon you want us to start?"

"As soon as you can. I know March is right around the corner, but I think this cold's going to hang around for a while, yet."

"I'm with you. Here's what I'll do. I'll come out in the morning and we can pick the location for the shelter. Then, I can have a couple of my guys come out and set the forms for the slab."

"You can come out tomorrow, but we'll have to take out a bunch of trees before the floor could be poured. There's not a lot of clear space on either side of the drive right now."

"Thanks for reminding me, Max. I didn't think about that. I'll call and arrange to have a tree removal guy I trust meet with us, also. Once we pick out the right spot, he can get the trees downed and my guys can still come out the next day to set the forms and dump a rock base inside them."

"Will your tree guy remove the trees and the stumps entirely? I don't want to have the floor cracked in a few months by them coming back."

"I'll make sure he brings all the equipment he'll need to grind the stumps, too. And I'll have my guys bring a plate compactor with them so they pack the dirt before they dump the rock. Then, we can get the floor slab poured a couple days after that. Shouldn't take much to finish it, just a quick troweling and cover it with plastic and straw to help keep it from freezing before it's set. While the slab sets, we can build the shelter in my shop and bring it out on our big trailer, ready to assemble on the slab. Bolt the walls to the slab, put on the roof, solar panel and heater, and presto, happy boys."

"Sounds like a good plan to me, John. Call me when you get close tomorrow and I'll meet you at the end of the drive."

"See you then, Max."

I still had a couple hours before I needed to head to the school for my meeting, so I grabbed my book and curled up by the fireplace to kill a few hours. When it was time to leave, I got dressed and headed to the school. I found the visitor parking and, after entering the school, I stopped a teacher in the hall and asked for directions to the principal's office. Directions fresh in my head, I set off down the locker-lined hall. I was met by a perky and cheerful young lady when I entered the office.

"May I help you, sir?" she asked in a high pitch sing-song.

"Good afternoon, my name is Max Sanders and I have a meeting with Ms. Carling."

"One moment, sir. If you'd like to have a seat, I'll page her."

"Thank you." Perky and cheerful made the page and we waited quietly. A minute later, a well-dressed, middle-aged woman came into the office followed by two women and a man. I stood as they headed my direction.

"Mr. Sanders, I presume. I'm Valerie Carling, the school's principal, and these three are your sons' teachers. Michael is in Mrs. Young's class, Thomas is in Miss Klaus' class, and Mr. Thomas is Joseph and Alexander's teacher." We all shook hands as Valerie made the introductions. "Why don't we step into my office?" Valerie led the way and then closed the door when we were all inside. "Please, have a seat everyone. Now, Mr. Sanders, what can we do for you?"

"First, you can stop calling me Mr. Sanders, please. My name is Maxwill and I go by Max."

"We can certainly do that, Max. And please, call me Valerie."

"I will, thanks. Second, one of the first things I asked the boys when we got to my house Friday night was if they wanted to be called by their full names. All of them said no and asked to be called Joey, Alex, T.J. and Mike. If you could make that adjustment here, that'd be great."

"We can sure do that, right folks?" she asked, looking to the teachers. Nods from all three teachers signaled their agreement.

"Okay, continuing on, as I told you during our call yesterday, over the weekend, I became the legal guardian of the boys and I'm in the process of adopting them. Since I'm obviously new to this whole 'being a parent' thing, I just thought it would be good idea to come over, meet the folks responsible for my sons' education and find out what's expected or needed of me."

"I wish all our parents took their jobs this seriously. All our lives would be so much better if they did. But, really, Max, all we look for from parents is to be involved in their children's education. Set aside some quiet time every day and help them with their homework. If you see them having any problems, let us know so we can see what we can do here to provide additional assistance. Also, attend the parent/teacher meetings so you can meet directly with their teachers and relay any concerns you may have. These meetings are also a way for the teachers to pass information, directly to the parents, of any issues they may be seeing."

"I can certainly do all that. Are there any problems I should know about now?"

"I'll let the teachers address that question. Why don't you start, Ken?"

"No real problems with the twins. They do like to be the class clowns, though, and can be disruptive at times. Usually, all it takes is a gentle reminder and they calm back down. Other than that, their grades are among the top five percent of the class. Both are highly intelligent and might possibly be bored with certain subjects at times, most notably, math. I've noticed both seem to daydream when we're working in that subject, but their grades don't show it. You might consider having them tested and see if we can move them up a grade level. Other than that, I don't see any problems."

"Excellent, Ken. Peggy, how is T.J. doing?" Valerie said.

"Well, he's only been in my class since January, remember, but from what I've seen so far, he seems to be doing well. His reading, spelling and math skills all seem to be where they should be. His science grade could be improved a bit, but he's not horribly behind. I'm sure some of that comes from the school he came from. They use a different textbook for the subject and I'm sure he's playing a little catchup."

"One thing I noticed with T.J.," I interjected, "very soon after our first meeting a few weeks ago, he's very outspoken and doesn't seem afraid to share things that maybe he shouldn't. Has that been an issue?"

"Only a couple of times, and that was very early on. He seems to have learned to refrain from speaking out in class without permission."

"Thank the gods for that," I laughed. Peggy joined me with a quiet giggle.

"Your turn, now, Anita," Valerie interjected. "Any problems with Michael? Oh, I'm sorry, I should have said Mike. Old habits die hard, Max."

"No problem." I turned to Anita to hear her report.

"Mike's been in my class about the same length of time T.J. has been in Peggy's and he's been very quiet and reserved during that time. His skills seem to be about where they should be, maybe a little behind, but not too bad, I think. My biggest concern is his socializing with his classmates. He doesn't seem to be making any friends."

"Are you aware of his history before joining your class, Anita?"

"What history? Apparently not. What did I miss?"

"I'm surprised the agency didn't pass this on, so I'll do it now. Mike was subjected to severe physical and mental abuse by his parents. He was removed from their care and their rights have been severed. There is no chance of them getting him back."

"Oh, my, I was completely unaware of that. Now, it all makes sense."

"What makes sense?" Valerie asked.

"Some of the other boys in class tend to pick on him because he's so small. When they do it, Mike just cowers at his desk or in a corner. I've tried to stop them, and they won't do it when I'm watching, but if I turn my back or I'm busy helping another student, they just start up again. I moved the problem boys to the other side of the class and that has reduced the issue there, but at lunch and on the playground, I've no control over them."

"I wish you'd told me this was happening, Anita," Valerie said. "It looks like I need to have a little chat with these boys. Right after lunch, won't you please send them here? We'll get this situation resolved today."

"May I join that meeting, Valerie?" I asked.

"I think that would be a good idea, Max."

"Great, now, I have one more thing I think you all should be aware of. This stays with the four of you. If I hear of this spreading through the school from any of you, you'll be sued."

Valerie abruptly stood up behind her desk with an indignant look on her face. "Max, I don't think you need to be threatening us like that."

"It's not a threat, Valerie, it's a promise. Please sit and I'll explain." She sat back down and crossed her arms over her chest, clearly upset. "Thank you. Now, you don't *need* to know this as it's not really pertinent to the boys' education, but I think you should. I'm gay."

"And just how could that have any effect on our responsibilities?"

Valerie asked.

"One of the main reasons I'm being allowed to adopt these four is, according to their case worker, they are gay, also."

"Oh, don't give me that garbage," Valerie countered. "They can't possibly think something like that at their ages."

"What makes you say that, Valerie? How many gay people have you talked to about when they knew who they were?"

"Well, none."

"Then, I'll be the first. I've known since I was Joey and Alex's age, so I have no doubt about who they say they are. The reason I'm telling you this is so you will know what to watch for from other students. I will not allow these boys to be bullied by anyone, students or staff, over this or any other reason. Do we understand each other?"

"First of all, there's no need to threaten, or promise, to sue us to have us enforce our rules. We have very strict anti-bullying policies and they are enforced equally, regardless of the type of bullying. We have no room for that in our school. Second of all, as I've already said, there is no way they can *know* that at their ages. Impossible."

"What about you three, do you also think it's impossible?" I asked, looking to the boys' teachers.

"It's absolutely possible, Valerie," Anita responded. "My son, Steve, first told me he liked boys when he was five. I didn't believe it, thought it was just a silly phase he was going through, but here we are 20 years later, and you know what, he still likes boys. Well, men, but you know what I'm saying."

"I suppose anything's possible," Peggy said.

"What's your opinion, Ken?" I asked.

"Well, I never thought much about it, but now that I do, I guess I've known since I was about same age, also. So, I'd have to say the boys know what they're talking about."

"Wait, you're gay, Ken? You didn't disclose that information when we hired you," Valerie said with a look of incredulity on her face.

"You didn't ask, and more importantly, it's illegal for you to do so."

"Be that as it may, this information could seriously affect your ability to retain you job."

"Ken," I interrupted, "if that happens, you let me know and I'll give you the name of a hard-nosed attorney who has never lost a case and loves nothing more than suing a bunch of sanctimonious pricks."

Ken leaned forward to look at me and answered, "Thanks, Max, I'll do that." He looked back to Valerie, "You were saying?"

"Nothing," she fumed. "I think we're done here."

"Do you still want me to send down the boys who are picking on Mike so you can talk to them?" Anita asked.

"Not today. We'll deal with them later. Get out of here. All of you."

"Thank you for your time, Valerie," I said politely, "it's been very educational. Fitting, I suppose, seeing as we are in a school."

"Whatever. Just go!"

As we exited the office, I turned to the other three and asked, "Can I count on you three to help?"

"Certainly, Max. My son went through hell growing up and I want you to know that Mike will not have to worry about that as long I can help it."

"Thanks, Anita, I appreciate it." I turned to Peggy, "How about you?"

"Of course, Max."

"And Ken?" I asked as I turned to him.

"Bet on it, Max."

"I want to thank you three for taking your lunch time to meet with me. It was my pleasure to meet all of you. Don't hesitate to call or e-mail me if any of you have problems with the boys."

Anita and Peggy both thanked me and turned to head to their classrooms. I started to leave and felt a tap on my shoulder. "Ya gotta a minute?" Ken asked.

"Sure, Ken, what's up?"

"I think we're going to have some problems with our fearless leader."

"What kind of problems?"

"She's obviously homophobic beyond belief. I picked up on her feelings during my first interview almost two years ago. That's why I've kept my mouth shut about being gay. I knew she wouldn't like it and would use any reason she could to not hire me or let me go, and I really need this job."

"Well, Ken, don't worry about it. They can't fire you for being gay."

"I know they can't, but I don't have tenure, yet, and she could use just about any excuse she can think of to deny me that."

"I don't know what to tell you except don't worry about it. She doesn't want to take me on. I may be kinda new to all this, but I don't intend to let anybody treat us like we're not humans."

"Thanks, Max. I'll watch out for the boys. All of them."

"Thanks to you, too, Ken. Have a good afternoon and if you need anything, call me."

I left the school and headed to my meeting with Carol, but since I had plenty of extra time, I decided to grab some lunch on the way. After a couple beef, bacon and cheddar sandwiches at Arby's, I continued on to the agency's office and my meeting. I was greeted by Marcy, the receptionist, and asked to have a seat to wait while Carol finished her current meeting. Ten minutes later, Carol entered the lobby escorting a smiling young couple and, after saying goodbye to them, she waved for me to follow her. I tagged along, weaving our way through cubicle after cubicle to finally find her office along an outside wall of the building.

"Afternoon, Max, have a seat, please."

"Thanks, Carol, how are you today?"

"Great!" she smiled. "That happy couple you saw with me is in the process of adopting a baby and we were going over some of the final details before their court appearance Friday."

"That's great, Carol. I'd imagine they're happy."

"Well, after six months of waiting and a bungled background investigation, they are now."

"A what?"

"Oh, the moron that did the first background check screwed it up and delayed the adoption about four months."

"How'd that happen?"

"The gentleman's name is fairly common, something like John Smith, although that's not his real name, but along those lines. You know, lots of other men with the same name."

"Unlike Maxwill Sanders, right? Not too many of us around, is there?"

"Exactly. The original investigator stopped his search when he found a man with the same name in prison down south somewhere. Didn't cross reference any other info like wife, family, date of birth, nothin'. Well, as you know, a felony is automatic removal from any possible adoption."

"So I've been told."

"Well, when the idiot faxed in his report, the dimwit here who retrieved it from the machine just flagged *this* gentleman as a criminal and he was kicked out of the program as ineligible. It took me months and a new investigation with a competent individual to get it all straightened out. We're finally back on track."

"What a nightmare for them, and for you. I couldn't imagine how I'd feel if that had happened to me."

"Well, we've removed that particular investigator from our list of approved sleuths and the in-house dimwit is out pounding the pavement looking for a new job. Best I can see her getting is a job where every customer is asked 'you want fries with that?'," she laughed bitterly. "I'm sorry, you don't want the hear about my problems. What can I do for you today? Is anything wrong?"

"Nope, we're good, but I may have a solution to your problem."

"What are you talking about, Max."

"I just happen to know an enterprising young man who is about to resign his current law enforcement job in favor of something in the private sector. He says he's interested in opening his own private investigation agency and he's going to be looking for some clients to help pay the bills. I told him I'd do some checking around to help him fill that need. So, tell me, do you know anyone who could make good use of a top-notch investigator?" Carol's eyes had been growing wider during my speech.

"Are you talking about Tom? He's quitting he Sheriff's department? What brought that about?"

"Yes, it's Tom. He and I have fallen for each other, hard. He's going to talk to his sergeant, Dylan, this afternoon after his shift, and turn in his resignation. As to how it happened, we had a long talk Sunday night and I asked him if he was married to his job. He told he loved it but was scared to death every day that he wouldn't be going home each night. When I told him I loved him and didn't want to risk losing him every day, he admitted he felt the same way about me and told me he'd already decided to turn in his papers today."

"Oh, my God, what have I done!?" she screamed.

I got up and quietly closed her door to avoid attracting any unwanted attention from the rest of the office, then returned to my seat. "You haven't done anything to be ashamed of or worry about, Carol. When we met in the Mueller's driveway Saturday, it was fate that brought us together. Besides, you did say you thought we'd make a cute couple, didn't you?"

"That wasn't fate, that was me, meddling in the lives of two people I barely know."

"You call it meddling, we call it fate. Whatever you want to call it, it was meant to be. We both feel like we've known each other our whole lives and we want to thank you for helping bring us together. Now, how about an answer to my original question, you know anyone who needs an excellent investigator with connections to law enforcement?"

"You're serious, aren't you?"

"Deadly."

"Let me call Anna and see if she can join us." She dialed Anna's extension and after brief conversation, said she'd be here in just a moment. She still had a dumbfounded expression on her face and it was priceless. A few minutes later, there was a light knock and Anna joined us.

"What's up Carol? Oh, I'm sorry, I didn't know you had a client with you."

I turned to face Anna and said, "That's okay, Anna, she's gone a little mute at the moment as she tries to absorb the news I just gave her."

"Oh, hi, Max, I didn't know you were coming in today. How's everything going with our boys?"

"Just great. They've settled into their new home and are back in school today."

"That's excellent, I'm glad to hear it. Now, can you please explain Ms. Lost in Space over here?"

"I'll do my best. Do you know a sheriff's deputy by the name of Tom Wright?"

"We've never met personally, but I've talked to him on the phone a few times and I know Carol has had his help several times."

"That's the one. Well, Carol called him Saturday to help me with the Muellers and, I guess the best way to say it is, things have kinda snowballed and he and I are now a couple. Ms. Lost in Space is worried she's meddled in our lives and, I think, feeling guilty about it."

"Is that why you're here?"

"Actually, no. I did come to talk to Carol about Tom, but not about her supposed 'meddling'. He's decided to resign from the Sheriff's department and open his own private investigation firm. I told Tom that I would talk to a few people to see if I could help create some business for him and I decided to talk to Carol first. As it turns out, I just happened to come in as she was escorting out a couple whose background investigation was screwed up by an incompetent investigator. I thought my timing was good, but now I'm thinking maybe not. Or maybe it was just too much at one time."

"Well, first, I suppose, congratulations are in order," she said as she gave me a hug. "And second, I think Tom will be a fine investigator and I'm sure we will be making use of his new services."

"I'm glad to hear it, Anna. We are both encountering major changes to our lives now and I think this will help ease one of his concerns. He really doesn't have to work as I'm well-off financially, but I believe he thinks he's taking advantage of me somehow. It's kinda hard to explain. I'm hoping adding Tom to the household won't have any effect on the boys' adoptions."

"Oh, don't worry about it, Max. We all go through changes in our lives, it's how we deal with those changes that make us who we are. And, no, adding Tom to your home shouldn't change anything with the adoptions. I'm sure the background checks he's been through to get his job are more thorough than what we do. Now, any suggestions on how to retrieve her from planet Catatonia? She looks like she's really out of it."

I looked back at Carol and said, "Wait, I think I see a glimmer of recognition in her eyes. Yes, there it is, come on Carol. Back to Earth, yeah, that's it."

She looked at me with fear in her eyes. "Oh, Max, what have I done? Sure, I thought you two would be a cute couple, but from meeting to being a couple in just a few days, how is that possible?"

"I told you Carol, we both feel like we've known each other forever and we just clicked. Hasn't that ever happened to you?"

"Once, about six years ago, but it didn't work out like I'd hoped. Turned out he loved his drugs more than me and I wasn't sticking around to watch him kill himself."

"So, you know it happens. Don't be so surprised it happened with us. You were absolutely right. I love him and so do the boys and he loves all of us, too. We're all going to be just fine. Now, can we get back to his doing investigations for you?"

"Yeah, right, investigations." She turned to Anna, "What do you think, Anna? I know the hassle we've had finding and keeping good investigators. Do you think we could use Tom? I know we need somebody good for background checks, but I also don't want it to look like we're using him just because of connections."

"I'm sure we can. And I'm not worried about 'connections', providing his checks are thorough and accurate. We can't have another debacle like this last one. That ass almost killed that adoption before it even got started." Anna turned to me and asked, "Any idea when Tom will be ready to start his new venture?"

"Not yet, but I should know tonight. He's turning in his resignation this afternoon after his shift ends. I guess it depends on his sergeant and what he says. I'm sure it will be at least two weeks."

"Well, please keep us informed as to his status and make sure he comes in when he's ready to get started. We're always needing background checks done and I'll have some waiting for him when he's ready."

"I will, Anna. Thanks." I stood to leave, then turned back to Carol and added, "I was serious about wanting to thank you for arranging our meeting. You're a good person, Carol Ward, and you do excellent work. Keep it up."

"Th-th-thanks, Max," she stammered.

"Well, I need to be on the way home so I can be there when the bus arrives. I don't want the boys to have to walk the half-mile to the house. You two have a great afternoon."

"Thanks, Max, you too," Anna said.

I left the office and hit the road for home. My timing should work out just right to arrive about five minutes before the bus would. As I drove home, my thoughts swiveled to Tom and the discussion he would soon be having with Dylan. I was hoping Dylan would accept his resignation, but I also knew he wouldn't want to lose a well-trained deputy. I'd just have to wait until Tom got home to find out. It turned out I was right on time to meet the bus as it turned up the road to the house right behind me. I pulled in the drive and waited for the boys to get off and join me in the car. Once they were settled in, we continued on to the house.

16

"Did you guys have a good day at school?"

"The morning was good, but this afternoon got kinda weird," Joey answered.

"What happened this afternoon?"

"Ms. Carling sat in our class, taking notes of some kind."

"Mr. Thomas was pretty upset over it," Alex added. "He didn't say anything about her being there, but we could tell he wasn't happy about it at all."

"What about you two?" I asked Mike and T.J.

"Fine," T.J. said.

"It was okay," added Mike.

"Good to hear, boys. Any homework to do tonight?"

"Alex and I have some since we missed yesterday, but it's only math. We'll have it done in no time."

"And I have some spelling words to work on. Can you help me with them, Dad?" T.J. asked.

"Sure thing. What about you, Mike?"

"Nope, nothin'," he chirped happily.

"All right," I said as I pulled in the garage. "Why don't we get set up at the kitchen counter and let's get the homework out of the way. Then you have the rest of the evening for a swim or whatever."

"Yeah!" they all yelled.

Once in the house, I said, "Get comfy and I'll meet you all in the kitchen." I headed to my bedroom and got undressed. As I returned to the kitchen, I was met by the four boys scampering to their stools. I gave Mike a couple blank sheets of paper and a pack of colored pencils from my study and asked him to draw something while the others worked on their assignments. I started T.J. with writing his spelling words three times each. While he did that, I checked on Joey and Alex. Ken was right on the money about their math skills as they were putting answers to paper while barely looking at the problems in their books. They were finished in no time and when I checked their work, I found no errors.

"How did you two get so good at math?" I asked.

"Not a clue, Dad," answered Alex. "It just comes to us."

"Well, it's a good skill to have. Are you bored in the class?"

"Most of the time, yeah, but our grades are perfect," Joey said.

"That's what Mr. Thomas said. He also said I might want to consider some testing for you. If you did well on the tests, you might be able to start working on a higher level. Do you think you might want to do that?"

"Sure, why not?"

"I'll get in touch with him and get it set up." T.J. had finished writing his spelling words, so I quizzed him on them and he got them all right. "We'll run through those again before bed to make sure you still got 'em, okay?"

"Sure, Dad."

"When's Tom gonna be here?"

"Not a clue, Mike. He had to talk to his boss this afternoon."

" 'Bout what?" T.J. asked.

"I think I'll leave it to him to tell you. It's his news, after all."

"What's for supper?"

"How do hamburgers grab ya, Joey?"

"Sounds great."

"Good. Why don't you four get the table ready and I'll get the burgers ready to put on the grill when Tom gets home?"

"But Dad, I'm not done with my picture yet," Mike whined.

"You go ahead and finish your picture and you can put the silverware out when you're done."

"Thanks."

The other three had the table ready in short order and I had the burgers ready for the grill soon after. Mike had finished his picture and proudly showed it off. He had drawn a nice-looking house with six people lined up in front of it, two taller people on the ends and four shorter ones in the middle. He'd carefully written the names of each of us under that person's figure on the drawing. At the very bottom, he'd written 'My New Family'. It was all I could do to not cry.

"This is a great picture, Mike. I'm going to have to get some magnets so we can start putting artwork on the fridge. Until then, I'll keep it in the study, okay?"

"I'm glad you like it. It's not very good."

"You did a great job, son. I'll put it away for now, but let's make sure we show it to Tom when he gets home."

"I will!" Mike squealed with joy.

I headed to the study, placed the picture on the desk so it wouldn't get dirty and noticed the envelope with the shreds of the picture of the twins' parents. I smacked myself on the forehead, hard. I couldn't believe I'd forgotten about it. I left myself a note on the desk as a reminder to make some calls on it in the morning.

As I headed back to the kitchen, the drive sensor went off. I was hoping it was Tom or there was going to a mad rush for us all to get some clothes back on. I looked out the front window and saw him climbing out of the car and breathed a sigh of relief. He turned towards the passenger side and it was then I noticed someone else getting out of the car. I quickly headed to the bedroom to get dressed, telling the boys they needed to do the same. They took off for their rooms as I disappeared down the hall to mine. I heard the front door opening just as I reached the bedroom door.

"Max, you here?" Tom called.

"Be right there, Tom, I'm in the bedroom. The boys are in their rooms and should be back out shortly, also."

"Okay, Dylan came home with me. Hope that's okay."

"Not a problem." I returned to the living room just as the four boys were coming back down the hallway to join us.

"Oh, there you are, Max. You remember Dylan from Saturday, don't you?"

"Of course, I do. I'm not senile. Not yet anyway," I laughed. "Good to see you again, Dylan," I said as I shook his extended hand.

Tom turned towards the boys, "Come here guys, I want you to meet my boss. Dylan, I want you to meet the boys I've told you about. From left to right, we have Alex, Joey, or is it Joey, then Alex? Either way, I guess. Then, Mike and T.J. Boys, this is my boss, Sheriff Dylan Brock of the Sangamon County Sheriff's Department."

"It's good to meet the four of you. Tom's told me a lot about you this afternoon. You guys all settled in your new home?"

"We sure are, Mr. Brock," Joey answered.

"How does it feel to have a new dad and brothers?"

"Great!" they yelled.

"Whoa, boys, we're all in the same room, inside voices, please."

"Sorry, sir," Alex apologized, "we just really like it here."

"Yeah, Max is gonna be a great dad," Mike answered.

"I'm glad to hear it. Now, I hate to ask this, but would you please excuse us for a few minutes so I can talk to Tom and your dad?"

"Sure thing, Mr. Brock," T.J. answered. He turned to me and added, "We'll be in our rooms, Dad. Let us know when supper's ready."

"You know I will." I turned to Tom and Dylan, "Welcome, Dylan, I didn't know you were coming out this afternoon."

"Sorry, Max," Tom answered, "I didn't have a chance to call."

"Not a problem. Would you like to join us for supper, Dylan? We're having hamburgers."

"I'd like that, Max, thanks for the invite."

"Well, why don't we sit by the fireplace and have that talk." I led the way and after we were seated, I asked, "So, what would you like to talk about?" I noticed Tom was looking at the floor and avoiding eye contact.

"About this bonehead leaving the department," Dylan answered, hooking a thumb in Tom's direction. "He's the best guy I've got out there and I don't want to lose him."

"You're talking to the wrong man, Dylan. This is entirely his decision."

"You mean to tell me you had nothing at all to do with this?"

"I asked one question Sunday night and he told me that he'd already made his decision. My only input was to tell him that now that I'd found him, I sure didn't want to lose him."

"Yeah, that's the same thing he told me he said to you." He turned to Tom, "Well, Tom, it sounds like I'm not going to talk you out of resigning, am I?"

"No, sir. You know I love the job, but it scares the hell out of me these days. There's just too many lunatics roaming loose and raising havoc. I need to start doing something where I don't have to worry about coming home alive every night. I've been thinking about it for a while and meeting Max and the boys just solidified what I'd already decided."

"Well, it's sure hard to argue with that logic. If I was living here, I'd sure want to make sure I came home every night, too," Dylan chuckled. "As much as this sucks for me, I'm happy for you two. I know how difficult it is for a gay man to find the right guy and connect."

Tom shook his head in surprise and asked, "Wait, *you're* one of the guys you mentioned Saturday?"

"Of course I am, Tom. And had I been there Saturday, instead of you, it would have ended a whole lot worse for the Muellers than it did. And, of course, I could see the way you two were looking at each other. I knew right then something was happening. Apparently, it took you two a little longer to figure it out."

"Not too much longer, Dylan," I responded, "When was it, Tom, Sunday afternoon, right?"

"Pretty much. I'm sorry, Sarge, really, but I have more to live for than the job, now."

"Damn right you do, and don't you ever forget it. So, what's your plan from here?"

"I'd been thinking about starting my own private investigation agency and I'm pretty sure that's what's going to happen. Max said he'd talk to a few people and see if he can find me some clients to help get started."

"And I found your first one today," I said.

"What?! Who!?"

"The agency Carol works for. I stopped by today and talked to Carol and Anna. They've had real problems finding competent people to handle background and abuse investigations. In fact, when I got there, Carol was with a young couple in the process of adopting a baby whose adoption got delayed several months because of a botched investigation. They were ecstatic about finding someone they think will do a more competent and comprehensive job."

"Oh, my God, that's great!"

"That's good news, Tom. And an excellent cause. I'd be inclined to allow the use of some department resources to help ensure mistakes like that don't happen again."

"You're kidding me, Sarge, you won't even allow the local police departments to use our computers."

"That's because most of those guys are ham-handed apes who don't know their asses from holes in the ground. You, young man, are way above them. You have the brains and innate curiosity that makes for a good investigator. I'm more than willing to help you succeed. Besides, if you do well, that reflects well back on me and I look brilliant for having hired you in the first place." We all enjoyed a laugh at that remark.

"Thanks, Sarge, I appreciate it. So, when's my last day?"

"Can you stick with it for a couple more weeks? That'll give me a chance to look at schedules and see who I can shift to your patrols."

"Yeah, I can do that. I owe you that much."

"It's a done deal then, Tom." Dylan turned to me, "You're one lucky mothe..., uh, dude, Max. You better take good care of all these fellas or you're gonna have to deal with me. And I don't think you want that, do you?"

"Not at all, Dylan. Thanks for the warning."

"Don't mention it. Now, I have one more thing to tell the both of you."

"Oh, shit, here it comes," laughed Tom.

"Congratulations. On meeting each other and finding those four lucky boys. I think you are all going to be very happy together."

"I think we are, too, thanks, Dylan."

"Yeah, me too, Sarge."

"Well, if we're done with that, shall we eat?" I asked. I received nods from both men, so I headed to get the boys and let them know to get ready to eat.

T.J. came to the end of the hall and asked, "Uh, Dad, can you come here?"

"Sure." I walked to where he waited and asked, "What's up, son?"

He wiggled his finger for me to come down to his level. When I knelt, he whispered in my ear, "Is Mr. Brock 'other people'?"

"I'll find out, go wait with your brothers and I'll let you know in a minute."

While T.J. skipped his way back to the twins' room, I headed back to Tom and Dylan and Tom asked, "What's that all about? Don't tell me they're suddenly getting shy."

"Not at all, they just want to know if Dylan is 'other people'."

"Oh crap, I shoulda' known, shouldn't I?"

"What's that mean, Max? Is that like 'don't talk to strangers'," Dylan asked.

"Uh, not exactly, Sarge."

"Well, clue me in so we can eat. I'm getting hungry."

"I got this, Tom." I turned to Dylan and explained the house rules to him.

Dylan laughed heartily when I finished my explanation. "Hell, if they don't care, I don't care, either. Tell 'em it's fine with me."

"Tom, why don't you get changed while I tell the boys the good news. Then I can start cooking." I headed to the hallway and called out, "It's okay boys, he's one of us." A resounding chorus of acceptance cheers rang from the twins' room and as I turned to the kitchen to start the hamburgers, the first boy emerged wearing only his birthday suit. I just shook my head and pulled the burgers out of the fridge. I had just put the first one on the grill when I saw Tom had returned, wearing nothing but a cheesy grin. "Et tu, Brute?"

"Like you said the other night, 'when in Rome'."

Dylan laughed again. Until Joey looked him square in the eyes and asked, "Aren't you gonna join us, Mr. Brock?"

The laugh quickly turned into a cough. "Um, I don't think so, boys."

"Why not?" Alex quizzed him.

"Yeah, why not?" T.J. echoed.

"I told you guys he'd be too chicken," Mike chimed in.

Dylan was now seriously blushing, although it was hard to tell for sure due to his darker skin color. "Well, it seems your dad is remaining clothed and I just think I should, too."

"That's not going to work, Dylan. Not with them, anyway. Besides, as soon as I'm done cooking food that's spattering hot grease, I'm joining the crowd."

"Guess I'm outnumbered, then, aren't I? Okay, where can I put my clothes?"

"Tom, why don't you direct him to the empty bedroom. There're hangers in the closet if he wants to use them."

"Sure thing, Max. C'mon, Sarge, this way."

Dylan followed Tom into the bedroom so he could also get comfortable.

"Really, Sarge, you don't have to do this if you don't want to. I know it's gotta be weird for ya."

He removed his shirt as he said, "It's all good, Tom. Been a while since I've been naked around anyone else, you know. Hope nothin' comes up that shouldn't, if you get my drift," Dylan said as he removed his pants.

"Oh, I got it alright. If it does, it won't be a big deal, we're slowly getting used to it, too. Besides, shit happens, don't it?" Dylan had just removed his boxers and Tom got his first look at his boss nude. "Okay, I take that back, maybe it will be a big deal," and laughed.

"I shoulda' warned ya, Tom. Bet you thought you was the 'big man on campus', didn't ya?"

"Not no more, Sarge. Damn, how the hell do you walk?"

"Very carefully, my man" Dylan answered with a laugh, clapping Tom on the shoulder. "And I'm no longer Sarge. No uniform, no rank, okay. Dylan's fine."

"Well, if you're ready, let's go back and rejoin the others. Burgers should be about done."

"Lead the way, Tom."

By the time Tom and Dylan had returned, the boys had added another place setting, ketchup, mustard and pickles to the table and set out three different kinds of chips. I had just finished the hamburgers and was about to set the tray on the table when the two entered the kitchen. I literally dropped the tray the last two inches to the table after catching a glimpse of Dylan as he stepped out from behind Tom. The boys all whistled in appreciation and I heard one of the twins whisper 'holy shit'.

"I believe I'll get comfortable before I sit. Go ahead and get started. I'll be right back."

I returned just in time to hear T.J. ask, "Are all black guys as big as you?"

"Thomas, that's not a question you should ask," I scolded.

"Whoops, sorry, Dad. Sorry, Mr. Brock."

"No problem, son, it's normal to be curious about others," Dylan chuckled. "I've heard that exact same question in many a locker room from many a white guy over the years. I'm used to it and take it as a compliment nowadays."

"Well, are they?" T.J. persisted.

"Thomas, please." I groaned, trying to end his interrogation of our guest.

"To answer your question, T.J., no they're not. Most I've seen are more like your dad and Tom. I'm one of the rare exceptions. And remember, most men would be offended at your question and not be as nice about it as I am. You need to be more careful who you ask questions like that, understand?"

"Yes, sir," he answered, hanging his head.

"Can we please eat now?" I asked, hoping that full mouths would hinder any further questions. That seemed to finally do the trick, and everyone dug into their burgers. As usual, when we were done eating, the boys cleaned up the table, stacking the dishes in the sink. Once that task was completed, they returned to the table to join our conversation.

"Hey, Uncle Tom, Dad said you might have some news for us when you got home," Joey said.

"Yeah," Alex added, "what's that all about."

Tom looked at me, "You didn't tell them?"

"Nope, I thought that since it's your news, you should be the one to tell 'em."

"Okie-dokie, then." He turned to face the boys and continued, "Boys, I'm leaving the Sheriff's department. That's the main reason Dylan is here tonight. He was gonna try to talk me out of quitting."

"But why you quittin', Uncle Tom?" asked Joey. "I thought you liked bein' a cop."

"I do, but it's a very dangerous job and now that I have you guys and Max in my life, I want to make sure I can come home every night. I can't stay a cop and do that."

"We don't want to lose you, either, Uncle Tom," T.J. said. "We love you, too. I'm glad you're quitting."

"What are you gonna do now?" asked Alex.

"I'm going to open my own private investigation office."

"What're you going to be doing?"

"Well, Max went to see Carol and Anna today, and part of what I'll be doing is background checks on foster parents and folks who are adopting. We want to make sure all the kids who need new homes, temporary and permanent, are going to good ones. I don't ever want to see a kid living with someone like the Muellers."

"That's great, Uncle Tom. People like them don't deserve to have any kids, ever," Joey said.

"What can we do to help?" asked Alex.

"Nothing I can think of," Tom chuckled. "Investigations like that are an adult's job."

"But we can help," Joey protested. "We knew the Muellers were bad people right off, but we couldn't take the chance of being split up."

"Yeah living there sucked big time, but we didn't know what would happen to us, so we didn't make any problems. Besides sleeping in the same bed," Alex said while he grinned mischievously at Joey.

"Alexander, mouth."

"Sorry, Dad, but it did suck."

"Boys, Dylan's going to help out, too. He's promised to allow me access to the county's computers to help out. He doesn't let just anyone do that."

"It's for a good cause and I trust you to not abuse the privilege."

"It's still going to help out a lot, Dylan, and I can't thank you enough."

"Oh, Mike, why don't run into the study and grab the picture you drew so Tom can see it? It's right on the desk." He took off in a flash and quickly returned, picture in hand, which he proudly showed to Tom.

"This is great, Mike. You did a great job."

"You like how I named everybody?"

"It's just perfect. We'll have to put this on the fridge."

"As soon as I can get some magnets, Tom," I answered.

Dylan leaned over to see the picture and commented, "You have some real talent there, Mike. I wish I had a picture like that to put on my fridge."

"Can't your son draw you one like I did?"

"I suppose he could if I had one, Mike. I'm not married, though, and I don't have any kids. Someday, maybe," he added wistfully.

"So," I interrupted, "who's ready for a swim?" Everyone but Dylan raised their hand. "Oh, c'mon, Dylan, a little dip won't hurt ya."

"Seems to be a little cold out there for a swim, Max, I think I'll pass."

"Follow me." I led Dylan to the glass wall facing the pool and turned on the outside lights illuminating the pool shelter.

"Well, that changes things. I do believe you've talked me into it."

"Boys, grab towels for seven, please." They scampered off to the laundry room, returned with the towels as requested and we headed out for our swim. The boys tossed their towels on the table and jumped right in. Tom, Dylan and I were a bit calmer in joining them, but once in the water, we were smothered by four very happy, squealing and squirming boys. Joey and Alex were working over Dylan, Mike had jumped on Tom and T.J. attacked me. We spent the next thirty minutes playing with four giggling boys before we excused ourselves to calmer waters in the deep end of the pool.

"Whoa, what a workout," Dylan panted. "Those twins are brutal."

"Yeah, they are," Tom agreed.

"No harm done," Dylan chuckled. "Ya won't mind if I ask you a personal question, will ya, Max?"

"Oh, hell, why not? Whatever it is couldn't be too bad, could it?"

"Okay, where the hell is all your hair?"

I laughed at the question. "I see curiosity isn't limited to us white boys. The boys asked the same question the first time we were all nude together, wanted to know why Tom was all hairy and I wasn't. The quick answer is, obviously, I shave or keep it trimmed real short."

"Can I ask why?"

"I like the look and feel of it, Dylan. Just some weird little kink in my brain. It's not for everybody, I know."

"When did you start?"

"I guess I was about twenty, maybe twenty-one."

"That surprises me. At that age, body hair, one spot especially, always seems to be important to a guy. Tryin' to reinforce the fact that they're now a 'man', ya know?"

"Yeah, and when the hair first started sprouting, it was important, but once I got out on my own and wasn't dealing with locker rooms daily, it became less and less a thing I cared about. I tried shaving a couple times and then let it grow back, but eventually decided I preferred life without it. Plus, with being on the swim team in college, it was pretty much expected. I just continued and haven't been in a locker room since," I chuckled.

"I'd imagine. You'd be questioned about that just like I'm questioned about black guys and the size of their equipment. It does get tiresome."

"Well, Dylan, you're welcome to come out any time and make use of the pool. I don't think you have to worry about any more questions here, will he, Tom?"

"Not from me. Can't really say for the boys, though," he joked.

We spent another forty-five minutes in the pool relaxing and chatting while the boys played before I called out time for showers, snacks and bed. The boys hopped out of the pool, grabbed their towels and headed for the house, quickly drying themselves before leaving the warmth of the shelter. The three of us were a little more relaxed in our return to the house. By the time we reached the kitchen, the boys were coming back from their showers and climbing up on their stools for their snack. I set them up with sliced apples and juice tonight and they dug in. Once the snacks were completed, Tom and I excused ourselves for a few minutes to tuck the boys in and give them their nightly goodnight kisses.

"Dad," Joey started, "We really like Dylan. Do you think he'll come back?"

"Yeah, he was a lot fun, especially in the pool," Alex said.

"Boys, I don't know if he'll be back or not. All we can do is ask."

"Night, Dad, night, Uncle Tom. We love you."

"We love you, too," I responded.

"See you in the morning," Tom added.

We stopped to check on T.J. and Mike on our way back to the living room and heard them snoring lightly. What a sweet sound that was. After quietly saying good night and kissing their foreheads, we rejoined Dylan in the living room where we found him admiring the Ansel Adams print over the fireplace.

"Dylan, can I interest you in a cup of coffee or hot chocolate before you head for home?"

"Coffee sounds great, Max. Thanks."

I headed to the kitchen to brew a fresh half-pot and when I returned,

Tom and Dylan were sitting next to the fireplace and in deep conversation.

I passed them each a steaming cup, took a seat and said, "You two sound like you're planning a complete overhaul of the juvenile criminal justice system." They both laughed at my comment.

"Nothing quite that grand," Tom replied, "but we do want to see what we can do improve the background checks for Anna and Carol."

"Yeah," Dylan continued, "That situation you described earlier should have never happened. We need to work together to make sure it doesn't happen again."

"Mind if I make a suggestion?"

"Sure thing, Max," Tom answered. "The more people we can get involved in this, the better off we'll be."

"Well, in the past couple weeks, I've met more gay people and folks who know someone who's gay than I've met in the last twelve years. And that includes those four boys sleeping down the hall. Part of that, I'm sure, is just getting the hell out of this house."

"Wait a sec," Dylan interrupted, "they're all gay?"

"So they say. That's the main reason Carol felt comfortable placing them with me. She wanted them to have a friendly and positive environment to grow up in. I know not every kid realizes who they are at the same age, but for me, it was when I was about seven or eight. Tom told me he was about eleven or twelve when he figured it out. How about you, Dylan?"

"Thirteen. I remember that night like it was yesterday. I was having a friend, Malcolm White, spend a weekend with me, camping in the back yard. Today's parents would say I was molested, but nothin' happened I didn't want happenin'. And after that weekend, I knew I'd never climb in bed with a woman. I loved every second of those few days, and the many weekends that followed. He and his family moved away when we were both 16, but if he hadn't, I bet we'd still be together. Damn, I really loved him, and I miss him dearly."

"Well, that was a little more than I was looking for, but it proves my point. After I started the process of trying to adopt, and then finding out the boys were gay, I started to wonder how many other gay kids are out there, living in situations they shouldn't be."

"My god, Max, I can't believe I hadn't thought about that myself," Tom exclaimed.

"I'm not saying you should focus solely on gay kids but should make the extra effort to ensure those that are or think they may be are placed in accepting homes. I don't think the adults need to be gay, necessarily, but they should definitely *not* be like the Muellers or my parents. That's the worst thing that can happen with these kids."

"You're right, of course," Dylan said. "I think we can do that."

"I'm in complete agreement," Tom said. "Once I start the new job, I'll talk to Carol and see if she can help identify kids needing special placements."

"That sounds like a plan to me," I agreed.

"Oh, by the way," Dylan started, "with everything else this evening, I forgot to tell you something I think you're both going to enjoy hearing."

"What's that, Dylan?" I asked.

"I went to see a judge today and walked out of his chambers with summonses for both Frank and Iris Mueller. When I explained to the judge what happened with them on Saturday, he was disgusted. Both have been charged with obstructing and destruction of personal property. They appear in court next week to enter their pleas. I personally delivered the papers to their home. You wouldn't believe the look on their faces when I handed each of them their summons. It was priceless."

"Whoo-hoo!" we hollered.

"What date and time?" I asked.

"Next Thursday at ten. Tom will have to be there since he was the officer on the scene and you may be called as witness, Max."

"Excellent, I'll be there. I can't wait to see them get what they deserve."

We spent the next hour chatting and getting to know each other better. I really enjoyed Dylan's company, and he had a great sense of humor along with a very outgoing personality. About ten-thirty, he suddenly stood and said, "Well, fellas, it's long past the time I should be getting home, I have an early meeting in the morning and it wouldn't do for the boss to arrive late. I better grab my clothes and skedaddle." He headed to the spare bedroom to retrieve his clothes and was back sooner than I thought he would be. It took me a moment to realize he was carrying his clothes instead of wearing them.

"Um, Dylan," Tom said, "I think you might have forgotten something."

He looked startled and then looked closer at the bundle in his arms. "Let's see, pants, shirts, belt, socks, shoes, gun, cuffs, radio. No, it looks I got it all."

"You're not wearing it?" Tom asked incredulously.

"Eh, why bother, I'll just have to take it all back off when I get home."

"I can't believe this," Tom muttered. "What if you get stopped on the way home?"

"I'm driving a marked car, Tom. Who the hell's gonna stop me? Besides, I do this all the time," he laughed. "My garage is connected to the house, so I can get from the car into the house without being seen."

"Please don't let the boys know about this, Dylan," I pleaded, "It's hard enough to keep them in clothes as it is. I don't need it to be even more difficult."

"Good luck with that," he laughed. "Well, I want to thank you both for a wonderful evening, I can't remember the last time I enjoyed myself as much as I did tonight. Max, you're a lucky man and I envy you. Tom, I'll see you in the morning. Remember, though, I'll be your sergeant again, and I'll expect proper respect on the job."

"I'll be there, boss, with bells on."

"Your regular uniform will be fine, Tom. The bells might be saying just a bit more than you want," Dylan cracked.

"Dylan, I'm glad you had a pleasant evening. I was serious about you returning, and I know the boys would like you to come back, also."

"I may just take you up on that offer, you never know. Adios, amigos." With that, he turned and headed out the door, shiny, bare, black ass reflecting the lights outside the front door.

"Well, that was interesting," Tom said while shaking his head in disbelief. "I've worked with him almost every day for the last five years and never picked up a hint Dylan was gay."

"Sounds a lot like you and me, bubba. The few people I've told so far never thought it was a possibility, either. Nice to get to know people away from work, isn't it?"

"Yeah, it is. And to find out he had no problem with the nudity was an even bigger surprise."

"Tell me, Tom, if you had his equipment, would you ever have a problem being naked around other guys. The truth."

"No, I guess not. But, damn, I feel for sorry for any guy he hooks up with. He could kill someone with that thing."

"I hope he felt welcome enough to come back. Dylan's a great guy."

"Yeah, he is. It'd be nice to know him outside the job."

"Okay, enough about him. Are you ready to go to bed?"

"Not really. We never got our showers after swimming and I need to get the chlorine off me before I turn whiter than I already am."

"Head on in, I'll put our cups in the dishwasher and meet you there."

"Best offer I've had all day," he said as he turned and headed down the hall.

"Better be the only offer you've had today, smartass," I called to his back as he giggled his way down the hall.

His back was to the door when I entered the bathroom a minute later and the water was running over him as he bent over to hang his head down. I quietly stepped in the shower, slid in behind him, and whispered, "Guess who?"

"Brad Pitt? No, too small. I know, George Clooney. No, too big. Damn, who could that be, knockin' at my back door?"

I grabbed his arm, spun him around and asked, "Really?"

"Ah, Maxwill Sanders, perfect in every way. Where've you been all my life?"

"Living right here, among the trees, patiently waiting for Mr. Right to find me. If you see him, would you point him my direction, please?"

"I love you, Max Sanders, and I can't wait to spend the rest of my life with you."

We embraced under the water and held each other as we started kissing and our hands roamed freely. One thing led to another and we were soon ensconced on the bed. After slipping a blindfold over my eyes, Tom spent the next thirty minutes massaging me from my toes to head. He had to help roll me from my front to my back since I was unable to accomplish the task myself due to his ministrations. When the time was right, he straddled my body and slowly took me inside him. We were both in heaven and our time entwined was much too short for our liking.

"Oh, my god, I have waited so long for that," he whimpered after he laid down beside me. "The 'aids' I had were okay, but nothing like the real thing. I'm so glad you were the first to share the experience with me."

"I'm with you, in more ways than one. I don't think a hand will ever suffice again."

"We're going to find new territories of pleasure together, you and me. I hope you're ready."

"Been ready for years, Tom, I just needed to find the right guy. I'm happy I finally did."

"Me, too. Even happier it was me," he laughed.

"By the way, where'd you get the blindfold and oil?"

"You remember that little box I grabbed from my apartment the other day?"

"Yeah, but you stashed it as soon as we got home, and I forgot about it. What else are you hiding from me, young man?"

"You'll find out," he laughed.

"Um, I think we both need another shower."

"Come on, lover, let me get you cleaned up."

We headed to the bathroom and lovingly cleaned each other. Once we dried off, we climbed back into bed, curled up together and fell into a deep, dreamless and contented sleep. Until the alarm went off early the next morning.

17

The alarm went off at six to announce the beginning of our new day. Tom and I crawled out of bed, took care of our morning bathroom needs and rinsed our mouths to clear away the morning breath.

"Good morning, lover," I whispered as I leaned in to give him a kiss.

"Mornin' to you, too," he grumbled and returned the kiss.

"Ooh, someone's a grumpy bear this morning. Are you like this every morning?"

"Only until I get some caffeine in me."

"Well, you get dressed and I'll get some ready for you, okay?"

"I'll be there."

I headed to kitchen, got the morning pot brewing and headed across the house to wake the boys. I went into T.J. and Mike's room to find Mike's head on T.J.'s shoulder and T.J.'s arm protectively wrapped around his younger brother. I put a hand on each boy's shoulder and gently shook them to wake them up. When their eyes were at half-mast, I said, "Breakfast in ten, get up and get dressed for school."

I headed to the twins' bedroom to find the covers tossed on the floor again and a jumble of arms and legs in the middle of the bed. I reached in to shake them awake, only to have my arm grabbed by Alex and I was pulled onto the bed with them amid a gale of laughter from both boys. I extricated myself from the tangle and told them it was time to get dressed for school and come out for breakfast.

When I returned to the kitchen, Tom was working on his first cup already and I could see his eyes were much brighter now. "Would you please go put some clothes on so I can leave the house this morning. If you stay like that, I won't want to go anywhere."

"Nice to hear some cheer in your voice. That caffeine works wonders on you." I turned and headed to the bedroom to find a pair of sweatpants. When I got back to the kitchen again, I found four boys lined up on their stools ready for breakfast. "Pop-Tarts sound okay this morning?"

"Sure, whatever," Joey mumbled.

I pulled out the toaster, loaded it with four tarts and soon had one in front of each boy as I started round two in the toaster. Tom had poured milk for them while I dealt with the tarts. I turned to Tom and asked, "What about you? You interested?"

"No, thanks. I'll stop at a Mel-O-Cream on my way through town and grab some doughnuts."

"I shoulda' known. Cops and their doughnuts," I laughed.

"Well, don't expect that to stop when I'm done being a cop. I can't seem to stay away from the things."

Pop-Tart round two was soon ready and I set each of the boys up with their second one.

"Well, I gotta scoot," Tom started, "or I'll be late. You four have a good day at school and I'll see you tonight."

"Bye, Uncle Tom," Joey said.

"Be careful out there," added Alex.

"I'll be careful, don't worry." As he started to walk away, he wiggled his finger for me to follow him. As we headed to the door to the garage, he said, "I hate to ask, but since Dylan and I came out in his car last night, I don't have a vehicle this morning. Do you mind if I take the Shelby so I can get to work?"

"Hell, I didn't think about that. Sure," I said as I reached in my pocket to retrieve my keyring. I separated the Shelby fob from the Flex fob and handed it to Tom. "I better call my insurance guy this morning and get you added on my policy."

"Humph, haven't even left the garage and you're already worried about me wreckin' it. I tell ya, that's love, that is."

"Oh, don't be such a smartass, Tom. I'm not worried about you, it's all the other idiots out there."

"I know, Max, just yankin' your chain."

"If you're not careful, you'll be yankin' your own chain, buddy."

"Heaven forbid," he mocked. "Not that!"

"Get outta here and be safe, you hear me."

"I hear ya. Thanks, Max, I love you."

"Love you, too, you big goober." We gave each other a kiss and he turned for the garage. "One more thing, hotrod, that car's got a lot more power than you're used to, try to keep it under a hundred."

"Yes, Daddy," he smirked. "I'll be good, I promise." And with that parting comment he was out the door.

I got back to the kitchen to find the plates and glasses rinsed, stacked in the sink and no boys. I hollered, "Boys! Coats, hats, gloves, backpacks, we gotta roll." Just as I finished, I spotted all four were coming down the hall, ready to go. "Oh, sorry, I guess you're waiting on me, aren't you?"

"Yeah, Dad, c'mon, we gotta roll," T.J. parroted with a laugh.

"Be right back." I pulled on a shirt and shoes in the bedroom, grabbed my coat and we headed to the garage. Once the boys were loaded up and belted, I headed to the end of the drive to wait for the bus. As the bus was coming up the road, we got out of the car and I gave each boy a hug and reminded them, "Have a good day and learn something new." They all moaned in defeat as they climbed on the bus and took their seats. When the bus was out of sight, I returned to the house and headed to my study to see what I had to deal with today.

The first thing I found was the envelope containing the pieces of the twins' parent's picture, waiting for some desperately needed repair. I hopped on the internet and did a search for photo repair services in the area. After finding a few with good reviews, I started making my calls. The first two places showed no interest in attempting the project, but I finally hit pay dirt on my third call.

"Ed Clark Photography, this is Ed. How may I help you?" he answered.

"Good morning, Ed. My name is Max Sanders, how are you today?"

"I'm doing well, Mr. Sanders, how about yourself?"

"I've had better days, but I'm hoping you can help make this one better for me."

"Tell me how I can do that."

"I'm in the process of adopting two boys who lost their parents four years ago. The last thing they had of their parents was a photo of them and, unfortunately, their former foster parents tore the thing to shreds and the boys are quite upset, as I'm sure you can imagine."

"That's horrible. How many pieces are we talking about?"

"Fifty to sixty. I haven't actually tried to count them. Do you think there's any way you can repair something with that much damage?"

"I'll be honest with you, Mr. Sanders, I've never tried. Not that heavily damaged, anyway. Usually the worst we deal with is scratches or water marks."

"Well, hell."

"Hold on, now, I didn't say I wasn't willing to try. I obviously can't promise results but I'm more than willing to give it a shot."

"You're a lifesaver, Ed. When can I bring it in?"

"Let me check my schedule, hang on." He returned a minute later, "Okay, I have a couple coming in at ten for a portrait shoot and that usually takes about half an hour. That's all I had scheduled today, so any time after that should be just fine."

"Is the address I found on the internet current?"

"My studio's in Sherman. Is that the one you have."

"It is. Thanks, Ed, I'll see you about ten-thirty."

I next called my insurance agent to get Tom added to my policies. That only took ten minutes and I found out I needed his driver's license number to complete the process. I let them know I would have Tom call to give it to them later today.

Since I had a few spare hours, I grabbed a new book from the study and curled up in my chair by the fireplace to read for a while. The ding of the drive sensor roused me from a stupor forty-five minutes later and I shook my head to clear the fog. I suddenly remembered my contractor, John, was coming out this morning to discuss the shelter at the end of the drive. Fortunately, I hadn't undressed after the boys left so I grabbed my coat and keyring and zipped out to meet him. When I arrived, John was already out of his truck and looking at areas he thought would be a good location for the shelter.

"Hey, John," I called as I got of the car, "Sorry I wasn't waiting for you. It slipped my mind that you were coming this morning."

"No problems, Max. I just got here. I was just about to call and let you know I was here."

"I know, the drive sensor announced your arrival."

"Forgot you had that." We shook hands and John asked, "So where're you thinking, north or south side of the drive?"

"I think the north will be best. As I recall, the main power feed back to the house runs down the south side and there's not a lot of room over there to begin with."

"North side it is, then. I sure don't want to worry about the power line. Is the fence over there your west property line?"

"It's about five feet this side of it. The line itself is about the middle of the ditch. I was thinking we should leave about eight feet clear between the fence and the shelter. What do you think?"

"That sounds good, that way we have some extra room to work in. You want the trees cleared out eight feet all around, also?"

"I think so. My lawn guy can have it mowed quickly when he does the rest of the property."

"Great, let me show what I drew up as a plan and you tell me if it's close to what you're thinking about." He retrieved his case from the truck and pulled out a small stack of paper, then handed it to me. I looked through the pages, making mental notes as I went. "So, what do you think, Max. That what you're looking for."

"Just about perfect, John but let's make a couple quick changes. Let's move the door to the east wall and center the window in the south wall instead of having both on the same one."

"Easy change to make. You want the door centered or set in one of the corners?"

"I think the south corner of the east wall with the hinges to the left side so it swings in against the wall. That leaves the rest of the inside open space. I'll probably put some fold-up chairs inside so the boys will be able to sit while they wait. We'll need to make the window tall enough they can see outside while they're sitting."

"Sounds good to me. Anything else?"

"This is going to sound stupid, but I want the siding on it to match the cedar I have on the house and I think a metal roof. Between those two things, it should be pretty maintenance free. The only other thing would be a push-button lock for the door. I know the boys can easily memorize five or six numbers and then I don't have to worry about lost keys."

"Music to my ears, Max, because everything you want is just jacking up the price," he laughed.

"I know, but I want it solid and make sure it lasts for fifteen or more years with minimal upkeep."

"Oh, it'll be solid all right and probably be sitting here long after you're gone. We'll frame the walls, get the exterior sheathing on 'em, then spray in the foam insulation. We'll cut the inside sheathing so once the walls are bolted to the slab, we can slap it in place with minimal effort. I assume you wanting something decent on the inside. Do you want us to paint the inside? And if so, what color?"

"That wouldn't hurt, John, and I think just plain white or an off-white would be fine. Two more things I'd like done is to have the heater on a timer so it runs as automatically as possible. That way it won't be running the battery down when nobody's inside. The other thing I'd like done is to tie a push button into the driveway sensor so the boys can let me know when they get here. That way I'm not just sitting down here waiting. Either of those sound like problems?"

"The timer doesn't. We'll just install a programable thermostat, but the dinger button's a little trickier. I'll have to get someone out here to locate the sensor first. Once it's located, we'll have to dig down to it to tie the button into the system."

"I can make it even easier for you, John." I led him to a tree on the south side of the drive and pointed to a small gray box hidden behind it. "That box contains the circuits for the sensor. The wire to the house was buried in the same trench with the power line. You should be able to tie in there without having to do any locating or serious digging."

"Max, you're a smart man. That was damn good planning."

"Thanks, but you really need the tell the sensor folks. They set it up this way in case I ever had any problems with the thing. They were making it easier for themselves if they ever had to do a repair."

"Well, I think that about covers everything except for getting the trees cleared out. If my tree guy would show up, we can let him know the area to be cleared."

"Speak of the devil, John, I think he just arrived," I said as a truck pulled up with the name, Abe's Tree Service, painted on the side.

"About time, I was starting to think he got lost." Two men got out of the truck and joined John and me.

"Morning, John, how ya doin' today?" the driver asked.

"Finer than frog's hair, Justin, How 'bout yourself? Besides bein' late, that is?"

"Sorry, John, Willard's car wouldn't start this morning and I had to run by his house to pick him up, so it's all his fault."

"No worries, Justin, just messin' with ya. I want you to meet Max Sanders, the owner of the property."

"Good morning, Max. Understand you need some trees removed and stumps ground. Tell me where and we'll get started."

"Morning to you, too, Justin. Judging by the name on your truck, I assumed your name would be Abe."

"Long story, Max and I'm sure you don't want to hear it."

"Okay, then. Well, John and I have selected a spot right over there," I said, pointing in the general direction to the area to be cleared. We walked over to the spot. "John's gonna be putting an eight-foot by eight-foot shelter here for my boys to use while they wait for the bus in the mornings. And I want eight feet cleared on each side of the building, so we need a cleared area of twenty-four feet by twenty-four feet, coming east from that fence and north from this side of the drive. Think you can handle that?"

"That's a pretty big spot to clear in a day, but most of these don't look too big, so, yeah, I think we can get it all done today."

"My only concern is I need to leave in about half an hour, so I can't have any trees over the drive for a while. Once I'm gone, I probably won't be back until later this afternoon, after three or so."

"Not a problem, it'll take a while to get going anyway and when we do, the first few are pretty small. We should be able to drop 'em right along the edge of the drive and keep 'em outta your way."

"Great. How do you want to handle payment since I'll be gone most of the day and you might be gone before I get back?"

"I'll just leave the bill in your mailbox and you can mail me a check."

"You sure that's okay?"

"Hey, if John says you're good for it, I'll take his word. And if you don't pay me, I'll send another bill to him," Justin laughed.

"Perfect. Thanks Justin, I'll get out of your way and let you get started." I turned to John and signaled him to follow me. We walked to my car and I asked, "You need any money up front for materials to get started?"

"Nah," he answered, "I can handle this, and we'll settle up when we're done."

"If you change your mind, let me know."

"Will do, Max, thanks. I think I got all the info I need. I'll call the lumber yard as soon I get back to my office to get everything ordered. We'll be able to start on the walls in the shop tomorrow morning and two of my guys will be out about nine in the morning to start compacting dirt and settin' the forms for the slab."

"Perfect, John. You have any problems, call me." I hopped in the Flex and headed back to the house. I saw John talking to Justin in the rearview mirror as I pulled away.

When the time came, I grabbed the envelope with the shredded picture in it and headed to Sherman to meet with Ed. I was hoping he would be able to pull off a bit of photographic magic. True to his word, Justin had kept the drive open, so I didn't have any problems getting out of the drive and I waved to Justin and Willard as I rolled by. When I entered the studio forty-five minutes later, I saw Ed was still working with the couple from their shoot, so I browsed the studio admiring his work.

When the couple finally left, Ed turned to me, "You must be Max. Nice to meet you," he said as he extended his hand.

I shook his hand while saying, "That's me, good to meet you, too. I hope you can help me."

"Well, bring it over here and let's see what we're dealing with." We walked over to the counter and I emptied the envelope's contents onto the glass. "Oh, my, they really did a number on this. However, it looks like they used a pair of scissors or a knife on it instead of just ripping it. That should make it a bit easier to achieve a good result. Let's get all the pieces flipped over."

We spent a minute turning pieces over and arranging them a bit to create the border. There was a small studio logo visible in the bottom right-hand corner piece of that border. "This picture is one of mine!" Ed exclaimed, "That's my logo." Then, Ed's hand flew out, picked up a stray piece of the picture and pulled it up close to his nose. He stared at the fragment for a moment, then looked at me with a strange look of wonder and concern. "Can I ask the name of the boys this picture belongs to?"

"Sure," I said, "they're Joey and Alex Allison. I have no idea what the parent's names are, though."

"That's it!" he exclaimed. "I'll be right back," he quickly added as he disappeared into his office. True to his word, Ed returned in a few minutes carrying his laptop and a CD-ROM disk. He set the laptop on the counter and inserted the disk. In a few moments, we were looking at a screen full of thumbnails. Ed double-clicked one and it opened to fill the screen. "I bet this is the picture we have in pieces before us." On the screen were a handsome young man and woman and I could see the resemblance to both boys in their parents.

"My god, Ed, how did you figure that out so quickly?"

"Well, my logo on the corner was the first clue. But, when I saw this," he continued, holding the piece he'd picked up in front of my face, "I recognized this locket. The name just wouldn't come to me."

"I'm guessing we don't have to put the rest of the puzzle together then, do we?"

"Nope. I can reprint the picture from the original on the disc. I'm so glad I started storing my work on CDs. It makes reprints a piece of cake."

"When was this picture taken, Ed?"

He squinted at the screen and replied, "The date on the file is a little over four years ago. Why?"

"Well, the boy's parents were killed in an auto accident right about the same time. These may very well be the last pictures ever taken of them."

"Oh, my God!"

"Well, since you have the original, how soon can I get the reprint?"

"Do you have an hour?"

"Sure."

"Get comfy in one of the chairs over there and I'll get it going for you right now. How big do you want it?"

"Well, the original's an eight by ten, so I think the same size would be fine. Can we look at the other pictures real quick? I may want to get some more."

"Sure." We continued scrolling through all the pictures on the disk and found an excellent outdoor shot of Mr. and Mrs. Allison, along with two mischievous looking young boys standing in front of them. "Oh, my, I'd forgotten the boys were with them that day, but now that I see them, I remember them all too well."

"Let me guess, they were a handful, weren't they?" I chuckled.

"You know it. Those two were all over the place. It was all the parents could do to get them to stand still for this shot. I'm just glad they weren't wearing white that day 'cause they sure wouldn't have stayed that way." Ed laughed at the memory and I laughed with him.

"I can tell you that they haven't changed a bit. Tell you what Ed, why don't you give me a sixteen by twenty of this picture also, and a five by seven of each of the others?"

"I'll be happy to do it, Max. It'll take a little longer, though."

"No rush, Ed. Do you have some frames for the two bigger pictures?"

"Of course, I do. Let me get the prints running and I can show you what I have. We can pick the frames you want, and I'll have the pictures in them as soon as they're done printing." Ed disappeared into his office and returned shortly with a couple different brochures showing the different frames he stocked. "Okay, the printer's running and here's a brochure to see the frames I stock." I perused the selection and settled on two different ones. I selected a rather basic frame for the picture of their parents alone and a slightly more ornate one for the family photo. I hoped the twins would approve of my choices.

As Ed promised, the pictures were all printed, framed and ready to go in an hour and a half. "What's the damages, Ed?" I asked.

"No charge, Max."

"What are you talking about?"

"Exactly what I said, no charge."

"You can't do that. I expected to pay for these when I walked in here and I'm not walking out without doing so. So, give me a total or get ready for a long-term guest."

"Consider it my gift to the boys in congratulations for being adopted. They've been through so much, losing their parents at such a young age, it's the least I can do. I'm giving you a copy of the CD, too, and you have my permission to reprint any picture on it."

"I appreciate the thought, but that's not how I work, Ed. I expect to pay my share wherever I go. If you don't want to keep the money yourself, donate it to a good cause, but I *am* paying you for these."

"Oh, fine. I know a good charity that can always make good use of some cash." Ed gave me a total for the frames and pictures and I gave him cash as payment so he could do what he wanted with it.

"Now that that's all settled, I want to ask another question. The adoption process is supposed to be finalized in about five or six months and I'd like to get some new family pictures taken when it happens. Are you interested?"

"You bet. I'd love to see those two monkeys again. They probably won't remember me, but I'd still consider it an honor to commemorate the happy occasion."

"That'd be great. If it's okay with the court, I'd like to get some pictures taken during the final hearing and have some more taken at my house at the party afterwards. That won't be a problem, will it?"

"I don't know if the court will allow cameras inside, especially juvenile court, but we can sure ask. The worst they can do is say no. The party afterward is no problem. Where's it going to be?"

"At our home on the other side of Springfield. As we get closer and I have an actual date, I'll let you know and we can firm up arrangements then. Sound good to you?"

"Perfect, Max. I'll look forward to it."

"I'm glad the first two places I talked to weren't interested in helping and I called you. I'd promised Alex and Joey I'd get the picture fixed, but I didn't have a clue how I was going to be able to follow through on the promise. You've saved my ass."

"Glad I could help. Those are lucky boys to be with you. I'll look forward to hearing from you in a few months."

I grabbed the pictures and headed for home, stopping in Springfield for lunch on the way. Since I had a little extra time before I needed to be home to collect the boys when they got off the bus, I also ran by Walmart really quick to pick up an assortment of animated movies I thought the boys would enjoy. After picking out ten movies with the assistance from the department manager, I headed for home, pulled in the drive and waited for the bus. Justin and Willard were still clearing the area for shelter, but it looked like they were close to being done. It was a short wait again today and the bus showed up just a few minutes later. The boys climbed in the car chattering about their day as I waved to Cal.

"What's going on here, Dad?" T.J. asked.

"Just a little something," I deflected. "Don't worry about it. Good day, guys? Any homework tonight?"

"Weird day, Dad," Joey responded.

"What happened?"

"Mr. Thomas wasn't there, and we had a substitute."

"Was he sick? You do know teachers get sick sometimes, don't you?"

"Sure," said Alex, "We've had subs before, but they've always told us the regular teacher was sick."

"They didn't say anything this time except Mr. Thomas wasn't gonna be there and they made it sound like the sub is gonna be here a while," Joey added.

"And we really like Mr. Thomas. He's really cool and one of the best teacher's we've had."

"Well, let me see what I can find out in a little bit. What about you other two?"

"Nothin' for me," T.J. answered.

"Me neither," Mike added sullenly.

"Well, it looks like you have the night off for other things, then," I said as I pulled in the garage. "Come on, let's get inside and you can have a snack."

As always, the promise of a snack got them moving. I knew they'd be distracted for a few minutes as they put their things in their rooms and got comfortable, which would give me time to get the new pictures stashed in the study. I really wanted to give them to Joey and Alex now, but thought I should wait until Tom was home so he could be part of it, also. After stashing the pictures in the study, I went to my room and got undressed, then headed to the kitchen to set up snacks for the boys. When I arrived, the four were already waiting at the counter with expectant looks on their faces. Today's snack was apple slices with milk.

"Boys, I need to make a couple phone calls. Can you amuse yourselves for a bit?"

"Sure thing, Dad," T.J. answered.

"Great, I'll be back shortly."

18

I headed to the study and pulled out the school directory. My first call was to the main office.

Perky and cheerful answered the phone, "New Berlin Schools, how can I help you?"

"Good afternoon, this is Max Sanders. We met yesterday when I came in for a meeting with Ms. Carling."

"Oh, good afternoon, Mr. Sanders, how are you today?"

"I'm not sure. Joey and Alex told me that their teacher, Mr. Thomas, wasn't at school today and they're worried about him. Was he ill today?"

"I'm sorry, Mr. Sanders, I'm not allowed to discuss that situation."

"And what situation is that? According to the boys, he's the best teacher they've ever had, and I hate to see the school lose a good teacher."

"As I said, sir, I can't discuss it."

"Well, may I talk to Ms. Carling, please?"

"I'm sorry, Mr. Sanders, but she's in a meeting that I believe will run quite late. I'll be happy to leave her a message you called."

"Please do, I'd like to find out what's going on."

"I'll let her know you'd like to talk to her. Is there anything else I can do for you today?"

"I guess not. Thanks." We hung up and I picked up the school directory again. I looked up Ken's information, found a home phone for him and dialed the number. After four rings, I got his answering machine or voicemail.

"You've reached Ken Thomas, please leave a message after the beep and I'll return your call as soon as I can."

"Ken, this is Max Sanders, Joey and Alex's dad. The boys just told me that you ..." I was interrupted by the click of someone picking up the phone.

"Mr. Sanders, is that really you?"

"Of course, it is, and please call me Max. Then tell me what's going on. The boys said you weren't at school today and they had made it sound as if the sub was going to be there a while. Are you sick?"

"No, I'm not sick. I'm sure your boys told you Valerie was in my class all afternoon yesterday."

"They did. And they said you didn't seem very happy about it, either."

"I wasn't. That evil witch was looking for some reason to get rid of me. I knew it was going to happen after my little announcement during our meeting. You saw how she reacted."

"I did. Then what happened?"

"After the students were gone for the day, she left and went back to her office. I was just finishing up straightening my desk and getting ready for today when she came back in. She told me that after witnessing my performance for the afternoon and making several phone calls, it was decided that my contract was terminated, immediately. That bitch fired me, just like that."

"She can't do that, can she? Doesn't the school board have to meet to make those decisions?"

"I sure thought so, but she apparently had a conference call with four of the seven members and talked them into canning me. I have no idea what she told them, except it had to be lies. Schools never dump teachers in the middle of a school year unless it's something really major."

"Did she tell you which board members were on the call?"

"She only told me about the board president, wouldn't give me any other names."

"Well, I think I need to make another phone call. Fortunately, the board president is listed in the school directory. Thanks for the info, Ken. I'll make good use of it."

"Max, you don't need to get involved in this."

"Yes, I do, Ken. My sons' educations and futures are at stake and I'm not going to have it screwed up by some misguided and vindictive woman just because she doesn't approve of who we love."

"Well, I wish you good luck, then, 'cause you're going to need it."

"Don't worry about me, Ken. I'm a big boy and I know how to take care of myself. Thanks again for the information. I'll let you know what I find out."

"Thanks, Max."

We hung up and I called the board president at his home.

"Speak," a gruff male voice answered.

"Good afternoon, is this Steve Franklin, the president of the New Berlin school board?"

"It is, who's this?"

"Mr. Franklin, my name is Max Sanders. I am the father of four boys enrolled in your school and I have a question I'd like to ask."

"Go ahead."

"My two oldest told me this afternoon that their regular teacher, Mr. Thomas, was not at work today and they're worried about him. They really like him as a teacher."

"I'm sorry, Mr. Sanders, but I can't discuss personnel matters outside of a board meeting."

"Well, it's my understanding you did just that yesterday afternoon, so you broke your own rules. Now, tell me what's going on."

"No can do."

"Excuse me, Mr. Franklin, but have you ever heard the name Clarence Cantrell?"

"Can't say that I have."

"Well, you should know that he's my attorney. And he's one hard-nosed son-of-a-bitch. I'm prepared to retain him to represent Mr. Thomas in a course of action against the school district, Ms. Carling and the entire school board."

"You can't do that."

"Sure, I can. When Clarence is done with you, you'll all be lucky to get new jobs at Burger King. I believe I know why Ms. Carling instigated this witch-hunt and I intend to stop it right now."

"What are you talking about?"

"Let me explain what happened yesterday." I relayed the reason for my meeting yesterday and how it broke up with no warning. "I believe Ms. Carling fabricated any excuse that she could use to get Mr. Thomas fired yesterday afternoon and I want to know what that reason is. If it's serious enough to get a qualified teacher fired in less than an hour without an actual board meeting, it's bound to come out in the news."

"There won't be any news because the situation's been dealt with."

"There will be news after Mr. Cantrell digs into it, I promise you that.

Do you want to take that risk? Think of the damage that will be done to the district if the board is charged with a false termination. Now, tell me what excuse she used, or my next call is to Mr. Cantrell and I assure you that you, Mr. Franklin, will be his first call."

"Fine. Ms. Carling told us that Mr. Thomas was touching students inappropriately during the afternoon. We can't have that behavior in our school and we acted to protect the students."

"Do you have any other witnesses concerning this supposed behavior, or did you just take her word for it? Did you talk to Mr. Thomas to see what he had to say?"

"We took her at her word. And, no, we didn't talk to Mr. Thomas."

"Would you listen to two students who were in that classroom yesterday afternoon and hear what they have to say?"

"We don't normally do that, especially with third graders. But if you think they can shed some light on the matter, I'll listen to what they have to say."

"Good, we'll be right back." I stuck my head out the study door and called for Joey and Alex to join me. While I waited for them to appear, I switched the phone to speaker so we could all hear what was being said.

"Yeah, Dad, what's up?" Alex asked as the twins came through the door.

"Boys, come here, please. I'm talking to Mr. Franklin, the president of the school board, about what happened in your class yesterday afternoon. Mr. Franklin, I'd like you to meet my sons, Alex and Joey Allison. Say hi, boys."

"Hi, Mr. Franklin," they chimed.

"Hello, boys. Your dad thinks I may have been lied to yesterday afternoon and since you were in the class with Mr. Thomas and Ms. Carling, I'd like you to tell me what you saw."

Joey started, "Well after lunch, Ms. Carling came in, said she'd be observing the class for the afternoon and then she sat in the back of class taking notes of some kind."

"Yeah," Joey added, "Mr. Thomas didn't seem too happy to have her there, either."

"Boys, I need to ask a question that I normally wouldn't ask over the phone, especially of children, but I need an honest answer. Will you promise to tell me the truth?"

"Always, Mr. Franklin. Dad says it's really important to always tell the truth," Alex answered.

"Your dad's right, boys. Lord, I can't believe I'm doing this. Okay boys, here's the question. Did either of see any kind of inappropriate contact between Mr. Thomas and any of the students in the class? Do you know what I'm asking?"

"Yes, sir, we know all about that. I didn't see anything, did you, Joey?"

"Nope. Nothin' like that happened. It couldn't have."

"Why do you say that?" Steve asked.

"Because Mr. Thomas never left his desk after lunch, right, Alex?"

"Yeah, he was either at the board or his desk all afternoon."

"Did any of the other students go up to his desk?" Steve asked.

"No, sir, we were working on math all afternoon, studying for a test we were supposed to have today," Alex reported.

"We both do real good with math, so we kinda let our minds wander when we're supposed to be studying it. I didn't see anybody get anywhere close to his desk," Joey added.

"Thank you, boys, I appreciate your honesty. Can I talk to just your dad again, please?"

"You two run along. Thanks." I waited until they left the room, then closed the door and picked the phone back up. "Now that you've heard from them, what do you think now, Mr. Franklin?"

"I must ask my daughter about this. She is also in Mr. Thomas' class, but I do believe I was lied to yesterday afternoon. Do you have any idea why that may have happened, Mr. Sanders?"

"I have a very good idea. During my meeting yesterday with Ms. Carling and the boys' teachers, I explained that I was gay and there was a good possibility my sons are, also. I was trying to make sure they all knew that I would not allow the boys to be bullied by anyone at the school, including staff, for any reason. When Ms. Carling said it was impossible for them to know that at their ages, I explained when I knew I was gay. When Ms. Carling asked the boys' teachers for their opinions, Mr. Thomas explained that he knew he was gay around the same age as Joey and Alex. At that point, the meeting ended abruptly with Ms. Carling essentially kicking us out of her office."

"So, you believe this all comes down to the fact Mr. Thomas is gay and Ms. Carling doesn't approve."

"That's exactly what I believe. And, if that is, indeed, the case, it's perfect grounds for filing an unlawful termination lawsuit. And I firmly believe Mr. Thomas would win the suit. The damages to the school in terms of financial and personnel costs would be catastrophic, not to mention the damage to its reputation as a good school district."

"I agree with you, Mr. Sanders. I want to thank you for bringing this to my attention. I'm going to talk to my daughter and make a few phone calls myself to see what I can find out. Will you be home this evening in case I have some news to pass along?"

"We're not going anywhere, Mr. Franklin. And I'd love to hear from you. Thank you for your time and I appreciate you hearing us out." We ended our call and I headed out to find the boys. I found them in the twins' room playing UNO.

"Where did you guys find that game?" I asked.

"We had it at the Mueller's. It's one of the few they let us have," Joey answered.

"Great. I used to play that growing up, too. We'll have to play together some time. Alex, Joey, I want to thank you for talking with Mr. Franklin."

They looked at me and Alex asked, "So what's going on?"

"I'm not 100% sure right now, but it looks like Ms. Carling went to great lengths to get your teacher fired yesterday."

"Fired!? Why would she do that, he's a great teacher," Joey yelled.

"I didn't tell you yesterday, but I had a meeting with Ms. Carling and all your teachers to find out what would be expected of me now that I'm your dad. During the meeting, I informed them that I was gay and the four of you probably are, too."

"What!?! Why the hell'd you do that? We ain't told nobody yet."

"Calm down, Joey. I was trying to impress on the four of them that I would not allow anyone to bully you four for any reason, whatsoever. When Ms. Carling didn't react well to that, saying there's no way you could know at your age, I told her when I knew I was gay. Then, Mr. Thomas told her when he knew about himself." I saw Joey and Alex share a knowing grin.

"Ms. Carling kinda lost it and kicked us all out of her office. After school was out, she fired Mr. Thomas."

"I told you he was," Alex said, "but you said no-o-o-o."

"Okay, okay, I was wrong, and you were right. Happy little mister smarty-pants?" Joey whined.

"Very. Ha! Maybe next time you'll believe me," Alex crowed, sticking his tongue out at his brother. "So, what's gonna happen now? Is Mr. Thomas coming back?" he asked, looking back to me.

"Mr. Franklin's going to talk to his daughter, who's also in your class, and then make some phone calls himself. Beyond that, I don't know."

"I sure hope he comes back." Joey said.

I heard the ding of the drive sensor and headed out to see who was here. I was relieved to see the Shelby come down the drive and pull in the garage. "Boys, Uncle Tom's home. Let's get ready for supper." Four lads ran to the kitchen to start setting the table while I waited for Tom. When he came in the door, I met him with a hug and kiss, whispering in his ear, "Glad you're home safe. I missed you."

"Missed you, too, lover." We headed to the kitchen where he was attacked by the four wild monkeys. "Whoa, down boys, I just got here."

"But we missed you, Uncle Tom," cried Mike.

"We were hoping you didn't get hurt." T.J. added.

"I missed you, too. And I'm just fine. If you'll give me a couple minutes, I'm going to hang up my uniform and get comfy. I'll be right back, okay?"

"Hurry, Uncle Tom, it's almost time for supper."

"Two minutes, okay?" He looked at me and asked, "What's for din-din, Boss?"

"I thought we'd have pork tenderloins and fries. Sound okay?"

"Sounds great. Be right back to help." He planted another kiss on my cheek as he headed to the bedroom to get undressed. I had just plugged in the fryer when he returned and I asked him to turn on the oven to keep our food warm as I couldn't fit everything in the fryer at one time. "Boys, we'll need ketchup, mustard and pickles, too. T.J., why don't you get the buns out?" Joey and Alex hopped off their stools and carried the items to the table while T.J. retrieved the buns from the pantry. When I had enough tenderloins and fries for six hungry guys, we took our places at the table. I was really getting used to all of us eating together and was starting to look forward to it every afternoon.

With our appetites sated, the boys cleaned the table and stacked dishes in the sink while Tom and I cleaned up the fryer and associated mess. With that task completed, I asked, "Why don't you four sit at the table for a minute. I have something for you. Tom, come help me." Tom, puzzled look on his face, followed me to the study to retrieve the pictures and new movies I'd picked up earlier. I told him what I had, and he nodded his head in understanding. On our return to the dining room, I laid the wrapped eight by ten picture in front of Joey and Alex and the sack of movies in front of Mike and T.J.

"What's this?" Joey asked.

"Open it and find out. But be careful, it's fragile."

Joey and Alex carefully removed the paper while T.J. and Mike watched intently. When they had removed enough wrapping to recognize what was inside, they both broke down in tears. I walked over to the twins and wrapped my arms around their shoulders.

"How'd you get this?" Joey cried.

"Yeah, it was trashed," sobbed Alex.

"I had some luck today. The man I found to try and repair the picture turned out to be the same guy who took it originally. He still had the original in his files and was able to reprint it. And we have another one for you." I had Tom present them with the sixteen by twenty and we stood back for the unwrapping. The paper was carefully peeled back and the tears started flowing again, dripping on the glass. Tom handed me some paper towels to dry the picture and the twins' faces.

When the tears subsided again, Joey looked to Alex and said, "I remember this," he whispered. "We weren't very good that day."

"Funny you should say that Joey, that's exactly what Ed, the photographer, said."

"I don't 'member it," Alex replied.

"You will, I'll help you."

"Thanks."

"We'll figure out where to hang them later."

"Thanks, Dad, this means a lot to us."

"I'm glad you like them." I looked to Mike and T.J. and asked, "So, did I do okay picking out some movies for you?"

"You did great, Dad, I love the Cars movies," Mike squealed in joy.

"Yeah, these are cool, can we watch one tonight?" T.J. asked.

"Why not? Pick one and we'll get it started."

After some serious debating, they finally agreed on Real Steel with Hugh Jackman and Dakota Goyo. I led them to the theater and while they took their seats, I got the movie going for them. Once they were settled in for the show, I went back to the kitchen to rejoin Tom where I found him wiping tears from his eyes.

"What's wrong, Tom?"

"Nothin'," he mumbled.

"Don't try to bullshit a bullshitter."

"That thing with the pictures is about the nicest thing I've ever seen someone do for someone else. I can't believe you did that."

"Why not?"

"Well, you're gonna be their new dad. I didn't think you'd want a reminder of their real parents around the house anywhere."

"Why wouldn't I. Sure, I'm their new dad, but I'm just continuing the work their real mom and dad started almost nine years ago. I don't want them to ever forget where they came from. While I hate the fact they lost their parents the way they did, deep inside, I'm kinda glad, too. Otherwise, those two wouldn't be here right now. Does that make me a sick, heartless bastard? Probably, but, I'll learn to live with it."

"You're too good to be true, Max, you know that, right."

"Time will tell, Tom."

The phone chose that moment to ring, cutting off any further conversation on the subject.

"Max Sanders," I answered.

"Mr. Sanders, Steve Franklin."

"Good evening, I hope, Mr. Franklin."

"Can we dispense with the 'Mr.'? Call me Steve and, if it's okay, may I call you Max?"

"That depends on what you have to tell me, sir."

"I figured as much. Okay, here's what I've discovered. In my conversation with my daughter, she backs up what your sons told me over the phone and I believe the three of them. She was not at all hesitant to answer my questions, and I'm pretty good at knowing when something doesn't quite have that 'ring of truth' with her. Seems she thought yesterday afternoon was a 'bit off', as she put it, also. After making a few phone calls to relay what I learned from your sons and her and receive more input from the other board members involved in the conference call yesterday, we've come to a decision."

"And what would that be?"

"I just got off a phone call with Mr. Thomas, apologizing profusely to him, and letting him know that we expect him to return to his job as of tomorrow morning."

"Is that really going to solve the problem?"

"That, in itself, won't, but the call I made before talking to Mr. Thomas will."

"Go on, please."

"I called Ms. Carling, told her we had an emergency meeting of all seven members of the school board at my home this evening and by a vote of seven to zero, her contract as principal of the elementary school has been terminated, effective immediately. I am meeting her at nine in the morning to supervise as she removes any personal belongings from her office and then I will personally escort her off the property. The police will also be present to ensure she complies."

"You've had a busy night, Steve. I believe you've come to the correct decision and I thank you for that."

"Ha, I must have said the right thing, you called me Steve."

"Yes, sir, you did, and I did. I always prefer to refer to my friends by their first names."

"I'm glad to hear that, Max. In the interests of fostering that new friendship, would you have time to meet with me in the morning, say around ten? I think the unpleasantness should be over by then."

"I'd be happy to, Steve. I'll look forward to it."

"Excellent, Max. Thank your boys for me and tell them they'll see their favorite teacher again in the morning. Thanks again for bringing this issue to my attention. We can always use input from our student's parents. I hope you and your boys enjoy the rest of your evening and I'll see you in the morning."

"Thanks, Steve, you, too. I'll look forward to meeting you." Tom had been watching and listening to me for the entire conversation, confusion etched deeply on his face.

When I finally hung up the phone, he wasted no time in asking, "What the hell was that all about, Max. Since I could only hear your side of the call, I'm confused." I told Tom what the twins had told me after school and the calls I'd made when we got to the house, then what the call from Steve had been about. "Somebody's been busy tonight, haven't they?"

"I guess so. I'm tired of seeing gay people treated like shit in this country and I guess I've decided to do something about it."

"Good for you. Hope you leave some time for us."

"Don't you worry, I will. Shall we go tell the boys the good news."

The phone rang again and I answered it on the first ring.

"Is this Max?" a shaking voice queried.

"It is, may I ask who's calling?"

"Ken Thomas, Max. I've been trying to get you the last half hour."

"Oh, hi, Ken, are you feeling better about things now?"

"Much better, thanks to you. I don't know what you said to Mr. Franklin, but it worked."

"I just explained the facts of life to him, Ken. He decided he would rather avoid a lawsuit and the resulting publicity by righting the wrong perpetrated on you yesterday."

"Well, it's more than that, Max, way more. Not only did he tell me I was expected back in my classroom in the morning, the board has also authorized a one-time payment of $250,000 to me, and I quote, 'in thanks for not filing a lawsuit we're certain to lose'."

"Good for you, Ken. You deserve it for being abused the way you were. Valerie had no cause for what she did and now she gets to pay for it. Good riddance to bad rubbish."

"I couldn't agree more, Max. Thanks again for your help."

"You'll really need to thank the twins and Steve's daughter for their help. They were the ones who told Steve the truth about what happened yesterday afternoon and got him to see yesterday's event for what it was, a colossal mistake."

"I'll make sure to pass my thanks to those three, also. Well, you guys have a great evening. I have to go wash some clothes so I can go to work tomorrow."

"Good night, Ken. I'll talk to you soon." I ended the call and turned to Tom.

"Ken, huh, is he cute? Do I have competition?"

"Yes, Tom, he's cute, but he's no competition for you. He's the twins' teacher I helped out today and he was just calling to say thanks. And you won't believe what the school board did."

"You mean besides firing and re-hiring him, all in the space of twenty-four hours?"

"Yeah, besides that little faux pas. They're paying him a quarter-million dollars, basically to keep his mouth shut about the whole situation."

"Whoa, bet he loves that."

"I'm sure. Now, shall we give the boys the good news?"

"Let's go. I wanna see this."

We walked to theater where I grabbed the remote and paused the movie. Four boys turned to look at me with daggers in their eyes for interrupting what must be a good show.

"Hey, what's the big idea, Dad?" asked Joey.

"Yeah, it's almost over," added T.J.

"I wanted to tell Joey and Alex some good news, but if the movie's more important, we'll just forget it. Bye." Tom and I turned to leave.

"Come back here and spill it, bucko," Alex called to my back.

I spun back around and said, "Bucko, huh. Now I'm never gonna tell ya. Be nice or you get nothing."

"I'm sorry, Dad, will you please tell us your good news?" Alex whined.

"Since you asked so politely this time, I will. Mr. Thomas will be back at school in the morning. And Ms. Carling will be gone."

"What!? How'd you do that?" Joey asked.

"Yippee!" yelled Alex. "I didn't like that sub at all."

"Actually, I just made a phone call. It was you two and Mr. Franklin's daughter that really made things happen. Since you three told him the same story about what happened in your class Tuesday afternoon, he realized that Ms. Carling had lied to him and the other board members, and they had made a decision based on bad information. They've corrected their mistake. This is a good example of why you should always tell the truth."

"We will, Dad. Thanks," Joey said.

"Okay, I'll let you finish the movie now and when it's over, shut everything down and come out for your snacks."

"Thanks again, Dad," Alex called as we left them to their movie.

Tom and I headed to the living room and sat by the fireplace.

"Well, you've heard about my day, so tell me, how was yours?"

"Unusually quiet. I drove around all day and did nothing but write one speeding ticket."

"Good, I hope the rest of your days on the job are just like today."

"Me, too. I really want to come out the other side in one piece."

"We all want that, Tom. We're both long overdue for something good in our lives."

"What's going on out at the end of the drive. I saw the big, cleared area. You buildin' another house to get away from us all?"

I laughed and answered, "Not a chance, Tom. I'm in for the long haul. No, I'm having a shelter built for the boys to be able to wait for the bus without freezing or getting wet."

"That's a big bus stop. They must have cleared a thirty-foot square area."

"The building's only going to be eight by eight, but I wanted a decent clear space all around it."

"How much is that thing gonna cost?"

"Not a clue. Can't say I really care, either."

"Damn, I don't know if I'll ever get used to that."

"What?"

"Not having to worry about money. I've worked five years as a cop, drive a ten-year-old car and consider myself lucky to have about ten grand in a savings account. And here you are, dropping at least that much just so the boys won't get cold or wet."

"Nothing's too good for our boys, Tom. If I can provide it, I will." Tom started to tear up. "Now what are you crying about?"

"What you just said, 'our boys', I guess it hadn't really hit me just yet.

Hearing you say it just drove it home. I've been pinching myself several times a day since Sunday, making sure all this ain't just a dream. I know it's not, but, sometimes, I have to wonder."

"Nope, not a dream, you big softy. Tom Wright, this is your life." I sat next to him, took his hand in mine and gave him a wet sloppy kiss on the cheek. I immediately heard giggling from behind us and turned to find four hungry boys standing there. "Movie's over, I take it?"

"Yep and we're ready for that snack now," Mike said.

"Okay, kitchen boys, we'll be right behind you. C'mon, softy, we have some hungry monkeys to deal with." I helped him up and we followed the boys to get their snacks. "You guys okay with cookies again tonight?"

"Please," answered T.J.

"And thank you," added Mike.

"Ah, manners, nice to know at least two of my sons have some."

"Hey, we got some, too," complained Joey.

"Yeah, we just don't like to use 'em much," Alex chipped in.

"We're gonna have to work on that, aren't we?"

"Yes, sir," they responded.

I set out the cookies for each while Tom poured their milk. As they munched on their snack, Joey and Alex were enthusiastically talking about Ken being back at school in the morning. I'm sure T.J. and Mike were wanting to add something to the conversation, but the other two wouldn't let them get a word in edgewise.

When all four were done with their snack, I said, "Go brush teeth and jump in bed. Tom and I will be in to say goodnight after we clean up the munchie mess."

They slowly ambled towards their rooms while Tom and I cleaned up and loaded the dishwasher. That small chore completed, I said, "Well, let's go check on the boys and make sure they're settled."

The light in T.J. and Mike's room was off when we entered so I turned on the light on the dresser. The two were curled up together, T.J. holding Mike, sleeping peacefully. We kissed both on their foreheads and headed for the twins' room. They were stretched out on the bed, waiting for us to pull up their covers. After pulling them up to their chins, we leaned over, gave both quick kisses on the forehead and said, "Love you guys. Lights out in five."

"Love you, too, Dad, Uncle Tom," Alex answered.

I quietly closed the door and asked, "You ready for bed big guy?"

"With you? Always. Lead the way, lover," he replied with a slick grin.

I grabbed his hand in mine and led the way to our room. After one last stop in the bathroom, we curled up together for a good night's sleep.

19

Thursday morning dawned with the alarm going off at six. Tom and I were both pretty grumpy this morning as neither of us had slept very well. I stumbled to the bathroom first, then headed to the kitchen to get the caffeine going while Tom used the bathroom and got dressed. With the coffee started, I headed down to wake the boys and get them moving, finding Mike and T.J. curled together and the twins in their normal pretzel configuration. That chore accomplished, I headed back to the bedroom to pull on some sweats and check on Tom.

"How ya doin' this morning, big guy?"

"I'm ready to roll."

"That's the spirit. Now, let's go attack our day."

"Point me to some coffee and I'll make a concerted effort."

"Follow me and I'll get you all set up."

"To the ends of the earth, lover."

Tom followed me to the kitchen where he greeted the boys and poured himself a cup of coffee.

"Morning, boys, cereal okay this morning?" I asked. I received four nods and mumbles of acceptance, so I fixed each a bowl and poured myself a cup of coffee, also.

"You guys ready for school?"

"Not really," Joey answered.

"Never will be," Alex chimed.

"Do we have a choice?" asked T.J.

"I'm ready, dad," added Mike.

"No, sorry, you don't have a choice. At least one of you is ready. That's better than none. How 'bout you, Tom, you ready for your day?"

"As ready as I'll ever be," he grumbled.

"C'mon guys, it's a beautiful day. You need to enjoy it."

Tom shook his head and complained, "How can you be so dang cheery in the morning?"

"I'm just glad I woke up this morning. It's so much better than the other option. You eatin' here, Tom, or is it doughnuts again this morning?"

"Doughnuts, what else is there? Breakfast of champions." he laughed. He headed to the garage asking, "Okay if I use your car again today."

"No problem, you still got the key?"

"You bet. You're gonna have to pry that from my cold, dead fingers."

"Hey, aren't you forgetting something, mister?"

"Well, just where are my manners?" He returned to the kitchen, gave us all a kiss and said, "Hope y'all have a good day. Boys, learn something new at school," receiving moans from the four monkeys, then added, "Max, don't tilt any windmills today, okay?"

"Only if they get in my way. I don't go looking for trouble, ya know."

"I know, but it seems to find you, anyway. Love you all and I'll see you tonight."

A chorus of 'love you, too, Uncle Tom' from the boys followed Tom down the hallway.

"You guys about ready to roll? We're running out of time. Grab your stuff and I'll meet you in the garage." I headed to the bedroom to get a shirt and shoes, then headed to the garage. The boys were already loaded in the car and belted, so I climbed in, backed out of the garage and headed to meet the bus. When we arrived, I noticed John's guys hadn't shown up yet to start work on the compacting and forms. That wasn't a big surprise, really, as it was only seven-twenty and I didn't expect them to be here until nine, according to John.

"Tell us what's going on over here, dad," Alex said as he pointed out the window.

"Can't, it's a surprise. You'll just have to wait to find out."

"That's not fair, man. You're supposed to always tell the truth," Joey tossed out.

"I am telling the truth. It's a surprise and you'll just have to wait to find out."

"That ain't right," Alex muttered.

"Okay, everybody out, here comes your ride." We got out of the car and I gave each boy a hug before the bus stopped. They climbed aboard after Cal opened the door and I gave them a wave. As the bus pulled away, I got back in the car and turned back to the house to wait for my meeting with Steve at the school.

I read by the fireplace until it was time to leave. John's guys had shown up and were compacting the dirt in preparation for placing the forms for the floor slab and I gave them a wave as I rolled by. I arrived at the school about five minutes early for my meeting and found one of the town's police cars still parked in front of the school, lights flashing. I was just in time to see Valerie carrying a box and being escorted to her car by a man I can only assume was Steve. I waited in my car until she had left the parking lot to avoid meeting her and after she and her car disappeared around the corner, I got out and headed inside for my meeting. I found perky and cheerful behind her desk in the office with a smile on her face.

"Ah, good morning, Mr. Sanders, I understand we have you to thank for this morning's change in personnel. Such a glorious day. It should have happened a long time ago."

"I know not what you speak of."

"Huh? Oh, I get it. Funny. You're here for a meeting with Mr. Franklin, correct?"

"I am."

"Go on in, he's expecting you."

"Thanks." I entered Valerie's former office to find a rather large man sitting at the desk. "Good morning, you must be Mr. Franklin, I'm Max Sanders," I said in greeting as I extended my hand.

Steve came from behind the desk, grasped my offered hand in both of his large, meaty and calloused hands for a long handshake. "Good morning, Max. It's a pleasure to meet you, face to face. I want to sincerely say thank you on the behalf of the entire school board and the district. You have saved us from what would have certainly been a very costly and embarrassing chapter in the district's proud history." He waved me to a chair and added, "Please, have a seat. And remember, it's Steve."

"Thanks, Steve. It's a pleasure to meet you, too. I trust Ken is back in his classroom this morning."

"He is, and very happy to be there. He should be after what we did for him."

"You mean allowing him to retain his job or buying his silence?"

"Both, I guess, although I prefer to not refer to the monetary gift as 'buying his silence'. Tuesday's events are still quite unsettling. I'd never dreamed Valerie was capable of such destructive thoughts and actions."

"Well, hopefully, you won't have to worry about that any longer."

"Oh, no, it'll come back to haunt us. As I was escorting her out of the building, she was vehemently protesting her ouster and promising to file a lawsuit against the district. For unlawful termination, of all things. Guess she should know all about that."

"Yes, no doubt. I'm sorry for inciting all this, Steve. I never intended for anyone to lose their job. Had I known that would happen, I would have kept my mouth shut."

"Don't worry about it, Max, it's water over the dam now. We'll deal with it and move forward."

"So, what can I do you for you. You wanted to meet me for a reason."

"I did, and I thank you for agreeing to come in. Especially after what has transpired. First, I wanted to ask if you're the author, Maxwill Sanders, or is the name a coincidence?"

"Nope, no coincidence, I'm the author."

"Excellent. Have you had any college or background in education?"

"Actually, I was writing my first book as I went to the U of I to get my teaching degree. I'd always planned on being a teacher, family curse, I guess."

"Your family was in education?"

"Yes, my mom and dad were both teachers, and I guess I felt I felt obligated to follow in their footsteps. Unfortunately, I never finished my degree. I dropped out the last semester as the book had been released and my travel schedule to promote it was causing me to miss too many classes. I figured I'd be better off dropping out than failing."

"You were right about that. Colleges don't look too kindly on folks who fail. Have you ever thought about returning to complete your studies?"

"Not really. After the success of the first book, I just kept writing. Teaching didn't have the same allure that it had before."

"Would you consider it? Finishing your degree, that is?"

"I suppose, what are you thinking?"

"I'd like to hire you as a high school English and advanced literature teacher. It would do wonders for the district to have such an esteemed author on staff."

"Whoa, Steve. I'm not too sure about all that. I have a lot of changes happening in my life right now and my first priority is to make sure the four boys I'm in the process of adopting are taken care of properly. I'm starting to think I may have bitten off more than I can chew."

"I understand, Max. But please think about it. Now, may I ask you a personal question?"

"Feel free to ask, but I may not give you an answer."

"No pressure, Max, just curiosity."

"Shoot."

"If I heard everything correctly last night, you're gay. Is that correct?"

"It is. Do you have a problem with that?"

"Not at all. And from what you just said, you're also in the process of adopting four boys."

"Also, true. May I ask where you're going with this?"

"Simply, it was my understanding that the state and adoption agencies wouldn't allow a single gay man to adopt, especially a gay man adopting boys. Can you explain why it's being allowed in your case?"

"As I mentioned in our call last night, according to my case worker, Carol Ward, all four boys, despite their ages, have shown that they are most likely gay, also. Carol has been trying for quite a while to find a home where they could grow up to understand and embrace who they are. When I showed up, looking to adopt, she said she'd finally found it."

"May I ask the names of the other two boys? I kind of met Joey and Alex on our phone call, but you didn't name the others."

"T.J. Stults who's in the second grade and Mike Bell who's in first grade. Why do you ask?"

"Well, I'm going to make sure that your boys aren't abused by anyone while they're at school, be it other students or the staff."

"I thank you for that, Steve, but why?"

"My sister is a lesbian with a daughter who is going through hell because of her mom's sexuality. I am going to make sure you and your boys don't have to go through that."

"Well, guess I have to add another one to the list."

"Excuse me, Max, what list is that?"

"The list of people I've met in the past couple weeks who are either gay or know someone who is."

"You're going to find that list will continue to grow. Now, back to your sons for a moment, if we could. Do you believe they are gay, also?"

"Who knows for sure, Steve? They've only lived with me since Saturday, so we're all still trying to figure things out. From what little I've seen and heard so far, though, I'd have to say it seems highly likely."

"Not to sound like a total idiot, but, as young as they are, could they really know?"

"You're not an idiot, Steve, just uninformed. Like I told Valerie, I knew I was different from other boys around the same age as my sons. If I can know at that age, they can, too. It could just be curiosity, but I tend to doubt it."

"I do, too. I have one more question for you today I'd like you to seriously think about before answering."

"And that is?"

"I want to raise awareness among our staff about gay youth and their acceptance in our school and our lives. In light of that, I'd like to have, for lack of a better word, a workshop with them to discuss the issue and how we can better acknowledge and accommodate our gay students. Your sons can't be the only four enrolled in this school who are or may be gay. If the workshop goes well, I'd like to extend that education to all our students and their families."

"And how would that affect me?"

"I'd like you and your sons to be involved."

"How?" I asked with a look of surprise on my face.

"I guess as an example of how things should be."

"While I applaud your desire to do this, I hardly think I'm the right guy to hold up as an example. I've only recently accepted who I am and I'm not really ready to start sharing it *that* openly."

"May I ask how many people you've trusted with the news so far, and what their reactions have been?"

"I'm not sure, let me think." I took a few moments to come up with a number for him. "I'd guess about eighteen or twenty so far. Reactions have been about seventy-five percent positive, twenty-five percent negative. Of course, two of those negatives are my own parents."

"And for the people who've read your books and are anxiously awaiting the next one, how do you think they'll react when they find out?"

"Who knows, hopefully no worse than what I've seen so far."

"Well, regardless of your answer, I'm going to push ahead with it. Teen suicide for gay youth due to a lack of positive role models is extremely high. With my personal connection with the issue, I feel a need to combat that problem and the only way to do so is to face the issue head on. I intend to do just that and would truly appreciate your assistance in making a positive change in our small corner of the world. We've been lucky here so far, and I want that to continue."

"I'll have to give this some thought and give you my decision later."

"Oh, I didn't expect an answer this morning. Take your time. I'd like to meet with our teachers in a few weeks, so, the sooner the better."

"Thanks, Steve. Is that it?"

"One last thing before we break up. When your adoption is finalized, I assume you are going to have a party to celebrate."

"You know it," I grinned.

"If I'm not being too forward, I would like to join the celebration."

"I'll be sure to include you and your family on the guest list," I laughed.

Steve stood, signaling an end to our meeting, "Again, thanks for bringing this gross injustice to my attention. I'm glad we could resolve the situation in a positive manner. If you ever need anything, don't hesitate to call me."

"Would it be acceptable if I stopped by Mr. Thomas' classroom on my way out?" I asked as we walked out of the office. "I'd like to see how he's doing."

"Of course, I'm sure he'd appreciate it."

"Which way?" I asked as we stepped into the hallway.

"Let me take you there. It's kind of hard to find it in this maze we laughingly call a school." I followed Steve as he led the way through the building's various additions until we reached Ken's classroom. He knocked lightly and pushed the door open. "Mr. Thomas, I have someone here who would like to see you. Do you have a moment?"

"Sure," he responded. "Class, I'll be right back." He started towards the door while Steve stood aside and gave me a gentle push through the door. When Ken saw who was there, he scooted over and wrapped me in a bear hug. In the background, I heard two voices say 'Dad?' while I heard Ken whisper in my ear, "Thank you so much. I owe you big time."

"Don't worry about it. Glad I could help." As we separated, I could see tears in his eyes. "Pull yourself together, Ken, we have witnesses," I said as I pointed to the class.

"Oh, crap," he muttered quietly. He turned his back to the students and quickly dried his eyes. That task completed, he turned back to the class and said, "Class, you owe your thanks for me being back today to this man. Well, him, his sons, Joey and Alex, and Mr. Franklin's daughter, Andrea." A round of light clapping ensued and Joey, Alex and Andrea stood to accept it.

"I'll get out of here and let you get back to work, Ken. Congratulations."

"Thanks again, Max. I'll be in touch."

I waved to the boys and headed to the door where Steve waited. As we headed down the hall towards the front door, I told Steve, "Let me talk to my sons and boyfriend tonight about your proposal and I'll let you know our decision tomorrow."

"That's fair, Max. It's a lot to ask, I know, but I think we stand a better chance of success with a person of your stature being involved with the program. If your partner could be involved, that would be wonderful."

"I think he's going to be pretty iffy. His job may not allow it, but I'll ask."

"What does he do?"

"At this moment, he's a Sangamon County deputy, but he's just turned in his resignation and has two more weeks on the job."

"Is it a true resignation or is it one of those 'resign or be fired' types since he's gay?"

"Oh, no, it's entirely his decision. His boss is okay with Tom being gay."

"You must be taking about Dylan."

"Yeah, you know him?"

"He's been to the school on several occasions to talk to the students about driving safety. Seems to be a good man."

"He is."

"Let me talk to him. I'm sure he'll be willing to help with the workshop, also."

"If you can get him involved, you can count on me to be there, too. I don't know about my sons or Tom, but, like I said, we'll talk about it tonight and I'll let you know."

"Thanks, Max, I appreciate it. I really want this to succeed." We'd reached the door to the parking lot and Steve added, "Thanks for coming in this morning. And, again, for helping me correct a major mistake."

"No thanks necessary, Steve. A bad decision was made based on bad information. I'm just glad we were able to fix it before it went on too long. Thanks for listening to my sons and believing what they said."

"I hated to drag them, and my daughter, into an adult situation, but it seemed appropriate at the moment. I'll look forward to hearing your decision on the workshop. Have a great afternoon, Max."

"Thanks, Steve, you, too."

I left the school and headed for home, stopping at the end of the drive to talk to John's guys. "How's it going, guys?"

"Good, Mr. Sanders. We finally got the dirt compacted where the shelter's gonna sit and we're starting to set the forms for the floor slab."

"You got the right spot?"

"Pretty sure we do, but since you're here, you want to check it real quick to make sure?"

"Why not?" I got out of the car and walked over to check the location. "It looks like you might be closer to the drive than I intended, but that's okay. Do you have enough form material to set up for a sidewalk to the drive?"

"We should. Didn't plan on it, but this would be the time to do it. Where's the door going to be?"

"This corner, right here," I answered as I pointed to the location.

"No problem. It's only about six feet to the drive. You want it three feet wide?"

"That should be good. Make sure you tell John about the change so he can charge me more," I laughed. "No seriously, I want to make sure he orders enough concrete to pour the floor and walk at the same time. No sense trying to get a truck out for just the walk later."

"I'll make sure to let him know when we get back. Anything else, Mr. Sanders?"

"Nope, I'll get out of your way. If you need anything, drink, bathroom, whatever, come on down to the house. I'll be home the rest of the day."

"Will do. See ya later."

I hopped back in the car and drove on to the house, parking the car in the garage. I decided that for once, I would keep my clothes on since I may have unexpected company later if John's guys needed something. For some odd reason, the thought popped in my head that I had no idea what the boys' birthdays were. I decided I needed to fix that lapse of knowledge and called Carol.

"Carol Ward, how may I help you?" she answered the phone.

"Carol, Max here, how are you today?"

"Great, Max. Not having second thoughts, are you?"

"Not a chance. But I just realized I haven't been a very good dad just yet."

"Well, I think you've done just fine. What horrible thing have you done that puts you in the 'bad dad' category?"

"I don't have a clue when the boys' birthdays are. I can hardly have parties for them when I don't know when to have them, can I?"

She laughed and said, "I knew I was forgetting something else, now I know what it is. This all happened so quickly, I didn't have time to create the information folder we usually put together for all our new parents. Please don't fire me, Max."

"Not a chance, Carol. I still need your help," I chuckled.

"Give me just a sec to grab their files." I heard the rustling of papers as she dug through her desk. "Okay, got 'em. Ready?"

"Ready and waiting."

"Okay, Joey and Alex's birthday is March thirteenth, T.J.'s is April twenty-third and Mike's is May fifth."

"Glad I called when I did. Looks like the first party will be happening in three weeks. We'll expect you to be here."

"I wouldn't miss it. Anything else you need?"

"Well, since you asked, I do want to run something by you, see what you think. Got a few minutes?"

"Always have time for you."

"Good." I relayed the information on the workshop Steve wanted to have at the school about supporting gay youth. "So, what do you think? And more importantly, what do you think about me and or the boys being involved?"

"I think that's a wonderful idea. Teen suicide among gays is becoming an epidemic and something needs to be done. I don't have a problem with you being involved, but it might be asking a bit too much of the boys right now."

"I was feeling that way about T.J. and Mike, but I think Joey and Alex would be fine. I know they're only eight, almost nine, but they certainly seem to know who they are and the path their lives are taking."

"Now that I think about it, you're right, those two would probably be okay, but I'd keep the other two out of it. For now, anyway."

"Thanks, I plan to talk to them tonight and see what they have to say. I'll let you know what we decide."

"Thanks for the call, Max. Be sure you let me know when the party is."

"I will, Carol. Thanks for the info and have a great evening."

We hung up and I grabbed the book I'd been reading on the way to my favorite chair by the fireplace. I was interrupted about an hour later by a ring of the doorbell. It had to be one of John's guys because the drive sensor hadn't gone off. I opened the door to find both men standing on the porch.

"Sorry to bother you, Mr. Sanders, but could we please use a restroom? It's a little too cold out here to just whip it out and pee on a tree."

I laughed and said, "Sure, down the hall there, last door on the right."

One took off for the john and I asked the one waiting his turn, "You guys want some coffee to help warm up a bit?"

"I wouldn't turn down a cup, and he'd probably like one, too."

"Be right back." I headed to the kitchen and returned shortly with a Styrofoam cup for each of them, noticing the two had swapped places. "How ya doin' out there?"

"Just about done, sir. Got the floor area formed and we're getting ready to do the walk now. Since we hadn't started the forms when you stopped by, we moved it a couple feet further from the drive so it should be closer to where you want it. We're nice and square so when we bring the building out, we should be able to just drop it in place."

"That sounds great. Any idea when the concrete will be poured?"

"I think John's scheduled it for next Monday, depending on the weather. We'd like the temp to be above freezing when we do it and Monday's supposed to be forty degrees or so."

"How soon can you set the shelter in place after it's poured?"

"That's scheduled for the next Monday. John wants give the concrete at least a week to set."

"Sounds like he has it all planned out. Thanks for the info." His work partner returned, and I handed his cup of coffee to him.

"Thanks, Mr. Sanders, I needed that," he said pointing down the hall. "Need this, too," he added, holding up his cup. "Okay, let's get out of here and get this done. See ya later, sir."

"Thanks guys, have a good evening," I said as they headed back out into the cold. I headed back to the fireplace to continue my reading. At three-thirty, I decided to head out to meet the bus and check on John's guys. When I arrived at the end of the drive, they were already gone. I got out to check their work and once satisfied everything looked ready for concrete, climbed back in the warm car to wait. I didn't sit there long as the bus pulled up three minutes later, disgorging four laughing boys.

They eagerly climbed in the car and we started the short trek to the house.

20

As we headed toward the house, I asked what was quickly becoming my daily question.

"Did you guys have a good day, and do you have any homework?"

"Ours was great," Joey started, "since Mr. Thomas is back."

"Yeah, thanks for helping him, Dad," said Alex. "Oh, and no homework for us since we had the math test today."

"I have to review my spelling words for our test tomorrow. Will you go over them with me, Dad?" T.J. asked.

"I'll be happy to, T.J. What about you, Mike?"

"No, I'm good," he mumbled in response.

"Something wrong, munchkin?"

"Not really. Nothin' you can fix, anyway" he said as I pulled into the garage.

When we got inside the house, I said, "Mike, why don't you come tell me what's going on while the other three hang out in their rooms for a minute?" I nodded my head towards the twins' room and saw Joey, Alex and T.J. duck in while Mike and I headed to the living room to sit by the fireplace. I took my favorite chair and had Mike climb up in my lap. When we were both seated and comfortable, I started with, "Okay, young man, I can tell something's bugging you. If you won't tell me what it is, I can't do anything to help."

"It's just these other boys in my class. They keep picking on me. They been doin' it ever since I started comin' to school out here."

"Ah, yes. Mrs. Young said something about that during our meeting Tuesday and with everything else that happened, apparently nothing has been done to correct their behavior. What're their names and I'll see if I can do something about it?"

"Andy, Mark, and Billy. I try to stay away from them so they won't bug me, but it don't matter what I do or where I hide, they find me."

"Now that I know who's causing the problem, maybe I can help fix it."

"Okay, Dad, thanks. The teacher tried. She even moved them to the other side of the room, but they still find me."

"Okay, run along, get comfy and tell your brothers it's time for a snack. I'll make a call about the problem while you eat your cookies." He hopped off my lap and headed down the hall to tell the others it was time for snacks. When the four came charging into the kitchen, I already had their milk and cookies laid out and ready for them. Once they were seated, I said, "Eat your snack while I get comfy and make a phone call. T.J., find your spelling word list and we'll work on them when I get done."

"Okay," he called to my back as I headed down the hall.

I called the school, and perky and cheerful answered the phone, "New Berlin Schools, may I help you?"

"Good afternoon, it's Max Sanders, is Mr. Franklin still around?"

"Oh, hi again, Mr. Sanders. He was just about to leave, hang on."

I was put on hold for a brief moment before Steve answered, "Afternoon, Max, what's up? You make a decision on the workshop already?"

"No, Tom's not home yet. Sorry to bother you this late, but I have another small issue I'd like to discuss if you have a couple minutes. With everything else that's happened, I'd forgotten all about it."

"I've got all the time the for world for you, my friend."

"One of the things that was briefly discussed with Valerie and my sons' teachers Tuesday was a few boys in Mike's class have decided he's a good target for getting picked on. Anita said she's tried to stop the problem and has moved the boys in question to the other side of the classroom, but Mike reminded me tonight they're still causing a problem. Valerie had said she would deal with the issue Tuesday after lunch, but she ended up with bigger fish to fry. I was hoping you might be able to help ease the problem."

"That's the least I can do for you after what you did for us. Do you have the names of the boys involved?"

"Mike tells me it's three boys named Andy, Mark and Billy, no last names."

"Are they doing this because they think Mike's gay?"

"No, I don't think it has anything to do with that. I'm pretty sure it's just because he's the new kid in class and smaller than they are, so he won't fight back."

"I shouldn't need last names, Anita will know who they are. I'll deal with this first thing in the morning, Max. Thank you for bringing it to my attention."

"Please let me know if there's anything I can do. Thanks, and have a great evening, Steve."

"You, too. I hope to hear your decision on the workshop tomorrow."

I hung up and when I returned to the kitchen, found the snack plates and glasses rinsed, stacked and waiting in the sink. I got them in the dishwasher and headed off to find T.J. to review his word list. I found him in his room, hugging a crying Mike.

"Mike, what's wrong?" I asked as I pulled him into my lap after sitting on the bed.

"I just get tired of those jerks. I don't know why they won't leave me alone. They been on me almost every day since I got here."

"Well, hopefully, it will stop soon. I just got off the phone with Mr. Franklin and he said he would talk to them first thing in the morning and he'd let me know what happens."

"I hope he makes them quit. I can't take much more of it."

"Don't worry, son, we'll take care of it. Why don't you go play with the twins for a few minutes so I can work with T.J. on his spelling words, okay?"

"Sure, Dad." He shuffled out of the room looking for the other two.

"C'mon, young man, let's get this done with." I sat on the edge of the bed with T.J. sitting right next to me and I started giving him words to spell. When we reached the end of the list, he had missed only two out of twenty words on the list. I asked him to write each word ten times for practice and we'd check them again after supper. I was headed to the kitchen to start preparations for supper when I heard the drive sensor go off. I stopped at the front door just in time to see the Shelby pulling in the drive towards the garage. Tom was home in one piece again tonight, thankfully, and I continued to the kitchen to start supper.

"Honey, I'm home!" echoed through the house as he came in from the garage. Cheers followed his announcement and as I stuck my head out of the kitchen, I saw Tom getting mugged by four rowdy lads. When they finally released him from their grasp, he headed to see me in the kitchen. "I've always wanted to say that. Hey, lover, how was your day? And what's for supper?"

"Right for the heart, as usual. I had a great day and lasagna with garlic bread. How was your day?"

"Sounds delish. Another successful day as a cop. Didn't get shot and didn't have to shoot nobody."

"I'll be glad when I don't have to worry about you being out there every day."

"You and me both. The boys, too, I'm sure. They 'bout squeezed the stuffing out of me just now."

"That's just 'cause you're just a big damn softy." We kissed each other on the cheek. "Why don't you get comfy and come back. We have something new to talk about this evening."

"Oh, shit, here it comes," he laughed as he turned towards our bedroom and I laughed along with him this time. I got the lasagna in the oven and when he returned, I had him gather the boys so we could talk. We settled around the fireplace for our discussion, four grumpy boys and one uncertain adult.

"This is good talk for once, so turn those frowns upside down, please." I got half-smiles before I continued. "You all know I met with Mr. Franklin this morning at the school. He has proposed something I think we should be involved with, but I want to hear what you think."

"After the way they treated Ken, I'm not too sure about that," Tom commented.

"*That* wasn't his or the board's doing, that was all Valerie. Actually, he came up with the idea because of Valerie's shenanigans. He would like to hold a workshop with the school's staff to enlighten them about the issues faced by gay youth and the problem of teen suicide due to coming to terms with that. He's asked me to be involved in the workshop, along with the boys and you, Tom, if you're interested."

"Dad, what's suicide?" asked T.J.

"It's when someone is so sad, they take their own life."

"That's horrible," Alex said.

"Yes, it is. That's why Steve wants to do the workshop."

"But why does he want us involved?" asked Tom.

"Obviously, so we can relate what it's like to be gay in this country. I think he considers us a positive role model of how things *should* be. He thinks that since I'm gay and now raising gay sons, we can provide a first-person point-of-view the staff hasn't had the opportunity to see and know."

"But, Dad," Joey started, "we haven't told anybody we're gay yet."

"Yeah, and I don't think we're ready to," Alex added.

"You don't have to go if you don't want to. But I still want you to think about it. Remember Steve and your teachers already know because of what's happened the last couple days. They've promised me they won't say anything to anybody, but once I stand up and tell the rest of the staff about myself, you know they're going to start wondering about you, too. It'll only be a matter of time before they figure things out for themselves."

"I'll do it," T.J. stated flatly. "I don't care who knows."

"Are you sure? That's a big step to take, especially in front of a crowd."

"Yeah, I'm sure. I want them to know kids our age *can* know we're gay. Most people don't think we can."

"It's your choice, T.J. If you want to be there, I'll be glad to have you with me. What about you, Mike? What do you think?"

"Huh-uh, I don't want no part of it."

"That's fine, son. This isn't mandatory." I had noticed Tom had been very quiet so far so I looked to him and asked, "What about you, big guy?"

"I don't know, Max. When's this supposed to happen. I don't want to do anything that could have any effect on my job."

"Probably two weeks from now, after you're done being a cop. And I should warn you that Steve knows Dylan and said he was going to call and ask him to be involved, too."

"You're kidding me. Why the hell would he do that? Do you think he knows Dylan is gay?"

"That's not the impression I got, but who knows? He said Dylan's been to the school several times to do a presentation on driver safety. I think he wants to get a law enforcement perspective involved to provide some statistics along with what parents and teachers should be aware of to help prevent suicides."

"I guess that makes sense. I'm sure I'll hear about it tomorrow when I see him."

"No doubt about it." I looked back to the boys and said, "Okay T.J.'s in, Mike's not, Tom's a maybe. What about you two? Have you thought about it yet?" I asked looking to the twins.

They looked at each other, shrugged their shoulders, and looked back to me.

"We're in. This is more important than keeping who we are a secret," Joey answered.

"Yeah, and like you said, it won't stay hidden very long, will it?" Alex asked.

"Probably not. If you both accept who you are, there's no real reason to hide it. I'm proud of you and I'll be happy to have all the backup I can get. Okay, I'll call Steve in the morning and let him know our decision. I'll leave you as a maybe, Tom, until I hear from you."

"Can we eat now?" Mike asked.

"Now, there's a lad after my heart," Tom piped in. "I'm starved."

"Okay, okay," I caved. "Boys, would you set the table and get the drinks, please? You four can have soda, if you'd like, but I'd like a Corona, please," I added as we all headed to the kitchen.

"Same for me, please," Tom said.

"Tom, would you get a basket and put the bread in it? I'll pull the lasagna out of the oven and get it cut."

"Lasagna?? I love that stuff," Mike yelled as he grabbed the silverware.

"That's good to hear, Mike. Do you like parmesan cheese on it?"

"What's that?"

"It's a finely grated cheese a lot of people add to pasta and pizza."

"Don't think I've ever had it but I'll try it."

"Excellent. I think you'll like it."

With everyone working together, we were ready to eat in very short order. I sprinkled a little parmesan on a corner of Mike's lasagna so he could try it before I covered the whole piece. After one bite, he begged for more, so I covered the rest of plate with a light dusting.

"That's yummy, Dad. Thanks."

"Glad you like it. Well, dig in people."

By the time everyone was done stuffing their faces, the lasagna was all gone, along with the bread, ruining my plan of having leftovers for lunch tomorrow. The boys got busy cleaning the table, then rinsing and stacking the dishes in the sink. I took care of the lasagna pan and Tom cleaned up the rest.

During the process, I called out, "T.J., between."

"Huh?" he answered with a confused look on his face.

"Your spelling word, between, spell it."

"Oh, yeah, b-e-t-w-e-e-n."

"Perfect, now around."

"A-r-o-u-n-d."

"Right, again. Good job. I think you're ready for your test tomorrow."

"I hope so."

"You'll do just fine, young man." We sat back at the table and I started a new conversation with, "I called Carol earlier and she gave me some very important information she had neglected to pass on when she was here this past weekend."

"What's that, Dad?" T.J. asked.

"I understand we have a birthday coming up soon."

"Really, who and when?" Tom asked.

Joey and Alex raised their hands while grinning wildly.

"There ya go. The big day is March thirteenth and they'll be nine this year. Anything special you'd like to do, guys."

"Can we have a party?" Alex asked.

"Yeah, the Muellers never let us have a party," Joey complained.

"I think a party is a grand idea. Since the thirteenth is a Thursday this year, we'll have the party on Saturday, though. I know Carol wants to be here for it. Are there any friends you'd like to have come over?"

"You bet. How many can we have?"

"Give me a list of ten to twelve kids, I'll contact their parents and make sure they're all invited. Now, what kind of cake do you like?"

"Chocolate for me," Alex said, "with chocolate icing."

"White with white icing for me," Joey added.

"Okay, we can do that. And we now have another way to tell which of you is Alex and which is Joey. We'll have either two cakes or a half and half cake. I'll talk to a bakery and get that taken care of. Now, what's missing?" I asked.

"Decorations!" yelled Mike.

"Drinks!" was T.J.'s contribution.

"Presents!!" yelled Joey and Alex.

"Ear plugs and body armor," Tom said as he added his two-cents worth with a grin.

"I'll make sure to add those to the list, Tom," I laughed. "Now, do you think you'll want to swim? If so, I'll need to make sure we have someone on hand who's a certified lifeguard. While Tom and I can handle the four of you with no problems, sixteen screaming kids in the pool will require more attention than we have."

"Well, duh, we'll definitely want to swim, won't we, Alex?"

"You bet. That'll be a bunch a' fun."

"Okay, that's another call I'll have to make. Anything else? Keep in mind, there'll still be snow on the ground and it'll probably be cold, so we'll be inside most of the day."

"How about a movie?"

"That's a good idea, Alex. Anything in particular?"

"We'll have to think about it and let you know," Joey said.

"The sooner, the better, in case you pick something we don't already have. Okay, I think we have the basics set. Get me your list of kids to invite and I'll contact their parents and make arrangements. Now, on to another subject, your rooms."

"What about 'em, Dad?" T.J. asked.

"Well, they're pretty plain. I set them up that way when I had the house built so anyone who spent the night wouldn't be assaulted by wild colors or anything. I think it's time to change that."

"Really, we can do that?" Mike asked.

"Of course, you can. They're your rooms, now, and they should look the way you want them. First, I want to ask if you want to keep sharing the same rooms the way you are now? You two asked about having separate rooms the first time we met," I said while pointing to the twins.

"Joey and I are fine just the way we are, Dad. It might be good to have a separate space, just so we can work on our homework alone or whatever."

"But we still want to sleep in the same bed. We love that bed and we love sleeping together. But a separate space is a good idea. Much as I love Alex, sometimes I just gotta get away from him," Joey laughed.

"Hey!" Alex yelled as he punched his brother's shoulder, "That wasn't funny."

"Here's my idea for you two, then. I know a good builder and I can have him make some changes to the bedroom Carol used to make it the way you want it. When he's done, we'll move you in there. Sound okay?"

"That'd be great."

I turned to T.J. and Mike, "Okay, they're taken care of, what about you two? Do you want stay in the same room together or do you want separate rooms?"

They looked at each other for a moment, exchanged nods and then turned back to me. "I think we want to stay together, Dad, right, Mike?" T.J. answered.

"Yeah, I like the way you hold me close at night. I feel safe when you do that."

"Well, you're my brother, you'll always be safe with me." I could see tears welling in Mike's eyes after that statement.

"Do you want a separate space from each other like Joey and Alex."

"That'd probably be a good idea, Dad. Especially since our homework is different. I'll still help Mike when I can, but it'll be good to have our own desks."

"I like the way you think, young man. Here's what we'll do. We'll get Joey and Alex's room done, get them moved into it, then redo the room they're in now for you two. That'll leave the spare room between you. Does that sound okay?"

"Sounds great, Dad. When will it happen?" Joey asked.

"I'll get in touch with John in the morning and we'll see. It'll depend on if he's busy with other projects. With luck, we can have the twins moved into their room by their birthday."

"Sweet, we can show our friends then," Alex said.

"Okay, that's settled. Now, who's ready for a swim?" I asked. Six hands shot in the air. "Grab your towels and we'll meet back at the door to outside." Tom and I saw nothing but four bare backsides as the boys took off in a flash. We ambled to our room to grab our towels and the shelter key, then returned to meet the boys. They were bouncing up and down with impatience as we made our way across the living room. Once we were all assembled, I led the way to the pool with Tom bringing up the rear. Once the shelter door was unlocked, the boys squeezed past me, tossed their towels on the table and jumped in.

"In a hurry, aren't they?" Tom asked.

"They always are," I chuckled. When we reached the pool and got in, we were immediately surrounded by four boys ready for battle. Instead of their normal two-on-one attack, they decided to work together tonight and all four jumped Tom. I lounged against the side of the pool and enjoyed the action. It took almost five minutes, but they eventually managed to get Tom's head shoved underwater.

Their mission accomplished, they changed targets and turned their attack towards me. I tried to get away, but they were just too quick and soon had me in their clutches. I knew what was coming and had just managed to take a deep breath before they were on my back and pushing me under. Tom finally came to my aid and pulled me back up, sputtering for air.

"About time you rescued me."

"I didn't see you rushing in to help me. Turnabout's fair play, bubba."

"Hey, Mike," I called, "how do you feel about teaching your brothers to swim?"

"I can do that, Dad."

"No, you can't," Alex whined.

"Yeah, you're too small," T.J. complained.

"I ain't listenin' to him," Joey added.

"Mike, why don't you show these doubters that you can help them?" He promptly took off, swimming the width of the pool four times without stopping while the other three stared in awe. He finally came to a rest at the side of the pool and looked at his three brothers while sticking out his tongue and blowing raspberries in their direction. "Now, do you still think he can't help you?" I asked.

"Maybe he can," they all agreed.

"Good, from now on, whenever we go swimming, Mike will spend at least thirty minutes working with you, understood."

"Yes, Dad," they mumbled.

"Mike, it's your class. Take charge." Tom and I headed for deeper water to relax and I felt a disturbance behind me. Just as I turned around to see what it was, Mike jumped out of the water, wrapped his arms around my neck and his legs around my waist. He whispered in my ear, "Thanks, Dad," kissed my cheek, then dropped back in the water and swam back to rejoin his brothers.

When Tom and I had settled in along the wall, he looked at me and asked, "Have I told you how good you are and how much I love you?"

"Several times, but I never get tired of hearing it. I love you, too, you know."

"I do. So, you think Steve's serious about this workshop?"

"Yeah. After what Valerie almost cost the district with her bullshit, he's serious. He was not a happy camper. He really wants you there, too. I don't think he was really quite ready to hear me use the term 'boyfriend', but he covered it pretty well," I chuckled.

"That's one of the things that really bugs me about straight folks. They don't have a problem with saying 'boyfriend' and 'girlfriend', but heaven forbid, the world's gonna end if we do the same."

"Just more of the same old double standard, Tom. At least we can legally get married, nowadays."

"Holy crap, did you really just say that?"

"Uh, yeah, I guess I did. That should give you a hint of where I think we're headed. You good with that?"

"You have no idea. When I accepted being gay, not being able to get married and have kids was the only thing I hated about it. That's what made it so hard to tell Mom and Dad, the fact that they could forget any hope they ever had about me giving them grandchildren. I mean, you know how every parent wants to become a grandparent someday."

"Tell me about it. That's the biggest issue my mom had when I came out, she wasn't gonna get to be a grandma. You'd have thought the world was ending. She didn't give a shit about me, just how it affected her and her social standing to have a 'faggot' for a son."

"Well, hopefully she'll get over it. Mine eventually did. It didn't happen overnight, mind you, but slowly. Think glacial. That reminds me, I need to call Mom and Dad and let them know about us, the boys, resigning and everything that's happened this week."

"You don't think it might be a little early for that?"

"Nope. My mind is running on the same wavelength with you. Is it sudden? Damn right it is. Was it expected? Hell, no. Does it feel right? Abso-fuckin'-lutely."

"I'm right there with you."

"So, you really think we could end up married with children?"

"As long as I'm Al and you're Peggy," I laughed.

"Oh, god, really? I hated that show," Tom groaned.

"Well, I think it's time to get out of here and get the boys on the way to bed. I'm starting to get waterlogged and wrinkly."

"That's not the water, Max, it's your advanced age," Tom laughed as he pushed off the wall and swam away.

"I'll get you for that, mister."

"Promises, promises. Catch me if you can, you old fart."

"Boys," I called, "shower time, then snacks." They jumped out of the pool, dried off quickly and ran to the house to take their showers. Tom and I followed at a much more relaxed pace, pausing for a long hug and kiss before returning to the house. Tom took our towels to our bedroom while I turned into the kitchen to get the snacks ready. Tonight's munchie was half a Halo orange and a glass of milk. I had them set and ready for each boy as they came in and took a seat at the counter. When Tom returned, he stopped and pulled a Corona from the fridge for each of us.

"Thanks, Tom." I turned to the boys and asked, "You all ready for school tomorrow?" All four mumbled an unenthusiastic acceptance of their fate. "Oh, cheer up, it's Friday and then you have the whole weekend free."

"Whatever," groused Joey. The other three nodded in agreement.

"Well, when you're done with your snack, hit the john and climb in bed. We'll be there in a few to say goodnight."

One by one, they tromped off to their bedrooms and Tom and I followed after finishing our drink. We stopped at T.J. and Mike's room first to find them sitting in the middle of the bed and playing a little UNO.

"Come get your hugs and kisses goodnight." Both boys crawled across the mattress and got to their knees in front of us. We wrapped our arms around them and kissed their foreheads, then swapped places so both received a kiss from each of us. Once they had their hugs and kisses, I said, "Lights out in five minutes, boys, tomorrow's still a school day. Sleep well, we love you."

"We love you too, Dad, Uncle Tom, night."

Tom and I headed to the twins' room to take care of our goodnights there. Surprisingly, when we reached the door, the lights were out, and we heard no sounds emanating from within. We quietly entered the room and turned on the small dresser light so we could see. We found Alex and Joey sleeping soundly, covers shoved to the end of the bed, twisted in a pretzel as usual. Tom and I pulled the covers back over the two, kissed each on the forehead and crept quietly from the room, turning off the light as we passed the dresser.

As we walked down the hallway towards the living room I asked, "Didn't you have a call you wanted to make?"

"*Want* would be the wrong word. Need would be more accurate."

"I'll grab a book and stay out of the way. Why don't you use the phone in the study?"

"Oh, no you don't, you big chicken. I want you there with me. If I'm going to tell them everything, I want some damn backup, and I ain't calling Dylan for it."

"Fine, let's go." When we entered the study, I had Tom sit at the desk while I took a chair on the other side. He put the phone on speaker and dialed the number. While we waited for the call to connect, I asked, "Where do your parents live? You've never said."

"Just outside of St. Louis," he answered as the phone rang.

"Hello?" asked an older lady in a cautious voice.

"Hi, Mom, it's Tom. How're you?"

"Fine, now that I know it's you. I recognize your voice, of course, but didn't know the name and number on the caller ID. Who the heck is Maxwill Sanders?"

"He's why I'm calling, Ma. I need to tell you and Dad something. Is he there?"

"Sure, hang on a sec." We heard her call in the background, "Bill, pick up the phone, it's Tom," and heard him respond, "Hang on, Estelle." His mom came back to us, "Wait a second, Tom. I just remembered why that name, Maxwill Sanders, is familiar. He's an author, isn't he?"

"He sure is."

"Well, you must be moving up in the world, hobnobbing with famous authors. Why are you calling from his home? You at a party?"

"No, Ma, but wait 'til Dad's on the line, okay?" At that moment, we heard the click of an extension being picked up.

"Tom, you there? What's up, son?"

"Hi, Dad. Look, I know you two weren't very happy when I came out to you, but I think we've pretty well cleared that hurdle, haven't we?"

"Yes, dear," his mom said.

"Not easily," his dad added, "but, yeah."

"Good, because I have something important to tell you and I don't want you freaking out."

"Spit it out, boy," his dad said.

"I've met someone and fallen in love with him." You could have heard a pin drop in the silence that ensued. "There's more. Max is in the process of adopting four boys. If this ends up where we both think it is, you're going to be their grandparents. One set of 'em, anyway."

"Oh, my, Tom, that's a lot to take in," his mom said.

"I know it is. A lot has happened in the last week."

"A week. You can't fall in love in a damn week, Tom," Bill claimed.

"Yeah, Dad, you can. You've told me, yourself, that within days of meeting mom, you knew the two of you would be together the rest of your lives. The same thing's happened to me."

"That's true, Bill, and you know it. I suppose congratulations are in order, son," his mom said. "If you're sure about this. Is this Max a good man?"

"The best, Ma, and he's sitting right here. Say hi, Max."

"Hello Mr. & Mrs. Wright. It's a pleasure to meet both of you. I want you to know that you've raised a fine man and I've fallen deeply in love with him."

"Oh, hello, Mr. Sanders. We didn't know you were there, too," Estelle replied.

"Please, Mrs. Wright, call me Max. Mr. Sanders is my dad."

"O-o-kay, I guess I can do that," she stammered.

"Dad, you still there?"

"I'm here, just a little stunned."

"Sorry, but there wasn't an easier way to tell you."

"Oh, don't worry about that, we'll adjust to this, just like we adjusted to the news about you being gay."

"The other thing you need to know is I'm resigning from the force."

"Are they forcing you to because of, well, you know?" Bill asked.

"Not at all, Dad. My boss is real cool and me being gay has nothing to do with it. This is entirely my decision. Having met Max and his new sons, I want to be sure I can come home in one piece every night. I can't do that and stay a cop."

"That makes sense, son," said Estelle. "I knew you never liked that part of being a cop. I never liked it much either. I was always worried about you."

"What are you going to do now, Tom?" Bill asked.

"I'm going to open up my own private investigation service. And I already have a client."

"Who's that?" they both asked.

"The agency handling Max's adoption. They had a guy who screwed up a background check several months ago, and he almost killed an adoption because of it. They're going to start using me for background checks and abuse investigations."

"That should keep you busy," Bill said. "A lot safer than being a cop, too."

"Oh, Tom, that's such a wonderful thing for you to do. I'm happy for you," Estelle added, "for everything."

"I'm glad to hear that, Mom. Really."

"We hope you'll be happy, son," Bill said.

"I am, and I will be. I'd like it a lot if you could come up and meet everyone."

"Are you sure?"

"Yeah, I am. The twins' birthday is coming up on the thirteenth next month and we're having a party for them that Saturday. It would be great if you could be here. I'd really like them to meet their new grandparents."

"We'll have to talk about it and let you know. Is that okay?"

"That's fine, Mom, and I'll understand if you can't make it. Love you both and hope to see you soon."

"Bye, son, we love you, too."

Tom disconnected the call and looked at me. "That went better than I thought it would."

"I'm glad for you, Tom. They sound like nice folks."

"They are, just a little outdated in their thinking, but they're a lot better than they used to be."

"Way ahead of my parents. Now, do you have any interest in going to bed?"

"Don't I always?" he asked with leading tone. "Lead the way, lover."

We headed to the bedroom and, after a quick shower to rinse off the chlorine from the pool, curled together for a good night's sleep after a long day.

"I love you, Tom Wright," I whispered in his hear.

"Love you more, Max Sanders," he whispered back.

21

Friday began like all the other days this week, alarm blaring in my ear at six. Of course, if it wasn't, it wouldn't wake me up. I hopped out of bed, took care of my morning bathroom needs and shook Tom to wake him.

"C'mon, big guy, rise and shine!"

"Five more minutes, please," he grumped as he rolled over and pulled the covers over his head.

I headed to the other end of the house to wake the boys, receiving much the same greeting I had just gotten from Tom. When I finally managed to get them moving in the right direction, I headed back to work on Tom some more. I found him sitting on the edge of the bed holding his head in his hands.

"You okay, Tom?"

"Yeah, just a freakin' killer of a headache. You got Advil or anything?"

"You bet. Behind the mirror in the bathroom. Bring some with you and I'll have coffee ready for you when you get to the kitchen, okay?"

"Sounds good, I'll be there shortly," he moaned.

I pulled on some sweatpants and headed to the kitchen to get the coffee and some breakfast going. After looking over the available options, I decided on scrambled eggs this morning. I was just dishing the eggs onto plates when the boys straggled in to join me. I got them set up with their eggs, some toast, and glasses of milk and juice, then headed back to check on Tom since he hadn't made it to the kitchen yet. I found that he'd managed to get dressed, but that was about it.

"Are you sure you can work today?"

"No, I'm not, but I can't call in sick during my last two weeks on the job."

"Sure, you can. Want me to dial the number for ya?"

"Nah, I'm okay, just need some caffeine and Advil and I'll be fine."

"If you're sure, then you better get a move on."

"Yes, Dad," he said, oozing sarcasm.

I grabbed a shirt, socks and shoes so I could be ready to drive the boys out to meet the bus and headed back to the kitchen to check on their progress. They were just finishing their breakfast when I returned. While I pulled on my shirt, they started rinsing and stacking their dishes in the sink. As Tom came for his cup of coffee, they took off to their bedrooms to finish getting ready for school. Tom grabbed his mug, popped a couple Advil into his mouth and followed it with a big gulp of the coffee.

"Holy shit, that's hot, why didn't you warn me?"

"It's coffee, Tom, it's supposed to be hot," I deadpanned.

"I know, but still, you coulda' warned me."

The boys picked that moment to come back, all seemingly ready to go meet the bus.

"You don't look too good, Uncle Tom."

"Just a bad headache, Joey, I'll be fine. Well, I better get going or I'll be late." We each got our hug and kiss, the boys on their foreheads and mine on the lips, much to the delight of four whistling boys. "I assume it's okay to take the Shelby, again?"

"Get outta' here, ya big goof."

"I gotta tell ya, Max, that is one fun car to drive. All the guys at the cop shop think I musta' won the lottery or something."

"We both won the lottery when we met on Saturday."

"Yeah, I guess we did. Hey, I need to go to my old place this weekend and get some things. We can get my car then."

"So, you're really moving in?"

"Can't think of any reason not to, can you?"

"Not a one."

"Good. Love you guys and I'll see everybody tonight." With that, he headed down the hall.

"Bye, Uncle Tom, be careful out there," Alex called to his back.

"Thanks, I will."

"Okay, you boys got everything you need?"

"Yes, Dad, coats, gloves, hats and backpacks," T.J. answered.

"Good, get in the car, let me get my shoes and coat on and we'll be off." I met the boys in the garage to find them buckled in and ready to roll. When we got to the end of the drive, we still had a few minutes to wait for the bus to arrive.

"So, you're still not gonna tell us what's going on over here, are ya, Dad?" Joey asked.

"Nope, it's still a secret."

"It looks like you're having something built," Alex said.

"Maybe, you'll just have to wait to find out," I teased.

I saw the bus coming up the road and we got out of the car. When it finally stopped, I gave each boy a hug, reminded them to be good and learn something new, then pushed them to board the bus. I waved hi to Cal and bye to the boys as I got back in the car and headed back to the house. I had a busy morning ahead with several calls to make. After I got undressed, my first call was to John, my builder.

"Good morning, John, Max here. How are you this bright and beautiful Friday?"

"Great, Max, how 'bout yourself?"

"Just dandy. How's work going on the bus shelter?"

"We have the walls built, insulated and ready to attach to the slab. Next, we'll get the roof framed and shingled. I'm going to leave the siding off and the door and window separate until we have it sitting on the slab and anchored. Don't want to have to deal with all that extra weight while trying to position the framework and anchor it to the slab."

"That sounds great, John. Is the slab and sidewalk still going to be poured Monday?"

"That's the plan. I'm glad you thought about adding the sidewalk from the shelter to the drive. I should've thought of that myself."

"Well, it didn't make much sense to have a nice warm and dry place for the boys to wait for the bus and then force them to walk through mud to get to it. Now, I've come up with a couple more projects and wanted to see if you're interested."

"I'm always looking for work this time of year, Max. What's on your mind?"

"I need some modifications done to a couple bedrooms in the house so they'll be more what the boys want and actually look like a kid's room."

"What kind of changes you thinking about?"

"I have two boys in each room and they've asked for separate desks and a space they can call their own. I also want to get some painting done in whatever colors they choose."

"That sounds simple enough. How soon do you want this done?"

"The twins' birthday is coming up on the thirteenth next month and I'd like to get their room done and have them moved into it by then. Once they're settled in their new room, we can redo the room they're in now for the other two boys."

"Sounds like you've given this some thought, Max. And it sounds like a workable plan. How soon can you have the furniture out of the first room?"

"I plan to move it out this weekend."

"Perfect. I'll be out Monday morning for the pouring of the shelter slab, anyway. When that's done, I'll come on up to the house and you can show me the rooms we'll be working on. I'll draw up a few options and come back that evening so we can show them to the boys, see what they think."

"You're a good man, John. I can't thank you enough for making this happen so quickly."

"Don't worry about it, Max. It's not like I'm really that busy at the moment. I'll take any work I can get right now, even busy work. Still got to pay the bills, ya know."

"I know, John. I still appreciate the way you've jumped on these projects. Well, have a great weekend and I'll see you Monday."

"Thanks, Max, you, too."

My next task was to try and locate a lifeguard for the twins' birthday party. I didn't have a clue where to begin, so I started my search by calling the YMCA in Springfield.

"West Iles Y, this is Brad, how can I help you?"

"Good morning, Brad, my name is Max Sanders, I'm looking to hire a lifeguard and I was hoping you could point me in the right direction."

"Good morning, Mr. Sanders, I'm sure I can help you. Are you looking to fill a permanent or part-time position?"

"Definitely part-time. *Very* part-time. My twins' ninth birthday is coming up on the thirteenth next month and they want to have a pool party at our home the afternoon of the fifteenth with about ten or twelve of their friends from school along with my other two sons. I feel comfortable with watching my four, but I think fourteen or sixteen will be a bit much for two adults to handle."

"You got that right, especially if they're all boys. I deal with that here all the time and they can certainly be a handful. What hours did you need somebody?"

"I'm thinking from maybe one to three. Two hours in the pool should have them all pretty well worn out and ready to relax for a movie."

"I would hope so. How much were you thinking about paying?"

"In all honesty, I hadn't thought about it and I have no idea what a lifeguard should be paid."

"Well, sir, we usually get twenty-five or thirty dollars an hour when we're actually pulling lifeguard duty here. That offsets with ten bucks an hour to answer phones and greet members."

"I'd be willing to pay fifty bucks per hour for the two to three hours of the party."

"I'll tell you what, Mr. Sanders, I'll ask for that afternoon off from here and I'll be your lifeguard. I'm fully trained and Red Cross certified. I'd love to do it, sounds like it'll be fun. And very different to being here all day."

"That's great, let me give you my phone numbers and address." I passed on the info he would need to get in contact if needed. "If anything happens that you won't be able to make it, just let me know. Otherwise, we'll see you about one on the fifteenth, Brad."

"Looking forward to it, Mr. Sanders. Thanks, and have a great day."

My next call was to a bakery I'd used before to talk about the birthday cake. After about ten minutes on the phone, we had everything settled and two cakes would be ready to pick up, a smaller one Thursday afternoon and a much bigger one on Saturday morning.

After the bakery, I called a catering service to arrange for them to provide and serve the food and drinks for the Saturday party. I didn't want to miss any of my sons' first birthday with me because I was too busy with food and other things.

"Good morning, Carol," I said when she answered.

"Morning, Max, what's up?"

"Thanks for telling me about the boys' birthdays. You'll be happy to know that the twins are ecstatic about getting to have a party."

"That's great, Max. When's it gonna happen?"

"Well, since their actual birthday is on a Thursday, we're going to have the big party Saturday afternoon, starting about noon. I know you wanted to be there."

"Oh, I do, but I can't make it that afternoon. I already have plans with my parents that day."

"Well, do you think you might have time to come out Thursday night? We're going to have a smaller, family only event then."

"Oh, that'd be great. I really want to see how the boys are doing, anyway, and that will be a good time to do so."

"Perfect, Carol. They'll be happy to see you."

"I'll look forward to it, Max. See you then."

"Bye, Carol, have a good day."

I had just hung up the phone when it rang. I recognized the number as the school's and answered, "Max Sanders."

"Max, Steve here, how are you today?"

"Doing well. How about yourself."

"Not bad. I wanted to call and let you know I've talked to the three boys in Mike's class who are causing problems for him. I've also talked to all their parents so they know what's been going on."

"How did that go?"

"I'm pretty sure I've impressed two of them, Mark and Billy, that their treatment of Mike is unacceptable and I expect it to stop immediately. Andy, however, is going be a tougher nut to crack."

"Why is that?"

"After our talk this morning, I'm pretty sure Andy is being abused at home and he's taking it out on someone smaller than him who likely won't fight back. I just don't know what I can do about it."

"Have you reported the situation to the authorities?"

"I don't have any evidence abuse is happening, so no, I haven't."

"What kind of evidence do you need?"

"Bruises or marks of some kind, but I just can't have him lift his shirt up here at school and check him over."

"Maybe I can help out with that."

"How do you propose to do it?"

"Why don't you give me the parent's names and phone numbers of all three boys? I can have Mike invite all three over tomorrow afternoon. I'm pretty sure we could talk the boys into going for a swim and that would be a good opportunity to check him over."

"That sounds pretty devious, Max. But, I like it. Here ya go." I wrote down the info as Steve gave it to me. "You'll let me know if this works."

"Bet on it."

"The other reason for my call was to see if you'd made a decision as to whether you'd be joining us in the workshop I want to have."

"I'll be there, along with Alex, Joey and T.J. Mike was adamant he wasn't coming, which is fine. I didn't expect he'd want to be there. I'm not sure about Tom at this moment."

"Oh, Tom will be there."

"Really, does he know that?"

"I don't know. But I did talk to Dylan earlier and he's agreed to participate. He's the one who told me Tom would also be here."

"Ah, the old five-watt bulb just flickered to life. Okay, I guess that makes five out of the six of us. Have you picked a date and time yet?"

"Wednesday, March twelfth at nine-thirty. That day is already scheduled to be an off day for other reasons. That way, nobody has to give up an evening to attend."

"I'll have to have my sister stay with Mike, then. That's all right, though, she's been wanting an excuse to hang out with the boys, anyway. She'll only have one that day, but she'll still be happy to do it, I'm sure."

"Sounds good, Max. I'd like to talk about it some more before it happens, see if you have any ideas beyond what I already have."

"I have one now you may not know exists. My sister is the assistant director of an organization called ICASA. While they deal mostly with rape crisis centers throughout the state, they may have some resources and information we could use."

"ICASA? Never heard of it."

"Not too surprising. ICASA stands for the Illinois Coalition Against Sexual Assault. I'm sure they'd be happy to be involved. If you'd like, I can check and let you know."

"That'd be great. We might get a better reaction if you made first contact, especially since your sister works there."

"I'll call Lee this evening, then."

"Thanks, Max. Let me know what she says."

"I will, Steve. And thanks for trying to help with Mike's issue. Hope you have a great weekend."

"You to, Max. Adios, amigo."

With all my calls completed, I realized I had nothing to do until it was time to meet the bus after school. I fixed myself a quick bite to eat for lunch and then settled in my chair by the fireplace with my current book. I was about to doze off when the drive sensor announced an incoming visitor a little before three. I zipped to the bedroom to pull on my shorts. Just as I was sliding them up my legs, I heard, "Honey, I'm home!" echo through the house. With a sigh of relief at Tom's safe return, I slid the shorts back off and met him in the living room.

"I like coming home to find a naked man in my living room," he laughed when he saw me.

"And I like an armed man in uniform finding me in such a state. Shall I raise my hands over my head and assume the position?"

"Dressed like that, you can assume just about any position you'd like." We headed to the bedroom where Tom started to get undressed. "When do the boys get home?"

"The bus doesn't get here for another forty-five minutes or so. Why."

"Good, come here lover." Tom grabbed my arm and pulled me in a bear hug, grinding his hips into mine. He backed up to the bed, pulling me with him, and we fell onto it in a heap when our legs hit the edge of the mattress. We spent the next half-hour intimately exploring every nook and cranny of each other's bodies.

As we sprawled on the bed in our post-carnal bliss, Tom mumbled, "God, you're gonna kill me one of these days with that shit, but what a way to die."

"I know what you mean. For a guy with little to none supposed real-life experience, you certainly know how to work wonders with that tongue of yours."

"You're not complaining, are you?"

"Absolutely not. I only hope that someday, you'll teach me some of those tricks." I looked at the clock real quick, "Oh, shit, I've got to meet the boys at the bus." I rolled over and gave Tom a hug and kiss before jumping out of bed and pulling on sweats, shirt and shoes and darting out. My timing was almost perfect as I had just put the car in park when the bus stopped and the boys flew out, running madly towards me. After they were in and buckled, I made the U-turn to return to the house.

As we pulled in the garage, Joey was first to notice that the Shelby was there. "Is Uncle Tom already home?"

"He is. He had an early end to his day. Any homework for the weekend?"

"Nothing for any of us, Dad," Alex answered.

"How'd your spelling test go, T.J.?"

"Got a 100 on it, Dad, thanks to your help."

"You could have done the same without my help, but that's what I'm here for. Any time you want help, all you have to do is ask." We entered the house and the boys stopped in their rooms to drop their backpacks and get comfy. I headed to the bedroom to do the same. As I passed the kitchen on the way, I saw Tom rummaging in the fridge for something to eat.

"You hungry, big guy?"

"Starved. What's for supper?"

"I thought we'd get pizza from Capone's tonight. I don't feel much like cooking. Sound okay to you?"

"Perfect. The sooner, the better, too." At that moment, four nude boys ran past me and wrapped Tom in a hug, Alex and Joey on each side, T.J. to the rear and poor Mike got the front. I turned towards the bedroom with a laugh as I headed to join the comfort crowd. When I returned, the hug had finally broken up and I asked the boys if pizza was good with them tonight. With all in agreement, I placed the order and was informed our supper would be ready to pick up in about forty-five minutes.

"While we wait to pick up supper, let's have a seat, guys. I need to pass on some information I learned today."

"I know part of it," Tom commented.

"I'm sure you do."

"I know part of it, too," Mike said.

"How does he know, and we don't, Dad?" Alex asked.

"Because he's the reason for some of it." We all sat in the living room around the fireplace, the boys on the couch and Tom and I in chairs facing them. "First, Mike, some of your problems with Andy, Mark and Billy should be resolved. Mr. Franklin told me he talked to all three today and Mark and Billy both seemed to understand that the way they've been treating you is unacceptable and he expects they'll stop."

"Yeah, I think they will. At lunch, they both came over to sit with me and they told me they were sorry. They were just following Andy because he's their friend."

"Did Andy do or say anything?"

"No, not today, anyway."

"Well I have an idea that may help smooth things over with him, too."

"Really, what's that?"

"I think you should invite the three of them over tomorrow afternoon and give all four of you time to get to know each other better."

"Wait, you want me to have those jerks over here so they can pick on me at home, too?"

"I think once you four spend some together, they'll stop that. They'll see you're a regular kid, just like them. You might actually end up liking each other."

"Don't think that's gonna happen," he scoffed.

"Mike," Tom interjected, "There's an old saying, 'keep your friends close, but keep your enemies closer'."

"What's that mean, Uncle Tom??"

"It means, if you become friends with these three, they won't be your enemies anymore and should stop picking on you."

"That kinda makes sense. I guess it won't hurt to try. But I don't know how to get a hold of them."

"I do," I said. "Mr. Franklin gave me their parents' names and numbers this morning. Why don't we call them after supper and see if they'd like to come over?"

"Okay, if you think so, Dad," Mike grumbled. "I don't think it's gonna work, but I'll try."

"Good. The other thing Mr. Franklin and I discussed was the workshop. I let him know that Alex, Joey, T.J. and I would be there, and he told me that Tom would be there."

"Yeah, thanks for that."

"Hey, don't blame me. From what he said, it sounds like Dylan volunteered you."

"He did, told me this morning right after he got off the phone with Steve. Told him he had the 'perfect guy' for him."

"Well, you are the perfect guy for me. For the workshop, I'm not too sure. We'll just have to wait and see."

Tom leaned over, smacked the back of my head and laughed.

I turned back to the boys and continued, "You three who are going to be involved need to think about what you want to say between now and then."

"When is it?" T.J. asked.

"March twelfth, the day before the twins' birthday. It was going to be an off day at school already and Steve thought it would be a better way to spend the day than what was already scheduled."

"What about me?" Mike asked. "If you're all going to be over there, what am I gonna do?"

"I'm going to call Aunt Lee tonight and see if she'd be willing to spend the day with you."

"Oh, goody, that'll be fun."

"Wait, if Aunt Lee's gonna be here, I don't wanna' go," Joey whined.

"Sorry, Joey, but you've already committed to being there and we don't back down from our commitments."

"Dang it."

"Maybe we can convince her to stay for supper when we get home."

"Yeah, okay."

"I think that settles all that for the moment. Why don't you guys get the table set for supper and I'll go pick it up?"

"Hurry, Dad, we're hungry," T.J. called to my back as I headed to get dressed again for the trip out.

"Be as quick as I can." By the time I returned with supper, Tom and the boys were sitting at the table, silverware in hands, looking at me with hunger written all over their faces as I placed the pizzas and bread sticks in front of them. "Dig in, I'll be right back." I went to the bedroom to get comfy again and returned to find all five of them stuffing their faces.

"Oh, I see how y'all are. You're just here for the food and to heck with me."

"Gotta have your priorities straight, Max," Tom laughed around a mouthful of bread stick. "Food first, souls second."

I filled my plate and joined the others in chowing down. When we were done eating, the boys cleaned up the table while I retrieved the names and numbers of Andy, Mark and Billy's parents so we could make our calls and invite them for tomorrow. While Tom and the other three headed to the theater to start a movie, Mike and I sat by the fireplace to make our calls. I put the phone on speaker so I could hear the whole call, but told Mike it was up to him to do the talking.

"Let's call Billy, first," Mike said. "Even though he was with Andy and Mark, he really never did much and I think he's the nicest."

"Billy, it is." I dialed the number and we waited as the phone rang.

"Hello?" an adult answered.

"Hi, is Billy there?" Mike asked.

"Just a sec."

"Hello," came a timid voice.

"Hi, Billy, it's Mike, from school."

"Oh, hi, Mike. I was wonderin' who was callin' for me. What's up?"

"Look, I know I'm not, like, your best friend or anything, but I wanted to find out if you wanted to come over tomorrow."

"Really? After what we done to you? You want me to come over?"

"Yeah, I think we could have some fun."

"You askin' Andy and Mark, too?"

"Plannin' to. I wanted to start with you. Figured if you'd want to, they would, too."

"Cool. What're we gonna do?"

"We could walk through the woods, watch a movie, play a game, swim, whatever."

"Swim!? It's way too cold for that."

"We got a pool that's covered, Billy, and we swim all the time. It's great. C'mon, it'll be fun."

"Let me ask my mom, hang on." He set the phone down and came back in a minute. "My mom says it'd be okay, but she wants to talk to your mom or dad, first."

"My dad's right here."

"Hi Billy. Put your mom on," I said.

"Who's this," she asked.

"Hi there, I'm Max Sanders, Mike's dad. How're you?"

"Oh, hi Max. I'm Sarah White, Billy's mom. You really want him to come over tomorrow?"

"I assume you know of the problems the boys have had."

"I do, and Billy's been grounded because of his involvement. He knows better than to treat people like that."

"I'm glad to hear that Sarah. But, I'd like you make an exception in his grounding for a day. It's my hope that if all four boys involved spend some time together, they might become friends. Do you think you'd allow that?"

"I think so. Now, Billy said something about swimming, but it seems the wrong time of year for that." I explained about the pool and its heated shelter. "Aha, now it makes perfect sense. But, he's not a very good swimmer."

"That's all right, Sarah, if we do swim, I'll be there, too. The boys can't use the pool if I'm not there with them."

"You have more boys?"

"Four. And I'm sure they'll all be swimming."

"Sounds like you have your hands full."

"I do, but I'm loving it. Why don't you give me your address and we'll pick up Billy about one tomorrow? Would that be okay?"

"That'd be just fine, Max. And thanks. Billy doesn't have many friends."

I got the address and thanked Sarah. We called Mark next, and then, Andy. Both were surprised at being invited but accepted after talking to their parents. Everyone would be bringing swim trunks to use, and I just hoped I could convince my four to wear theirs.

"See, Mike, that wasn't so hard, was it?"

"I guess not. I really hope we have fun."

"I do, too. Now, there's something I want you to do for me tomorrow."

"What's that, Dad?"

"When Mr. Franklin talked to the boys this morning, he got the impression it might be difficult to get Andy to stop his bad behavior."

"Did he say why?"

"He thinks Andy is being abused at home, but he has no proof to call the authorities. He thinks he might be picking on you because he's being abused."

"Oh."

"I'd like you to talk to him and see if you can find out anything, then let me know."

"You bet I will. After what I've been through, I don't want anyone I know to go through it, too."

"I knew you'd help me out. Thanks, buddy. And please, don't tell your brothers. I don't want them all riled up about it, okay."

"You got it, Dad, thanks. It'll be fun."

"Great, now let's go join the others and watch a movie, okay?"

"Can I get a ride?"

"Sure thing, munchkin, come here." I grabbed him under the arms, then lifted and spun him around so he could sit on my shoulders. When we rejoined the others, I set him down and he hopped in the chair with T.J. while I sat next to Tom.

"How'd that go," he whispered.

"Well, it took a little convincing, but all three of the little troublemakers will be here tomorrow. I'll go pick them up about one. I'm hoping Steve's concerns about Andy are unwarranted, but we'll find out tomorrow."

"What are you talking about?"

"Sorry, I was gonna tell you when you got home, but something distracted me and I forgot all about it. Not that I'm complaining." I filled him in on Andy and his possible situation.

"I hope you're not forgetting what I do for a living for the next week. If I suspect anything, I'm obliged to investigate."

"No, I haven't forgotten. In fact, I'm counting on it. I'm hoping you might pick up a hint of something the rest of us might miss."

"I'll do what I can. And if I suspect anything, I'll let you know, right after I call Dylan."

"Good, it's nice to have some backup."

We settled back to enjoy the rest of the movie and when it was over, I asked if they wanted to watch the next Star Wars movie. After boisterous agreement from the boys, we headed to the kitchen to get popcorn and drinks for the show. While we waited for the popping to end, I explained to T.J., Alex and Joey about our visitors for tomorrow afternoon.

"Okay, guys, Andy, Billy and Mark are coming over tomorrow after lunch to play with Mike. If Mike wants it to be just the four of them, I expect you to honor that. If he wants all of you all to play together, I expect you to join in. Any problems with that?"

"Nah, that's cool, Dad," T.J. answered.

"Next, since they obviously won't know about our dress code out here, I'll expect you all to be wearing shorts and if we swim, you'll wear shorts in the pool, also."

"Oh, man, that sucks," moaned Joey.

"Mouth, son."

"Sorry, Dad, but it does."

I looked to Tom for some support. What I got was, "Don't look at me, he's right, it does."

"Fat lot of help you are." He just shrugged his shoulders. I looked back to the boys and continued, "Look, it's going to be their first visit here and I don't want them freaking out and telling their parents we're all a bunch of weirdos."

"Okay, Dad, we'll be good," Alex said.

"Thank you. Now, let's go watch a movie."

We headed back to the theater and I started the show. T.J. and Mike were sitting together, and the twins were sharing another chair. Before I sat, I remembered I needed to call Lee and let Tom know I'd be back shortly. I headed back to the kitchen and got on the phone.

Lee's husband, Carl, answered the phone, "Joe's Bar and Grill, what's your pleasure?"

"Hey, Carl, how ya doing?"

"Great, Max, how about yourself? You survivin' the week as a new dad?"

"Barely. These guys are keepin' me on the run, but we're all still kicking, so there's that."

"Glad to hear it. I thought Lee had dipped into the good shit when she told me you were adopting four boys. Never imagined that happening."

"Ha, neither did I, Carl. Maybe we both snuck into your stash."

"Sh-h-h-h, careful what you say, Max, you never know who's listening."

"Mum's the word. Hey, is Lee there? I need to run a couple things past her."

"Yeah, hang on just a sec." I heard him call Lee to the phone and he came back, "She'll be right here, Max. Good talkin' to ya. Hope to see you and meet my nephews, soon."

"Anytime, Carl."

"Here's Lee. Talk to you later."

"Hey, Max, what's up?"

"Got two things for you. First, I need to find out if you'd be available to stay with Mike on March twelfth. The rest of us are going to be involved in something that Mike doesn't want to go to."

"Yeah, I could probably do that. I have some time I can take from work for a day."

"That's great. I don't know who else I could call to do it."

"Well, if it turns out I can't, maybe Carl would do it."

"Either one of you will be great, Lee. Thanks. That's one down, now for the second thing. The reason I need someone to stay with Mike is the rest of us are going to be involved in a workshop at the school that day."

"What's that all about?"

"Well, there was some excitement at the school this week and now the board president has asked me to be involved in a workshop with the school's staff to discuss the issues faced by gay people in general and, more importantly, the problems gay youth face while growing up. Coming to terms with who they are, and the risks of suicide related to that."

"That sounds like a great thing to be involved with, Max, but, are you sure you all are ready for that level of exposure?"

"Not really, but this sounds way too important to ignore."

"Oh, don't get me wrong, it's super important. Suicide among gay youth is on the rise. What's your involvement supposed to be?"

"Well, I think our main purpose of being there is to let the school staff know of the issues gay kids face that they are most likely unaware of and may not understand. As Steve said, despite the smallish size of the school, my four boys can't be the only gay students in the school and he hopes bringing the subject out in the open will help.

"Tom's boss Dylan is going to be there to provide a law enforcement point-of-view and I thought maybe ICASA might want to get involved, also. I know this isn't normally the type of thing your office deals with, but you might be able to provide some important insights into other issues."

"I'm sure we can. Let me talk to Allison about it tomorrow and see what she says. I can't imagine her not wanting to help out, but we'll see."

"That'd be great, Lee. Thanks for not telling me to take a hike. And thanks for staying with Mike that day. Maybe we can all have supper afterward."

"I'm sure Carl would like that. I know I would, too. We can talk more between now and the twelfth to come up with a real plan."

"Great, sis, I knew I could count on you. You two have a great night. Talk to you later." We ended our call and I headed to the theater to rejoin my family for the rest of the movie. I sat next to Tom and took his hand in mine. When the movie finally ended, we discovered we had four snoozing boys again. We got Joey and Alex in bed first, then took care of T.J. and Mike. Once they were all safely tucked in their beds, Tom and I headed to bed, also.

"You ready for sleep?" Tom asked. I shook my head, grinning madly. "Good, I'm not ready for sleep, either. What's on your mind tonight, lover?"

"I want to see what else was hidden in that little box you snuck in the house."

22

"I like the way you think," he said as I closed the bedroom door. He pulled open the nightstand drawer, retrieved an assortment of what he had euphemistically called 'aids' and spread them on the bed. They ranged in size from a rather smallish item to another that almost put Dylan to shame. My jaw dropped, and eyes opened wide with surprise.

I laid down on the bed and turned myself over to my lover. After half an hour of his sweet and delicate attention with the two smallest items from his tool chest, I experienced an orgasm like none I'd ever felt before. My entire body twitched and jerked with delight as snaps of electricity coursed through me from my toes to the top of my head.

"I'm guessing that's never happened without touching yourself."

"Never. God, what a feeling."

"Yeah, I know. My first time was unreal, too."

"I think we need a shower. C'mon, let's get cleaned up and get to bed. We have three more rugrats here tomorrow afternoon, remember?"

"Oh, yeah. Whose bright idea was that?"

"Guilty. I figured between helping Mike get along with those three and seeing if Andy's being abused, it's worth it."

"You're right, of course."

"Of course, I am, get used to it," I laughed.

We finished our shower and climbed in bed, me holding Tom, and fell into a deep sleep. The morning sun was streaming through the window into my eyes when I realized a pair of very intense hazel eyes set in a field of freckles was staring at me.

"Morning, munchkin, what's up? Where's your brothers?"

"They're all still in bed. I had to pee and didn't want get back in bed with T.J., so I came to see if you was awake yet."

"I am now, hop up here." Mike jumped up on the bed and crawled over to give me a hug, which I gladly returned. I lifted the cover between Tom and me and said, "Crawl in." When he was settled, I curled up behind him, pulled him into my arms and promptly fell back to sleep. My next waking moment was to someone violently shaking my shoulder.

I rolled over to find T.J., jumping up and down, screaming something about Mike gone missing. Tom sat up straight wanting to know what was going on and I pushed the covers down just enough to show T.J. that Mike was safe. "I appreciate your concern, T.J., but please stop screaming."

"Oh, thank god, I was scared to death. We've looked everywhere and couldn't find him. I thought he sneaked out."

"More like he snuck in. Feeling better now?"

"Yeah, loads."

"Okay, scoot on out of here and we'll be out in a few minutes."

"Okay, Dad. I'll tell Joey and Alex I found him and they can stop the search." T.J. disappeared through the door and I turned to find Mike giggling in the middle of the bed.

"Oh, you think that's funny, do ya?"

"Yeah, the look on his face was wicked."

"Well, do ya think this is funny?" I asked as I started to tickle his ribs.

"No, stop, I gotta pee again!"

"Well get outta' our bed and go, ya little booger." He tossed the covers off all of us and proceeded to crawl over me. He left the room at a run, giggling as his bare behind turned the corner into the hallway. "C'mon, big guy, time to get moving. We've got a long day ahead of us."

"Yeah, yeah, I know."

We crawled out of bed, hit the john, washed faces and hands and headed to the kitchen to rustle up some breakfast.

"How do pancakes sound this morning, folks?"

"Yeah!!"

"Well, get the table set while I make the mix and heat the syrup."

The boys hopped off their stools and proceeded to take care of getting everything on the table but the pancakes. By the time they had everything in place and their glasses of milk and juice, the first pancakes were ready to be eaten. I gave each a couple to get them started, thankful I had the big griddle plate that covered two burners on the stove. As fast as I could get them made, the boys were wolfing them down. When they finally slowed down, Tom and I got our turns to enjoy breakfast. When the boys finished, they started cleaning their dishes and waited patiently while Tom and I finished with ours. With the meal completed and the dishes ready for the dishwasher, it was time to make plans for later this afternoon.

"So, what are your plans with your guests this afternoon, Mike?"

"I'm gonna sic my brothers on them. Let's see if they like getting picked on," he grinned evilly while rubbing his hands together.

"Now, as fun as that might sound, you're trying to turn them into friends, not create bigger enemies."

"I know, Dad, I was just kidding. Maybe we can take a walk in the trees, see if we can find the deer again. Definitely wanna' swim for a while, then could we watch a movie?"

"Sounds like you've got a full afternoon, there, but I like it. Do you want your brothers with you for any of it?"

"Well, sure. Maybe we can all be friends. That'd be cool."

"Alex, T.J., Joey, do you want to help Mike with his guests?"

"Why not, what else we gonna do? Sit around and watch them have all the fun?" Joey asked.

"I thought you might rather join in the fun than not. Thanks, I appreciate it. Mike, I think we should leave here about twelve-thirty to start picking them up. You'll be ready to roll, right?"

"Yeah, Dad, I'll be ready."

"Good, now, why don't you four go watch some TV for a while before lunch." They took off to the theater, leaving Tom and I alone. "Are you ready for this?"

"As ready as I'll ever be. Will we still have time this evening or tomorrow to go get some things from my apartment?"

"Oh crap, I'd forgotten all about that. I'm glad you reminded me. We'll take care of that tomorrow. We'll go in the morning and make as many trips as needed to get the things you want now, including your car. With your car and the Flex, we should be able to get quite a bit."

"I don't really have a lot there I'm worried about. It's not like I'm going to need a thirty-two-inch TV or my stereo. Hell, you got bigger screens in the bedrooms here than what I had in my living room. Same goes for the few dishes I had. Don't really need that junk out here, do we? Or my furniture, either. None of it would really fit in with what you already have.

I'm beginning to wonder if I really do belong here, despite how much I want it."

"Tom, don't be like that," I said as I gave him a hug. "We'll bring everything out and decide later what you want to keep. We can rearrange, replace, add, whatever. We're in this together and we'll work it out."

"Thanks for that, Max. As much I've grown attached to you and those four boys over the last week, I still have moments where I wonder if we're really doing the right thing."

"Don't you doubt that for one second. I've never felt so right about anything in my life. Sure, a lot has happened in a very short time, but it's all good things. I *want* you here, the boys *want* you here, we all love you, too."

"But I'm not bringing much to the party, am I?"

"You're bringing the most important thing you can, yourself. The rest is just stuff. We can deal with stuff, yours, mine and the boys."

"I thank Carol every day for calling me to help you last Saturday."

"Me too, bubba, me too. Hey, I've got an idea for ya."

"Oh, shit, here it comes. Again," he laughed.

"Laugh it up, fuzzball," I said as I smacked him on the shoulder. "You know the bus shelter we're going to have soon. What do you think about putting some of your stuff out there for the boys to use? No reason it can't be nice, is there?"

"That's a good idea, Max. It sure beats the hell out of trying to sell it or give it somebody. And I sure can't leave it where it is. Oh, crap, I need to let the apartment manager know I'm moving. I hope they don't screw me for breaking the lease."

"Don't worry about it, Tom. If they want anything, I'll pay it."

"Whoa, I'm not here for a free ride. I expect to pay my fair share."

"And you will, but don't stress yourself over the penny-ante shit."

"Easy for you to say mister rich and famous author. That's big shit to regular folk like me."

"Tom, you live here now. You're a part of this family, and I hope to make that official as soon as we can, so you better get used to 'rich and famous'." He whipped his head around and stared in my eyes, mouth wide open in surprise. "What?" I asked.

"That almost sounded like a proposal. Did you just ask me to marry you?"

"Um, maybe. I guess that depends on your answer."

"Well, I had planned to wait at least another day before asking you. I mean, it's not even been a full seven days since we first met and I think that's rushing things a bit, don't you? Eight days would seem to be much more appropriate, don't you think?" His grin grew wider with every word.

"Well, gee, since you put it that way, maybe we should wait a little longer ... Okay, long enough." I got down on my knee, grabbed Tom's hand and said, "Tom Wright, I've never met anyone who makes me feel like you do. You complete me. I love you and want to spend the rest of my life with you. Will you marry me?"

"Get up here, you hopeless romantic." As I stood, Tom wrapped his arms around me and pulled me in for a hug. "Yes," he whispered in my ear.

From behind us, we heard, "Would you two get a room, please? This is embarrassing." We both turned to find Joey opening the refrigerator.

"What are you doing in here? Eavesdropping again?"

"Nah, just came to get us some drinks. I'll be gone soon and you two can carry on," he smirked. After Joey returned to the others with their drinks, Tom and I busted out laughing. Over our laughing, we could hear cheers of joy escaping the closed theater door. Said door fairly burst open as four exuberant lads ran out and surrounded us.

"Is what Joey just told us real?" yelled Alex.

"Depends on what he told you," I answered clamly.

"He said you two was gettin' married," T.J. said.

"Then, yes, it's real. I asked Tom to marry me and he said yes." Their cheers practically raised the roof off the house.

"When?"

"We don't know, it just happened, we haven't had time to discuss a date just yet. When we do, we'll be sure to let you know, okay?"

"Cool. Will we get to be in the wedding?"

"I'm sure you will." I looked at the clock and realized lunchtime was creeping up on us and I asked if hotdogs and chips would be okay for a quick lunch before leaving to pick up Andy, Mark and Billy. After receiving agreement from everyone, I got the dogs on a griddle while the boys set the table and got the buns, ketchup, mustard and relish out and Tom dealt with the chips. With the feeding frenzy completed, the boys cleaned and stacked the dishes to go into the dishwasher and I noticed Mike and I had to get a move on so we could pick up his guests. "Mike, let's get dressed so we can get out of here. The rest of you, please, please, please, have some clothes on when we get back home. I don't want to scare these three when we get here." Mike and I headed to our rooms to get dressed and met back in the living room. "You ready, munchkin?"

"Yeah, Dad, let's go."

"Be back in about a half hour, guys" I called over my shoulder as I put my hand on Mike's shoulder and led him out to the garage.

❊ ❊ ❊

"So, Uncle Tom, when you two get married, what are we gonna call you then?" Joey asked.

"Yeah, Uncle won't seem right, and we can't call you both Dad," Alex commented.

"How 'bout, 'big guy', you know, since he's so big down there?" T.J. laughed.

"I don't know, yet, guys. We'll figure things out as they need to be."

"I hope it happens before we go to court for our adoptions," Joey mused.

"That would be nice, but we'll just have to wait and see."

"It's gonna be great having two dads," Alex said.

"Two really cool dads," T.J. added.

"Thanks for that, boys. Well, Max, Mike and the others will be back shortly, and we told them we'd be decent when they got here, so let's get some shorts on and be ready for them, I guess. Actually, if you're going to go for a walk through the woods, you might as well put on some warm clothes so you'll be ready to go when they get back."

"Okay, Daddy," T.J. said as he came over and gave me a hug. With that, the three took off down the hall to get dressed and I headed to my bedroom to do the same, wiping tears of joy from eyes.

✲ ✲ ✲

Mike and I arrived at Billy's home and headed to the door. I had Mike knock to announce our arrival while I stood behind him. Sarah answered the door with her son standing behind her, holding a backpack.

"Hi, there, you must be Max and Mike."

"We are," I answered. "I'm obviously Max and this munchkin is my soon-to-be son, Mike," patting him on the head. "It's a pleasure to meet you. Is Billy ready to go?"

"Right here," she said, guiding her son in front of her. Sarah knelt in front of Billy and said, "You be a good boy and do as Max says, you hear me?"

"Yes, ma'am. Thanks for letting me go."

"What time will you bring him home?" she asked, turning back to me.

"I think around sixish, if that's okay with you?"

"That'll be fine. I'll hold off fixing supper until then."

As soon as Billy was out the door, he and Mike sprinted for the car. They were both in and buckled before I joined them, then we headed to Mark's home to repeat the process. When we arrived, both boys hopped out of the car and ran to the door. Mike had knocked and Mark's mother opened the door before I was able to join the boys on the porch.

"Hi, Mrs. Reynolds, we're here to pick up Mark," Billy said.

"Hang on." She turned back into the house and yelled, "Mark, your friends are here. Get a move on, young man." She turned back to the door and asked, "Hi there, I'm Peggy. Are you Mr. Sanders?"

"That's me, I'm Max and this is my son, Mike. I assume you know Billy."

"Hi Mike, nice to meet another one of Mark's friends. Hi, Billy, how are you today?"

"I'm good, Mrs. Reynolds. We're going to Mike's to swim."

"I know, Mark hasn't shut up about it all morning. Are you sure you're ready to handle four boys for the afternoon?"

"Actually, it'll be seven. My own four plus Mark, Billy and Andy."

"You're either very brave or very crazy," Peggy joked.

"I'd prefer to think brave, but it's more likely I'm crazy," I laughed.

Mark appeared at his mom's side at that moment.

"You got everything you need, son?" Peggy asked.

"Yeah, Ma."

"Swimsuit, clean clothes, including underwear?"

"Ma-a-a-a! Not in front of the guys," he whined as he turned pink with embarrassment. I turned my head to hide my chuckle.

"Well, get out of here, then, and go have some fun. And you listen to Mr. Sanders and do as he says. I don't want to hear you've been bad."

"I'm sure he'll be fine, Peggy." With that, the three boys ran to the car and got ready to go pick up Andy. "I'll have him back around six, is that okay?"

"That'll be fine. Thanks, have fun and good luck."

I joined the boys in the car and we headed to Andy's home. Before we got there, I told the boys that I would go to the door by myself this time. They weren't happy with that, but they'd have to live with it. When we got there, I got out of the car, walked to the front door and rang the bell. The door opened to reveal a rather large and gruff looking man.

"Yeah?" he grumbled in disgust.

"Good afternoon," I said politely. "My name is Max Sanders and I'm here to pick up Andy. Is he ready to go?"

"What the fuck you want with that pain-in-the-ass kid? The old lady didn't say nothin' 'bout him goin' nowhere."

"Well, my son and I talked to your wife last evening and we invited Andy to come to our house to spend an afternoon with my son and two of his other friends, Billy and Mark."

"I ain't married to that skank. If you really want him, take him, I don't give a fuck." He turned to the inside of the house and yelled, "Yo, shithead, get your ass in here. Your loser friends are here to take you away."

"We're going to my house so the boys can go swimming and watch a movie."

"I don't care what he does, just get the little turd outta my sight for the day and I'll be happy." Andy had come up behind the man and was trying to sneak around him to get out the door. "You better not fuck up kid or you'll pay for it when you get home."

"I know, sir. Bye, sir."

"Come on, Andy, the others are waiting in the car." I put my hand on his shoulder as I turned towards the car, but I turned back to the door and said, "I'll have him back home about six or six-fifteen. Is that all right?"

"Why the fuck would I care? His mom'll be home then, and she can deal with his sorry ass."

I could feel Andy shrink under my hand as we walked to the car. "The middle seat's full, Andy, why don't you hop in the front with me?"

"Really, he never lets me sit in the front."

"Well, you're not supposed to, but we're not going that far."

"Thanks, Mr. Sanders."

As we pulled away, the boys all said hi to each other and it sounded like they might actually enjoy themselves this afternoon. After they had calmed down, I asked Andy, "Does your dad always talk to you like that?"

"He ain't my dad! He's just mom's boyfriend."

"He doesn't seem very nice."

"He ain't and I wish she'd get rid of him."

"Okay then, sorry you have to deal with that."

"It ain't too bad as long as I stay in my room when he's around."

"What's his name?" I asked.

"Russ Weedman, or something like that."

By that time, we had reached the drive and I'd made the turn to the house.

"Hey, where we goin'? Nobody lives back here," Andy said.

"I do," Mike called from the back.

We'd just reach the clearing in the center of the trees and the boys got their first look at the house.

"Whoa, you live here, Mike?" Mark asked.

"Yep, with my dads and brothers."

"Cool place. Never knew it was back here," Billy said.

"Wait 'til you see the inside," Mike said proudly as I pulled in the garage. "C'mon, guys, let's go."

All four took off for the house, hauling their backpacks with them, as I followed in their footsteps. There was no need to announce our return as I'm sure the others could hear the peals of laughter as they charged down the hall. I found Tom in the living room holding his hands over his ears and I had to laugh.

"What, you expected quiet? Dreamer."

"Hey, don't burst the bubble, man, it's my dream," he retorted.

Mike and his guests came into the living room at a run after dropping their backpacks in Mike's room.

"Hey, who's the other dude, Mike?" Andy asked as they came to a sudden halt.

"He's gonna be my other dad as soon as they get married."

"Two guys can't get married," Andy protested.

"Why not?"

"It's just wrong, that's why not."

"Boys, come here and Mike can introduce you."

They came closer and Mike started with, "Uncle Tom, this is Andy, Mark and Billy. They're in my class at school."

"Hi, guys, nice to meet you. I hope you have fun this afternoon."

"He's a cop and if you're bad, he'll haul you off to jail." Mike added.

"I'll be good, sir," Billy started, "I don't wanna' go to jail."

"Me neither," Mark added.

"Don't worry boys, I don't take kids to jail."

"Hey, Dad, can I show 'em the theater?" Mike asked as he turned to face me.

"Sure, but weren't you planning to go on a walk to look for deer?"

"In a minute, I want 'em to see where we're gonna watch a movie later."

"Okay, go ahead." They scooted off and returned in a few minutes chattering wildly. "You guys ready for your walk now?"

"Yeah, can we go swimming when we get back?"

"You bet. Are your brothers going with you?"

"I think so. They said they would."

"Okay, if you do find deer, remember to be careful around them and don't get too close."

"We won't, Dad." The four headed to Mike's room to get ready for their walk and came back shortly with T.J., Alex and Joey following.

"Alex, Joey, watch after them and don't let anybody get too far apart. I don't want to have to send out a search party later to find you. And make sure you stay away from where the bodies are buried," I joked.

"We'll keep an eye on 'em, Dad," Joey said.

"And we'll stay away from your secret corner, too," Alex added while grinning evilly and rubbing his hands together.

With that, the seven lads turned and headed for the front door. As the door opened, I heard 'Is he serious? About bodies out there?' Tom and I chuckled as the door closed.

"So, how did picking up the boys go?"

"Getting them was fine, taking them back is going to be another story."

"Why?"

"Let's just say I don't think we'd be doing Andy any favors taking him back to that house." I told Tom what I heard from the man who answered the door.

"Do I need to call Dylan?"

"Not yet. Let's see if we see any bruises or marks on Andy when we go for a swim."

"Just say the word and I'm on the phone."

"I know, Tom. Thanks."

❋ ❋ ❋

"So, Mike, how long has Mr. Sanders been your dad?" Billy asked.

"We got here last Friday. Didn't know for sure we'd get to stay until the next day, though."

"Yeah, we thought we'd be going back to our foster homes on Sunday," T.J. said.

"You guys like it here?" Mark asked.

"What's not to like? We got a great house, theater, pool, everything we ever wanted," Joey answered.

"Yeah, and most of the time, we don't have to wear no clothes," Alex tossed into the conversation, then promptly clapped his hands over his mouth when he realized what he'd done.

"Dang it, Alex, you weren't s'posed to say nothin' 'bout that."

"I know, sorry," he mumbled as he hung his head and stared at the ground.

"Wait, you guys run around naked all the time?" Andy asked, surprise showing on his face.

"Since big-mouth screwed up and let it slip, yeah, we do," Joey said.

"Ain't that weird?" Mark asked.

"A little at first, maybe, but now we been doin' it for a week, so not no more," Mike answered.

"What about your dad and the other dude?" Billy quizzed. "They don't wear no clothes, either?"

T.J., Mike, Joey and Alex exchanged a glance with each other. Finally, T.J. shrugged his shoulders and said, "Yeah, them, too. Why wouldn't they?"

"Wow!" Billy said. "I ain't never seen my dad naked."

"Me either," Mark added.

"I don't even know my dad," Andy mumbled, looking down at the ground. "And I sure don't want to see Russ naked. He probably looks as nasty as his moods are."

"Look, guys," Joey interrupted, "we weren't s'posed to say nothin' and you guys ain't s'posed know about it. You can't tell no one," he begged.

"Yeah, if you say anything, it could screw up our gettin' to stay here. We don't want that to happen," Alex said. "We *can't* go back to where we were."

"Please, say you won't say nothin'," T.J. pleaded.

"Hang on, I ain't too sure 'bout that. This don't sound right," Andy said. "Mark, Billy, come here a sec."

While Andy, Mark and Billy huddled into a serious talk, Joey turned to Alex, "Man, Alex, you really fucked up this time."

"I know. I'm really sorry guys, I just hope they keep their mouths shut."

"We'll find out soon enough. Here they come," T.J. said pointing towards the other three.

"Okay, here's what we'll do. I think you'll like it. We'll keep your secret on one condition." Andy said.

"What!? That sounds like you're gonna blackmail us," Joey responded.

"Call it what you want. You wanna' hear the condition?"

"Probably not but spit it out anyway."

"Okay, we'll keep quiet if we get to join you when we get back to the

303

house."

"Wait, you guys wanna go naked, too?" Mike asked.

"Why not?" Billy asked. "None of us got anything special to hide, do we?"

"Not compared to Uncle Tom, we don't," T.J. giggled.

"Oh, and one more thing," Andy said, "Your dad and that Tom dude have to get naked, too."

"Uh-oh, that could be a problem. I don't think they'll do it with you three here," Alex said.

"That's the deal, take or leave it."

"It's our turn to talk, Andy, give us a minute, okay?" Joey said.

My four made their own huddle and returned shortly with a plan.

"Okay," Joey started, "Here's what we'll do," and he explained the plan. "You think that'll work?"

"It's worth trying," Andy answered as he grinned mischievously.

After about thirty minutes of being outside, we heard the front door open as the seven boys returned.

"Hi guys, did you enjoy the walk?"

"Yeah, it's pretty neat out there," Andy said.

"Even though we didn't find any deer or dead bodies," Mark laughed.

"You got any more trails out here?" Billy asked.

"Several of them. You'll have to come back when it's warmer and try them out."

"That'd be cool. Thanks, Mr. Sanders."

"You want some hot chocolate before we go swimming?"

"That'd be great, Dad," Mike answered.

It took Tom and I five minutes to get the warm drinks made and set on the table for the boys. "Tom and I will get ready to swim while you warm up a bit. Don't forget to put your cups in the sink when you're done."

"We will, Dad," Alex answered.

Tom and I headed to our bedroom to change. When I closed the bedroom door, I looked at him and asked, "Does something seem a little off to you?"

"What? I didn't notice anything."

"It might just be my imagination, but they seemed awfully quiet when they came back in from their walk. Especially for seven boys."

"That's fine with me," Tom laughed. "Beats the hell out of hearing them screaming in the pool."

"We'll see." We got our swim shorts on, grabbed towels and headed out to the living room to wait for the boys to be ready. As we passed the kitchen, we noticed the table was empty, so we assumed the boys were changing in their rooms. Tom and I sat by the fireplace and we didn't have long to wait before we could hear the giggles of seven boys coming down the hall from their rooms. I'm not sure why, but I was shocked as they turned the corner into the living room and formed a line in front of us, towels tossed over their shoulders.

"Okay, Dad, we're ready, let's go," Mike grinned.

23

"Um, I do believe you're forgetting something," I said to the lineup of seven nude boys as Tom buried his face in his hands to hide his laughter, earning him an elbow to the ribs. "I told you they were up to something," I whispered. The boys looked at each other, giggling, then looked back to Tom and me, goofy grins on their faces.

"Nope, we didn't forget nothin'," Joey said.

"Would you please explain where your swimsuits are?"

"Ours are still wet and they forgot to bring theirs," Alex answered.

"I'm not buying that, and you know it. Now, what gives. I thought I was pretty plain when I laid out the rules for this afternoon."

"You were, Dad, but Alex screwed up while we were on our walk," Joey answered.

"What'd you do, Alex?"

"We were just tellin' 'em what it's like to live here and it kinda slipped out how we go naked most of the time. Sorry, Dad."

"That still doesn't fully explain why you're all standing there without swimsuits."

"Well," Joey started, "we told 'em they couldn't tell nobody or they'd screw up our adoptions. And they told us they'd keep quiet only if they could get naked, too. It seemed like a good idea to us. We don't like wearing clothes and they wanted to try it, too."

"I have the distinct feeling I'm still waiting for the other shoe to drop."

"Uh, we ain't got no shoes on, Dad," Mike giggled.

"Well," started Alex, "youhavtajoinus," he mumbled to the floor.

"Excuse me, I didn't quite catch that."

"Fine," he said, then looked directly into my eyes and repeated, "You. Have. To. Join. Us. Did you catch it all that time?"

"Loud and clear, young man." Tom was practically rolling on the floor with laughter by now. "You really think this is funny, fuzzball?" I asked as I turned to him for some help.

"Yeah, I do. I figured they'd come up with some way to get us all naked this afternoon. Nice to know my finely-honed powers of detection are running true to form."

"You could have warned me."

"Qué? No hablo Inglés, señor," he responded and cracked up again.

"Fine, I can see I'm outnumbered here. I've created monsters, I tell ya."

"Yeah, c'mon, Dad, it ain't no big deal, right?" T.J. asked.

"Okay, c'mon, bubba, let's join the crowd." We stood up, pulled off our shorts, dropped them on the chairs and turned to face the boys. "Okay, you happy? Can we please go swimming, now?"

"Yeah, let's go!" yelled Mike.

I led the way since I had the shelter key and I heard a voice whispering behind me, 'Man, you weren't kidding, T.J., Tom's got a big one'. I unlocked the shelter and the boys tossed their towels on the table as they ran past me to jump in the pool. Tom caught up with me and we headed for deeper waters. I said, "I'm not sure this is such a good idea, Tom," I commented as we slipped into the water.

"Why not? You see anybody picking on anybody? They're all playing together and having fun. Who cares if they're not wearing their swimsuits. They sure as hell don't. They're all equal in each other's eyes right now. I think this may actually help solve Mike's problem at school."

"We can hope. But, we're not all equal. I heard one of them whisper to T.J. on the way out that you 'have a big one'. Not exactly what I expected to hear today."

"He ain't lyin', is he?"

"No, I suppose not," I laughed. "You realize, I hope, that we could be setting a dangerous precedent here."

"And...?"

"I imagine the twins are now going to expect to have their upcoming birthday party nude."

"Oh, crap, I didn't think about that."

"Bet you are now," I laughed. "By the way, I thought of something I wanted to ask you about."

"Go ahead."

"Last Saturday when Carol called you to come help me out at the

Muellers, she said you owed her a favor. What'd she do that you owed her for?"

"Oh, that," he said as he blushed.

"Yeah, that. Fess up, big boy."

"Well, shortly after she got to town, I was sent to her apartment complex on a call. There was a B & E in an apartment down the hall from hers and I was assigned to get witness statements from all the residents on the floor. When it was her turn, she invited me into her place to have a cup of coffee while we talked. Since she was the last person I needed to interview, we ended up talking quite a while and during the conversation, I swung my arm or something, hit my coffee cup and dumped it all over my lap."

"Ouch, I bet that stung."

"More than you know. I was burning and, without thinking, I just stood up and dropped my pants and boxers to my ankles. God, it was embarrassing, standing there in her kitchen with my roasted junk on display."

"I'd imagine. So, what happened next?"

"Well, she turned her head, but she'd already gotten the full Monty and I was in some serious pain. She really felt bad about it because she'd just refilled our cups, so she gave me a towel to cover myself and had me sit back down on a dry chair. Then she got me an ice bag to help with the burning issue and tossed my clothes in her washer. So, there I sat, in a strange woman's apartment, bare-assed, ice bag and towel covering my crotch for the next hour and a half while she washed and dried my clothes. We talked about a lot during that hour and a half."

I couldn't help but snicker at the image that had formed in my brain while he told the story. "When my clothes were finally dry and the burning in my crotch had finally receded, I excused myself to the bathroom to get dressed. When I came back, she was sitting there in her kitchen, just giggling her ass off. When I thanked her for everything and started to leave, she stopped me, gave me a kiss and asked me for a date."

"Oh, my god, Tom. That's freakin' hilarious."

"Eh, not so much, man. I had to break her heart and tell it could never work out for us since I'm gay. She freaked, initially, but slowly regained her composure and apologized for kissing me and just assuming I was straight. I told her it was no big deal. I mean, I'd just sat there for what seemed forever, almost naked, in a strange woman's apartment, and me being gay just didn't come up. What can I say? She swore she'd take the secret of that night to her grave."

"That story makes something she said last Friday make a whole more sense."

"What was that?"

"I'd just gotten out of the pool and was drying off when she asked, 'Why are all the hot guys gay?'. I couldn't understand, then, where it came from, but now it makes sense."

"Nice to know the ladies think I'm hot, not that it does them any good."

"Don't worry, Tom, I think you're hot, too."

"Thanks, Max, I think the same of you."

"So, you owed Carol a favor for keeping her mouth shut, huh? Are you paid up yet?"

"Not by a longshot. I'll owe her for that the rest of my life," he laughed.

We continued lounging and the boys played for another half-hour when I asked, "Well, shall we get out of here and get a movie going?"

"Sounds like a plan to me, lead the way."

We climbed out of the pool and headed to grab our towels.

"Boys, time to get out and start your movie." All seven climbed out and grabbed their towels to dry off before heading back into the house. "T.J., why don't you shower with the twins today and Andy, Mark and Billy can jump in with Mike."

"Why do we have to take a shower, Mr. Sanders? Isn't the pool clean?" Billy asked.

"Oh, it's clean, but you don't want to spend the rest of the day coated with chlorine, do you?"

"Didn't think 'bout that, I guess."

"That's why we take showers after every swim, Billy." They all took off to get cleaned up while Tom and I got popcorn and drinks ready for the movie. I'd half hoped the boys would come back from their showers dressed, but was pretty sure that wasn't going to happen. I was not disappointed when seven nude lads crossed the dining room, chattering away, on their way to the theater. "Mike, why don't you pick out the movie you want, and Tom and I will bring refreshments in a minute. Make sure all the chairs have towels down before you sit."

"Okay, Dad."

"What're the towels for?" Mark asked.

"They keep the chairs clean when we sit on them. All nudists do that," I answered.

"Are we nudists, now?" Andy asked.

"I don't know about when you're at home, but it looks like you are when you're visiting here. Are you enjoying it?"

"Yeah, it's cool," Andy answered. "I spend so much time in my room because of Russ, maybe I can do it at home, too."

"That may not be a good idea, Andy. Russ probably wouldn't like it if he found you that way, would he?"

"Yeah, you're pro'lly right," he answered dejectedly. "He'd beat my ass with his belt just like he does when I do anything else he don't like."

"Does that happen a lot," Tom asked in his cop voice.

"Oh, crap, I shouldn't a said that. 'Specially 'round a cop. I don't want to make no trouble and give him another reason to beat me."

"Andy, come here, please," I said. "The rest of you get settled in the theater and we'll be there shortly." The other six headed to the theater while Andy came into the kitchen with Tom and me.

"Andy, I'm going to ask you some questions and I want you to tell me the truth, okay?"

"Yeah, okay," he mumbled in response while looking at the floor.

"Does Russ really hit you with a belt?"

"Sometimes, but only when I'm bad."

"What does he consider 'bad'?"

"You know, not taking out the trash, not keeping my room clean, staying up too late, whatever."

"Come a little closer, Andy." He hesitated, and I added, "Come on, Andy, we're not going to hurt you, we just want to check you for bruises and other marks. I promise, that's it." I guess he finally decided we were okay and came over to us. We knelt down to his level and looked over his front side and saw nothing of concern. Then, I asked him to turn around so we could check his back side. Tom and I were appalled at what we saw. Faded bruises were very apparent on his lower back, buttocks and upper thighs. They were barely visible now, which explains why we hadn't noticed them earlier in the pool, but with him this close and dry, there was no doubt that Andy had been severely beaten. Multiple times.

"Thanks, Andy. Does Russ hit your mom, also?" I asked as he turned back around to face us.

"Yeah, but not with a belt. He uses his fists on her."

"You don't like it when he hits you or your mom, do you?"

"I hate it, but he's way too big for me to fight and I can't do nothin' to make him stop. I been afraid to say anything to anybody 'cause who knows what he'd do to me if he found out."

"Maybe you can't stop him, Andy, but we can. And we will. You've done the right thing in trusting us. Now, why don't you go join the others in the theater and we'll be right behind you?" Andy scampered off while Tom and I grabbed bowls of popcorn and drinks in cups with lids and followed in his tracks. Mike had selected the movie *Cars*, and once I had it playing, Tom and I retreated to the kitchen.

"I knew that man was trouble the instant he opened the door."

"Am I making a call?" Tom asked.

"Damn right you are, this shit stops right now."

"You know Dylan's gonna come here first and he'll want to know how we know, don't you? Are you ready for that explanation?"

"I'm not worried about Dylan. He, of all people, knows how we live out here and he also knows that there's nothing wrong with it."

"As long as you're sure." Tom picked up the phone and dialed Dylan's cell phone.

"Sarge? Deputy Wright here."

"I have to assume, since were using titles, this is an official call and not a social one."

"Absolutely. We have a situation out here that needs your attention."

"Where's here, Tom?"

"Max's home."

"What's going on?"

"Mike has some kids over from school to try and make friends with them this afternoon. Max picked the boys up and had a bad feeling about one the kids."

"What kind of bad feeling?"

"The man who answered the door was verbally abusive towards Andy and after our swim, he said that Russ beat him with a belt at times. He also told us this guy also beats on his mom with his fists. Max and I checked Andy over and found fading bruises on his back, behind and thighs."

"Dare I ask how you found bruising on his behind?"

"Well, you know how the boys are."

"What the hell, Tom. Can't you keep clothes on anybody out there?"

"It's a long story, Sarge, but we need to deal with this before the boys go home. We won't leave Andy at that house with this guy."

"Did you get anything for a name besides Russ?"

"Andy said it was Weedman, or something like that," I answered.

"Okay, let me do a search and see what I can find. I'll be out there in a little bit."

"Thanks, Sarge, we appreciate it."

I turned to Tom and said, "We need to let the boys know that Dylan's coming out and we all need to get some clothes on. Normally, I wouldn't worry about it, but with this being an official call, I think that'd be best."

"They ain't gonna like it. Especially since Dylan's been here before."

"I know, but that was social, this is business. They need to start learning the difference as to when being nude is acceptable and not."

"You're right, let's go tell 'em."

We headed to the theater and paused the movie to get their attention. "Boys, Tom's boss will be here shortly."

"Mr. Brock's comin' out, too? Can we go swimmin' again?" T.J. asked.

"He's not coming for that kind of visit. He's coming out to help fix Andy's problem."

"Really, Mr. Sanders?" Andy asked with wide eyes of surprise.

"Really, Andy. And we all need to have clothes on when he gets here."

"Why, Dad, he knows we go naked all the time. He even joined us the other night," Alex said.

"That was what we call a social visit, boys. This is a business visit. You need to learn that we sometimes need to wear clothes at home. This is one of those times. Why don't you all go pull on a pair of shorts and a shirt, then you can come back and continue your movie until he gets here? Go!" Seven bare, white behinds flew by Tom and me as they took off to get dressed. "I guess we need to follow suit and pull something on, too."

"If this dude, Russ, is as big as you say he is, I should probably put my uniform on and go with Dylan so he's got some backup. I don't want him going there alone."

"That's probably a good idea. We know he beats women and little kids, but there's no telling how he'll react to the cops showin' up on his doorstep."

After we got dressed, we met the boys in the theater and got the movie going again, then Tom and I returned to the kitchen to wait for Dylan.

"Do you think I should call Carol and get her out here, too? We are dealing with child abuse and that's part of what she does."

"That'd be a good idea. With the situation, she could provide more grounds for whatever Dylan and I end up having to do with Russ."

I dialed Carol's number and waited for her answer.

"Hello, Max, ready to return the boys?" she laughed.

"Not on your life, lady. Listen, Carol, we have a situation here and I think you should be involved."

"What's going on, Max?"

"Mike has some boys from school over this afternoon and one of them shows signs of abuse."

"What signs?"

"He has bruising on his back, behind, and thighs, and he was the leader of the three who were picking on Mike at school."

"And just how did you see this bruising?"

"We all went for a swim this afternoon and ..."

" 'Nuff said, Max. Give me twenty-five to thirty minutes and I'll be there. Do I need to call law enforcement?"

"Already done and Dylan's on the way. He should already be here by the time you get here."

"Good, I'm on the way. Don't do anything until I get there."

"Thanks, Carol. See you soon." I turned to Tom, "Okay, she's on the way and said not to do anything until she gets here."

"Good, it'll be nice to have her input."

Twenty minutes later, the drive sensor announced an arrival. I went to the door and saw a Sangamon County Sheriff's car pull in and Dylan get out of the car. I opened the door as he was coming up the walk and said, "Afternoon, Dylan, how ya doin'?"

"I've had better days. How 'bout yourself, Max?"

"Hectic, but you have to expect that with three extra boys in the house."

"How's Tom?" he asked as he stepped through the door.

"Ask him, yourself. He's waiting in the kitchen."

"He's here already?"

"He should be since he living here now."

"Guess he forgot to file a change of address form with the department," he grinned.

"Give him a break, will ya, we've been busy."

"I guess so." We'd reached the kitchen and Dylan said, "Afternoon, Tom. How's the new living quarters workin' out?"

"Great, Sarge. Thanks for asking."

"Why're you in uniform? You're not on duty today."

"Max said this Russ dude's pretty big and mean. I'm not letting you go there alone."

"Good, 'cause with what I found out on the search, this is one sick mothe..., uh, individual."

"What'd you find?" I asked.

"First, I need a description of the guy you saw to make sure I got the right info 'cause the last name is different from what you said."

"I'd guess about 6'-1", 225 to 250 pounds, brownish hair, tattoos on both arms that I could see, ugly."

"Sounds like a match to me. Let me show you the picture the system spit out." Dylan pulled a mugshot out of a folder and slid it across the counter to me.

"That's him, no doubt in my mind."

"Good. This guy's bad news. Multiple arrests for drunk and disorderly, assault, burglary, etc., etc. He has multiple warrants out on him right now, including drugs, armed robbery, another assault. We've been looking for him for a while, but he's been flying under the radar. Nice to finally know where the scumbag's been hiding. It'll be good to get his ass off the streets."

"Glad I could find him for you. Pure luck."

"I'll take what I can get. Now, I need to speak with the abuse victim."

"You'll have to wait a few more minutes, Sarge."

"Why? I want to get this guy while we know where he is."

"That's my fault, Dylan. After Tom talked to you, I called Carol since we thought we were dealing with abuse only. She's on her way out and told us not to do anything until she gets here. She wants to be here when we talk to Andy."

"Didn't think about that, sorry for jumping the gun. She's absolutely correct that she should be here. I can't question a minor without someone there to protect their interests, no matter what."

"So, boss, while we wait for Carol, there's something I need to tell you," Tom muttered.

"Spit it out, boy."

"I've moved in with Max and we're going to get married."

"I knew the first since Max told me that at the door, but the second is certainly news. When did you two make that decision?"

"This morning, boss."

"When's it gonna happen?"

"We haven't gotten that far yet, Dylan," I said. "We're hoping we can make it official before the adoptions are finalized so both our names can be included on the court papers."

"Whenever it happens, I better be invited. Congrats to both of you. I wish you nothing but the best, for all of you."

"Thanks, boss." Dylan gave each of us a hug just as the drive sensor dinged to announce Carol's arrival. I met her at the door and led her into the kitchen to meet with Dylan and Tom.

"Well, afternoon, boys. How's everybody doing?"

"Great, Carol. I'm glad you're here," Dylan answered. "This guy is bad news and we need to get him out of that house."

"Do you have grounds to do that, besides his abuse of the young man visiting here this afternoon?"

"Plenty, but if we can throw another charge at him, it'll keep him jail and away from his victims even longer."

"Victims?? I was only told about the one boy, who else?"

"Andy told Tom and me that he beats his mom, also," I replied.

"Okay, let's talk to him and get this show on the road. Can we use your study, Max?"

"Of course, why don't you and Dylan head in there and I'll bring Andy along in a minute?"

"We'll be waiting. Thanks, Max. Come on Dylan." Carol and Dylan headed for the study while I turned to the theater to get Andy.

"Andy, I hate to interrupt the movie, but would you please come with me for a little bit?"

"What's up Mr. Sanders?"

"I have a couple of people who need to talk to you."

"Do I have to?"

"If you want Russ out of your home, I think you should."

"Okay, let's go," he said dejectedly. I rested my hand on his shoulder and guided him to the study. After entering, I closed the door behind us.

"Andy, I want you to meet Carol Ward and Sheriff Dylan Brock of the Sangamon County Sheriff's department. Carol is working with me on the boys' adoptions and she's here to help protect you. Sergeant Brock is here to help get Russ out of your house. They need to ask you some questions and they need truthful answers."

"Okay," he mumbled.

"Thanks, Max," Dylan said. "We'll take it from here. Can you wait outside with Deputy Wright, please?"

I'd turned to leave when I felt Andy grab my hand and he pulled me back by his side. "If he ain't stayin', I ain't sayin' nothin'."

I knelt in front of him and said, "Andy, it's okay. Just answer their questions and they'll take care of everything else."

"I'll tell 'em whatever they wanna' know, but not without you here, Mr. Sanders." I looked to the others and received nods of acceptance from both. I sat in my chair behind the desk while Carol and Dylan took seats on the other side. Once I was seated, Andy crawled up in my lap and made himself comfortable.

Carol started her questions with, "Andy, can you tell me your last name, please, and your mom's name?"

"My mom's name is Arlene and our last name is Cox."

"Okay, good. How long has Russ been living with you?"

"Since before Christmas."

"Do you know where your mom met him?"

"Not a clue."

"That's all right, Andy. Now you told Mr. Sanders that Russ has beaten you and your mom. Is that true?"

"It sure is. He uses a belt on me and his fists on my mom."

"How many times has he done this?"

"He's hurt me five or six times since he showed up, but he's hurt mom lots more."

"Okay, now I need to ask you a question that you won't like, but I need a truthful answer."

"What?"

"Has Russ ever touched you in a place he shouldn't?"

"What, you mean, like, my di ...?"

"Unfortunately, yes. I know this is uncomfortable, Andy, but I need to know if anything like that has happened."

"NO! Never!"

"I'm sorry to upset you, but I need to know these things. Now, I need one last thing."

"Now what?"

"Max told me when he called this afternoon that you had some bruising on your lower back, behind and legs. You're not going to like this, but I need to see the bruises and take pictures of them for evidence."

"No way! I ain't showin' you my butt and you sure ain't takin' no pictures of it!"

"Andy, I know you don't want to do it, but if we're going to punish Russ for hurting you, we need to have proof that it happened. Without proof, we can't put him in jail."

"Well, get your proof some other way 'cause I ain't showin' you my butt."

I held up my hand to interrupt Carol and said, "Andy, remember, you already let Tom and me check you out all over."

"Well, yeah, you're guys, that's different."

"Can we do it this way? We can ask Carol to step out of the room, then you can show Dylan the bruises. That way, we can get the proof we need, and Carol won't see your behind."

"I guess that'd be okay. I mean, you already seen it, and he's a guy. Yeah, that'll work."

"Will you let Dylan take the pictures they need?"

"I don't want to, but I guess so. If it'll help get that jerk outta my house, I'll do it."

"Good deal, Andy. Carol, would you excuse us for just a few minutes, please?"

"Sure. I'll be waiting outside the door," she answered with a light smile of understanding.

"Thanks." She left the study and closed the door behind her. "Okay, Andy, she's gone, can we do this now?"

"Okay," he grumped.

He jumped off my lap, turned around, lifted his shirt and dropped his shorts to the floor.

"Can you see the bruises, Dylan?"

"Barely, it's hard to tell if their bruises or shadows from this angle. Any chance of getting better light on the area?"

I knelt in front of Andy and gently said, "Andy, I know this is embarrassing, but we need to get more light on your backside. Will you let me lift you up on the desk so we can turn on the desk lamp and make the bruises easier to see?"

"Oh, why not? Hurry up and get this over with."

I put my hands under his arms and lifted him up so he was standing on the desk, his shorts dropping off his feet and remaining on the floor. I then turned on the light and directed it to illuminate the proper area.

"There ya go, Max. That's perfect. Okay, Andy, I'm going to take the pictures now."

"Just do it," he mumbled.

Dylan took the pictures he needed of Andy's back side, then had him turn around so he could verify there was no bruising on his front side.

When we were done, I set Andy back on the floor and he pulled his shorts back on.

"Andy," I said, "I know you didn't want to go through that and it's embarrassing as all get out, but I'm proud of you for doing it."

"Me, too, Andy," Dylan added. "It takes a big man to let other people see you vulnerable like that. You did great."

"Thanks, Mr. Sanders, Mr. Brock. If it'll get that jerk gone and keep him from hurting anybody else, it was worth it."

"Consider it done, young man," Dylan responded.

"Can he go back to his friends, now?" I asked.

"I don't see why not." He knelt in front of Andy and said, "You did a great thing, young man, and I thank you for helping out the department today. I promise that nobody will ever see these pictures unless they can prove to me it's absolutely necessary. And once Russ is in jail where he belongs, I'll personally destroy them. Now, why don't you go back to your movie and let us take it from here?" Dylan held out his hand, Andy gave him a quick shake and ran out of the study.

Carol came back in and asked, "Well?"

"There is definitely bruising. It's pretty faded, but still visible, so there's another charge we can use against this loser."

"Do you need anything else from me, Dylan?" Carol asked.

"Well, Max said the boy's mother wasn't home when he picked Andy up, so I don't if she'll be there when we go get Russ. Since you're already out here, you may want to go along and check out the home after we get him out of the way."

"That's a good idea. Shall I take my own car, or should I ride with you?"

"You'll probably want your own car there since mine will be occupied with the scum of the earth."

"Good point. If I had to be in the same car with him, I'd kill the son-of-a-bitch."

"Whoa, Carol, take a deep breath and relax. I don't want to have to arrest you, too. Okay, I'm going to call for another car to meet us at the truck stop and then we'll continue on from there. Once we have Russ under control and in the car, we'll search the house and make sure whether the mother is or isn't home."

"Sounds like a plan to me, Dylan," I said. "Anything I can do?"

"You've already done it by calling us, Max. It's our job now. You stay here and take care of the boys until Tom gets back."

"I can do that. Thanks, you two."

"No, thank you, Max. Like I said, we've been looking for this guy, just didn't know where he was hiding. Now, we can get his sorry ass off the streets and in a jail where it belongs. Let me go out to my unit, make a call to get more help and we'll be ready to go."

We left the study and as Dylan headed outside, Carol and I returned into the kitchen where Tom was waiting.

"Hi Carol. Where's Sarge?"

"He went out to call another car to help you two corral Russ."

"Good. The more, the merrier."

"So," Carol began, "How're you two doing? And how's our boys?"

"We're great, Carol, and so are the boys. We do have a little bit of news to give you since you're here, though."

"Will I like it?"

"I hope so. And I hope it won't hurt the adoptions."

"Oh Lord, what have you two done now?" Carol asked with exasperation.

"This morning, before I went to pick up Mike's friends, I asked Tom if he'd marry me."

"And I said yes."

"Oh, my God! Congratulations to both of you. I'm so happy for you."

"You're not freaked?" I asked. "You were pretty shook up earlier this week when I told you about us getting together, but this you're okay with?"

"I'm over that, Max. You're both grown men and can make your own decisions. I realized after you left my office that I was overreacting. And it should have no effect whatsoever on your adoptions."

"That's good to hear." I looked to Tom and, with a sly wink, asked, "So, what do you think? Should we invite her to our wedding?"

"Gee, I don't know, Max. She seems like quite the troublemaker to me," he grinned in response.

"Look, you two, if I'm *not* invited, that will most definitely hurt the adoptions," Carol responded sarcastically.

"Don't worry, milady, you will most certainly be invited. It was, after all, you who brought us together. It's all your fault."

At that moment, Dylan came back in. "Okay, another unit's on the way, we better get to the truck stop and be ready to roll. Ms. Ward, I'm going to ask you to stay in your car until we have the situation under control."

"No problem, Dylan."

I followed Dylan, Carol and Tom to the door and after Dylan and Carol had stepped outside, I grabbed Tom and spun him back around. I wrapped my arms around him and whispered in his ear, "You be careful and come home in one piece, you hear me?"

"I hear ya. I'll be back soon." Then, he turned to join Dylan in the car and I slowly closed the door. With nothing else to do, I headed to the theater to wait it out with the boys.

24

Time seemed to crawl as I sat there, dark thoughts swirling through my brain, and I simply couldn't focus on the movie. When *Cars* ended, the boys asked if they could watch another. Since we had nothing but time, I let Andy select the next movie. He chose *The Spiderwick Chronicles* and I got it started, then retook my seat and sat in a daze waiting to hear from Tom or Carol.

※ ※ ※

"So, you and Max are getting serious pretty quick, aren't you, Tom?" Dylan asked while we waited for our backup to arrive.

"I know it seems like it, Sarge, but we really do feel we've known each other our whole lives. Everything just seemed to click between us and fall into place."

"I am truly happy for you, Tom. Maybe, someday, I'll get lucky and find the right guy, too."

"If it can happen for me, Sarge, it can happen for you."

"From the mouths of babes ... Ah, here's our backup. Let's have a chat before we go get this loser." We got out of our cars and met for a short discussion. "Afternoon, Doug, Neil, you ready for this?"

"Afternoon, Sarge, Tom. What do we got?" Neil asked.

"We have a suspect, Russ Weder, holed up in a house in town here. We've been trying to find him for months and got a tip this afternoon that he'd been located."

"Where'd the tip come from? Is it a reliable source?"

"Anonymous to you guys, but I know the man and believe his information is good. Tom and I will attempt to come in through the front door. I want you two to take positions at the back corners of the house so you can see everything that goes on back there and keep sight lines up each side, also. I don't want this guy getting away, again. And I want him alive, got it?"

"You got it, Sarge."

"Ms. Ward will be waiting in her car while we get the suspect under control."

"What's she doing here?" Doug asked.

"Well, in addition to all the other problems for Mr. Weder, she's adding domestic and child abuse to the pile. It turns out our felon likes to beat on women and kids, too."

"Well, let's quit wasting time and go get him."

"Okay, let's move out. No sirens or lights. No sense announcing our arrival before we have to."

"Got it, boss. Lead the way."

We climbed back in our cars and took off. When we arrived at the house, Doug and Neil took their positions at the rear and once they were set, Dylan pounded on the front door. A voice from inside yelled, "Who's there and what the fuck you want?"

"Police, Russ. Come outside so we can talk, please." We immediately heard loud crashing like a herd of buffalo had been turned loose inside the house. Dylan kicked the front door open and we charged inside just in time to see Russ darting through the kitchen on his way to the back door. As soon as he flew out into the cold, sunny afternoon, we saw Russ raise an arm and a flurry of gunshots ensued. We continued on through the house and met Doug and Neil in the back yard, with Russ writhing on the ground and holding his right thigh.

"What the hell's goin' on back here? I said I wanted him alive."

"Look, boss, he's still alive. Can't you hear his pitiful moaning?" Neil asked with a grin. "Besides, when he hit the door, he had a gun. He raised his arm like he was gonna shoot Doug, so I took the shot and hit him in the leg. He lost his gun when he collapsed and it flew over there," the deputy recited as he pointed to the gun laying on the ground ten feet away.

"All right, good work, Neil. Now, put cuffs on that piece of shit and find something to tie off his leg. I don't want him bleedin' out. Doug, call an ambulance. Tom, why don't you get Carol after you check inside and make sure there's no other bad guys in there."

"You got it, Sarge." I turned to follow my instructions and just as I did, a man in camouflage burst through the door, gun raised, aimed directly at me. I pulled mine just as he fired his first shot and managed to get a shot off before I collapsed to the ground, then heard another flurry of shots as my partners dispatched the late arrival. Then, the lights went out.

※ ※ ※

I still hadn't heard anything from Tom, Dylan or Carol and was getting antsy. They'd left only forty-five minutes ago, but they didn't have that far to go. I should have heard something by now. The boys were engrossed in the movie, but I couldn't concentrate on what was happening on the screen.

"You guys want a drink or anything?" I asked in a lame attempt to distract myself from the nasty thoughts swirling around in my head.

"Juice sounds good, Dad, you want some help?" Alex asked as he turned in his chair.

"You bet, big guy, thanks." We headed to the kitchen and I retrieved seven juice boxes of assorted flavors from the fridge.

"When's Uncle Tom coming back home?" Alex asked as we stabbed the little straw into each box.

"I don't know, Alex. Soon I hope," I answered as we carefully carried the juice boxes back to the theater. We handed one to each boy and, again, I took my seat behind them and continued to stew in silence.

※ ※ ※

The next thing I knew, Dylan was crouched over me, one arm reaching to the left side of my head and his hand holding it still, yelling, "Wake up, dammit. You ain't dyin' on my watch."

"Whoa, Sarge, I'm here. And quit screamin' would ya, my head's killing me."

"As it should, mister. You got a hell of a crease down your left temple and just above your ear. Good thing you got a damn hard head."

"How bad is it? Will I still need to part my hair when I comb it?"

"You'll end up with a nice scar once they get you stitched up, but I think you'll be okay. They'll have to shave this mop you call hair to fix you up, though."

"Who gives a shit about that, it'll grow back. As long as I'm still in one piece, more or less, that's all that counts. Crap, I gotta call Max and let him know what's happened."

"Don't worry 'bout that, Tom, I'll take care of it. By the way, good shootin', Tex. You plugged that bastard right in the heart."

"Nice to know all that practice was good for somethin'. Five years on the job and I've never had to pull my gun, and then it has to happen in my last week. Just my damn luck. Go figure."

"Now that you're awake again, you hold this compress to your head while I deal with the mess we've created."

"Thanks, boss, I'll just lay here and bleed all over the yard."

"Best thing you can do right now, Tom." He stood and got on his radio, "Dispatch, this is Brock, we need another ambulance and a meat wagon at this location, pronto."

"On the way, Sarge, Neil already called it in," the dispatcher replied.

"Good." He turned to Neil and said, "Neil, check the house for any other idiots who think they want to die today. If it's clear, get Ms. Ward so she can check out the house and see if the young man who lives here can come back home tonight."

"On my way, boss."

The first ambulance finally arrived, and as the paramedics came around the house and headed towards Russ, Dylan directed, "Oh no, you don't, that asshole can wait for the next one. You take care of this man, first. And you better do it right. He's got a man and four boys waiting at home for him."

The crew exchanged confused looks but headed my direction anyway. They gently lifted me on the gurney and took a quick look at the crease in my scalp. "Sergeant Brock," one of them began, "we better get him to the emergency room. They'll want to do some scans and make sure there's no internal damage."

"Then load him up and get him the fuck outta' here!" Dylan screamed.

"Yes, SIR! You got it." The paramedics carefully loaded me on a gurney, then started wheeling me through the yard and when we rounded the corner at the front of the house, we met Neil leading Carol inside.

"Oh my God, Tom, what happened?" she cried as she ran over to see me.

"Just a scratch, Carol, I'll be fine," I managed to mutter through teeth tightly clenched from the pain ripping my skull in two.

"You better be fine or I'm gonna kill ya. You got a wedding to plan."

"Damn right I do. You take care of Andy and make sure he's safe."

"I will." She turned to the paramedics, "What the hell are you two waitin' for, an engraved invitation, get him outta' here."

"Well, we just heard something about a wedding, so, yeah, we're waiting for our invite."

"I'll personally hand-deliver it to you, *if* you get going? Happy?"

"We're gone, lady." With that, we were on the move again.

Once on the road, the paramedic in the back with me asked, "You feelin' okay, Deputy?"

"You mean besides feelin' like my melon's been split in half and throbbin' to beat all hell? Yeah, other than that, I'm just peachy dandy fine."

"Good, we'll be at the ER shortly. Just lay back and enjoy the ride."

"Yeah, right. No siren though, okay, I don't think I could take that right now," I joked as my lights went out for the second time.

✻ ✻ ✻

"Come on, Ms. Ward," Neil called, "let's get inside so you can see what you need to, just don't touch anything you don't have to. We have more units on the way with a search warrant and we need to keep any disturbance to a minimum."

We stepped inside, and I immediately retched at the stench that permeated the house. "How can anyone live in a hellhole like this, Neil?"

"Not a clue, ma'am."

"Well, I can tell you right now there's no way I'm allowing Andy back in this house, not tonight anyway, this is despicable. Even without his abuser being here, this place isn't fit for anybody to live in."

"No arguments from me, ma'am," Neil answered.

"I need to find his room and get him more of his clothes and some other things. Can you help me with that, please?"

"Those are my instructions, ma'am, let's get on with it."

※ ※ ※

"Doug," I started, "Get a sheet or something from the house and cover that up," I said, hooking a thumb over my shoulder to the lifeless body sprawled on the ground behind me. "I'll keep an eye on Mr. Weder. Not like he's in any shape to run away, is it?"

"You got it, Sarge."

I pulled my cell phone from my pocket and dialed Max's number for the call nobody ever wants to make.

※ ※ ※

I heard the phone finally ring, jumped from my chair and ran to the kitchen to answer. I didn't recognize the number on Caller ID and felt my worst fears welling up from deep inside.

"This is Max, who's this?"

"Max, it's Dylan."

"This can't be good news. Not with you calling."

"Not the worst possible, but not great, either. We got the scumbag we came for and one of his pals will be worm food soon."

"I don't give a shit about them, tell me why Tom isn't making this call."

"Well, these morons must have thought they were at the OK Corral and came out with guns blazing. Tom took a crease to his temple, but the paramedics say he should be okay. He's on the way to the ER to get checked over and stitched up."

"Fuck! I just knew something bad was gonna happen today. Which hospital, Dylan? I'm on the way."

"Memorial, but you can't really go anywhere, Max. You got seven boys out there with you, and three of them aren't yours."

"Shit, shit, shit! I wasn't thinking. What am I going to do?"

"You stay there with the boys. I'll go to the hospital to take care of Tom when I'm done cleaning up this mess."

"Okay, fine, what about Andy? Is Carol there?"

"Hang on one sec, here she comes now." Dylan handed his phone to

Carol.

"Max, is that you?"

"Yeah, what's the story with Andy?"

"He's not coming back here tonight. This place is a pigsty."

"What's gonna happen with him?"

"This late on a Saturday, I don't know. I'll have to find an emergency placement for him for the weekend and then something more permanent on Monday."

"What if he just stays here? Would that solve your problem?"

"Sure, it would, but don't you have enough to deal with already?"

"Oh, what the hell, Carol? I'm just a glutton for punishment and love a challenge. Besides, he's already here and if that place is as bad as you say, it sounds like he won't be going home tomorrow either. If he stays here, he won't have to miss any school."

"Yeah, okay, I guess that'll work, Max. Let me call Anna, get her input, and I'll let you know, okay?"

"I'll be here. For a while anyway. I'm gonna call my sister and see if she'll come watch the boys so I can get to the hospital and be with Tom. And I have two other boys here who still need to get back home."

"Tell you what, Max, I'm about the head your way with more of Andy's things. You call your sister, and when I get there, you can go on to the hospital. I'll stay with the boys until your sister can come out. Then, when she gets there, I can take the other two back home for you."

"I like the way you think, Carol. Thanks, you're lifesaver. See you soon."

I hung up with Carol and called Lee.

"Lee, thank god you're home. I need some help and hope you have the time."

"What's going on, Max? You sound stressed."

"Too much to tell you right now. Is there any way you could come out and stay with the boys for a while? I need to get to the hospital."

"Hospital? You sick?"

"No, not me. It's Tom. He went with Dylan and two others to arrest a local loser and Tom ended up getting shot. I need to get there to be with him."

"Oh, Lord, Max! I'm so sorry. I hope he'll be okay."

"Dylan, his boss, says it's just a crease and he should be fine, but I don't want Tom there alone."

"Good, glad to hear it. We'll be there as fast as we can, Max. I'll drag Carl along, too. He needs to get the hell out of the house, anyway."

"Good idea, Lee, especially since there's three extra boys here this afternoon. Carl will be good help. See you soon, and thanks." I hung up before she could ask any other questions and headed to the theater to tell the boys what was going on. I was not looking forward to this conversation.

I paused the movie and pulled a spare chair around in front of the boys.

"What's going on, Dad?" Joey asked with a tremor of fear in his voice.

"Well, good news first, I guess. Russ is gone, Andy, but it looks like you won't be going back home for a while."

"Why not?"

"Because Ms. Ward won't allow it. Part of her job is protecting kids from bad homes. She said that until your house is cleaned up, you're not going back there."

"But where 'm I gonna go?"

"It looks like you'll be staying here until she thinks it's safe for you to go back home or finds another foster family for you to live with."

"That'll be cool. I like it here."

"What else is going on, Dad," Alex asked warily.

"God, this is hard," I mumbled as I looked down to the floor for a moment. I looked back up, took a deep breath and continued, "Okay, I don't know all the details, but Tom's been hurt and is on the way to the hospital."

"C'mon, we gotta go!" T.J. yelled as he jumped out of his chair.

"No, we can't, T.J. Tom will be in the emergency room and there are too many of you take in there. And Mark and Billy need to go back home shortly."

"But, what're we gonna do, Dad? We can't leave Uncle Tom all alone," Mike cried.

"We're not. I've called Aunt Lee and she and Uncle Carl will be out soon. I'm going to the hospital to be with Tom while they stay here with you."

"But what about Mark and Billy? How're they gonna get home?"

"Carol's bringing some more things for Andy. She'll stay here until Lee and Carl get here, then she'll take Mark and Billy home."

"What are we supposed to do? Just sit around with our thumbs up our butts?" Joey asked.

"Maybe Lee and Carl will let you swim for a while, or you can play some Xbox, or Uno, whatever. I'm confident you'll find something to do to entertain yourselves. I want you to be good for Lee and Carl while I'm gone. Understood?"

"Yeah," the twins grumped, upset at having to stay home.

"Good, now I have to get ready to leave." I resumed the movie and headed to the bedroom to change clothes to something more suitable for a hospital. Just as I pulled on a clean shirt, I heard the ding of the drive sensor. I met Carol at the door and took the bag with Andy's things from her.

She gave me a hug, then asked, "Where're the boys?"

"In the theater watching a movie. How was Tom?"

"Tryin' to joke about it, but you could see the pain in his eyes."

"So, at least he was conscious."

"He was when I saw him. Dylan told me he was out for a bit right after it happened, but he was awake when I saw him."

"Thanks, Carol, I appreciate everything. I'm gonna get out of here. I'll call you when I know something. Lee and Carl should be here soon."

"Go be with Tom, Max, we'll be fine. Oh, and I spoke with Anna after talking to you and Andy will be staying here until we can find another foster home for him."

"Thanks, Carol. I just want to make sure he stays safe." I gave her a kiss on the cheek, then ran to the garage, hopped in the Shelby and took off for the hospital.

✳ ✳ ✳

"Hey, Sarge," Doug called from inside the house, "You need to see this."

Since Russ had been taken away in the second ambulance with Neil as his chaperone, and I was just waiting for the medical examiner to show up, I headed inside. That poor schmuck wasn't going anywhere. "What ya got,

Doug?"

"A whole stash of drugs and guns in the crawlspace. This dude was into some serious shit. Probably dealing both to support his own bad habits."

"Wonderful. Tag it all and get it out of here. Make sure you have pictures of everything that comes out of there."

"Will do, boss. Glad we finally found him."

"Yeah, me, too. Any word on the boy's mom yet?"

"Yeah, good idea to put out a BOLO for her. Last I heard, she'd been spotted at Walmart and was leaving the parking lot, assumed to be headed home. Could be here anytime."

"Let's stash our cars where they won't be seen until she's in the driveway. I don't want her rollin' by and us miss her. She had to know what Weder was doing here. No way you have that much shit under the floor and not know it's there."

We moved our cars to a more hidden spot and I waited quietly at the back of the house while Doug and Neil resumed their work inside. I didn't have to wait for long until Ms. Cox pulled in the drive. As soon as she got out of her car, I stepped away from the corner of the house and announced my presence.

"Afternoon, Ms. Cox. How are you today?"

"Fine. Who the hell are you?"

"I'm Sergeant Brock of the Sheriff's department."

"What're you doing here, pig?"

"Well, just waiting for you. Seeing as Russ is on his way to the hospital and his buddy is laying in the back yard with a sheet over him, I had nothin' else to do."

"Russ is at the hospital? Cal's dead?" she asked, then abruptly changed her tune, "Don't know 'em. Was they robbin' my house? And where the hell is my son?"

"Oh, no, nothing like that. But you already know that. You ain't got nothin' in there worth stealin'. And don't you be worrying yourself about Andy. He's safe and sound. You won't have to worry about him for a long, long time, lady."

"What're you talkin' 'bout? I want my son."

"Shit in one hand, wish in the other and let's see which gets filled first.

You're in deep and apparently don't have a clue."

"What? I didn't do nothin'."

"Including protecting yourself and your son from lowlife scumbags like Weder and 'Cal', you said? You can't expect me to believe you didn't know what your man was doing. What with all the drugs and guns in your crawlspace, and his beating you and your son whenever he felt like it. Now, you get to join him in jail, 'cause that's where you're both going. Well, after he gets out of the hospital, that is."

"I ain't goin' nowhere."

"You really don't have a choice. Put your purse on the ground and your hands on the hood of the car. Be gentle, now, we've already shot two people here today, one more won't faze me a bit." She did as she was told, and I carefully rounded the car to put cuffs on her. Just as I cleared the front bumper, she struck out at me like a demon possessed.

Now, I don't normally condone hitting women, but when they're coming at you, spitting and hissing, claws extended and aiming for the eyes, there's only one thing you can do. I clocked that bitch right on the chin and she crumpled to the ground like the lifeless heap of trash she was. I rolled her over on her front side and cuffed her. "Doug, get your ass out here!" I yelled.

"What's up, Sarge?" Doug asked as he exited the house.

"Put this *lady* in the back of your car with leg irons and get her outta' here. I want her booked and locked up, ASAP."

"Gladly, Boss."

"You guys about done in there?"

"I think so. We're still checking out the crawlspace and the boy's room, but I think that about all that's left."

"You think the others got a handle on it?"

"They should. Why?"

"I want to get to the hospital, check on Tom and see how the scumbag who lived is doing."

"Go ahead, boss. I'll stay long enough to meet the ME, then I'll head out to get her to the County Building and processed."

"Excellent. Good work today, Doug. Appreciate your help."

"Well, except for Tom getting hit."

"Yeah, except for that. We'll have to sit down and discuss what happened today and see what we can do to avoid situations like that again. I'm headed to the hospital. Get things wrapped up here and I'll see you Monday." I hopped in my car and took off for the hospital.

※ ※ ※

It was a good thing I knew where most of the Sangamon County cops were this afternoon as I arrived at the hospital twenty minutes after leaving home, a trip that would have normally taken thirty-five to forty minutes. This felt like the perfect time to let the 'Stang stretch its legs for a bit. I found a parking spot and headed inside to find Tom. After a few wrong turns, I finally found the ER check-in and walked up to the counter.

"Good afternoon, sir, how may I help you?" the receptionist asked.

"I'm Max Sanders and I'm looking for Tom Wright. He's a Sangamon County cop who was brought in a little while ago with a gunshot wound."

"One moment, sir." She tapped on her keyboard a few times and came back with, "Yes, sir, he's here, in treatment room one."

"Thank you," I said and started to walk away from her.

"Hold on, sir," she called as she stood up and moved to block my way to stop me from proceeding. "Are you family, or with the Sheriff's department?"

"Not yet, no."

"What, exactly, does that mean?"

"Well, if you must know, it means we're getting married, so we'll be family soon."

"Sorry, sir, you're not allowed into the treatment area. Only family members are allowed in with patients."

"Look," I said, trying to hide the frustration that was building inside me, "his parents live down by St. Louis and can't be here right now. Hell, I haven't even had time to call and let them know their son's been hurt. I'm the closest thing to family he has in the area and I'm going back there." I started to move around her and as I did, she moved to block me again and wiggled a finger over her shoulder. She was soon joined by a hulking man in uniform and a name badge signifying he was hospital security.

"What's seems to be the problem, Mabel?" he grumbled.

"This gentleman is attempting to enter the ER when he has no *family* in there."

"I'm sorry, sir, you'll have to wait out here. Only family members are allowed in with patients."

"Look, I just told her that Tom and I are going to be married soon and his parents aren't in the area. I'm going in."

"No, sir, you're not. You are going to sit in a chair over there and wait. If the patient is admitted, you can go to his room, otherwise you'll have to wait out here until he's released from the ER."

Fuming internally, I acquiesced and took the nearest empty seat I could find to the ER doors. Apparently, these morons had not moved into the 21st century just yet.

✷ ✷ ✷

I sat in the theater with the boys, waiting for Max's sister to arrive and take over. When I heard the ding of the drive sensor, I headed to the front door to meet her. Upon opening the door, I was met by a lovely looking woman with short brown hair and a handsome man with short and spiky blonde hair.

"Hi, I'm Carol Ward, you must be Max's sister. Thanks for coming out so quickly."

"Hi, I'm Lee Nichols and this is my husband Carl. It's nice to meet you Carol."

"Nice to meet the two of you, too. Too bad it had to be like this."

"Tell us, have you heard anything about Tom?"

"I was there when it happened and talked to him before they took him to the hospital. He should be okay."

"Thank God, Max didn't have time to tell me much of anything, just that he'd been shot and he needed to get to the hospital. We jumped in the car and headed right out. Thanks for waiting for us."

"Oh, no problem. Well, let me get the two extra boys out of here so I can get them home."

"Wait, Max said there were three extra boys here this afternoon? Did one go home already?"

"Unfortunately, no, he'll be staying here with Max and his boys. It was his house where Tom got hurt and the inside of it looked like a bomb had gone off. Absolutely disgusting. I can't let him go home and Max volunteered to let him stay here for the time being so he won't miss any school."

"And the hits just keep coming, don't they?" Carl asked.

"It sure seems that way, doesn't it? Well, the boys are watching a movie, why don't we interrupt them?"

"No time like the present."

"Boys, your Aunt Lee and Uncle Carl are here," Carol called after opening the door to the theater.

"Yay!!" my four yelled and ran to smother Lee with hugs.

They shied away from Carl until he knelt down to their level and said, "Come on, guys, don't be strangers, I don't bite, ya know. I've been wantin' to meet y'all since Lee told me you were here. Besides, every hug is worth a buck to ya."

"Carl, stop that," Lee reprimanded, smacking her husband on the back of the head. "Make a promise like that, they'll never let go, and we aren't that rich."

"Bah, what's a few bucks for some hugs?"

"Mark, Billy, get your things and let's hit the road," Carol called out. "I'd like to get back home sometime tonight."

"We're coming." Mike followed them to his room to make sure they got everything that was theirs, including their unused and dry swimsuits.

Once they had all their belongings, Billy said, "Mike, thanks for having us over. We had a great time and I hope we can do it again sometime."

"Yeah, we really were jerks to you and we're sorry. I hope we can be friends," Mark added.

"Sure thing, guys. I'm glad we had fun, too, and we'll do it again, for sure. Remember, you can't say nothin' about the naked thing."

"Lips are zipped, Mike. We want to be able to come back," Mark said.

"Yeah, my ma would have a cow if she knew 'bout that," Billy added with a conspiratorial grin.

The three boys headed to the front door to meet Carol and after waving goodbye to Carol and his new friends, Mike headed back to the theater to rejoin the rest of the family.

※ ※ ※

Twenty-five minutes after taking my seat, Dylan stormed into the ER and headed to the reception counter. I got up from my chair and joined him.

"I'm here to see two people, Tom Wright and Russ Weder. Where can I find them?"

While Mabel retrieved the info from her computer, I tapped Dylan on the shoulder to get his attention. He spun around in surprise.

"Max, what the hell are you doing out here, you should be in there with Tom."

"I'd love to do just that, but Miss Mabel, here, and that rent-a-cop over there don't agree with you, spouting some silly shit about me not being family."

"We'll see about that." He turned back to Mabel. "Would you please explain to me why this man is not in there with his fiancé?"

"He's not family and only family members are allowed in the treatment rooms."

"Did he tell you they're getting married?"

"Yes, but that means they're not married yet and, therefore, not family."

"If Mr. Wright's fiancée was a female, would she be allowed in the treatment room, or if Mr. Sanders' fiancée was a female would he be allowed in?"

"But, of course."

"So, tell me why the fuck he's still sitting out here like he's got the fuckin' plague or something."

"Sir, I don't care who you are, you will not speak to me like that."

"Do me a favor, Mabel. Remove your stuck in the middle-ages head from your fat, fuckin' ass and let this man be with his fiancé. And I'll talk to you any God damn way I fuckin' want to."

"Well, I never..."

"Obviously, lady, get with the modern world. C'mon, Max." Dylan turned and headed for the treatment rooms and I fell in step beside him, leaving a stunned Mabel in our wake. As we approached the doors separating the waiting area from the treatment area, the rent-a-cop stepped over to block our path. "Don't think you're stopping me, buddy."

"You can go anywhere you like, sir, but he's not going in," the guard said, pointing his finger at me.

"Look, you ignorant jerk-off, I've had a really bad fuckin' day. I've already shot two assholes who deserved it and punched a lady in the face. Get the fuck outta' our way."

"As I said, you're free to go where you like, but he's got no business in there."

Dylan looked at me while shaking his head in disgust and then turned back to the guard. He extended himself fully and dwarfed even the hulking silhouette of the guard, who seemed to suddenly shrink in stature. Dylan then put his nose inches from the guard's and quietly said, "Listen, dumbass, you really think you want to take me on, mister? My dog takes shits bigger than you, but if you want to try it, feel free to take the first shot. I'd love to throw another asshole in jail today." The guard shrank even further under Dylan's withering glare and he swallowed hard. He apparently decided common sense should prevail today and stepped aside to allow our passage.

As we passed through the sacred portal and into the inner sanctum, I said, "Thanks, Dylan."

"Don't mention it. I was dead fuckin' serious about being tired of dealing with assholes today. Also, just to clear up a wild rumor that's been making the rounds, I don't have a dog," he snickered. "Now, let's go find our man."

25

Dylan and I found the room where Tom was supposed to be, but it was empty. Dylan flagged down the first medical person he saw and asked, "We're here to see to Tom Wright, but he's not where he should be. Would you please tell us where he is?"

"The cop?" the nurse asked. "They took him back for a head CT about ten minutes ago. He should be back in about twenty-five or thirty minutes. You're welcome to wait in there until he comes back."

"Thank you. Can you tell me where I might find a Mr. Russ Weder, also?"

"He was taken up to surgery about five minutes ago. The cop that came in with him went up, also. Said he wasn't letting him out of his sight."

"Just as he should have. Thanks, again, for your help. We'll wait here for Tom to be brought back."

We took seats in the empty room to begin our wait.

"So, Max, you and Tom are getting married, huh?"

"Yep," I grinned. "You're cool with that, aren't you?"

"It seems to be a little sudden to me, but as long as you're sure it's the right thing for you, I'm cool with it."

"Good. We hope you'll accept our invite to the event."

"Of course, I will. I wouldn't miss it for all the tea in China."

"Excellent, Dylan. Now, please tell me exactly what happened today." Dylan relayed the afternoon's events and how Tom got hurt. "So, it was just the fact there was an extra guy you didn't know about."

"Pretty much. I feel like shit for putting Tom in danger like that, especially just after getting engaged."

"Don't worry about that, Dylan. He wasn't letting you go there alone, engaged or not. Besides, he's still a cop and he expects to do his job to the fullest until his very last day."

"Well, that day has arrived sooner than he thought."

"Huh, what do you mean by that?"

"Today *is* his last day. After an injury like that, his recovery will take longer than the week he has left. He's done."

"Well, I'm sorry for the department, but happy for me and the boys. I did nothing but worry about him all day while he was gone. Guess I won't have to do that anymore, will I?"

"Nope, you can both rest easy for the next couple of weeks. Tom a little easier, of course."

We sat in silence during the rest of our wait for Tom to come back from his scan. After what seemed hours, but was really closer to forty minutes, the gurney carrying his prone figure was finally wheeled back into the treatment room, followed by a doctor and a nurse who was carrying a tray of supplies. Tom's eyes were closed, and he appeared to be sleeping.

"Afternoon, fellas, I'm Dr. Hansen, who might you be?"

"I'm Max Sanders and this is Dylan Brock, Tom's boss."

"And what is your relationship to my patient?"

"He's my fiancé."

"Congratulations. I'm surprised Mabel let you back here since you're not married yet. She's a bit of a stickler for that stupid 'family only' bull."

"I have Dylan to thank for getting around that."

"And how, may I ask, did you accomplish that feat, Dylan?"

"I politely told sweet little old Mabel to 'remove her stuck in the middle-ages head from her fat fucking ass'." The nurse covered her mouth with a hand to stifle her laughter as she left the room. "I also had to knock your security guard off his high horse, but you'll be happy to know that no blood was shed."

"Good. We already see more than enough blood around here in a day, we don't need to add to it needlessly. Glad you were able to knock some sense into those two."

"Tell me, doctor," I started, "is Tom going to be okay?"

"He should be just fine. He was awake enough to let me know he's severely claustrophobic, so we gave him a mild sedative before feeding him into the machine down the hall. The CT scan showed no internal injuries and the crease in his scalp will heal up just fine once we get him stitched up. He'll have a pretty nice scar to remind him of this day, but that should be it. Well, that and a major headache for the next several days."

"Thank the gods for small favors. Will he be able to go home tonight?"

"As long as you can stay with him, I don't see why not. He probably has a slight concussion from the impact of the bullet against the side of his skull and he should be watched closely for the next twenty-four to forty-eight hours to make sure there's no complications, but I'm sure he'd rather do that at home than here."

"That's good news, doctor, thanks. Since we live together, I'll be able to keep an eye on him. I'll just have to make sure our boys stay quiet."

"Well, let me get his head put back together and we'll get you guys on your way."

"One more thing, doc," Dylan interrupted, "What can you tell me about another patient brought in with a gunshot wound, Russ Weder? What's the scoop on him?"

"Well, he's not quite as lucky as Mr. Wright, here. His bullet went through the fleshy part of his thigh and out the back of his leg, somehow missing the femoral artery, but still nicking the femur. Broke off several good-sized chunks of bone that will have to be dug out, and he's got some muscle and nerve damage, too. He's gonna be walking with a pretty pronounced limp the rest of his life."

"But, he'll still be able to stand trial when the time comes?"

"No reason he shouldn't. Be a week or more before he gets out of here, though. Then, I'm guessing, it's straight to jail, do not pass go, do not collect $200 when he does."

"You got that right. He'll need to be placed in a room that can be secured and has room for a guard to be with him. I don't want to take any chances that he'll skip. It took us months to find him and I don't want to have to go through that again."

"We can arrange that. Now, can I fix this man's head?"

"Please do," I said. He called the nurse back in to assist him and they quickly got to work, first carefully shaving the area around the gash in Tom's scalp and then proceeding to stitch it back together. Forty minutes and twenty-eight stitches later, the job was completed. The last step was to cover the area with a large gauze bandage with tape to help hold it in place.

"Okay, he should be good to go once he wakes up, which shouldn't be too much longer. It looks like I got the skin pulled back together pretty cleanly, so his scarring should be minimal. I'll give you some instructions on how to take care of him the next couple of days along with some pain meds and extra gauze pads. You can take him to his regular doctor in about one-and-a-half to two weeks to get the stiches removed."

"That's great, Doctor Hansen. I can't thank you enough. I'll call my sister and let her know we'll be home in a bit."

"You'll have to go out to the waiting room for that. You're not allowed to use cell phones in here."

"No problem, I'll be right back." Before leaving, I turned to Dylan and said, "Dylan, thanks for taking care of him this afternoon."

"Hey, don't remind me, he got hurt on my watch, not yours. Bet I know one person you won't be calling for babysitting services anytime soon," he snickered.

"Are you kidding me, the boys would love to have you come back out to the house. And Tom getting hurt wasn't your fault. That blame belongs to someone else. The main thing is, he's okay. Thanks again and go check on your other guy."

I passed the guard and Mabel on my way to the waiting room to make my calls, receiving dirty looks from both. I returned their looks of contempt with a wide smile. Once I was alone in a corner, I called Carol first to let her know what was going on. She was relieved to find out Tom was going to be okay and wanted to know when she could come out to see him. I asked her to wait a couple of days for his headache to diminish, but, after that, she was welcome anytime. My next call was to home.

When Lee answered the phone, I said, "Hey sis, how's it going out there?"

"It's about damn time you called," she harped. "We're just fine. How's Tom?"

"He's got twenty-eight stitches in the side of his head and the doc says he'll have a bad headache for a couple of days, but, other than that, he's good to go."

"That's good news, Max. I'm glad, for both of you."

"We'll be on our way as soon as he wakes up."

"They put him out for stitches? I've never heard of that before."

"No, they put him out for a CT scan of his head. Apparently, Tom's severely claustrophobic. I guess there's a lot we don't know about each other, not yet anyway."

"Okay, that makes sense, I guess."

"So, back to my original question, how's it going out there?"

"Oh, those boys are incorrigible."

"What'd they do now?"

"Nothin' I didn't expect, I guess. As soon as Carol was out the door with Billy and Mark, your four, no, make that five, said they wanted to go swimming, again. Carl said he'd go with them if I wanted to stay inside and close to the phone. I thought that was a good idea, so I told the boys to get changed and Carl went to your room to find some shorts he could wear. Carl came back into the living room in a pair of shorts just as the five boys rounded the corner, naked as jaybirds. I had to help Carl pick up his jaw from the floor."

"You weren't surprised, though, were you?"

"I wasn't sure what they'd do. I know we told them they could be nude when I was here, but I thought with Carl here, too, they'd maybe show a little more modesty. Boy, was I ever wrong. And that's only half of it. Once Carl recovered from his initial shock, he mumbled something like 'ah, fuck it' and pulled his borrowed shorts back off, then led the naked parade out the door to the pool."

I busted out laughing, garnering many strange looks from other people in the ER waiting room. "Damn it, Max, it's not funny. He won't even walk around his own house without at least a towel wrapped around him. And now, he's parading around here like he does it all the time."

"Sorry, Lee, I guess we're a bad influence," I chuckled.

"Oh, don't worry, you'll pay for it. I'm not quite sure how or when at the moment, but I'll come up with something."

"I don't doubt that for a minute."

"Look, you get back in with Tom and tell him we're thinking about him. Well, at least I am, I can't really speak for the lunatics in the pool. We'll see you when you get home."

"Thanks, again, for coming out on short notice. I love you guys." I ended the call and headed back to check on Tom, receiving daggers of disgust from Mabel and the rent-a-cop as I passed through the doors, chuckling quietly at the thought of straight-laced Carl skinny-dipping with the boys. When I got to Tom's room, he looked like he was still sleeping, so I quietly moved a chair closer to the bed and wrapped my hands around his.

"That you, Max?" he whispered.

"No, it's Brad Pitt and George Clooney," I joked.

"Good, that just proves dreams can come true." He lifted his head and grinned mischievously at me.

"Careful, big guy, I'm supposed to watch over you for the next couple of days. You don't want to piss off your caretaker, do you?"

"No, but I do want to get the hell out of here? I hate hospitals."

"Well, at least you know where you are. That's a good sign. Let me get the doctor. Hang on."

"I ain't going nowhere. Not in this damn thing," he said as he lifted the flimsy gown and exposed himself. I caught the doctor's attention and he headed our direction.

"Sleeping Beauty's awake and says he'd like to get out of here."

"We'll see about that." He walked to the bed and helped Tom sit up. "How you feeling, Mr. Wright."

"Not too bad, I guess, all things considered. Got a hell of a headache and I'm a bit dizzy, though."

"The dizziness should go away shortly. That's a residual effect of the sedative you received before the scan of your head, which came back clean, by the way. The headache's another story. You're going to have that for a few more days, I'm afraid. That bullet smacking your skull is about the same as hitting yourself in the head with a hammer."

"I wouldn't know, never done that."

"I don't recommend you do it, either. Not for the next few months, anyway. Let me take a quick look at your eyes." He shined a penlight in Tom's eyes, blinking it a couple times in each. "Pupils are good and reactive. I think you're going to be just fine, Tom. Take it easy for a few days. No work until those stitches come out."

"But I have another week to go."

"No, you don't," I said, "Dylan said you're done, as of today."

"Oh, he was here, too?"

"While you were getting your head scanned. He told me then, that today is your last day as a cop. He's beatin' himself up pretty badly over you gettin' hurt."

"Hell, it could have been any one of us. But I don't wanna' push my luck either." He turned to the doctor who was writing instructions in his chart. "Uh, doc, you got my clothes handy so I can get dressed. I ain't wearing this flippin' gown outta here."

The doctor chuckled and answered, "I'll have the nurse bring them back to you when she brings your discharge papers and pain meds. We put your belongings in a secure locker since you had your weapon on you when you came in."

"Thanks. For everything."

"Not a problem, Mr. Wright. All part of the job. Take care of yourself. And don't take this the wrong way, but I hope I never see you again."

"That makes two of us. Have a good life."

"The same to the two of you. Congratulations, by the way. I wish you both the best with your wedding."

I stood and shook his hand, "Thanks from me, too, doctor. Don't know what I would've done without him. I'm forever in your debt."

"Just take good care of him and be happy, Mr. Sanders."

With that, he turned and left the room. Tom and I waited quietly until the nurse showed up with his uniform, discharge papers and supplies.

"Here you go, Mr. Wright, you're all set. I need you to sign a few things, then I'll help you get dressed and you can be on your way."

"Thanks for that kind offer, but I'll have Max help me get dressed, if you don't mind."

"That's fine, but I did help get you undressed, so there's no mystery left in our relationship."

"Sorry, dear, but I'm already taken."

"Dang it. Oh, well, life rolls on. Let me get a few signatures from you and I'll get out of your way. Just let me know when you're ready to blow this pop stand and I'll bring a wheelchair in." Tom signed the pages where the nurse indicated, and she left, closing the door behind her.

"You ready, Tom?"

"As ready as I'll ever be. Slip my boxers and pants up my legs, then, you can help me stand up and get them the rest of the way up." I did as he asked and discovered he was pretty unsteady on his feet. I managed to get his shorts and pants pulled up and in position while he held on to the edge of the gurney. We then swapped the gown for his bloody t-shirt and I helped him sit in a chair so we could get his socks and shoes on. Last was his coat and he was ready for the road. I headed out to retrieve the nurse, and then left to get the car while she wheeled him to the door. After I pulled up to the door, we helped Tom get in the car, I thanked the nurse for her help and we hit the road for home.

Tom laid his seat back a few inches, rested his head on the headrest and closed his eyes for a much slower trip home. I took it very slowly as we headed up the road to our drive and down the drive to the house due to the potholes and general lousy condition of both. After I pulled in the garage, I lightly shook Tom to wake him up and get ready to go in the house. I walked around the car, opened the door and held onto his arm to help him out. He seemed to be a bit more stable on his feet, but I still didn't let go of him all the way into the house. Once inside, Lee joined us and helped me get Tom to a chair by the fireplace.

"The boys and Carl still in the pool?" I asked.

"Of course, can't you hear all the screaming?"

"Now that you mention it, it does sound like some wild animals are havin' a wicked party out in the back yard. Let me go out and I'll let 'em know we're home. Make sure he doesn't fall out of the chair," I said, pointing to Tom.

"Ha, ha, very funny," Tom replied.

I headed out the door to the pool and as soon as I opened the shelter door, five boys yelled, "Dad", and came running out of the pool to wrap me up in a wet group hug.

"Boys, calm down."

"How's Uncle Tom?" Joey asked.

"He's fine and sitting inside."

"C'mon guys, let's go," Alex called.

"Whoa, hold it right there! Tom's really unsteady right now, and his head hurts really bad. We'll go in, but you need to be quiet and calm, please. First, grab your towels and get dried off." By that time, Carl had joined us. "Evening, Carl, how ya doing?" I asked as I shook his hand. We walked to the table so he could grab his towel and get dried off, also.

"Fine, Max, how's Tom?"

"He'll be fine. His head hurts like hell and the doctor says he needs to take it easy for a few weeks, but he should be okay."

"That's good to hear. Lee's been pretty freaked out the last couple of hours waiting to hear something. She was afraid you were going to lose him."

"Can't say I was much better until I saw him at the hospital. Once I saw him, though, I knew he'd be fine. Did the boys give you any trouble?"

"Nah, they were great. In fact, I don't think I've ever as much fun as I did with them. They made me feel young again."

"Young enough to shed your inhibitions. And your clothes, apparently."

"Uh, yeah, I guess so," he answered as he blushed form head to toe. "When I first saw them coming around the corner to the living room in their birthday suits, I gotta tell ya, it surprised the hell out of me. But as I stood there, taking it all in, it hit me."

"What hit you?"

"I thought, 'yeah, what's the big fuckin' deal?', and I pulled off my shorts right there. Lee about collapsed in shock."

"I know, she told me when I called from the hospital. I don't think I've ever laughed so hard in my life and everyone waiting in the ER looked at me like I'd lost my mind. I bet she never thought you'd do something like that outside your own home."

"Her, hell, I didn't either, but with five other naked people right there, even though they're kids, it just seemed the natural thing to do. So, instead of fightin' 'em, I joined 'em. Best thing I've ever done in my life. *Now* I understand why you live out here in the middle of freakin' nowhere."

"You're welcome to join us any time, Carl. You know that. But only if you're prepared to see Tom and myself the same way."

"Thanks, Max. I'll take you up on that offer."

"In all the years you've been my brother-in-law, I don't think I've ever seen you nude, before. You really should do it more often, you've got a good-looking body." Whoops, there goes that full-body blush, again.

"Uh, Max, you know I'm straight, right," he replied rather seriously as he stared at me.

"Of course, I do, but that doesn't mean I can't appreciate a nice body when I see it, does it?"

"No, I guess not. It's kinda weird, but I guess I can get used to it."

"Okay, guys, let's get inside and remember, quietly and calmly." We walked to the house and the boys followed my instructions and kept it calm and quiet. Until they actually saw Tom with his bandaged head, that is, and then they took off at a dead run. He held his hand up as they ran towards him, telling them to slow down. They hit the brakes and slowly got closer.

"How ya doin', Uncle Tom?" Joey asked.

"Yeah, we were scared you wasn't coming back home," Mike whined.

"But, I'm here and I'll be fine after a while, but my head feels like it's in a vise."

"You need anything, Uncle Tom?" Alex asked.

"I could use a glass of tea, thanks, Alex. Max, can you get those painkillers they gave ya?"

"You got it."

"What's your head look like, Uncle Tom?" T.J. wanted to know.

"You'll have to ask Max that question, T.J., 'cause they didn't give me a mirror before they covered it up."

The boys looked to me for an answer. "It's pretty gnarly, guys. They had to shave the whole side of his head to stitch him back together. You can see it in a bit when I change his bandage," I responded as I pulled the pain pills out of the bag from the hospital.

"Cool."

"I'm sorry, Mr. Wright," Andy whimpered.

"What do you have to be sorry for?" Tom asked.

"Well, you only got hurt 'cause of me."

"Come here, Andy." Andy got closer and after Tom patted his thigh, he carefully climbed up into Tom's lap. "Don't you ever think that me getting hurt is your fault."

"But you were only there 'cause of me."

"No, Andy, I was there because it's my job. Well, it was. Being a cop is dangerous, make no mistake, but that's a risk we all take into account when we accept the job. We always try to be careful, but sometimes things happen we can't control. Today was one of those times and it just happened to be my turn. It's not your fault that Russ and his friend are bad guys, that's their fault. And you won't have to worry about either one of them ever again."

"Did ya kill 'em?"

"Not Russ, but his friend Cal, I did. He's the one who shot me. Russ is in the hospital and he'll be going to jail as soon as he gets out. And he'll be there for a very long time."

"Good. What happened to my mom?"

"I don't know right now, Andy, but we'll find out."

"Okay. I'm glad you're ok, Mr. Wright."

"Me too, buddy, me too. And since it looks like you'll be living here for the time being, why don't you call me Uncle Tom like the others?"

"Really, you'd let me do that?"

"You bet."

"Thanks, Uncle Tom. I'm gonna like living here. I hope I never have to go back to that house."

"Boys," I said, "time for showers and snacks. GO! Oops, sorry Tom, I shouldn't have yelled that." They took off for their rooms and I turned around to find Carl sitting in the chair behind me, still nude. "Have those boys converted you, Carl? I don't think I've ever seen you more relaxed and comfortable."

"They just might have done that."

"You better think about that again, bubba," Lee said, "you still have to go home with me. It's one thing for those boys to run around naked all the time, out here in the boonies, but don't go thinking you're gonna get away with it in my house. What the hell would the neighbors think?"

"Uh-oh, I'm sensing trouble in paradise," I laughed. "Oh, by the way, Carl, this is my fiancé, Tom. Tom, my brother-in-law, Carl."

"Hey, Carl, nice to meet ya. Hope you don't mind if I don't get up."

"Don't you dare move on my account. Good to meet you, too, Tom," he replied as he walked over and shook Tom's hand.

"Max, did you tell them our news?" Tom asked.

"What news?" I asked.

"I can't believe you've already forgotten. It just happened this morning. Hell, I got shot, in the head, no less, and *I* remember."

"Oh, *that* news. Sorry, no, I've been a little busy." I turned to Lee and Carl and told them about our upcoming nuptials.

"What!? And I'm just now finding out? What the hell kind of brother are you?" Lee asked as she punched me in the shoulder.

"Like I said, busy."

"That's no excuse, dammit," she laughed. "Congratulations you two. When's the big day?"

"No clue yet, but we hope before the adoptions are finalized."

"If you need any help with planning things, you let me know."

"I will, Lee, don't worry." I looked back to Tom and noticed he was starting to develop a bit of a list in his chair. "Hey, big guy, it looks like you're about ready for bed."

"Yeah, I am. I've had a lousy damn day and just want to go try and sleep it off. Maybe when I wake up in the morning, I'll discover it was all a bad dream."

"Can you wait until the boys come back so they can say goodnight and I can change your bandage? You know they want to see your head."

"I'll try."

"On that note, Max, I think Carl and I will take our leave. That's one thing I don't care to see right now." She turned to Carl and said, "Will you *please* get dressed so we can go home?"

"Oh, sure thing, honey, be right back," he replied with a chuckle, then headed to our bedroom to retrieve his clothes.

"I really don't know if I'm ready to handle this 'new and improved' Carl."

"You may not have a choice, Lee. You might even want to try it yourself. I think you'd enjoy it. You know I've never pushed the nudist lifestyle on anybody, especially in mixed company, but any time you feel the urge, my home is always open."

"I know, little brother, I just don't know that I'm quite ready to be seeing all of you naked, running around like a bunch of goofballs. And I'm sure all you gay men and boys don't particularly want to see a naked female running around, either."

"It wouldn't bother us in the least, sis." At that moment, Carl returned, dressed, and five boys rejoined us, freshly showered and nude. "Boys, say goodbye to Aunt Lee and Uncle Carl." The five swarmed the two to give hugs and say their goodbyes.

"Thanks for staying with us, Aunt Lee and Uncle Carl. It was great fun," Joey said.

"And thanks for swimming with us, Uncle Carl. You look good without your clothes on," Alex added with a smile. Carl blushed, again, at the compliment.

"Hope you can come back and do it, again," Mike exclaimed.

"Oh, I'll be back," Carl said, grinning wildly. Lee just shook her head and headed for the door, Carl trailing behind a few steps and I followed along.

"Thanks for coming out and running herd you two. You have no idea how much I appreciate it. Don't be strangers." After I closed the door, I turned to the boys and said, "Okay, guys, now's your chance to see what Uncle Tom's head looks like under that bandage. He needs to get to bed and I need to change it before he goes."

I grabbed the bag of supplies from the ER and started to carefully remove the covering over the wound. Once it was exposed, I had boys come over for a closer look.

"Oh, man, that's wicked," Joey said.

"Nice hairstyle, Uncle Tom. Can we get our hair done like that?" Alex asked.

"How many stitches are there, Dad?" T.J. wanted to know.

"Twenty-eight."

"That's a lot, isn't it?" Mike asked.

"I don't have any idea. It's the most I've ever seen in one place." I suddenly realized that I hadn't heard any comment from Andy and when I turned to look for him, I found him curled in one of the chairs, crying quietly. I went over to him, knelt beside the chair and put my hand on his back. "It's okay, Andy. Tom will be just fine."

"I know, but it's all my fault he got hurt."

"Andy, look at me." He lifted his head and turned to face me. "It is *not* your fault. It's Russ and Cal's fault. They're the ones who hurt you, your mom, Tom and lord knows how many other people. And they can't hurt anyone else ever again. In time, you'll see the truth in what I'm telling you."

"If you say so. I don't think I believe it, though."

"I do say so. Now come over and say goodnight to Uncle Tom so I can get his new bandage on, then get him in bed." I walked Andy over to Tom and all five boys gave him a gentle hug goodnight. I put some more antibiotic ointment on his scalp around his stitches, replaced the bandage and helped him to his feet. Once I got him upright, Alex and Joey insisted on helping me, so the three of us helped guide Tom to our bedroom with the other three following close behind.

Once we had him sitting on the edge of the bed, I said, "Okay, guys, I got it from here. Why don't you wait in the kitchen and, after I get Tom in bed, I'll be there to get your snacks."

"Oh, no you don't, Dad, we're all in this together," Joey said and started reeling off instructions. "T.J., Mike, you get his shoes and socks off, I'll take his shirt, Andy and Alex, when dad lifts him up, you two pull down the covers, and Dad can take his pants off after he lays down." The boys jumped to the tasks Joey had given them and we quickly had Tom laid down on his back. I undid his pants and slowly pulled them off his hips and down his legs.

I was ready to have Alex and Andy pull the covers over Tom when he said, "Get those damn boxers off me, too. If I wear those, they'll drive me nuts until I take 'em off myself." I grabbed the waistband of his shorts a slowly peeled them down his legs.

"Happy now?"

"I will be when you can join me." I finally let Alex and Andy cover him up and Tom closed his eyes and promptly fell asleep.

"Thanks for your help, boys, you made that a lot easier. Now, will you five go to the kitchen and wait for your snack? It's my turn to get comfortable and I want to make sure he's asleep. Then, I'll be right out." Each one gave Tom a kiss on the forehead and said 'I love you' before the fabulous five quietly padded out of the bedroom.

I picked up Tom's clothes and laid them across a chair, then got undressed myself. After a quick visit to the bathroom to wash my face and hands, I checked on Tom. He was breathing slowly as I brushed his forehead and gave him a kiss. Satisfied he was comfortable and down for the count, I headed to the kitchen.

I arrived to find five boys lined up on their stools at the counter, waiting patiently for their promised snack. I warmed some caramel dipping sauce in the microwave while I cut four apples into chunks and set everything on the counter along with five small forks. Five glasses of milk soon joined the rest of the snack.

"Have you decided where you're going to sleep, Andy? You can use the empty bedroom, or you could sleep with the others."

"Mike wants me to sleep with him and T.J."

"That's fine. If you change your mind, let me know and we can move you into the other room, okay?"

"Okay, thanks, Mr. Sanders."

"Listen, Andy, why don't you call me Uncle Max?"

"Why can't he call you Dad like we do?" Mike asked.

"Well, because I'm not adopting Andy. He's just living with us until Carol finds another place for him."

"But I don't want him to go nowhere else," Mike whined. "He's my friend, now, and I want him to be my brother, too."

"We'll just have to wait and see what Carol comes up with. What about you, Andy, do you think you'd want to stay here and live with all of us?"

"Yeah, that'd be great."

"I'll talk to Carol on Monday and let her know that. But, in the end, it's up to her and her agency."

After the snack was finished and cleaned up, I herded the boys to their beds, tucked them in, gave them their kisses and received kisses from each along with a lot of 'I love yous' passing back and forth. With the boys and Tom in bed, I collapsed in my favorite chair by the fireplace, lost in the thought that we'd almost lost Tom today. I know that I shouldn't feel this deeply about somebody after knowing him for only a week, but I couldn't help it and I started crying softly to myself. I was done trying to be strong for everybody else today and now it was my turn to feel something, even if I was alone.

After a few minutes of wallowing in my own misery, I felt a hand on my arm and a small voice asking, "Dad, you okay?" I opened my eyes to find T.J. standing there, a look of concern on his face. "I heard you crying and got worried."

"Not really, but I will be."

"What's wrong?" he asked as he crawled into my lap.

"I know we've all only known each other for a week, but I love each of you so much, it hurts when I think how close we came to losing Tom today. Now that we've all found each other, I don't ever want to lose any of you. I've been alone for too much of my life already, and I don't ever want to live like that again."

"We don't want to lose you either, Dad. Or Uncle Tom. We're all glad you two found each other. You two belong together. We all belong together."

"Thank you, son, that means a lot to me. How did you get to be so smart and caring?"

"Just lucky, I guess."

"No, I'm the lucky one. In oh, so many ways."

"You feelin' better, now, Dad?"

"You bet," I answered as I wiped my eyes. "Thanks for cheering me up. Come on, let's get you back in bed so I can go to bed, too." I carried my little angel back to his room and gently laid him on the bed so as not to wake the other two who were sound asleep. I whispered, "I love you, young man" as I pulled the covers over him, then kissed his forehead again and received a kiss back from him before turning out the light and closing the door.

I headed to our bedroom and used the bathroom before checking on Tom. He was snoring lightly as I kissed him goodnight and told him I loved him. Then, I carefully crawled in my side of the bed and fell sound asleep, holding the love of my life and thinking, tomorrow's a new day and I'm done wasting days.

To be continued ...

NOTE FROM THE AUTHOR

I WANT TO THANK THE READERS who weren't turned off or disgusted by this story's subjects and have made it this far. This saga began as a simple short story and it has grown well beyond those confines. As I continue my work on this project, I will cover many different topics that many people may find uncomfortable, though they really shouldn't be.

While the story itself is pure fiction, the situations and ideas aren't. Many of the situations you will encounter have happened in real life to someone, somewhere, possibly to someone you know and care about. If you know anyone who fits the mold I've created and described, reach out to them and let them know they are loved.

I would love to hear your thoughts and feelings on the story and welcome communications by e-mail to wcorgan@williamscorgan.name. I promise to respond to everyone who writes, whether your comments are positive or negative.

Made in the USA
Middletown, DE
25 May 2018